T0274095

LETHAL
KINGS

Books by Victoria McCombs

LETHAL
KINGS

VICTORIA McCOMBS

Published by Enclave Publishing, an imprint of Oasis Family Media, LLC

Carol Stream, Illinois, USA.
www.enclavepublishing.com

ISBN: 979-8-88605-162-9 (printed hardcover)
ISBN: 979-8-88605-163-6 (printed softcover)
ISBN: 979-8-88605-165-0 (ebook)

Cover design by Emilie Haney, www.EAHCreative.com
Typesetting by Jamie Foley, www.JamieFoley.com

Printed in the United States of America.

To Mom—

Thank you for all the ways you fought for me.

POWER
STRUCTURE
IN THE FAE REALM

MORTAL QUEENS

SEVEN FAE KINGS

THREE HOUSES
(Delvers, Low, Berns)

THREE HOUSE
REPRESENTATIVES

THIRTEEN LORDS

1

THEY SAY BEAUTY IS IN THE EYE OF the beholder, but the fae realm would be beautiful to anyone. Except Eliza, apparently. Her lips pressed furiously tight as the chariot glided onward, taking her on her first tour of the glorious realm where every country floated in the sky without roots, stars burned brighter than gems, and magnificence dripped from every dazzling mountain peak adorned with lanterns. We passed by a waterfall spilling from the edge of one country, sending an endless stream through the night, every drop pure white.

To Eliza, it might as well have all been burnt tundra.

Her shoulders pinched back as her hands gripped the rails, and her gaze made frequent trips toward the south where the mortal realm had disappeared and only darkness remained. I made a mental note to thoroughly explain that jumping off would not lead her to the mortal realm.

"When can we visit home?" she asked.

The three ambassadors in the chariot with us didn't hide their grimaces well. My stomach clenched. "We'll talk about that soon," I whispered.

As if our speaking had broken some rule of silence, the

silver-haired fae held out a slender hand. "I can take the bracelet. The lords of Bastian's court will be missing it."

My stomach sank further. The golden bracelet still clasped to my wrist was more than jewelry. Bash had stolen the enchanted jewelry at a great risk to his reputation and delivered it with the promise that I could use it to steal the power of an ambassador. In doing so, I'd become fae myself and escape the threat of impending death that all Mortal Queens are blessed with. It was to be my freedom. Or so I thought.

Shortly before my departure to the mortal realm earlier today, Odette informed me Bash was lying and that the bracelet would transfer the power to him, leaving me dead before I ever turned fae. That alone made me want to throw this bracelet into the abyss, but instead, my fingers tightened around it. It had great value to the lords, and that gave me power. "I'll hold on to it."

"To give to King Bastian?" By the way her brow lifted, she suspected a romantic relationship had formed between us, and it bothered her. She might have been right before, but now the relationship was weaker than my faith in survival.

"No. I'll give it directly to the lords."

Her hand wavered before dropping reluctantly. I held rank over her, and she couldn't argue. But as she spoke, her words dipped in displeasure. "See that you do."

The mental clock ticked in my head. Still hours until midnight. Thanks to my tenuous alliance with Lord Winster, the silver-haired fae was under obligation to say yes to anything I asked until that point, which would have allowed me to take her power as the ambassador—if only I had a way to hold the power.

I wondered if she knew what I had planned. By now, she must.

Beside me, Eliza crossed her arms. "Why didn't you visit us?" The accusation was clear in the tone of her voice, and it pulled me from my thoughts.

"I tried."

That sounded weak, but she didn't know the extent of it. I'd crafted deals with kings and alliances with those who made my skin crawl. I'd poured myself into the mysterious messages hidden within paintings. I'd spent days without sleep as I searched for answers. I'd thrown myself from the edge of the island, falling aimlessly, desperate to find home.

It had all been in vain.

But Eliza didn't know any of that. All she knew was that I left and didn't return. "You promised Malcom," she reminded me.

If Eliza pushed too hard, she'd see me cry. I straightened my spine. She shook her head and turned away. I tried to recall if I'd been this stubborn for Gaia, but all that did was make my insides twist harder until I struggled to compose myself. Her death still rested too close in memory.

Below, the shimmering lights of the Mortal Queens' palace came into view, nestled on the edge of a floating country with towering forests of amber trees growing behind it. The fae would be gathered there, and I appreciated the distraction from the tension in the chariot. I pushed myself close to the rails to see my fae home.

One thing piqued my interest above all else.

A mist of darkness blanketed the kingdom. The courtyard, though still far away, was ablaze with torch flames that gleamed from golden accents, but beyond the small palace, the kingdom lay in absolute darkness. The sort of darkness that swallowed even the night and sucked the beauty from everything around it. The kind that looked like death. It hadn't been like this before Gaia died. But now it was so bleak, I could hardly make out any details or see the trees. It was inhabited territory, but it ought to be lit up with the usual lanterns over polished wells, pathways of glittering stone, or quaint jars of shimmering light atop ivy-covered pedestals. The little I could see was coated in spiderwebs and layers of grey, like color refused to live there. It pained me.

What happened? Was the realm dying?

Talen's words came to mind. *We cannot live without our queens.*

It was more than the palace. The whole kingdom was drenched in despair so thick I could practically taste the bitterness of it, and my heart tore in two. It had been torn so often these past few hours that I wasn't sure it could be put back together again, and I bet if I were fae, I'd be the second one to have their glass heart shattered beyond repair.

We'd neared enough to hear cheering. To Eliza, the fae would sound nothing but happy. But I could hear the sorrow within them.

Welcome our new queen.

Mourn the old.

I'd been too blind to see their pain last year when the previous queen, Ivory, had died. But I felt it now, how Gaia's absence hung in the air like a shroud until it was all I could see. The fae were heartbroken. My kingdom was falling. I was returning to them—no longer as the hopeful, wide-eyed girl I'd been last year—but as a fragmented and lost person.

I almost didn't hear when Eliza spoke again. "What do we do?"

I shook myself to refocus on her. She was taking everything in, and, for the first time, looking awed at the crowds as the rigid line of her jaw smoothed. A distasteful fire still burned in her eyes, but now it was paired with curiosity.

My throat cleared. "We introduce them to their queen. Keep your mask on and your head high. Tell them how happy you are to be here." I put emphasis on that so she knew I meant to lie. "Don't let them see anything other than that."

"Simple enough."

But it wasn't. This world was so much more complicated.

The five of us were lowered into the thick of the cheering, with fae at all sides clamoring to be the first to see their new queen. The moment our chariot touched the stone ground, their cheers heightened. They'd left us a circle in the middle, right where I'd once played chess against King Brock and lost. Torches lined the arch, tall ones with claws holding the fire at the top, and spikes that dove deep into the stone. The ambassadors departed first, standing in a line near the back of the circle, facing the palace.

Smiles were present on the faces of every fae—in colors of gold, silver, and red. Earrings stretching to their shoulders, broaches as bright as the sun adorning their clothes, and gems threading through their hair. It was extravagance of the most luxurious kind.

I looked beyond them, to the windows I'd stared from while trapped inside for three months. The balcony where Bash would leave messages. To Gaia's room, where she'd died.

It would now be Eliza's, and she'd never know what we lost.

I slipped a hand into Eliza's and led her from the chariot.

"My fellow friends," I began. "I have returned to you with a whole heart." Lie. "My time away was short, but I missed you greatly." Bigger lie. "Now I have returned with one who will be such a blessing to us." That part might be true. I lifted Eliza's hand high as her eyes grew wide, taking it all in. "I present to you, your new High Queen of the East—Queen Eliza!"

As they cheered, I located the burning torch nearest me, one with an emerald handle. I drew it from its place in the ground, while gesturing for Eliza to take the flameless one beside her. As the fae gave voice to their approval, I ignited her flame.

She held it high. Eliza had once longed for this as much as I had, and had no doubt spent years playing pretend that she was a chosen queen. Now, I watched her raise a shield and put that disguise on— one of a fearless queen. A visible tremor ran through her arms, but she spoke confidently. "It is an honor to be selected as your new queen. I will forever thank the fae for choosing my name from the bowl, and I hope to serve you well."

Choosing my name from the bowl. My gaze darted to the silver-haired fae. She hadn't selected my name a year ago, and I'd known from how she had refused to show it to Gaia and instead burned the paper. Today, she had neglected to show me as well.

That treacherous being. My dislike for her grew.

I whispered to Eliza. "Walk past the seven thrones and through the doors. I'll meet you inside."

"That's it?"

"They'll get a full look at their new queen at a later celebration. For now, they get nothing more than a taste." I mirrored Gaia's words to me. Would this be how my final year went? Forever replaying the words of Gaia as I walked in her steps?

No, it wouldn't. Because last year, Gaia had hung her head low and retreated into herself, but I wouldn't succumb. Instead, I turned to the silver-haired fae—not caring who saw the altercation.

"Show me the name."

Her eyes widened, and she shot a look to those around us. I pressed, "Show me the proof that Eliza was rightfully chosen today. I want to see the paper."

She slipped two fingers into her pocket and brought it out. "That's right, my Queen. I forgot to let you kiss it. Do you wish to do so now, to wish her luck?"

I half-expected her to toss it into the flames, but instead, she handed it to me. I quickly opened it.

ELIZA NADINE NADELL

No. I flipped it over. The odds were too low. There were thousands of eligible girls on the center island. "It's a trick," I said out loud. "You came with her name in hand."

"There is no trick." She snatched it back. "Perhaps your luck has simply run out." She turned on her heel to sweep away into the thick crowd, but my hand shot out to grab her arm.

"Who ordered you to bring me to this realm?" I asked. "Will you answer me honestly?"

It wasn't what I'd intended to use my limited power over her for, but it would work nonetheless. I had until midnight to force her to say yes, and an opportunity like that shouldn't be squandered.

She went stiff, and her lips seemed to move with struggle. "Yes, someone did ask it of me."

"Tell me who."

She fought it, but the words escaped her lips. "A king."

I let go, and she took the chance to flee. I didn't chase.

A king.

Which king? Someone had been playing me from the start, and I intended to know why.

With both her and Eliza gone, I had nothing to distract from the madness around me. The courtyard was too loud. The fae too close. My head too conflicted. It all pressed against me until I could focus on nothing other than getting away.

Bony fingers pressed into my arms as the fae questioned where I'd been over the past few months and if I was going to leave again. Questioned Gaia's death. Questions I didn't know how to answer. The easiest ones were about Eliza and what sort of queen she would be. Cunning? Tricky? Illusive? *Practical*, I thought. Then spoke.

"It is not for me to say. You will get to know her tonight." I bent my head low and pushed through the crowds, until coming to the feet of the seven thrones where the kings sat.

They stared at me blankly, as if we were playing a game and I'd already lost. My eye wandered to the end thrones. Along with the seventh king, Bash was missing.

It was for the best. I wasn't certain what to say to him yet.

A king had called me here. Was it Bash? Or one of the others? I studied them again. *One of you is playing a game with me. I won't go down without a fight.*

Last year, I hadn't been frightened enough. I was now.

One year remaining.

2

I SLIPPED THROUGH THE GRAND
double doors and shut them behind me, blocking out some of the
noise. I knew what would happen next. The fae would leave, and
all would fall silent. Only the sound of the river would remain,
running from the two thrones and through the center of the throne
room, splitting it in two.

Eliza stood on the eastern side of it, staring at the chairs that
were once so magnificent. Now they were more like shrines.
Tributes to another time. My three stars were still embedded in
mine, but they barely held any remaining shine.

I walked along the western side, stopping before my throne and
looking over the stream to her. "I'm sorry." There was nothing else
I could think to say.

She wiped a tear from her cheek. It wasn't unusual to miss
home, but as far as I knew, every queen had felt as I had—excited
to see this realm and exploding with joy upon being chosen. I'd
walked into my role as queen eagerly, even though I missed my
brothers. I could almost laugh now at how eager I was to meet the
queens chosen from all the years prior, certain we'd have some
grand tea party together. But Eliza appeared immune to all things
fae. She hadn't been like this before. Even last year, when she was

already courting my brother, she longed to be picked. Something had changed within her, and it was recent.

"I shouldn't be here," she said, as if reading my thoughts.

"I saw your name on the paper." I reached a hand across the stream to her, but she didn't take it. "We will find a way to fix this."

"It should have been impossible," she spoke as if I wasn't there. "We made sure of it."

There was no way to be certain. Every year, they inscribed the names and placed them in the bowl the night before the fae came. And throughout the night, it was guarded by fifty soldiers. Every year, girls tried to sneak in and add their names in abundance, but they never got through. That bowl was more heavily protected than the governor himself. In equal measure, there would be no way to get one's name out.

But if anyone could do it, I'd bet my brother was smart enough to find a way. "Did Cal do something?"

She closed her eyes at the mention of him. Her words were a dainty breath, small and dry. "Show me the way home."

"I am going to get you home," I promised. "You will see Cal again."

"No, Althea. Now."

I swallowed, and she nodded as if I'd spoken.

"I knew it," Eliza said. "Something traps us here, doesn't it? It's not luxury that keeps the mortals in this realm, it is a curse." I didn't need to say anything for her to know that was true. She wiped another tear from her eye. "What now?"

I motioned to the grand stairwell on her side of the stream. The sweeping banister was less polished now, covered in cobwebs, and the stones cracked in places. It didn't give the same magnificent appearance it had when I first arrived. Instead, it was like pointing toward a coffin. "You are the High Queen of the East, while I rule the west." I indicated my own side that mirrored hers perfectly. "You'll go up those stairs and choose your first alliance."

She drew a hand down her face, tugging at her skin in a weary gesture. "Alliance?"

I wished to give her something simple. *Go up those stairs and enjoy some dates. We will visit the mortal realm tomorrow. All will be calm and joyful.* Instead, I found myself at a loss for words to describe this land she'd been dragged into. Still, I would try.

"We don't rule like we've read about in stories. There is no typical monarchy here. Instead, our kingdom thrives on power—the more power you have, the more your kingdom will prosper. Soil will be rich and harvest plentiful. Light will burn brighter. Civilians will feel healthier. And the way to gain this power is through alliances with others. Smart alliances with powerful people will acquire respect. Too many alliances dim the value of each one and put you at risk of them breaking away, but too few and you aren't strong enough. An alliance with a king is preferred."

"There are kings?" A hint of worry swelled in her voice.

"Not one that you must marry," I assured her. "You are queen in your own right and always will be. But yes, there are seven kings. One went missing a few hundred years ago, but six remain."

Her gaze swept over the drabby room. "Did you not have alliances?"

She couldn't know how that sent a blade into my heart. This was the room where I'd thrown parties. Where I'd tricked Bash into bowing at my feet. Where I'd celebrated with Talen and Odette. I made two of my alliances in this palace and announced my third here. But the room had fallen into despair.

"I had three," I explained, hoping she didn't notice how my voice thinned. "One with the House of Delvers, who rank right below the kings. One with Lord Winster, who tricked me into it. And one with a king, who was deceiving me."

When I summarized my time here like that, it sounded dejecting.

"So this world is a game?"

I nodded. "It's a game we will win. I promise."

She sighed. "I just want to sleep. I'll feel better in the morning when the light comes."

"Um, about that."

Eliza froze as she headed toward the stairs, then sent me a sharp look like she couldn't take any further bad news. I cleared my throat. "There is no light here. Only night."

She set her jaw and marched up the stairs.

"First door on your right," I called out, but she gave no reply.

Guilt dug into me. She'd be opening a door to an empty room and three fae representatives asking her to make her first alliance. If I'd thought about it, I would have sent her straight to my room to rest first. But the alliance would fill her room soon enough, and she wouldn't be saved by me protecting her from the realm. She had to meet it headfirst. That was how we'd win.

I stared after her, hoping she'd choose Talen. With his resemblance to Cal, she might. But I could not help her with that decision. And I had other matters to attend to.

Before I could, my name floated down from the west. Odette stood at the top of the stairs wearing an ivory gown and a pained expression like she felt every ounce of my sorrow. She'd been disappointed by the one she loved a long time ago. She cherished this kingdom just as I did. More than that, she felt my emptiness at losing Gaia. Every wound in my heart was mirrored in hers.

She flew down the stairs and wrapped her arms around me. "Talen and I have been searching all day for a way to get you back to your realm," she said. "We will not stop. You will live."

I tightened our embrace in thanks. Then I looked at her. "Take care of Eliza for me. She's like family."

"Of course." She combed her hands through my hair, smoothing it out.

"And make sure whoever she aligns with gets the softest mattress for her room, and a wool just as thick as mine."

She grinned. "I will." When I moved away, she caught me by the hand. "Where are you going?" She looked at me as if I were a fragile animal who might die in the wild without her protection.

I felt that way. But I summoned courage until a strength surged within me, along with an assurance to make smarter moves this year. Starting with making my peace with everything I'd just gone through.

"To pay my respects to Gaia." I wanted to say goodbye before

I moved on. My plan was to walk outside to have a moment for her since the courtyard should be cleared, but Odette held on to my hand.

"Then come with me. We have a special ceremony for our fallen queens." A tear came to her eye. "We always say goodbye."

I let her lead me to the east, not up the stairs, but under them. She moved a tapestry aside to push on the marble. The slab opened. A golden hallway stretched before us, covered in speckles of black dust with soot marks along the walls beneath dimly burning oil lamps. A musky scent filled my nose.

"What is this place?" I wrapped my arms around myself to shield from the sudden chill.

Her reply echoed. "A hallway only used once a year."

There were no paintings, vases, or signs of life. Nothing but dead rose petals at our feet, some freshly plucked and still ripe with red, others left from ages ago and now blackened, disintegrating underneath our steps. Petals for the fallen queens, years gone by. They collected in my skirts and stuck to the underside of my slippers as I walked.

After a hundred paces, we reached a second door, this one arched and built of driftwood. Or perhaps it had once been oak, but now was decayed beyond recognition. This was more than the damage to the realm from the queens who'd been missing for eight months. This hallway had long been soaked in death.

Odette opened the door, and I inhaled a breath of fresh air. The hallway led to a small pond at the back of the palace that glistened with still waters until it met the edge of the island, only held in by a wall of stone, or else it would spill into the endless sky. Fae gathered in the large courtyard, one that rivaled the size of the courtyard in the front. All of them looked to the pond. I wove through to get a better look before seeing the casket. It bobbed in the water. Fae came one by one to dip their hands in and mumble a few words, each paying their respects to the fallen queen.

Odette advanced with the crowd, but I stayed for a few minutes, staring at the casket.

Gaia. My sweet friend. I wasn't certain if we were true friends, but she was the only one who could have known what I was going through. She had been brave as she faced her fate and wore her death sentence with a strength I hadn't noticed as I ran wild looking for answers. She never crumbled. She never fled. She was a queen to the very end.

A lump rose in my throat, and like Odette, a tear slid down my cheek. Then another. Finally, I found the strength to step forward. She would be missed—by the fae, by me, and by her family. She would be remembered.

When all others had taken their turn, I dipped my fingers into the water and lifted my eyes to the casket. It was an old, leaden thing, with brass-bound spools up the sides and a handsome black fabric stretched tight between them. Decedent brocade wove throughout in silver thread. I pictured her inside. Dark hair clinging to the dainty curve of her shoulders, and seven golden earrings bound to her ear. That straight smile she always wore, now permanently etched on her lips. Her pure white mask still on her face.

Take it off, I thought.

I stood. "Take it off."

A few, startled by my sudden order, looked to me. I stepped into the pool, letting the frigid water swarm to my waist. Sharp rocks sliced against my slippers as I moved, but they didn't stop me. Nor did the shouts of the fae behind me. The somber mood shattered, and the silence fled, replaced with alarmed cries and splashing water as I shamelessly trudged to the casket while it rocked from side to side with the waves I created.

My fingers fumbled for the clasp, finding a silver latch and yanking upward. I trembled when I placed my hands beneath the lid to open it.

"My Queen, don't," Odette's voice came from behind me. She'd entered the water as well but stood several paces back. "She's gone."

"But she's not free," I said.

I lifted the lid.

Gaia lay inside, skin pale and body still. The fae gave a collection of gasps behind me, but none were trying to stop me. Thankful for that, I took my time reaching for Gaia's mask, then pried my fingers underneath it.

Masks are enchanted with some sort of fae power. Mine felt like skin to my fingers and moved as if it were. Now that Gaia was dead, I hoped hers would come loose. I was right.

Tenderly, I removed her mask and placed it beside her. For the first time in two years, she was free to be human again.

She was a captain's daughter, so her face was one I had known before she ever came to the fae realm, but she'd grown more beautiful in her years here. Even with her eyes shut, every trace of her features was perfect, with high cheekbones, silky hair, and a curve of her lips like she held a secret. Another tear fell, landing on her cheek. I brushed it away with a promise.

You will be the last Mortal Queen to fall. I will find a way to end this.

I sealed the lid. Then, as a hush fell over the fae, I pushed the casket to the end of the pond, right where the stone met the air. The edge of it grated against the rocks. I peeked over my shoulder until I found Odette, looking for confirmation that this was how they buried their dead—with an eternity among the stars. She nodded.

With a tight throat and damp cheeks, I pushed the fallen High Queen of the East over the edge and let the casket fall.

3

I TRUDGED BACK THROUGH THE
pond and climbed out, aiming for the drafty corridor. Odette
barricaded me with stiff arms and a hushed whisper. "Queen Eliza
will need your help. You should go to her."

"Eliza will have to manage," I said, passing by her to enter the
dark, dusty tunnel once more. A renewed sense of fight filled me—
determination not to end up like Gaia. "I have someone else to see."

"Thea." From the echo of her voice, she'd entered the tunnel
too. I quickened my pace. "You cannot trust him."

She hadn't even said his name, yet my voice came out strained.
"I know."

I moved too fast for further questions, or to form a proper plan.
All I knew was Bash had betrayed me, and if I'd gone through with
his idea to steal power from the ambassador today, they'd be pushing
a second casket off the island. I strode out of the tunnel, through
the throne room, and to the main courtyard. There, I flung my
hand up and waited for a chariot to spot me. It only took a moment
for one to glide down and settle on the tiles. I climbed aboard.

"Take me to King Bastian."

It took off. I grasped the rail as the wind caught my wet skirts
and plucked dead rose petals away, until droplets of water and

petals flew behind me. I checked my wrist for the ambassador's bracelet. Still there. Several fae had likely seen it at the funeral. There would be whispers soon, poisonous words darting through the night sky at a speed too fast to stop.

It would be Bash's neck on the line this time. Not mine.

I'd loved him.

He'd almost killed me.

Before long, the high peaks of Bash's home came into view. Snow capped the sleek, black mountains, and thick clouds brewed overhead to release flurries of brilliant white. Of all the places I'd been to in this realm, this palace remained the most breathtaking. Floor to ceiling windows carved into the side of the mountain with ever-burning lanterns of polished iron mounted along wooden rails. Lavish curtains hanging over ever-opened windows, the fabric billowing outward to dance in the wind. Fires burning to light various courtyards. The crimson glow bounced from my soaked dress as we neared.

My chariot settled on the wide, grey stone patio that backed to the edge of the cliffs. I stepped off, looking to the great double doors cast with metal.

"I'll be right back," I informed my chariot. The misty orb that guided the chariot glittered in response.

I pushed against the doors, not bothering to knock.

Just as in my home, his opened directly to his throne room. But the similarities ended there. Black floors at my feet. A wicked fire blazed along the north side, running the entire length of the space to illuminate a dark throne with two spindles on each end. And at the right-hand side of the throne, the cloche with his unbreakable glass heart. Red silk covered it now, but I knew what rested underneath. Solid glass. A sign that he'd never cared for anyone.

The stories about his heart should have been my sign to stay away. I'd received many warnings—from Talen, Odette, King Vern, and a server at my coronation ball. But I'd ignored them all for the thrill that came with being at his side.

I supposed it was true what they said—mortals weren't made for this realm. It was too intoxicating for us. I'd gotten my last taste. Going forward, I wouldn't let anything captivate me again.

Without thinking, I approached the cloche.

My fingers hesitated over the silk. Just when I'd determined to open it and see for myself, dark laughter sliced the air.

It was Troi's—Bash's faithful sister. She was also his protector, which meant she'd devoted her life entirely to keeping him safe, which did not bode well for me currently.

Troi wore a long ebony dress with a slit up the side, a sword on one hip, and a trailing-blade dagger on the other. Her smile was just as lethal as either of those. "Here we were, wondering how we'd get into the palace to find you, and instead you waltzed into our own home"—she glanced outside—"alone."

I was highly aware of her hand on the hilt. "You plan to kill me?"

Out of everyone in the realm, she might actually do it. She raked her gaze over me like she debated it now. "To get that bracelet back?" She gestured to my wrist. "Whatever it takes."

"I think I'll hold on to this," I said, wishing my earlier determination had come with an impulse to grab a weapon. If needed, I could grab the cloche and use that. I'd see if Bash's heart would break if thrown. "Leverage and all."

"Leverage? The only thing that bracelet is to you is a pretty accessory. You clearly failed to take the ambassador's power, and therefore have no further use of it." She stuck out her hand, stepping close enough for me to see the fine tips of her silver eyeliner. "Give it to me, so my king can make things right."

"No." My voice sounded surer than I thought it would.

"Do you care at all for him?" she pressed. "His kingdom falls without that. Hand it to me now."

From her tone, she wouldn't ask again.

Bash's voice came next, accompanied by heavy footsteps. "Leave us, Troi."

We looked at him in unison. He strode from a stairwell behind the throne, mostly coated in shadows. What I could see was the glint of his eyes and the steady way he walked, like he had nothing to be ashamed of. It made something twist inside me.

Had he no regret for what he'd done?

Troi hesitated before bowing. She gave me a final glare, then backed away.

As she left, Bash's movements slowed. For a moment, only the crackle of the fire split the tension in the air, while I held my breath in my throat. With him standing in front of me, my heart was somehow able to beat again, while I simultaneously felt like I was drowning. As if my body knew he was supposed to be my safe place, but right now I was sure to break.

Finally, I remembered how to speak. "You lied to me."

"I've been told not to trust the queens," Bash said as if he had not heard me. He wore the suit from when I'd seen him last, cut from smooth black cloth, adorned with topaz buttons, and lined over a red shirt that set off the flames in his eyes. "Warned not to align with them. They are so desperate to live, they don't care who they burn in their fall. Tell me, did you rejoice when I offered to steal such a relic from my own lords? Did you celebrate what you'd tricked a king to do?"

My brows shot up. "I tricked you? No. You tricked me. All your talk of eternity together as you plotted to end my life early. Does it pain you that I'm still here?"

His eyes flicked to the bracelet. "You showed it to the ambassador after I warned you how desperately I needed it to remain hidden. You've ruined me."

"She saw it on her own," I said, as if that made a difference. "But unfortunately for you, I didn't use it."

"For me?" His next steps were quick, bringing him from the darkness to the side of the throne, where firelight danced across his brown skin. Everything in me trembled. He was as striking as ever, threatening to collapse my resolve. It took everything to push aside my feelings and remind myself who he was.

He took in the sight of me. "Everything I did was for you."

I ripped the bracelet off and clutched it in my fist. "If I'd used this, I would have died, and you knew that."

"I would have been there in an instant to revive you." He reached his hand upward, and with a thundering boom, ripped one of the stars from the sky. "Did you forget I can pluck the stars like a petal from a flower? Surely I am strong enough to keep you alive. But you didn't give me a chance. Instead, you revealed the bracelet and thrust my kingdom into chaos."

"You do not get to make me the villain. You lied to me!" My voice rose. "You should have told me the bracelet would have taken all power and transferred it to you, killing me."

"Did you forget? I am your ally. I cannot lie to you."

I *had* forgotten. My anger turned to confusion while I sorted a new path. He'd still betrayed me somehow—bent the truth so it wasn't a lie. Led me astray.

He kept his voice as calm as the snowfall outside. "I enchanted the bracelet to not transfer power to me, but to keep it in you. You cannot hold that much power as a mortal, that much is true. But the moment you acquired the power, I'd have felt it, and been at your side in an instant to kept you alive long enough to turn you fae. Exactly as we planned. I can't save you from the fate of the Mortal Queens, Thea. But this would have. Instead of trusting me, you betrayed me."

He was twisting this to make me feel bad for not trusting him, when he'd failed to tell me this plan of his would leave me dead, and creating a fine story of how he would have saved me from such a fate.

I had no way to know if that was true.

He went on. "I didn't mention it before you left, but the lords already knew I stole the bracelet from them. They were doing everything they could to find it and slowly breaking away from my kingdom. I have no lands left. No one who trusts me. No one willing to align. Yet I didn't return the bracelet, even though you had vanished. Do you know why?"

Silence met him.

"I did it all so you'd have a way to survive."

His words punched a hole through me, and I fought to keep myself together. "I can't trust that you are telling me the truth right now."

"Why would I kill you?" His eyes met mine. "Thea, I loved you. And you—" He lifted his hands, then let them fall. "You left me with a kingdom in ruins."

When he said he loved me, I wanted to believe it was real and that he would have saved me. But in this fae realm, it was far more likely he'd used me as a siphon to get the power from the ambassador, not that a mortal girl had swayed the heart of a king.

The unbreakable glass heart.

My gaze went to the covered cloche beside me. I blinked my eyes dry. "You never loved me." That was the truth, no matter how hard I wished otherwise. And to think, I'd believed I'd be his fae queen. "You can't love anything."

To prove my point, I ripped the silk from the cloche to expose his unblemished glass heart.

It was cracked.

A deep, jagged crack ran through the depths of it, and the sight instantly shattered my own heart. Quickly, Bash yanked the silk from my hands and threw it over the cloche. His voice broke as he spoke. "Will you not allow me some remaining dignity?"

I had broken his heart. Me, a simple mortal girl, had found a place in the heart of a magnificent fae king, and I'd cracked it.

He'd been telling the truth.

I stumbled back. "Bash . . . I didn't know. I thought you were tricking me."

"I gave up everything for you." He was speaking more to himself than to me. "I broke my kingdom for you, and you walked away from me so easily."

"I'll use it now." I was unable to move my eyes from the cloche. "I'll find the ambassador and ask for her power."

Bash stepped away. "It is too late. The clock has struck midnight, and Lord Winster's influence over her has expired. As for us"—he was retreating, slipping back into the shadows—"our alliance is over."

A fierce desperation grew within me. "Don't do this. Please, Bash. I didn't mean to hurt you."

He was nearly out of sight, but I caught his words. "Too late for that. I don't need to learn lessons twice. Those close to the queens only get burned."

I became frantic. I threw the bracelet into the darkness after him. "Take it! Heal your kingdom." No reply came. My skin felt hot, and my breaths quickened. "What was I to do? This realm is all about lies that come from every direction, and alliances I can't trust. How could I not protect myself when I thought I would die? How am I to think rationally in a land such as this? Bastian, please. Let me fix this."

His voice drifted out. "There is nothing to fix. You played a game, and you played it well. The realm will praise you for your trickery."

"I don't care about that. Bash, stop!" I couldn't think. I couldn't breathe. The truth mixed with the lies until it was hard to see clearly, and something snapped inside me. I shouted, "I have one question left!"

From deep in the shadows of the stairwell, his figure turned.

"Upon making the alliance, you owed me the honest answer to two questions, and one remains. King Bastian, did you love me honestly?"

His voice rang of sadness and resolve. "Yes."

I'd never heard a word sound so much like goodbye.

He left me alone in silence as fear built within me that I'd just lost the one person in this realm who truly cared whether I lived or died.

4

THE RIDE BACK TO THE PALACE WAS

a solemn one where I repeated every memory with Bash in my head,
wishing I'd known how much he cared, as if the knowledge could
somehow summon his feelings to return. From the void expression
he wore when he looked at me, such emotions were long gone.

But mine weren't. My love for him rested too close to the surface,
where it could easily consume me. I'd hoped to have it tucked away
by the time the chariot delivered me home, but it was to no avail. I
pushed the two front doors open with an aching heart and a tight
throat. I glanced to the east. I ought to check on Eliza. But I craved
a moment alone.

What I found was anything but that.

When I opened the door to my chambers, Talen paced the floors
with his top hat in hand and the tails of his suit flapping with each
step. His white hair was rumpled like he'd been running his hands
through it too many times. Odette stood at the end of my bed,
opening her mouth each time Talen passed before snapping it shut.

Eliza was the only one who appeared at ease, her legs crossed
as she sat in the chair beside my paintings, staring at Bash's still
unfinished face.

Upon my entrance, Talen and Odette both sprang toward me.

Talen got words in first. "She won't align." He thrust an accusatory finger Eliza's way.

She gave a big sigh, clearly unbothered. "He's just mad that I won't align with *him*."

"You could align with Thomas for all I care." Talen spat the name. "But you must pick someone."

"Please don't align with Thomas. He's insufferable," Odette said. Then she neared Eliza. "My Queen, the House of Delvers would be a smart alignment. It's who Thea chose."

At that, Eliza lifted a brow. "And what have they done for Thea?"

I thought quickly. "Talen gave up his heart for me." There were many things I could have said, including hundreds I was certain I hadn't seen. Talen had filled me in once on everything he did to shield me from tricks and pave the way for my success, but none spoke to his devotion as much as the time he'd traded his glass heart to reduce the sentence King Brock had placed over me, buying back three months of freedom for me.

But Eliza only frowned at the words. "He's in love with you?"

"He's not in love with anyone," Odette snorted.

Talen fell to his knees. "I will love you, Eliza, if you align with my House." Behind his back, Odette rolled her eyes.

Eliza remained unimpressed. She leaned forward to speak firmly. "I will not align." She settled back. "If this world is a game, I refuse to play."

Now I understood Talen's pacing. He'd resumed it as Odette tossed up her hands to return to her position against the bed, biting her nails. I studied the two of them, then Eliza.

"Has a queen ever refused to play?" I asked Talen. It hadn't occurred to me to refuse my first alliance, but if I'd seen a fae so bothered by my actions, I would have done anything to fix what I'd done.

Eliza held no such apologies.

"Gaia didn't play in her last year," Talen said. "But even she was aligned. Your Highness, without an alliance with us, I cannot offer you any assistance—by deflecting mischief aimed at you, by bringing in new alliances, or by aiding your navigation through this realm. Do you know how many packages rest outside your door now—every single one likely ensnared with a trap of sorts? You'd be helpless. I can't even provide a bed for you to sleep on."

"She can sleep with me," I interjected.

Talen shot me a look. "Fine, you'll have a bed. But with everything else, you will be on your own." He looked at me again before I could open my mouth, and I thought better of it.

I would help Eliza as much as possible, but she truly would benefit from a real alliance. Additionally, the land required it. The queens needed to grow powerful again to heal the darkness that had settled over the realm, and I could not carry that weight alone. There was a balance that needed to be met.

But Eliza locked her jaw. "I am not here to play games. I am not here to make friends. I am only here for as long as it takes to find a way home. So thank you very much for the offer, but I don't accept."

"Eliza," I tried. "It's for your own good."

"Has playing by the rules of the fae worked out well for you so far?" I flinched. She knew the answer. "Then I will not play by their rules. I choose to start my reign here with no alliance."

Odette cleared her throat as if to make her pitch, but Eliza sent her a glare. "I have said no, and as long as I wear seven earrings, which, as far as I've counted, is more than any of you"—her glare sliced to me when I lifted my hand—"not you. Then I outrank you all. I will not hear of it again."

We all blinked at each other. My fear when bringing Eliza to this land was that she would be like Gaia. Temperate. Unsure. Someone I'd have to carry along as I tried to save us both. But Eliza was quite the opposite, and while at this present moment it was inconvenient, her strong will might be just what we needed to get out of the realm alive. Like me, she had something to get back to, and she had already shown she would not be deterred. Even where I'd been distracted by handsome fae kings, I suspected she would not be. She would never lose sight of our goal to return home, and together we could be smart enough to unravel the mortals' ties to the fae.

I gestured Talen and Odette toward the door. "Could you give us the night? We can convene in the morning to discuss our next steps."

"I would love to, but there is the matter of the coronation tonight," Talen said.

I groaned internally. Last year, the coronation was where I announced my alliance with the House of Delvers, created my alliance with Lord Winster, and met King Bastian. The fae craved to know their new queen. It would be a slight to rob them of that.

But judging the expression on Eliza's face, she would not go. I asked her anyway.

"No."

"Host the celebration," I told Talen. "Let's hope the fae settle for me."

Though obviously displeased, Talen and Odette nodded and departed. Eliza had returned to staring at my paintings, so I took the moment to quickly follow Talen.

"Wait," I whispered before they'd gone too far down the hallway. I shut my door behind me. "I have a task for you."

"We have a task for *you*—convince Queen Eliza to change her mind."

I gave a laugh. That would be as difficult as the task I was giving them. "I'll do my best. The task I have for you is . . . sensitive." As I tried to speak, the words were hard to find, like my mind wasn't yet certain they were true. It had only been today that I made two startling discoveries in the mortal realm—both from the lips of my father.

One, he was fae. I'd found that out when everyone froze after I pressed the dial on my watch, yet he did not. If I squeezed my eyes tight, I could almost transport myself back to that moment when I'd held on tight to my little brother, Malcom, for what might have been the last time. It still made my heart weak. Then my father moved, and everything I'd thought was true in life shattered.

The second discovery was just as shocking. My mother hadn't gone missing five years ago. After receiving a letter threatening that I'd be summoned to the fae realm one day, she'd willingly come here to find a way to defeat the Mortal Queens' fate before I stepped into this land. But I'd seen no evidence of her over the past year. If my mother remained in this realm, I needed to find her.

And if she had come into the fae world, she might have a way out.

But if she was here, it also meant she had spent the past year avoiding me, and I wasn't certain what to make of that. She had always been all things a mother should be—gentle, fiercely protective, loving. That image didn't pair well with someone who didn't acknowledge her daughter for a year. If she was here, she was either in hiding or detained. Or dead. Pieces of the story were missing, and Talen might be able to find them for me.

Talen and Odette watched me with concern as I struggled to say the words. "What is it?" Talen asked.

"My mother is in this realm." The words tumbled out, and both their jaws dropped. I hurried to answer the questions they'd surely ask. "I don't know how or where she is. But I am confident she is here and in trouble, and I need you to find her for me."

Talen blinked before he spoke. "I'll find her as soon as I can."

That was all I could ask. I debated telling them about my father but left it at that. One parent was enough to deal with tonight, and I had a festivity to prepare for. "Let me know if you need any help, and please keep this quiet."

They agreed and departed, and I went back to my chambers where Eliza waited, still as stubbornly expressionless as before. Instead of facing her, I crossed to the bed to throw myself flat upon it. I laid that way for a while, only shifting when I felt Eliza settle next to me. She'd let her hair down and sat with her hands in her lap.

Eliza spoke first. "I know you're not happy I am not aligning."

"You can do what you like," I told her, rolling over. "Truthfully, my alliances have turned into a big hassle."

She managed a small smile, but something else clearly bothered her. "Talen said Gaia refused to play *in her last year.*"

I tensed. I knew the question she was asking, and I dreaded answering it as much as she must dread saying the words. I sat up.

"I haven't seen her yet. Where is she? What happened?"

"She died." I whispered the words she already seemed to expect.

Her chest rose with a sharp intake of breath. She still wore the black satin dress from the mortal realm, with pearls sewn between the stitching in the neckline and lace adorning the sleeves in a way that was considered pretty back home, but here, it was out of place. The look on her face, however, was one I knew well from this realm—dread. It was one I couldn't fix.

"We are dying," I said, reaching across the sheets to grasp her hand. "But we are working on a way to solve that."

"How is that going?"

"It's complicated."

I hoped she was ready to hear this.

I told her everything.

About our two-year lifespan with the fae, about the kings, about my alliances, about Illusion Point and glass hearts and messages in paintings. About how hard I tried to get back home. About how my father confessed he was fae before we returned, and how he claimed my mother was here somewhere.

When I finished, she was silent for a long while. She didn't take her hand from mine, and I kept hold, wishing I could be a steady presence for her. In truth, I was reeling as much as she was, and I wasn't confident either of us would find a way to survive. But when her breathing slowed, a look of determination filled her eyes.

"Cal loved puzzles," she said. My eyes watered at the mention of my brother. "He would tell them to me every day, and I became as obsessed as he was with solving them. This is just like one of his puzzles."

I nodded. "Cal would do well here."

"*I'm* going to do well here," she corrected. "But I will solve this in my own way."

5

THE VACANCY OF THE EASTERN
throne filled the room, until it was all anyone could look at when
they entered from the courtyard, each fae faltering in their steps
and sweeping their gazes across the two sides, checking for Eliza's
presence, no doubt. She wouldn't show.

For appearances' sake, we'd polished the thrones as if to say
our magnificence couldn't be dimmed, but the rest of the room
remained so dark, the shadows swallowing the lanterns, and the
only glow coming from the three stars on my chair. After Bash broke
our alliance, I half suspected they would die, but they didn't. And
now that I sat on the chair again, they grew brighter by the minute.

It increased my confidence that I could heal the realm.

The fae didn't seem as confident. They slinked into the room,
shuffling through the dim haze until they approached my feet.
There, they bowed, laid baskets of jewelry, gowns, treats, or other
various gifts at the foot of the thrones, and then retreated to the
courtyard where the air wasn't as musty, and they could whisper
without me hearing them. I guessed what they said.

The queens have been gone for too long. The kingdom has faded.
No alliance could save them now.

Even though I tried not to, I compared this year to last year.

This was meant to be a party, not a display of how far the Mortal Queens had fallen.

I wore the darkest gown I could find, as if the swirling darkness around us was one of my own design and not a cage closing in around me. The dress had full sleeves of sheer fabric, a swooped neckline, and thick skirts that tumbled over the seat of the throne and covered my leather sandals. My nails were painted a deep red, my earrings all black, and a platinum nose ring finished the look.

The mood didn't heighten until the first king arrived—Thorn. He radiated a golden light as he strolled through the doors with a glow seeping from his bronze cloak, the tips of his white buttons, and the heels of his polished shoes. He looked like the sun itself. He flashed a smile, sending a buzz through the room. Even Odette straightened. At my side, Talen flinched.

Thorn kept his bronze eyes fixed on me as if he didn't see that Queen Eliza was absent. In his hand, he held a small box. When he reached my feet, he knelt.

"My Queen. A gift from Illusion Point."

A spool of energy shot through me at the mention of Illusion Point. Thorn had been the one to take me there first and unveil the world of magic it contained. The island was more of a carnival than anything, with narrow streets crowded by tents and booths, while endless chess games took place at its heart. I'd removed my watch earlier, the trinket I purchased from Illusion Point that gave me twelve extra minutes with my family, not to mention the information from my father.

A different watch that Gaia bought from the same island had hastened her death rather than save her as she'd hoped. Gifts from Illusion Point were a double-edged sword, so it was no wonder the whole room pulsed nearer to see what the king had brought me.

Thorn opened the box, and a crystal flute of pudding rested within.

"My personal favorite flavor," he said, passing it to me. "I figured it would be a while before you escaped outside to the food, so I brought something special for you."

I recognized the name on the side of the box and spotted the red dot on Thorn's finger. "Madame Rola took some of your blood again? Does she have no other payment method?" I asked, accepting the pudding and slender spoon he offered.

"It seems to be her favorite, and the fae don't seem to mind. In fact, there's been an increased number of customers recently, so she is doing very well for herself."

"Still, I'd like to know what she needs it for." I dipped my spoon into the pudding and took a bite. The cream had been blended perfectly to offer a sweet honey flavor at first that melted into a smooth mint. Thorn watched me expectantly.

"What does it taste like?"

I looked at him in surprise. "You said it was your favorite. Don't you know?"

"To me, it tastes like lavender so pure, it is like I'm in a field. But the taste mimics the eater's ideal flavor, so no two people taste the same thing."

"Fascinating." I lifted the flute closer to inspect its contents. "That sounds—"

"Expensive," Talen finished for me. "How much did it cost you, and what will it cost my Queen?"

His words reminded me where I was—in a land where nothing was given freely.

But Thorn's smile was so innocent, I almost believed his next words. "Nothing. Sometimes a king simply likes to shower his queen with gifts." I didn't miss how he called me *his* queen, and I knew what he wanted.

He wanted an alliance. It would be a fair proposal, considering I was down one alliance, but I wasn't quite ready yet. Perhaps part of me held out hope that Bash would come around and ask for me back, or I feared what he would think if I ran to Thorn in his stead. Either way, I plastered on a wide smile and pretended I believed Thorn had no ulterior motives.

"Thank you, my King."

At last, he glanced to Eliza's seat. "Has the new queen decided not to attend? You've scared her with stories of this realm, haven't you?"

I did my best to keep a straight face and not give away that he'd guessed it. "She feels ill with the excitement, that is all. We will host another party later to properly show her off to the realm."

"Indeed. And what House did she align with? Delvers again?" He turned to Talen. "If so, you might be in for a promotion."

"She leans that way," he replied stiffly. To his credit, that was probably true. If she were to align, I suspected she'd choose him. But with how I'd left her, it'd be a miracle if we managed to drag her out to the realm at all, much less convince her to pick an alliance.

Thorn's eyes danced as if he'd won a prize. "She chooses no alliance, then. Interesting. Perhaps she needs a king to change her mind." He looked toward the east wing as if he was going to ascend the stairs and ask her himself. Let him. She wouldn't be there. Even if she was, she certainly wouldn't be convinced by a mere pretty smile.

Instead, Thorn observed, "After the year we've had, the whole realm will be very interested to see what happens." He tipped his head. "Enjoy the pudding."

I watched him walk away. When he was gone, Talen noticeably relaxed, and I almost laughed. "You truly don't like him."

"He's not my favorite king."

"Is that because of his previous relationship with Odette?" I poked.

He grimaced. "One of many reasons. And many relationships he's had. That king is trouble."

"Which one isn't?" I mumbled. Each king came with his own warning signs, yet I tended to ignore all of them.

Speaking of kings, King Brock entered next with his fae queen on his arm. Her brilliant, bright hair twisted around her arm like a snake, rubbing against her dress of diamonds, while he opted for the simpler look of a black suit. The golden band on his forehead and his six earrings were the only indicators that he ranked above the rest of the fae. He took Eliza's absence in stride. They both approached.

"You are a welcome sight after many long months," Brock said. "I hope you visit my home soon, so we may properly celebrate you."

With his words, I remembered I still owed him one favor from when he beat me in chess. If visiting his home was all he would ask, I was getting off easily.

The stream of fae had slowed until no one else approached the thrones. I took the moment to lean toward Talen. "Truthfully, how bad are my lands?"

He appeared to chew the answer over in his mind before speaking, as if debating how honest he should be. Finally, he said, "Bad. The darkness is thicker than we have ever seen. Beneath it all, the land has dried up and all crops have died. Any who lived in your kingdom have fled to other regions, leaving you even weaker. If you don't impress the realm soon, I fear nothing will bring the lands back to life again."

Impress the realm. There was a need for balance here I couldn't see, and it demanded satisfaction. "What does it need? A good deal made? A chess match won against a king? A new alliance?"

Talen tilted his head. "You have three strong alliances, so I'd focus more on making good deals and perhaps a few tricks. Even making friends or acquiring favors could do it."

"Two alliances," I mumbled.

His eyes widened, and he made sure no one was around to listen before dropping his voice. "Two? Winster?"

"Still aligned." I took my last bite of pudding. "But Bash and I are no longer together."

"What happened?"

I tried not to appear bothered. "It simply didn't work."

"Was it because of the bracelet he stole for you, which you revealed to the realm?"

"If you already know, then why do you ask?" I set the flute down and stood. "I hurt him, and now I've lost him, and there is nothing more to be done about that. But I will find a way to fix everything else."

"Oh, Thea," he said, but I shook my head. As I tried to step away, Talen put his hand over mine. "I know how much he meant to you."

He didn't know the extent of it. I loved Bash, and knowing I'd cracked his heart hurt worse than any pain I'd ever felt. It was as if a chasm opened within me, and I was clawing my way out, but the distance was endless, as was my struggle. It gutted me. Talen couldn't know all that, but the tenderness in his eyes was so raw it threatened to pull the emotions out of me until they were sprawled on the floor for everyone to see.

"You can join Eliza if you wish and leave me to deal with everyone."

"Tempting," I confessed as I stepped past spools of fabric and jars of jellies, leaving the gifts behind. Perhaps the sight of all these would encourage Eliza to come downstairs. At least going through them would promise me a distraction from my thoughts. "Right now, I have a different task at hand. Let's turn this into a dance."

Talen looked to each side. "There's no music."

"Then make some. Or is the House of Delvers not powerful enough to create music?"

"It is, but we can hardly see the dance floor. The chandelier is lit, but none can see it beyond this dark shroud."

"We will dance anyway." The idea ignited within me like a fire. If this realm needed to return to life, it would start tonight, darkness or not. I would talk, I would laugh, and I would remind my guests why they loved the Mortal Queens. "How long until you can get the music started?"

Seeing my determination, he straightened. "Five minutes."

"That's all I need." I marched through the throne room to the courtyard threshold and looked around. It was easier to see out here, as the veil of black was thin enough to allow the torches to burn through. Hundreds of fae were gathered, with glasses of wine and smiles on their lips, each casting glances toward the east windows, as if hoping to catch a glimpse of their new queen.

I'd just opened my mouth when I spotted King Brock. He stood near the chess board in the center, watching his wife play. His dark skin glinted in the firelight, and warm eyes crinkled in the corners while a tender hand stroked his queen's shoulder. I checked for the other kings. Thorn stood by the champagne with a horde of pretty faces around him. Vern the farthest, under a veranda. King Leonard with richly colored red hair and blazing blue eyes, deep in conversation with King Arden.

Arden had been prepared to align with me before I aligned with Bash. He might be an option again now.

Other than Bash, the kings were all present. Yet only two had entered the throne room. Had the queens fallen so hard that the kings were distancing themselves so as not to get caught in their downfall?

I sucked in a breath and summoned my courage with it.

"Citizens of the fae realm," I said loudly. At once, all gazes swiveled to me. A year ago, I might have faltered. Now I did not. "You have been without your Mortal Queens for months, but I have returned to you, and I am not going anywhere. And with me, I bring a new queen to you, one who is stronger than any queen before, and who will change all of our lives. Queen Eliza is sorry to be absent tonight, but you will find she does things in her own way, and she is well worth the wait. As long as you have me, I say we celebrate the return of the Mortal Queens with a dance." I stretched out my arms and, as if planned, music began. Talen outdid himself. The sounds of an invisible orchestra paraded behind me, welcoming us all back into the throne room. When I looked, the instruments had peeled themselves from the wall, each made of marble, and each playing perfectly though no hands held them.

The sight was enchanting, and I hoped the music swept the fae along with it.

Thorn took the first steps to extend his arm to me. "May I have this dance, my Queen?"

I laced my hand through his arm. "I wouldn't have it any other way."

He led me through the doors and into the darkness of the throne room, where he wrapped a hand behind my back and led me through the simple steps. In our lead, others followed.

"Thank you," I whispered.

"Thank *you*," he countered. "It's not every night I get to spend dancing with a queen."

I tried to keep my eyes on him, but secretly watched the flow of fae into the throne room as the music swelled, until there were so many present I felt their skirts against mine and we hardly had room to spin. The darkness remained thick enough that I couldn't see beyond more than two or three people, but I reminded myself it would fade. Eliza and I would make it fade. This would feel like a home once more.

Thorn glanced around. "It's been a while since we all gathered like this." Sadness collected in his voice. At that moment, the music changed to a softer tone, and our steps slowed.

"What was it like when we were gone?" I asked him. From my perspective, mere minutes had passed, while time dragged into months for everyone else. For me, it was only this morning when I'd crossed this very throne room to follow Gaia to her chambers to make certain she was alright. Instead, I found a mess of a human—desperate to survive and convinced she'd found the way. Then she used her watch to speed up time. The hour hand spun. My head whirled. It flung us eight months forward, directly to the one-year mark of me living here. Directly to Gaia's death date.

Just like that, she died.

I'd run from the room to find the land drenched in this darkness, with webs and dust covering everything, a taste in the air as if death lived here, and the fae gathered in the courtyard to collect their new queen. They all thought we'd left them.

"The darkness came slowly," Thorn said, remembering. "Each day the air grew thicker with it, and lands began to crumble. Buildings that stood for ages fell. Rivers turned black. Wine turned stale. We've always known we cannot live without the Mortal Queens, but now none can deny it. We need you—always."

We need you—always.

The line, if said sweetly, could be charming. Right now, it sounded as haunting as a death sentence.

You feed off us. I'd thrown the accusation at Talen before leaving the realm. It still made me squirm. For some reason, the fae were dependent on Mortal Queens, and I needed to discover why—beyond the story I'd heard.

It was an unfair deal that they needed us, but we could not survive here. Yet, despite myself, I felt sorry I'd accidentally left them for so long.

Thorn and I spun with the fae, and in the darkness, it took a minute of fumbling to find each other again. I'd laugh each time I ended up in the wrong arms, and we'd sort ourselves out once more. When we did, Thorn held me closer. "Now it's like you'd never left."

"It's so dark I can hardly see the end of my skirts," I said.

He grinned. "True, but the energy has returned. We love you, Thea. And we love Eliza. Even from across the realm, I could tell when you'd entered our home again, because I felt whole. We all do. You complete us."

Another line that should be tender, but it was pretty words for the cage we'd been put in. Still, it gave me a sense of responsibility. This realm was under my caretaking, and I would do my best to support it until I found my way home.

"We are all better now that you have returned," Thorn added.

I wished that were true. "Not everyone," I mumbled. One fae was very much displeased by my presence.

"King Bastian," Thorn guessed.

"He's not happy with me right now." I spoke quickly so the words didn't have the chance to get tangled inside me.

The music changed to a faster pace, and Thorn easily kept up. "If it helps, I'm certain he will come around. I've never seen anyone so in love that their whole kingdom knew they'd found their queen."

"What of you?" I asked. "No queen for your kingdom yet?"

Something in his expression shifted, and his eye twitched. "Not

LETHAL KINGS   37

for me. My mother was killed by someone trying to hurt my father, and my father was later killed because of his new love." He said the words plainly, but a tightness suggested it was a wound not yet healed. "After two parents die because of love, it puts a bitter taste in your mouth."

I didn't know what to say to that. "How long ago?"

"About twenty years," he replied. "I've been king ever since. How about your parents? Were they in love?" He thrust the conversation away from his family in a way that told me not to prod further, and I regretted bringing it up.

"They loved each other," I replied, for that much was true. They were kind to one another, respectful, even loving at times. "But not in the way I hope to find one day." My dreams for the future included an art shop that my love and I would run together, where our days were filled with paintings of fields and mountains and our evenings built of laughter around a fire. It was a simple dream, but to me, it was everything. I still hoped to find that, but the odds grew smaller with each passing day, bringing me closer to the end of my two years. If I couldn't find a future for myself, at least I wanted to save all the queens who would follow so they had a chance of one.

Laughter bubbled from nearby, and I looked to see Odette in Talen's arms. Her auburn hair flowed down her back where her effortless soft curls brushed along her gentle curves, and his hands gripped her tightly. I smiled. If anyone had good odds of finding love, it was the two of them.

Then I realized something. I could *see* them.

The darkness was beginning to lift.

6

THE CHANGE WAS SUBTLE. LIKE THE

first rays of morning melting the shadows into something lighter, or the first sign of fall as leaves began to change color. The difference was almost unnoticeable. But I could see the chandelier, and the black fog didn't gather so tightly at my feet. Hope stirred within me. Change was already taking place.

The realm was welcoming its queens back.

As I looked, a figure drifted across the dance floor. They had no partner and moved with purpose, crossing from the thrones toward the doors. Their sage-green cloak billowed with the cowl thrown up so all I could see were the ends of her dark brown locks.

But something about how they moved . . .

I caught a glimpse of the side of their face, with a black mask set over high cheekbones and a sharp nose.

I stumbled. Black had been her favorite color. And the shape of that nose was more than familiar.

"Are you ill?" Thorn asked. I hadn't realized I was shaking. I backed up, finding myself more unsteady without his arms around me.

I was unable to tear my eyes away from the woman, even as the room swayed. Had Talen found my mother already? I didn't dare find him to ask and risk losing her. Perhaps she was here to see me at last. Maybe she'd always been here, visiting periodically to check up on me. Either way, she was leaving now, and I could not let her go.

Thorn placed a concerned hand on my arm. "My Queen?"

"Forgive me, I must go," I said, moving in the mysterious woman's direction as if controlled by another's hand. I was vaguely aware of Thorn following me, but all I focused on was that woman and seeing her face.

It had been five years since I'd seen her face. If it weren't for my popularity as queen, she might not know me on sight. But I'd never forget her.

She moved into the courtyard, took ten steps, and stopped.

I burst through the double glass doors behind her. "Mother?" My hands trembled so badly I had to clutch them together.

She didn't turn.

Thorn stepped around me and took a protective stance in front of my body, his wide shoulders halfway blocking her from view. "Who are you?" he asked.

Still, she didn't move.

Hairs stood up on my arms, and for a moment, I forgot about everything else—my broken heart, the darkness swirling around us, Eliza still up in my room. All that mattered was *her.*

The door opened again, the other four kings trailing out of the throne room, and behind them were those I recognized as the lords of the realm. Then Talen and the other two House representatives. They fanned out to form an arch behind me, all of them looking at the woman in the cloak. Each of us caught in a trance.

Only then did she turn.

My heart fell. It was not my mother. Yet something about her sent a thread of excitement shooting through my veins until I was holding my breath, waiting to hear her speak. She inspected us from beneath long, thick lashes and spread her lips into a sly grin. She flung her arms outward, and two things happened at once—the plumes of dark smoke fled and the doors to my throne room slammed shut, sealing the lot of us outside.

With the new light, we were able to see a twinkle in her eyes while she examined us. A hush claimed the group, all waiting for her to speak.

She did, and the sound was like rushing water and newly strung lyres. "One queen, five kings, three representatives, and thirteen lords. The power of all the fae rests in your hands." Her tongue clicked. "Though we are missing one queen and king. That is no issue. I trust word will spread to every ear soon enough. I want all players on board."

As she spoke, we moved closer. A thrill filled her voice, a small promise of excitement, and none could resist.

Thorn managed to speak. "Who are you?"

Her gaze caught on his, and her smile deepened.

"You will know me as the Gamemaster, for I have a game for you."

A chill swept over the courtyard. There was something terrible about this woman, and something sweet. I felt both equally, just as I felt with an undying certainty that she had information that would lead to my mother. I hung on every word.

"Let us play a game like never seen before, one that will stretch across the entire realm and change everything for us. I will leave you a series of clues, each bringing you closer to the end. A sole victor will be named, and our land will be forever changed."

Her words were like a riddle, and I fought to decipher it. Was this the first clue? What would the prize be? The Gamemaster lifted her bright eyes upward. I followed the look. Eliza had ventured outside and watched us from a balcony, a blank expression on her face.

Whispers rose from the group. Through it all, the Gamemaster turned in a slow circle until finding me, and there her gaze stayed. It was like a needle piercing into me, so sharp I couldn't move. I squirmed though, and Talen saw it. He drew to my side and placed himself between us, breaking the trance.

"What do we play for?" he asked the woman.

"You play for something that has never been available before." She lifted a slender arm and a gilded chariot descended to land before her. Unlike most golden ones, hers was white like snow. "You play for the power of the seventh king."

A gasp rippled through the courtyard. The seventh fae king had been missing for ages. No one knew where he was. In that time, his kingdom had sat idle. But now, she claimed someone could inherit his power, and hope ran through me. The power of a king in the hands of a Mortal Queen.

It could be enough to save me.

As the Gamemaster glided away, she gave us the start of the game. "Look for the first clue with the setting golden moon."

Then she was gone.

The game was on.

7

THORN WANTED TO TALK ABOUT
the Gamemaster and the game she'd just thrust upon us all, but I
sent him home. I sent everyone home. Then I filled two glasses of
cider and sat on the stairwell with Talen, talking about the riddle.

I stretched my legs outward and rested my head against the
wall. The ends of my long skirts fanned down the stairs. "A setting
golden moon. Which moon glows golden?"

"Not any of the moons in your kingdom," Talen replied, sipping
his cider slowly. "Nor any that I know. But I will find out before
tomorrow night and get you the first clue."

"You don't want it?" I asked, arching a brow over my glass.

He frowned. "I serve you."

"And I appreciate that, but you were given the game just as I was,
so it's fair if you pursue it alone. She said only one will be named
victor. And to have the power of a king . . . Well, it's tempting for
anyone. What could one do with that?"

"Anything," Talen replied. "The balance of the realm comes
with the seven kings, and favor always tips their way. If someone
came into that power, it would change everything for them. Their
lands would never dry up. Their riches never deplete. They'd be
granted wisdom by the realm that would make it much more

difficult to trick them and make it much easier for them to trick others. Invitations to every party they threw would be coveted and every female fighting to be the one at their side. And if a king acquired this duplicate power?" He whistled. "No fae should have that much power."

"A king won't," I said with far more determination than I should have. "It'll be you or me."

Talen was already shaking his head. "I don't need more power. In fact, I'm thinking of stepping down as the House of Delvers' Representative after this year." He swirled his drink a few times, glancing down the stairs to where Odette gathered the gifts for Eliza and carried them to her room in the east.

Odette had once confessed to me that she and Talen shared a relationship, but it fell apart when he reached for more power by coming into his current position. He wanted influence, and she wanted him to want her. I smiled. "She'd like that."

"I don't know what you're talking about." But by the dance in his eyes, he knew exactly what I was talking about.

I finished my cider and stood. "We aren't going to solve this tonight. Tomorrow I will go searching for the golden moon, but this has been all the excitement I can handle for one day."

He tipped his cup. "The queen's first banquets are always something."

Odette spotted me and hurried over with a bundle in her arms. "For Eliza," she said. "She must be hungry. Talen already inspected it for traps."

I lifted a brow at him. "I thought you wouldn't deflect trickery if you weren't aligned with her."

He shrugged. "Let's call it the goodness of my heart."

"Thank you." I took the parcel and bid them goodnight. Then I ventured upstairs to my chambers to find Eliza sitting on the bed. She'd changed into one of my outfits, a simple peach silk shirt paired with matching pants that complemented the pink of her skin. She brushed her hair absentmindedly, staring at something on the bed in front of her. It took me a few steps to identify it as Antonio.

My chest tightened at the sight. "Malcom gave me that little soldier toy before we left," I reminded her. "It's been an anchor for me during my time here."

She looked up, and a tear fell down her cheek. I sat beside her and offered the food. "Eat," I ordered. "We can't fix much right now, but that doesn't mean you should be hungry."

She pulled on the ribbon and the cloth opened. With the first bite, her tears dried, and before long, the thoughts of home appeared tucked away.

"Quite the event tonight," she said between slow bites of a flaky butter biscuit. "Are things always so exciting?"

"Usually," I replied, but as I thought about it, that answer changed to a yes. "I got shot with an arrow at one event."

Eliza's eyes widened. "You left that out of your story earlier."

"It was quite painful. I thought I was dying." I would laugh if the memory wasn't laced with Bash.

While Eliza ate, I changed out of my gown and crawled under the covers, then took hold of Antonio. My thumb stroked the rigid side of his armor, where paint had been peeled off and redone. Eliza put away the food and slid under the duvet as well.

"That king you were dancing with, which one is he?" she asked.

"Thorn."

"Is he good or is he using you?"

Is he using you? Already, she thought like a Mortal Queen should.

"None of the kings are particularly good. But there is some goodness to him." Truthfully, Thorn had surprised me tonight. He was there as a friend when I needed him, and he didn't ask for anything in return. Without a doubt, the request would come later, Kindness never flowed freely in a land such as this.

She propped her head on her hands. "And the Gamemaster?"

I fumbled the hem of the duvet, thinking over the strange woman who'd shown herself today. "No one seemed to know who she is. And out of all the kings, someone should have. It's curious that she could grant the power of the seventh king as if it's hers to give."

There were many questions attached to the Gamemaster, and I believed somehow, if we found the answers about her, we'd find the answers to the riddles.

"Maybe she can't."

"What?"

Eliza shrugged like the answer was right there, waiting for me to simply open my eyes and spot it. "Maybe she can't give you the power of the seventh king, but instead needs others to get it for her."

I rolled to my side to stare at her. I hadn't considered that. In truth, I'm not sure it would have occurred to me. "Eliza, you surprise me. You're more cunning than I remember."

She laughed. "Cal has had a great influence on me."

Sounds like Cal. How many times had I wished he was here to guide me through this? "You could be right. She might have the key to the seventh king's power, but not a way to access it, and she needs us to solve that." I grinned. "Want to search for the first clue with us?"

She wrinkled her nose. "After what I saw tonight, I'm more determined than ever that I don't belong here."

"You could change your mind. It has a certain way of feeling like home after a while."

Again, she disagreed. "I haven't forgotten where home is, and that's all I want."

Something tightened inside me, as if the words implied I didn't remember where home was, or I didn't love my brothers as much as she did. I looked away. I'd been just as determined as she was to get home when I arrived. But I also wanted to live. Everything I did here, all the times I stopped focusing on my brothers and started focusing on this realm, it was only to survive.

"I know you miss them."

I took in a tight breath, the guilt nesting in my bones. "How have things been at home?"

"Good," she said. "Better than good. Cal got accepted as a student by Abbas, and it's given him a sense of purpose. He's also discovered he's exceptional at making apple turnovers, which we have all benefited from."

My mouth hung open. "I didn't know he could cook."

"Me either. But when we discovered that, he went on a streak for months where he was making new dishes every night and forcing us all to sit around the table to try them, even your father. The ritual stuck, and now we spend the evenings as a family."

"Wow," I breathed. "I can't imagine my father sitting around the table anymore."

"He's changed."

Or perhaps that was always who he'd been. It was impossible not to try to imagine him in the fae land, and what he was like here. Did he play the games? Chase clues? Make alliances? Did he leave of his own volition or was he driven out? This realm held the answers I longed for, and I was determined to find them.

I opened my palm to look at Antonio. "Everyone's changed. Malcom got so much taller over the past year. He looks so grown up now."

"He draws too."

"Really?"

She nodded. "He's excellent. After you left, Malcom would lock himself in your room and wouldn't allow anyone to enter. We didn't know what he was up to, but soon he asked for more paint, and we realized he was using your old art supplies. He claimed he was doing it to feel close to you, but as the year went by, it became a hobby, then a full obsession. He's gotten really good too."

"What does he draw?"

"Us. Our faces. Our family. He's filled many walls with our smiles."

My heart warmed. That sounded perfect.

"Plus a few gruesome battles," Eliza added. "There's a healthy mix of those."

I laughed. "I'd expect nothing else." I wished I could see some of his work. Now, when I painted, I would be thinking of him too.

It had only been one year, but it felt like I'd missed many more.

Before I left to become a Mortal Queen, we were stealing food to survive, had a strained relationship with our father, and no prospects for our future. In my absence, and thanks to the stipend my family received from the fae realm, they had pieced themselves back together in a way that was whole, like mending a broken mirror until one couldn't see the cracks. Perhaps for the first time since our mother disappeared, they had started to live.

I couldn't guarantee I'd ever return. But I'd die fighting to be certain Eliza did.

She was so quiet for a while, I thought she'd fallen asleep. Then I felt her hand stretch out to find mine, and she squeezed. "We are going to get back to them," she whispered.

I swallowed the lump in my throat. "We will."

It was a promise we might not keep, but we let the illusion remain as we drifted off to sleep.

8

A NOTE FROM TALEN WAITED FOR

me in the morning, slipped under the door.

> *A land in King Brock's region
> is home to a kingdom built of
> solid gold. It has one moon,
> and that moon sets in two days.
> I have no doubt the clue will
> be there.*

I read the note to Eliza as she scoured through my wardrobe for something that fit her smaller frame. She poked her head out the door. "That seemed easy."

I tossed the note in the fire. The last thing we needed was someone scouring through our rooms looking for hints that we'd found the clue already. "I guess we're on standby for two days."

A hollow knock came from the door before Odette let herself in.

She carried a wicker basket and announced. "I bring breakfast!" She'd braided strips of her auburn hair to wrap them like a crown against her forehead, showing off her four earrings.

Eliza exited the closet wearing the simplest dress I owned, with thin woven straps holding up flowy cuts of olive-green fabric. She frowned at the window. "It's so odd to be eating breakfast when it's pitch-black outside."

"Lunch will be even odder," I informed her as I rummaged through the basket of warm honey rolls and sacks of tea.

"Speaking of lunch, King Vern has invited Eliza to a lunch at his home."

Eliza took a roll as if that meant nothing to her. But it meant something to me. "King Vern has never invited me over."

"But he did shoot you," Odette pointed out.

The muscles in my jaw twitched at the memory. "Still. Before that, I didn't receive an invite."

"That's because Lord Winster is one of his lords," Odette said.

"Ah. Understandable then."

"Who's Lord Winster?" Eliza asked.

"See that wool?" I pointed near the crackling fire, where two armchairs sat decked in red velvet, and spools of iron twisted around the mantel to hold sixteen candles. On the floor rested the thick wool. "He gave me one like that but poisoned."

"An intense sickness followed, only relieved by the promise of her first dinner," Odette explained. I shuddered. That had been the first time I realized I was ill-prepared for this land.

Eliza eyed us from over her teacup. "You two really make this realm seem enticing."

"You'll do better than I did. Want to meet a king?"

Eliza settled into one of the armchairs and leaned back, sipping her tea slowly. "Not even a little bit. Not unless it's that one." She indicated my unfinished painting of Bash. I should really cover that up.

I avoided his gaze through the painting. "That is Bash."

"I guessed from how you try to avoid the sight of it but continue to steal a hundred glances. I want to meet the king whose heart cracked because of you."

Odette dropped the basket. Honey rolls scattered across the floor. "His heart cracked?"

I cleared my throat. "A little."

Odette rushed to sit in the armchair beside Eliza and fanned out her skirts, as if it were story time. "What happened?"

"This realm happened," I muttered. I sat on the wool beside the fire, watching the flames spark. As I did, Bash's face came to mind—the moment he had stood beside the fire in his own home and told me to leave. I closed my eyes until the sight went away, and then I told her my tale.

"After I was to use the bracelet to steal the power of the ambassador, I would have lost my strength, just as you warned me. What I didn't know was he planned to heal me. Then he was going to turn me into a fae. We were going to stay in this realm together and rule." It was hard to look at Eliza while indirectly confessing that I hadn't planned to return home. "But I doubted him, and instead revealed the bracelet to the realm, saving myself while putting him in trouble. Now he is convinced I never cared for him, and he broke our alliance."

"And you broke his heart," Odette breathed.

"Cracked," I corrected. "A tiny crack."

"Still, that means something."

Odette reached into her chest to remove her own heart. A sharp sound ripped from Eliza's throat as she stared at the glass heart Odette had just taken out of her skin. It was the second time I'd seen Odette do that, but it didn't make it less unsettling. The skin separated like shards, pulling against the heart before finally letting go. Once freed, the heart sparkled in the firelight.

"Our hearts are made of glass, but they aren't easily broken. Only when we are hurt—deeply hurt—will the pain show as a crack in our heart. For King Bastian's to crack—even a little—is significant, especially since he has always been known as the king whose heart wasn't cracked." She had her own crack from Talen, and it stretched from one side to the other. Eliza stood to see it better.

"Does it still hurt?" Eliza asked.

Odette grew quiet with unseen memories before replying, "Only when he smiles at me." She pressed the heart back into her chest. "Fae hearts do not crack easily. For Bastian's to crack . . . he loved you deeply."

"I'm a Mortal Queen," I reminded her. "The fae are bound by the realm to love me."

"Not like that. Not in a way that cracks our hearts." She tilted her head. "Will you chase after him?"

I shrugged as if I hadn't debated that very thing a hundred times already. "He said no. He told me to leave. And honestly, it might be for the best that neither of our hearts gets hurt worse, for there is no chance this ends well for either of us."

I started to pick up the rolls and put them back in the basket. When I finished, Odette took it from me, and her eyes met mine. "It seems your hearts are already hurt. You might as well enjoy being in love too. I promise it's worth it." She placed a hand over her chest. "No matter how badly it falls apart."

"It's not up to me."

She pressed her lips together and swung to Eliza. "How about you, my Queen? Any stories of lost love or broken hearts?"

Eliza answered with a slight smile. "No. I only know of joy and tenderness."

"She is involved with my brother," I informed Odette, though I didn't want to hear about *tenderness* with him.

Odette's eyes widened. "Cal, is it? Congratulations. How serious?"

"Serious enough that me being chosen shouldn't have been possible," Eliza responded.

I squinted at her. "That's the second time you've said that. Did Cal do something? Take your name from the bowl? Rig the competition?"

Eliza stood with a shake of her head. "It doesn't matter now. Thea, you told me there was a queen who escaped?"

"In theory," I said, glancing to Odette. Eliza was sharing a lot from our previous conversations, but I'd failed to tell her I hadn't shared everything with Odette. Specifically, the messages in the paintings that unveiled Dhalia's tale. "I've heard a queen escaped, but I believe she did it at the subsequent Queen's Day Choosing Ceremony. I missed that chance."

"I heard she remained in the realm," Odette said.

I treaded carefully with my next words. "I have reason to believe, however she lived, it involved the day I will never get to see again. I die before the next one."

As Eliza's face blanched, Odette's narrowed in thought, as if silently asking how I came by this information. But she didn't ask out loud. Information was currency, and by my expression, she knew not to push this. I wouldn't know how to explain.

Though a thought struck me. If Dhalia escaped the realm, her descendants were not living here as I'd believed.

So who was sending the messages?

Eliza headed toward the door. The heavy fall of her footsteps ripped me from my thoughts. "There could still be another way."

"Where are you going?" Odette asked.

Eliza stepped into the corridor. "This is the home that all the previous queens stayed in, correct?" When we nodded, she said, "Then their secrets are hidden here. I'm going to find them."

We searched for hours. I'd scavenged the castle before while serving out my undesired three months of captivity. During those months, I failed to find anything remotely interesting other than tipped-over cushioned chairs, a room of chandeliers, and one parlor perfectly set for a tea party, though no one ever came to enjoy it.

Now, it was like an entirely new place. With everything coated in spools of thick shadows and dust, it was impossible to see the ends of corridors or know if I were about to walk into a wall or walk off a balcony. Cobwebs clung to corners, though no spiders hung there. Shelves of books wrapped along staircases, though all the pages were blank. Thick rugs made it feel as if we were walking through mud, and the tapestries were so coated that it was impossible to tell what they once showed.

Eventually, even Eliza appeared defeated.

"Did anyone ever live here aside from queens?"

Odette stopped in the corridor to run her finger down a painting. The canvas was black. "No. This palace constructed itself for the queens after the first one."

"What happened to her?" Eliza asked. "I don't know the story of how the queens began."

I swallowed. When I'd arrived, I was convinced the key to my survival lay with the first queen. "A king loved a mortal girl and married her. But his love was short-lived, and he betrayed her."

Eliza waited, and when I didn't say more, she raised a brow. "Then what?"

Odette and I exchanged looks. "She died," I answered. It wasn't the full story, but it was enough. "In punishment for losing their first queen, the realm decreed it would always have a Mortal Queen, but the queens only live as long as the first marriage lasted—two years. A punishment for the fae."

Eliza remained silent for a while, staying put even as Odette and I moved on. Eventually, with slow steps, she trailed us. I thought she was thinking as I did—about the unfair punishment that hurt the mortals more than the fae. But then she spoke. "How did the king meet the mortal girl?"

"Our lands used to be united," Odette told her. "We could come and go as we pleased. Now, only the three ambassadors can travel between realms."

"How do they do it?"

"There is no doorway, no bridge, and no key. They simply can."

Eliza heaved a sigh. When we stepped into another room, she tossed up her hands. "We've been here before."

I looked around. It was built of dark red bricks, with stained wood beams in square patterns on the ceiling, and black trim. A table had been hastily shoved into the corner, with several steps of footprints surrounding it. Our footprints.

"You're right. I remember thinking the ceiling looked like a chessboard," I said.

"I can't do this anymore," Eliza said wearily. "I'm going back to the room to think."

"I'll show you the way." Odette held the door and looked at me. "Are you coming?"

"I'll be right there."

"Suit yourself," she said before leading Eliza down the hall.

I couldn't be certain what led me back to the painting Odette had found. Perhaps it was the golden frame that refused to collect dust, as if it had been cleaned or made new. We'd found tapestries here, but this was the only painting. It had to mean something.

My fingers streaked across the same place Eliza's had, and I held my breath.

Nothing happened.

No vision. No jolt. No message. I was alone in a dark corridor with a painting that was only a painting, and nothing more.

My chest deflated. I couldn't hope for messages because I'd ignored the last one. Whoever left me the tale of Dhalia clearly wanted me to see that she'd escaped on Queen's Day, and I'd lost my chance for that. They had nothing left to show me.

Dhalia had gotten home, and I was still here.

I brushed aside the dust, wondering what once showed on the canvas beneath the grime. Perhaps it had been the image of a queen who once roamed these halls, whose beauty would only be remembered by those of years gone by. We deserved such remembrance. Each of us resided here for only two years, but we deserved to have our portraits on these walls for eternity.

I could give them that.

Without needing another moment to decide, I pried the painting from the wall and hoisted it under my arm. I would paint the queens myself, starting with Gaia. They'd be remembered forever that way, and when we were long dead, the fae could still walk through these halls and remember the mortals who put up a good fight to live.

It was almost cruel, now that I thought about it, how the fae lived for so long yet we fought to have just a fraction of those years.

I set the painting down in the main hall, leaning against the base of my throne. Then I fetched some paints from my chambers. Inside, Odette and Eliza spoke in low tones, pausing when I entered to look at me as if I was interrupting something important. I almost asked what they were up to, but something about Eliza's expression told me not to.

With paints and brushes in hand, I retreated to the throne room.

It had been a while since I'd painted, so I took extra time to set up the jars just how I liked and prepare my brushes. I dipped the hem of my dress in the stream and used it to wipe down the face of the dirty canvas, gently removing the years of dust. All the while, I pictured Gaia's face and how I wanted her essence captured forever. In the end, I decided to put her in a field with that serene look she always carried, hoping the flowers made her appear more peaceful than the throne ever had.

Before I started, I looked to her throne to picture her one more time. Her shoulders always reached just below the beveled swirl in the stone, and her eyes had been level with the curve of chiseled roses. The images were subtle, with her throne featuring more of the rose, while mine focused more of the thorns—the details rubbed away by hundreds of queens so the intricacies were only noticeable from up close.

At the bottom of Gaia's throne, a slice I had never noticed before caught my eye.

I peered closer. It wasn't a mark of craftmanship. It was cut hastily, with rough lines.

Eliza's words came to mind. *Their secrets are hidden here.*

I stepped upon the dais and pried my fingers beneath the stone. When I pulled, it moved.

It was a brilliant hiding place. Few visitors ever came to the palace unless we were home, and the area would be covered by our skirts then. But now, I saw it. Was this why Gaia always sat here and never mingled? She was hiding something?

I pulled harder, and the stone crumbled in a way that indicated it had been cut long before Gaia.

A thin slot had been sliced out, and I hungrily reached my hand into it, jumping despite myself when my fingers met something other than a stone texture. I took hold and withdrew a faded journal. The cover might once have been red, but it had browned over time, with the corners furling in upon themselves. I could make out a name, though, stitched in white thread. Cottia. A queen from long ago, I recognized, but that was all I remembered.

What could be written inside that was important enough for Cottia to hide?

With my breath in my throat, I opened the first page.

It crumbled. Both the pages and my hope fell in tatters as the paper broke apart in my hands. Slips of parchment crumbled to my feet, delicate enough that I didn't dare touch them. When I tilted the journal, the rest of the pieces fell out. Whatever it once said was now gone.

Something in the mess caught my eye, and I knelt to sift through the parchment until I found a scrap somehow still intact. I lifted it tenderly. The bottom was straight, as if that were the end of the page. But right above it, something was inscribed. I held it close and made out three words.

Found. Price. High.

Found what? What had she found? And what was the price?
I picked through the pile on the floor until finding another line.

We want to live. But if we want anything,
we must give up everything.

I didn't care for the sound of that. Hastily, I dug for more. After a minute, one final piece revealed itself, the words as much of a puzzle as the rest, giving me answers that only brought questions.

It chilled me.

The king is the key.

At that moment, the doors of the throne room grated open, and a king waltzed into my home.

9

I GRABBED THE BLANK CANVAS AND

tilted it against Gaia's throne, hiding the mess of parchment. My unease would be harder to mask.

Thorn wandered in, his golden crown wrapped around his forehead and his suit jacket left undone. He had a rakish way of moving, as if every room he entered were one he owned, yet a softness when he looked at me that implied he'd give up everything to make me smile. It was the way of the kings. And it was dangerous.

He slowed when he spotted me, and then his grin deepened. "You know," he said as he crossed the room, "I've yet to see you paint in action."

I dipped the brush to collect pigment and started the blue strokes of sky. "And I've yet to paint the piece of you I promised."

He waved his hand like that was nothing, but debts didn't go unpaid here.

"This is something, though." He bent close, as if I'd created a resplendent masterpiece, but it was nothing more than a few ragged lines.

"It will be Gaia when it's done."

He was silent for a moment, long enough for me to glance over and see the streak of pain in his expression. He covered it quickly.

"She was always fond of this place. It's fitting she lives in the halls forever."

Thankfully, he settled on the step of the dais at an angle that kept the shambled journal hidden in the scant light. I worked to finish the base coat while he mused.

"How do your lands fare?" I asked to fill the silence. "Have they fallen into this thick darkness as well?"

"My kingdom is farther." His eye roved over the blanket of shadows in the hall as he spoke. It was better than it was yesterday, not quite as garish anymore, but not close to how it should be. "The darkness touched us, though not enough to impair the lands. We are safe."

"That's a relief. Here, would you wash this?" I passed a brush and cup of water, then readied pigments to mix the yellow.

Before swirling the brush, he shucked off his jacket, giving the impression he planned to stay a while. I tried to decide how I felt about that. On one hand, it would be good to know his thoughts on the Gamemaster. But he was a king, and I found I'd quite lost my taste for those. My mind went to the note in the journal. *The king is the key.* The key to living? Or did she mean something far less important, such as the key to getting an invitation for a ball? Thanks to the motes of dust decaying the parchment, I'd never know for sure.

"You ought to visit sometime," he said, dragging me back to the present. "We have the only lakes with water so clear that you can see to the bottom, and peacocks that eat fruit from your hand."

I kneaded a stone into the dye. "I think you told me that before. I remember hearing it somewhere."

"Not from me. I only mention the peacocks when I'm trying hard to woo someone." A ghost of a smile crossed his lips. "How am I doing?"

My hand faltered before steadying itself. I was right last night—he aimed for an alliance. I could play that game to see what information he'd gathered about the new game given to the realm.

As long as I didn't let myself get swept away, my heart would be safe. I pretended to mull it over.

"I must admit, seeing a peacock would be fun. I've never encountered one."

"Truly? They are a thing of beauty. Simple little creatures, but not ones you want to miss."

"Perhaps I'll visit someday. Are any of your lords fond of poisonous wools that I should know about?"

"Not that I am aware. And right now, they are all quite waylaid by this Gamemaster." The name fractured the conversation, and I grabbed hold.

"What do you think she wants?" I set my brush down, facing him. If he knew something, I wanted to know it too.

His glib demeanor vanished, leaving behind a beleaguered tone. "That is the question of the day, isn't it? I went to each king last night, even yours, and asked about this Gamemaster." He rolled the name from his tongue, as if it were poison. I ignored how he called Bash *mine*. "None know her, and I don't trust that. But the seventh king's power has lain dormant for too long, suggesting it could be ripe for taking."

"How would one take it?"

"With his signet ring. But it went missing when he did. If she has it, she could use the power for herself, which begs the question— why would she give it away? What does she have to gain from that?"

I frowned. "That's all one would need? A simple signet ring?" My eyes dropped to his hand where he wore a golden ring crafted of three horns.

"In theory. Some kings can enchant theirs, though that's considered bad form. But truthfully"—he glanced around the room then leaned closer—"the missing king's lands are near my own, and they've quaked recently. They are ready to wake. I believe the time is right for the power to be taken again."

"So if she found the ring . . ."

He nodded. "The power of the seventh king truly lies at the end of this riddle."

Interesting. "That's big. Any leads yet?"

"Why, my Queen, are you trying to pry secrets out of me?"

"I would never," I joked. "But I worry that someone has already solved the golden moon, and we will have a late start."

"We?"

I hadn't meant anything by it, but the hope in his eyes was too innocent to squash.

"I'd hate to fly blind in all this. And I'm already at a disadvantage, being centuries younger than everyone else and not from this realm. And with only a year to solve all the clues."

Thorn dried the brush he'd cleaned on a rag and passed it back to me. "If it helps, you are only 163 years younger than I am."

My jaw dropped. "It does not."

His laugh floated through the hall. Then he grew serious and studied me. "I once asked you for an alliance," he began tentatively. "You turned me down. Would you do so a second time?"

I pretended to be very interested in picking at my paintbrush, churning the idea through my mind. "I'm not ready," I finally told him. "I don't want to make another poor alliance."

"Then I won't ask. But perhaps we can play the game together and see where it leads?"

I looked up at him. Thorn, from the outside, appeared to lack nothing. He was a powerful king, his lands untouched by darkness. I hadn't heard of him getting into rotten deals, and he had many strong physical attributes that made him popular among the females. What did he have to gain from an alliance with me?

"Why are you here? I have few alliances, fewer friends, and no advantage in this new game. A match with me is unhelpful."

The question, or perhaps the honesty of it, took him back. To his credit, he seemed to give it thought before responding. "I know what you want, and that is to live. It removes the guesswork from the relationship. And I've already seen what you look like when you fight for something, when you become fearless in all manners and put your entire mind into the game. I'd like to have that on my side."

That would have been enough to get me to agree, but Thorn went on.

"My father was a good king, but he wasn't as good about the deals he made or the people he got into relationships with. He led with his heart far too often. Father left me a great kingdom but with a legacy to heal and people who look to me to return them to the glory days of my grandfather. I want to do right by them. So, just as I can trust your motives, you can feel confident in mine. Everything I do is for my people."

There was an honesty to his tone that I didn't hear often, even in the mortal realm.

"Only one of us can get the power of the seventh king in the end," I reminded him.

He shrugged. "Let's make certain it's one of us."

The words sounded pretty. And they mirrored what I'd told Talen last night. It'll be one of us. To have Talen and Thorn on my side would give me an advantage in the game, which sealed the decision in my mind. "Let's do it."

A smile cracked his lips. "Good." He stood. "Because I know the answer to the first riddle."

10

"THE GOLDEN MOON?" I STOOD
beside him, leaving my brushes scattered on the marble. "I figured
it out too. It references the moon that sets over the golden palace
in two days."

Thorn shook his head. "I believe it references you." Before I
had a moment to absorb that shock, he went on. "The kings are
often referred to as silver, a color that rules the night while forever
longing for the warmth of the day. But our queens—they are worth
more than us. They are the heat of a sun and the gold in this realm.
Often in images you are symbolized as a blend between our realms.
A golden moon."

"You think the clue is somewhere in this palace?" My mind
went to the journal I'd just found beneath the throne of the queens.
If that was how well these clues were hidden, this would be a harder
game than I'd thought.

Thorn's gaze fixed on the stairs leading to the east. "I do, and I
think I know where. The place most touched by the queens. Your
chambers."

Unease snapped up my spine like a whip. "You want to search
my rooms?"

"Or Queen Eliza's."

"She's not home right now," I told him. Let him make of that what he would. "Let's search her side." I deliberately led him away from the painting and the journal, taking him up the stairs to the east. He obliged, moving at an ample pace to venture beside me, our movement leaving trails in the dust along the railing and breaking the untouched silence of this side. He hung back at the corridor's archway, giving me a chance to show him which door was correct, but the way his blue eyes clung to the polished oak and iron handle of Eliza's chambers, I suspected he already knew. He'd been in the queen's chambers before, at one time or another. I wondered which queen had let him in.

I'd been so adamant to keep him from my room, I'd forgotten about the last time I stood at this doorway.

Sorrow couldn't claim me now.

The hinges squalled as the door swung inward. We both stilled.

Everything was white, the kind so absent of color that it only reflected all else. Four walls hung close, leaving the room no larger than the width of two beds, and most of it was cluttered with gift baskets Odette had brought up last night. A simple lantern sat in the middle, with an orange light dancing through wrought iron bars, casting a glow to the curved ceiling.

"It is true, then," Thorn mused. "She has chosen no alliance."

I didn't confirm it, but the room did. Mortals Queens came into this realm with nothing, and it was their alliances that gave them a start. This room was proof Eliza was unwilling to play.

"I suppose that makes our search easier," was the only thing I could think to say.

We stepped into the room, examining bags, inspecting boxes, and riffling through layers of fabric. We couldn't be certain what we looked for—something as obvious as a note or as subtle as the wrong color thread stitched into a hem. I hoped it was the first.

After a while, Thorn rolled up his sleeves. "I don't see anything. Perhaps it's not this room?"

I wasn't eager to turn the focus to my room. Despite the fact that it would take significantly longer to search, I didn't enjoy the thought of Thorn riffling through my things. "Remind me why you thought it was in our rooms?"

"You are the golden moon," he replied. "And these rooms are most touched by you."

I considered this a moment. Our thrones would be a good place, but for other reasons, I didn't want him seeing those right then either. It had to be in this room. "Perhaps the window?" The glass was small, hardly as large as my face, but it was the only place in the room I hadn't run my hands over.

Thorn barely gave it a glance. "If that can even be called a window."

But I moved to it, positioning my fingers along the steel transom to feel for anything. Upon finding the occasional crack or grove, I'd bend close and pry at it before moving on. Thorn had resumed going through the packages we'd already searched three times. I found some woad-dyed slippers I might trade Eliza for later, but that was the only thing interesting in those gifts.

When the window yielded no results, I leaned against it. Through the narrow opening was mere darkness with the occasional chariot drifting by. The only constant light was a glimmer from below, and I looked there. The rooms held a direct view to the pond, where the queens were all given their funerals. The water lapped against the stone walls, as if kissing the last place the queens touched.

I straightened.

"The rooms are for the queens," I mused out loud. "But only half of them. Half of the queens never touched this side."

Thorn stopped sifting through things. "The throne room, then?"

Maybe. But . . . I glanced outside once more. The excitement within me grew. "The Gamemaster didn't just say a golden moon. She said it was setting. If we are the moon, where do the queens set? Where is our end?" I pointed out the window. "That is where the queens end, when we are pushed into the stars for eternity. Our reign ends in that spot, each one of us."

Thorn came to look. "Brilliant," he declared. "The golden moon sets there."

We moved quickly down the stairs and pried open the door to the hallway. It didn't give off quite the austere feeling it had last time, for this time it was part of an adventure. I had a purpose now, and I had a sense of direction. The dead flower petals flew up in flurries beneath our quick steps, until we emerged on the other side.

We stopped to catch our breath.

It was impossible to see the courtyard clearly last time, for it was crowded with fae. But now it was only me and Thorn, allowing us to see the gothic-style design sculpted into the floor, creating two roses intertwined. Sharp thorns burst from all sides. At the place where the two roses bent together, two dainty stars gathered. Overtop them, a beautiful crescent moon.

"It's glowing," I said before realizing it was water. The entire design was built into the stone in such a way that let water from the pond gather within the cuts, making it shimmer against the black quartz.

Thorn stepped between the various strokes to come upon the center. "And there is the moon." He knelt and I crouched beside him.

I caressed my hand over the surface, begging something to open. Nothing did. Thorn clawed at the edges, but nothing happened.

I stood, growing more irritated by the moment. "Where is it?" I muttered. It might not be here. It might not be in the palace. It could be anywhere across the realm, and all we had was one little quote to go on. But Thorn wasn't giving up, having now moved on to chip at the chiseled stars, so neither would I.

With my skirts in hand, I stepped into the water. The soft blue matched the fabric of my dress as it wafted in a circle around me, pulled sharply each time I took a step, my eyes fixed on the stones at my feet. This pond was the final place where a queen would be, so perhaps it was meant as literally as that. In fact, if we were getting technical, the stone wall that queens were pushed over was the last place they would touch. I waded to the wall, where little bits of water spilled over the edge.

Endless sky met me. I pictured Gaia as one of the stars, watching us play the game, guessing which way it would turn. I pictured her happy. I pictured her with the rest of the queens, begging me to solve this so they would not need to be joined by another.

Help me, I beseeched them. *Help me save the queens.*

As I bent my head, a bone-white flash caught my eye.

"Thorn!" I called out. "There is something here."

He came to my side and looked down. In a crack in the stone, a key stuck out, one embellished with seven stars. The final one was a brilliant white. Seven stars for the seven kings.

"That wasn't here before," Thorn confirmed. "I bet the next clue is inside that latch."

"Can you reach it?" But even as I asked, I knew he couldn't. The key was too far down, and even when he laid himself on the stone wall and reached as far as he could, he still came several meters short. Little grooves stuck out in the stone, and my stomach dropped. "I think we are meant to climb for it."

Thorn let out a low whistle. "Proving we are willing to give up everything for this." A wry look entered his eyes. "Remember how I have the fastest chariot?"

I nodded.

"I also have the most accurate." Before I could ask what that meant, he thrust up a hand. Within moments, his chariot had sprung into the sky to come fetch us. Thorn stepped atop the wall and jumped into the stern, then held out a hand for me. "Ready to get your clue?"

I took hold, and he hauled me and my dripping skirts beside him.

Thorn guided his chariot down slowly until we were upon the key.

"The honors are yours," he said. Slowly, I reached and twisted. The latch opened. Inside were envelopes, each stained deep black, with white flecks on them like stars. They were labeled with the name of each eligible player—the two queens, the six kings, the three House representatives, and I counted all thirteen lords.

I found mine and passed the bundle to Thorn.

He tucked his under one arm, then thumbed through the rest.

"Should we throw the others away?" I asked.

"That'd be against the spirit of the game, and I have no doubt the Gamemaster would punish us for that," Thorn answered. But his eyes flashed with delight. "Though I like the thought." Then his expression darkened. He passed the envelopes back. "One is missing."

"Whose?"

"King Bastian already has his clue."

11

"HOW? HE WASN'T IN THE COMPANY last night."

Thorn tore open his envelope. "Someone told him. I visited him last night, and he was already aware of the game. If we are lucky, he figured it out this morning and is only a step ahead of us. If he is lucky, he is well on his way to the next clue. Let's see . . ."

As he read, I opened mine, trying not to panic that Bash was ahead of us. I'd rather play this game with him, but that wasn't what bothered me. I'd thought he was home nursing a broken heart, and instead he was back into playing the games of the realm.

If he could move on so quickly, then I could too. I held up the contents of my envelope.

It was nothing more than a slip of parchment, thin enough to see through, with one solitary design upon it. A chess piece. A king, specifically. Black in color with a narrow crown upon his head.

"How many chess boards do you think are in this realm?" I asked Thorn.

"Millions," he replied. "But none identical to another. I suspect someone will recognize which piece this is, but it is not me."

"What do we do?"

He tucked his envelope away. "We go trading for information.

Someone on Illusion Point is bound to know something, and they are all barred from the game and cannot compete. It's a good place to start."

With my nod, we were off.

True to its nature, the chariot sped through the sky. I held tight to the crossbars, bending my head so the wind didn't break hard against my cheeks, and waiting for the moment we'd stop. When we finally did, I looked up.

Illusion Point. Where the fae went to be tricked.

It stood like a carnival with rows of tents assembled together, outlined by shops with vendors who had countless party tricks to sell. While I couldn't see it from here, in the center of it all was the grand chessboard and the majestic thrones for the kings and queens to sit upon while watching chess matches.

"It's been months since a queen has come here," Thorn said as the chariot set down. He held a hand out for me.

"I was here a few days ago," I replied. "With you."

Confusion crossed his face until he remembered. "It must be odd to have lost such a gap of time," he remarked as he led the way.

I had no answer, so I stayed silent.

The streets narrowed right from the start, making it impossible to walk side by side at some points. Banners hung from posts, each promising us riches or glory if we turned that way. The colors grew more vibrant with each street, and the noise was almost deafening.

We approached a familiar shop with the flaps open for us to duck under. Thorn gestured for me to go before him. As I stepped past him, he said in a low voice, "I have business to attend to in here. While I'm busy, you should ask around about that chess piece."

I nodded, but I was only half listening. The other half of my mind was fixated on the inside of the tent. Shelves lined the area, each with different trinkets, and a man with the mustache swept over to greet us.

"It's good to see our queen again," he said, inspecting me, then glancing behind me. "Only one?"

"The other one won't be convinced, it seems," Thorn said.

"One is better than none." The man faced Thorn. "Here for business?"

Thorn inclined his head, and the man led him away.

From the back of the room, a familiar face peered over a book, and his lips curled upward. He was the one who had stolen a memory of my mother. I could not recall which one.

He'd been fascinated with her and wanted to know where she was. I hadn't known why he cared at the time, but now I did. My interest piqued. He'd heard someone in my memory say *Uhnepa te,* meaning "I love you" in the language of the night. A language reserved for the fae. Bash had told me that part, and finally I could answer the remaining questions. She knew the language because it was my father's.

Though I had the answers the man sought, I wasn't interested in giving them away. Instead, I turned and walked back outside.

Thorn wanted me to ask about the chess piece, but I had a different idea. I took the parchment out to look upon it again. The clue might be to find this exact playing piece, but it might also be pointing us toward chess in general. Specifically, the most famous chessboard in the land.

And that board was here. Right in the center of the island, where fates have been decided by a match.

I could wait for Thorn, or I could report to him if I found anything. After I read the next clue for myself, of course. With my head ducked low to discourage anyone from waylaying me, I made my way to the center of Illusion Point, to the iron gate with its ravens, to the pillars of stone, and to the haunting melody that played over it all.

My slippers scuffed against aged granite as I paused to observe the space. One side hosted long rows of benches, set up for fae to watch the matches. They were empty. I walked through them, beneath archways of statues, showing those who had played here before. I recognized faces of kings and guessed which queen was which.

As soon as the chessboard came into view, it was all I saw.

Larger than any other, and more magnificent in design, it was carved into a table, with legs like a phoenix's, the claws on the feet holding up the weight of the marble. The board was set, though no one played. That was my first hint that my guess was correct. Thorn had said this place was always in use. For it to be emptied meant it served a greater purpose today.

Tentatively, I approached. I moved beyond the white side to find the black, each piece facing its opponents. I unfolded the clue and set it on the board, then cupped the black king piece in my hand.

It wasn't a perfect match. This one had the face of a man, with curly hair and a regal expression. Its crown was more decorative than comfortable, and his neck stretched high under the weight of it. The king in the clue was less obvious. Less demanding. More humble.

Though I searched him, he held no clue for me.

"I was wrong," I said aloud.

"Halfway wrong," a voice corrected. I spun to find Bash moving from behind one of the thrones where he must have been watching me. He wore a gaunt jacket over a crimson shirt and a black tie halfway undone. He flicked something my way, and I caught it.

The chess piece from the puzzle stared back at me. I looked closer and noticed a small crack splitting the face. I checked the clue. The crack was so subtle that I almost couldn't see it, but it was there.

"This isn't from this board. Where was it?" I checked the base of the piece and found a slot. But it was empty. I looked up. "Where is the clue?"

Bash held up a small slip of parchment before tucking it into his pocket. "The piece was one from a millennium ago, when Brock beat Vern in a match. Vern, who was younger and less composed, crushed the king in his palm and stormed out. Brock was always one for dramatics, so he had the piece fixed and sculpted into Vern's throne here." Bash lifted his gaze to the top of the throne, where a thick chunk of black stone made up the stiles.

It was a small victory knowing I'd been correct in where to

go, but there was no way I could have known that story. Thorn, however, should have.

As if reading my thought, Bash gave a small smile as he stood. "The king you arrived with might not have been the best to align with."

"Where's the clue?" I asked, sticking out my hand.

Bash merely buttoned his jacket. "There was only one this time, meant for whoever found it first."

My arm dropped. "How will the rest of us play if we don't have a clue?"

"You'll see."

He made to move past me, headed for the stairs. Desperation flooded me. I needed this clue. I needed this game. I needed the power at the end of it. There was a certainty within me that without it, I could not save the future queens.

I reached out to touch his arm. "Please, Bash. I need this more than you."

He turned. "I need this power to save my kingdom—the one you ruined."

"I need this power to save my life!" I searched for emotion in his eyes, but he was frustratingly calm. Within me, feelings raged. I steadied my breath. "If your lands need saving, let me help you. Align yourself with me once more, and we will figure this out together." I dared to reach for him again. "Bash, we are better together."

"We've been down this road before," he said. To his credit, I finally saw the pain in his expression. "I cannot trust that you will not double-cross me to save the Mortal Queens."

I tested his words in my heart to see if they were true. If it came to a choice between a life of eternity with Bastian or saving the future queens—which would I pick? Could I sacrifice my happiness for girls I'd never know? The answer was clear in my mind, and from the way Bash looked at me, he knew too. I'd always pick the queens.

"I wanted a life with you," he said. "I would have given you

everything. Your desire to save the queens leaves nothing for us."
He withdrew, and this time I let him.

Bash climbed the crumbling stairs while I stood there, frozen in
the moment. Wishing I could give up everything for him. When he
reached the top, he paused and glanced down. "I will not give you
the clue, but I will give you this. Practice your chess, and choose
your partner wisely."

Then he was gone.

I still stood there when Thorn found me later. He looked
at my hand.

"You found the chess piece." He beamed as he hurried down
the stairs.

I tossed it to him, where it landed in his palm with a soft thud.
"I did." I swept past him, my skirts brushing his ankles. "But Bash
got it first, and there was only one. Come, we need to practice
our chess."

12

WE PRACTICED FOR WEEKS. WE

also visited Bash—me, Talen, Thorn, and Odette—each individually, hoping for that clue. He sent us all away. When it was suggested that Eliza try, she merely shook her head.

"He might answer to his new queen," Thorn suggested.

"I didn't even want to meet you," was the only reply she tendered. Thorn grinned at that.

Eliza had watched us practice chess in the throne room for days, eventually coming close enough to sit at my side and converse. But we could not convince her to leave the palace. "I'm still figuring out the pieces of the realm. I'll venture out when I secure them."

"That'll take more days than you have," Thorn told her.

"Don't you have a party to go to?"

"I do." Thorn stood. "I say we take a day. Let me see what the other kings know. Bastian must have told someone something more helpful than 'practice chess,' and we need to find out what it was. I'll return when I discover more. In the meantime, keep practicing, and don't be afraid to use the rook. You could have won that last one if you weren't so obsessed with the knight."

I studied the board on which I'd just lost. "I'll do my best."

He left, and Eliza sat in his place. She reset the pieces for us. "I gather you'll be playing chess in a mass group, single elimination, and the winner gets the next clue."

"I think you're right," I sighed. That wouldn't bode well for me. I could practice all I wanted, but the other fae had centuries of practice. They'd beat me. "Bash did tell me something else—'choose your partner wisely.' I wonder what that means."

"Will Thorn be your partner?"

I looked up at the sour way she'd said his name, and she didn't try to conceal her frown. "You don't like him."

Once her board was set, she glanced up. "I think it's probable that the kings are killing the queens to siphon their power."

A cold feeling snaked down my back. "They aren't."

"Maybe not. But the realm almost died when it lost its queens for eight months. It's feeding off us, and that makes me not trust anyone." She moved her first piece. "It might not be the kings, but someone is killing the queens."

Talen came down the stairs with a note in his hand. His mouth quirked. "You know, Eliza, I do believe you are the cheeriest queen we've had."

"I'm practical," she countered. "But if it helps, I plan to explore the realm soon."

"It'll help if you align with me," he proposed for the hundredth time. Eliza didn't answer. He gave a dramatic sigh, then turned to me. "I have information." He darted a glance at Eliza, with humor in his eye. "See? That is what an alliance with me gets you. Information."

But when his gaze returned to me, it became serious. I'd seen Talen serious several instances during my time here, and it was never good. It meant his heart had been traded away. It meant I was dying. It meant something was wrong. From the darkness shrouding his eyes, this was no exception. I stood.

He pressed the note between his fingers. "I just received word that your blood is on the market, and it has caused quite the stir. Unfortunately, very few know why it is important. I am not privy to that information, but I promise you I'll find out where someone got it and why it is causing such an uproar."

I blinked several times, soaking in the news. "My blood?"

He nodded. "For some reason, it's marked as the most valuable piece of information right now, even higher than whatever was in Bash's clue."

It didn't take me long to put together the answer to the first question, and the answer to the second came a breath later. "Madame Rola's bakery—Rola's Rolls. I gave her a drop of my blood."

"That would explain it. It's not often she gets useful information from those drops."

"What else does she use the blood for?"

"No one knows. But every so often, she gleams something important from it—where you've been, what you've eaten, who you are. And when that happens, she sells it on the market. I suspect it's her sole reason for taking it in the first place. It's been eons since she's had information good enough to list so high. Twenty thousand marks," he said. "That's how high this is going for."

I was fuzzy with their currency system, but from the way he said it, I understood it meant a lot.

He mused further, "So she listed it on the market, but why should buyers care?"

Eliza's gaze flickered to mine, and she shook her head subtly. I debated it. But I trusted Talen with my life, so I could trust him with this. "I know that too." Behind Talen, Odette descended the stairs in time to hear me unveil this valuable slice of knowledge. "My father is fae."

Talen and Odette froze like statues, and Eliza's long sigh was all that could be heard.

"I just found out on Queen's Day," I told them. "And I don't know what to make of it. He's fae, but somehow he lives in the mortal realm and isn't fond of your kind."

Talen began pacing the room, while Odette studied my face. Talen stopped and turned to me. "What does he look like?"

"Pale skin for someone on the five islands. Blue eyes. Narrow face. Picture yourself on a battlefield with the opposing general removing his helmet to smile at you as if he'd won. That man is my father."

I thought it painted a clear picture, but Talen shook his head. "Doesn't sound familiar. How long has he been in your land?"

"I don't know."

"Why did he leave?"

"I don't know that either," I confessed. Before he could ask more, I said, "That's all I learned. He's there, and he's fae."

Talen crossed his arms. "Your father is there, and your mother is here. She's mortal, yes?"

I nodded, and Eliza's brows flew up. "Your mother is here?"

I swallowed hard.

"Apologies, that was careless of me." Talen looked abashed. "I assumed she knew."

"She should have," Eliza snapped. "Why didn't you tell me?"

"Because I didn't know what to make of it," I said. "And when we get you home to Cal, he deserves all the answers. I wanted to wait until I could give you some. All I know is that someone from this realm wrote to my parents years ago claiming that one day I'd be called into this realm, and through means I'm very curious to discover, my mother entered this realm to save me before I had to come."

Eliza had known my mother when she was younger as our families had been close. But when my mother disappeared and my father faded away, our families grew distant. She'd been there to see us fall apart. She knew how bad things were. "Your father didn't say how she got here?"

I held out my hands. "That's all I know."

"Okay. So Thea's mother is here," Odette said, "but we don't know where. Thea's father is fae, and that information was detected in her blood and is now for sale on the market. Can anyone predict how this could go poorly for us?"

Her question pulled us in, refocusing the group on the future instead of the past. "My father must have left here for a reason, and who knows what ghosts might return to haunt me once they discover my lineage."

"So we must figure out exactly who your father is, and what he's done. Anyone else?"

Talen answered next. "If Thea is fae, there is power in her blood. To hold something that's both fae and mortal—some fae will go after that."

The idea that I might be in danger hadn't crossed my mind, and it made my skin crawl. "What kind of power?"

"Anything," Talen answered promptly. "It could be small, or it could be large. It could be nonexistent. So far, you've presented as nothing but mortal, but you might wield some power normally reserved for fae, and that makes you valuable."

I wrapped my arms around myself.

Odette gave me a determined look, as if she could single-handedly protect me from whatever came. "Is there anything else?"

No one replied.

"Next question, then. How can we use this to our advantage?" Odette asked.

It was Eliza who spoke up now. "If you're part fae, will you die as a Mortal Queen ought to?"

My breathing faltered. If I wasn't entirely mortal, then maybe the curse over the queens wouldn't take me. My eyes snapped to Talen.

He tapped his chin. "It's possible."

Possible was a long shot, but I'd hold on to it.

"What else?" Odette pushed. "We have the most valuable information in the realm right now. How do we use it?"

We fell silent as we thought, Eliza staring straight ahead, Talen tapping his foot, and Odette watching the three of us until I spoke up. "We sell it."

"What?" Talen startled.

My spirits rose as the plan hatched and took form, filling me with confidence. My blood might have entered the market without my knowledge, but I was still in control. Determination flooded my tone. "Talen, you sell this. News will get out very soon, so we might as well be the ones to collect. You know more than the blood will tell, so you should sell the information for more than the blood is going for. Turn all eyes back to us and show that we are in control."

Talen was already shaking his head. "We should try to smother this and hope no one finds out."

"It's going to get out anyway. At least five people know—us and Madame Rola. It's not a secret anymore—it's valuable information that will find its way to the light whether we want it to or not. Let's be the ones to gain from this."

Talen stepped back, brushing himself off as if he wanted nothing to do with it.

"It's my decision. Go to the market and say you have a secret from your queen to sell. You do it, or I will."

"We just established it could be dangerous for people to know."

"I can handle them. Odette, you agree with me, right? If someone is going to collect twenty thousand marks, it should be us."

She sifted her gaze between the two of us, worrying her lip. "It will earn you prestige in the House of Delvers," she noted. "Perhaps promote you as one of the illusive five Heads."

"Heads?" I asked.

"Five fae rule each House, their identities often secret," Talen informed me. "They are the only step between me and a king, but"—he glanced at Odette, who gave him a pointed look—"I said I was taking a step back. I shouldn't be chasing power."

They looked at each other, unspoken conversation passing between them. Eventually, Odette sighed. "Thea is right. Her blood is already on the market, and very soon someone will know why. We should list this information and collect the money instead."

"It will go straight to you," Talen promised me. "And I'll buy you lots more pigment for paint." He turned to Eliza. "And whatever it is you fancy for yourself."

She didn't reply, seemingly lost in her own thoughts.

Talen looked at us. "So, we are doing this? We are selling the information that Thea is part fae?"

I didn't hesitate. "Yes. Do it."

"Alright." He tipped his top hat at me and strode toward the door. "I'll update you when I return. Prepare yourself for the madness that will soon ensue, for the realm is not ready for this news."

I willed steel into my spine, but as he left, all I could think was how I wasn't certain I was ready for this news either.

13

MY STOMACH TANGLED ITSELF INTO
a knot that had no intention of unraveling anytime soon.

"I need to paint." The portrait of Gaia was almost complete,
then I could move on to the next queen—until these halls were filled
with their faces, and my mind loaded with distractions.

Odette nodded, but her gaze remained glued to the courtyard,
as if she planned to stay there until Talen returned.

Eliza followed me as I clambered up the stairwell, but instead
of settling by the fire in my chambers like she often did, she fetched
one of my cloaks. A thick one with sleeves built in. Not for lounging.

"Are you going somewhere?"

She checked her reflection in the vanity. "You were right." The
forest-green cloak fell over her cream gown. "I've been inside here
for too long. I need answers, and they lie out there."

The knots tightened within me. I wanted her to explore the
realm until she felt confident enough to play the games with me, in
hopes that together we might find a path to survival. But now that
she was going, I imagined the potential traps awaiting her. Hungry
to prey on her innocence. I thought back to Gaia, to when she'd
finally broken from her shell and went out into the realm. She died

that night. She'd been different from Eliza, though. She had been erratic and desperate.

Eliza fastened the cloak with steady hands.

In that moment, she looked more marvelous than ever. Her hair waved effortlessly into soft layers over the cloak, landing a few inches below her shoulders. Her cheeks held a flush of rosy color, her back straightened, and a determined look in her eyes as if—even in a land as overwhelming as this—she knew exactly what she was doing.

I set my paints down. "Where should we go first?"

She shook her head. "I need to go by myself. You're too recognizable, and I can slip around better alone." She flipped up the hood of the cloak, covering her brilliant hair. "I'll let you know if I need help."

"Don't sell your blood," I said quickly, then added, "Don't remove your mask. Don't get into chess matches you can't win, accept gifts of any kind, or fall in love with fae kings."

She gave me a smile. "I've watched you navigate this for a few weeks. I'm ready to try."

A few weeks was nothing. But I let her go all the same. I watched out the window as she entered the courtyard, tossed up a hand, and was taken away by a chariot.

She will be fine, I told myself. I gathered my paints once more.

Odette remained just where I'd left her, standing in the throne room with a hand around the neckline of her tunic.

"He knows what he's doing," I reminded her.

"That doesn't keep my from worrying." But she pulled herself away to settle at my side.

I set two clay jars on the marble dais and began mixing pigments. When I was content with the shade, I readied the brushes and fetched the canvas. After my excursion with Thorn, I'd stashed the painting behind my throne, covering a place where I'd made a cut of my own, once more hiding what remained of Cottia's journal. Her words often rang through my head, tempting me with what they could mean. Until I answered the puzzle, the journal would stay there.

I opened my mouth to ask Odette if she'd known Cottia, but a different question came out instead. "Have you and Talen mended things?"

She groaned, but the corner of her lips twitched. "I don't know. I tried to stay away from him. I truly did. But something about him draws me in and I can't let that go." She leaned forward to watch me work, absentmindedly twirling a truss of her hair between her fingers. "I've got it bad."

"I get that," I said under my breath. One look at Bash the other day, and I was willing to do whatever it took to get him back. "So that's it, then? You're together again?"

She sobered and dropped her hair. "Maybe. We want to be, but we still want different futures that aren't able to be compromised without one person giving up too much. He wants this." She waved her hand around. "A life serving Mortal Queens, with the whole realm knowing his name. Being the first to know information and holding all the cards in his hands. But that's not what I want."

"What do you want?"

"It might sound silly, but I want ordinary."

It was a simple thing, but she said it as if it was everything. Her eyes lit up as she spoke. "Did you know there are people who live and die, and no one knows their names? They just exist. They don't play chess to determine their fate. They don't make deals with kings or trade away their glass hearts for protection. They are simply . . . happy. And that is enough for them. I want that. I want a life where the realm doesn't know my name, because they have no reason to."

"That doesn't sound silly at all."

"It's never been what Talen wanted, though."

"He wants *you*," I insisted. "I know he does. Ask, and he'd give it all up for you."

"But that's the problem. I don't want him to give up anything. I want him to feel as if he's gaining the world by being with me, not giving it up."

I paused. That sounded fair. And it made me respect her more. But my heart broke for her as she looked over to the window for Talen. She was clearly in love. And I had no doubt he felt the same way.

Yet, I couldn't blame Talen for wanting the life he had. He played the games well, and he deserved his high position in the realm. It was an honor to be where he was, and he should be proud of his accomplishments. But what Odette said about compromise made sense. Either one of them got what they wanted, or no one did, but there was no bargain without one of them losing their dream.

"He might change his mind," I suggested. "Or maybe you will."

"It's hard to imagine changing my mind about something as big as my future."

"How did you become part of the elite anyway?"

"Talen," she replied. "And my relation to King Vern. That's how I met Talen, and I rose through the ranks with him. Did you know I was almost the next ambassador?" She took a moment to relish the surprised look on my face before continuing. "I was set for the promotion at the same time that Talen was offered to be the representative for the House of Delvers. But being ambassador means staying for life, and I remembered my childhood dream of running to the outer hills and settling down there. I asked Talen to come with me. He said yes, and I turned down the position."

She didn't need to finish the story. "And he accepted his role."

Odette confirmed with a small smile. She placed her hand over her chest where her cracked heart was and breathed deeply. "I won't change my mind about what I want. Unfortunately, my mind also wants him."

"Maybe he'll change his mind, then."

She chuckled. "Doubtful. Did you see how quickly he ran from here to sell the information? He is overjoyed right now with the power this will bring him."

"He might yet decide differently." I picked up my brush again.

"I did. I thought I wanted a future in the mortal realm as a painter, living a quaint life with my family. But now?" I dabbed the brush, feeling Odette's gaze upon me as I fought to articulate my feelings. I didn't know what I wanted, but when I thought of staying here . . . I didn't hate the idea. "Sometimes I'm not sure."

Her smile grew. "I'm happy to hear we haven't utterly scared you away from our realm."

"Sometimes you have," I replied honestly. "But the realm always pulls me back in again."

She fell silent to her thoughts as I finished the darker shades of Gaia's skin before moving on to the highlights. A few more touches and I'd be done, and her beauty would grace these halls. I'd already collected more canvases for the next queens. They'd hang on the walls on either side of the throne room, the east or the west, depending on which side the queen ruled. Gaia would go on the east at the far side, with only enough room for one painting to the right of her. Eliza's. The final queen.

A thought came to mind. I lowered my brush. "I don't see representatives easily giving up their position. How did Talen get it?"

"It was a large scandal at the time. The last representative was found—murdered."

"Murdered? How?"

"The Mortal Queen he represented was the one to kill him."

A tremble shot through me. I'd always pictured the queens as images of grace and beauty, each one fighting to do the right thing to free everyone who would come after her. But they chose random girls. It was likely that some would not be as delicate, but still. "That's awful. What happened to the queen?"

"She died as he did, on Choosing Day. It was the first time we went a year with only one queen."

I wondered if it grew dark during that time, or if the darkness was reserved for when both queens were missing. It had been three weeks since we'd returned, and things still remained overcast with shadows that clung to the thrones and wafted about our feet. The water still ran bleak. The air still tasted stale.

But it had gotten better. I could clearly see Odette beside me, and I had no trouble differentiating pigment colors as I dabbed the last spots on the painting.

"It's done."

I set the brush down and let Odette admire it. I'd painted Gaia with her mask on, but it only hovered over her cheeks instead of sticking to them. Her smile stretched wide, and her face turned up to feel the sun.

"It's stunning," Odette said. "I like it more than the first one."

"Which first one? The Salvation's Crossing bridge?"

"No." Odette, who'd seen me clean my paint supplies enough times, gathered the brushes to be washed. "The one at the far end of this hall."

I glanced beyond my throne to where she pointed, finding a corner shrouded in webs. Amidst it, something glittered.

Anticipation lurched within me, and I itched to run there. I had no doubt what it was. Someone had sent another message.

"Which queen is it?" Odette asked.

"Dhalia," I guessed. The queen whose story I thought I'd finished. Did she have secrets left for me?

Odette's gaze cut to me. "You'd already heard of her then."

"Who?"

"The queen who killed the previous representative. His name was Morten, and Dhalia killed him."

I recognized the name. The fae who loved Dhalia, and whom she'd loved in return.

I dove headfirst into my mind to search my memories for every moment with them, every time he reached for her, every time I felt her pulse speed up at his nearness. I'd been inside her mind. Her feelings were true. Were his?

It was a struggle to remain calm, one I didn't master. "Could you take these up while I hang Gaia's portrait?"

Odette took the supplies and moved up the stairs. I waited until she'd gone into my chambers to run across the room and throw myself into the tangle of webs. I grasped an ornate, golden frame and blew against the canvas, clearing the webs.

The painting was different this time, almost as if done by another artist. It didn't depict a scene, but rather a portrait of Dhalia, staring slightly to the right, with her chin held high. A tall crown sat atop her head with spindles of thorns clawing upward. The artist had extended the thistle to become a background that gave the image a haunting look.

The girl before my eyes wasn't a killer. I was eager to find out who was.

I reached for it, and my realm melted away.

Dhalia stood in a room mirroring mine, staring out the window. From inside her head, I felt the expectation swirling as she stood, utterly transfixed by the chariots coming and going. Waiting for someone, I realized.

The last I'd seen of her, she was planning to escape during the next Choosing Ceremony. From the view into the courtyard, the three ambassadors had arrived, signaling they were ready to take her.

"Where is he?" Dhalia fretted.

"There." Morten stepped beside her, pointing into the night. I focused on her inner feelings, checking to see if the love for him was real. I felt only relief upon spotting whomever it was they waited for.

Morten's hand went to her waist, and he pulled her into him. "I knew he would come through." His tone held concern, however, and his eyes sought hers. "All will be well. We can succeed."

How? I pressed into her mind. *What is your plan? Why do you end up killing him?*

It would be today. I remembered that with a start. She would kill Morten today and die alongside him.

Everything in my body was on high alert, watching to see what would happen and how it would save me. She was meant to be the queen who survived. I'd followed her clues to learn how to trick the fae kings, holding on to hope that I, too, could survive. Had I been following the clues of a dead queen instead?

Had she only been leading me to my death?

She reached for the ruffled collar of Morten's jacket to pull his lips close. There was no lie in how she touched him, and his eager response seemed as genuine as hers. If they were playing each other, it was a total devotion to the charade.

He rested his forehead against hers. "The next time I kiss you, we will be in the mortal world, starting our new life together."

They planned to escape together. I knew that. I needed more. I needed the details.

"I am eager for you to meet my family," Dhalia replied.

Morten released her and reached for the door. "Let me go bring King Ulther up. It looks as if he's brought his son, but I'll entertain him while you sort through the details of the escape."

"Be careful," Dhalia said.

He flashed her a grin that looked so much like Talen's. "I always am."

Then he vanished out the door. Dhalia swept a gaze around the room, giving me a chance to note the single, packed bag among a perfectly cleaned space. She truly planned to leave today. When she looked down to her finger, a jolt ran through me. She wore a ring from Morten. She smiled at it.

This girl was no killer.

But someone was.

At that moment, King Ulther stepped inside the doorway. The two of them might have formed an agreement of sorts, but his presence still made me uneasy. Honey skin that glowed too bright, alert eyes that saw too much, and a cerulean blazer sitting too perfectly overtop a black shirt. He took in the sight of Dhalia. "It's hard to believe this is the last day our realm will get to enjoy your presence. You've been a delight to us all."

"We both know that's not true," Dhalia said. But she maintained her smile. Whatever bad blood had once been here had passed.

She moved to fetch her bag from the bed. "Though I will forever be grateful for your help."

"It is not given freely," King Ulther said. "Our deal still stands?"

"It does. The power of the Mortal Queens rests in your hands this next year."

He gestured to her fingers. "When you are ready, turn the gem on that ring. Once you're in the mortal realm, it will hide you from the sight of the fae so we can never find you."

Dhalia's brow creased as she looked down. "My engagement ring?"

"It's a gift from Morten. A promise of a free future."

I could feel the unease slithering through her at not having previous knowledge of this part of the plan, but I couldn't see a reason for her to be concerned. King Ulther hadn't touched it. In fact, he'd made it a point to keep far away from her, almost out the door.

She touched the ring. "Very well. It's been an honor playing the game with you, King Ulther. You were a worthy opponent."

He bowed.

She twisted the sage green gem on the ring.

It let out a piercing cry and released a green wall of light that sprang to the ceiling, then fell like a cage around the room. Dhalia's heartbeat sped up. "What was that?" She twisted the gem again, but it would not right itself. It stayed put, glowing green. Her eyes snapped to King Ulther.

He'd stepped out of the room in time. Now he looked at her like a prized pet kept in a pretty cage.

Anger flamed within her. "What is this?"

"A locked room you cannot leave," King Ulther replied. "Only a king holding the matching ring bids it."

"And you have the ring?" She glared at him.

"I do not, though I was warned not to be in the room with you when you twisted that." He admired the green glow, testing it by putting his hand against it. It did not pass through.

"Warned by whom?"

His eyes gleamed. "Who do you think gave you that ring?"

She stumbled back. "Morten would never."

"He has been inseparable from your side this past year, but he is not here now. And unless you let another touch the ring, he is the only one who could have cursed it."

Dhalia clawed at the ring to remove it and threw it against the glowing wall, but it only bounced back. It clattered across the floor. "You're wrong. It's a trick."

"It is a trick, but I am not wrong." King Ulther appeared to be greatly enjoying this turn of events. "This worked out quite in my favor."

Dhalia rushed in circles about the room, checking the wall at various points. She hurled a vase at the ceiling, and shattered clay fell around her. She flung a chair at the wall. She kicked at the barrier to the balcony. "If I stay here, I die." She ran trembling fingers through her hair. "You're going to kill me."

"Again, this is not my doing."

She sank to her knees with heaving breaths. "Why? Why would he trap me here?"

"Did you think he would give up the magnificence of the fae for the dry heat of the five islands just to live a few decades with you? Dhalia, you are not a child anymore. Naivety doesn't suit you."

He loved me. I heard her thoughts, though she didn't say them out loud. Instead, she sharpened her gaze and turned it upward to King Ulther. "You will not get the power of the queens now."

"I don't want your power," he said. "But I will free you. Though I will not send you back to your land. You see, I've solved your problem. You will not die." His lips curled into a smile much like the snarl of a wolf. "You will remain in this realm with me."

"I will never be with you."

He knelt outside the door, level with her. "You will choose me, or you will choose death."

I hardly heard his words. From inside her mind, all I felt was fear as it crept up her spine, and the ache in her hands as she pounded the floor and screamed.

14

I WAS ON MY KNEES WHEN I
returned from the vision, breathing deeply. Dhalia's painting stared
back at me. A single tear fell from her cheek.

I'd been wrong, but now I didn't know what was right. This
entire time I'd been leaning on these tales for support, but now I
wondered if I had the message wrong. It wasn't that a queen could
escape. It was that we never stood a chance.

Talen cleared his throat.

I scrambled to my feet to face him. As my mind wavered between
creating a lie and telling the truth, he spoke. "These paintings are
not just paintings?"

The question hung in the air between us before I confessed,
"They are not." I gave Dhalia's painting a second glance. "But I am
wondering if they hold anything valuable at all."

Odette's footsteps cascaded down the stairs as she cried out.
"You're back!" She practically threw herself at Talen, and he caught
her in his arms. "How did things go?"

I gave Talen a look, one I knew he'd understand. *Don't speak
of the paintings.* He gave me a small nod before answering Odette.
"Splendidly. I listed the information for twenty-five thousand marks
and had a buyer before I'd left Illusion Point. With that, I paid to

get your blood off the market, and now we are richer and appear in control of the whole situation."

Odette exhaled with relief, but I didn't relax. "Do we know who bought it?"

"Anonymous buyer," Talen said. "My guess is they will reveal your fae father in their own time. But every king was present today, so it came off looking very good for us to list something so high and sell so quickly."

"Every king?" I clarified.

Talen nodded and drew himself up. "And I was offered the position of one of the five Heads of the House of Delvers."

I gasped before remembering my conversation with Odette. Her skin had paled. Talen was quick to collect her hands in his. "Do not worry. I will not take it."

She took a moment to find her words. When they came, her voice was tremulous. "Being a Head at your age? How could you refuse?"

"I've got a pretty good reason," Talen said in a voice so soft I felt I ought not be there. I looked down, but not before seeing Odette's uncertain expression.

"Ah, but one thing I forgot to mention." Talen changed direction quickly, drawing our attention back to the sale from today. "There was a stipulation with the exchange." He reached into his pocket to withdraw three glass orbs. "We cannot spread the information to any other fae. Otherwise, the sale is reversed."

I eyed the orbs. They were small, no larger than the width of a ring, and unassuming. But if Dhalia had taught me anything, it was that small trinkets could demand a heavy price. "What do those do?"

"Bind you to the promise. Place your hand over it and give your word that you will not share the information of your fae blood with the fae."

I hesitated, then took the glass and spoke my promise. As soon as I did, a ruby red light glowed from within. Talen and Odette did the same. When we were finished, he took them back. "Good. Where is Eliza? She must make the promise as well."

"You're going to be delighted by this. She's out."

Talen almost dropped the glass. "Out? Where?"

"She didn't say." I moved toward the thrones, drawing them away from the portrait of Dhalia. I skirted the hiding place where I'd stashed Cottia's journal. I had little pockets of secrets all throughout this room that I had to keep to myself.

Talen wasn't Eliza's alliance, but the worried look on his face matched the times when I'd gotten in trouble and needed him to rescue me. "When did she leave?"

"Right after you. She took a cloak with a thick cowl and doesn't plan on being spotted. I believe she is merely exploring."

"A cloak?" His eyes narrowed. "That dark green one you like?" When I nodded, he groaned. "She's on Illusion Point. I saw someone there wearing the cloak and it created a ruckus, but I was in the middle of the sale, so I couldn't investigate. So foolish." I couldn't tell if he meant him or Eliza.

Panic set in my chest. Illusion Point was the absolute worst place for a new queen to go when she had no experience with the realm. Frankly, I was surprised Talen let me go there unsupervised.

He marched toward the door. "She can handle herself," I called to him.

"I know that. Because I'm going to help her."

"Fine. I should find Bash to see if I can convince him this time to let me see the clue."

At that, Talen turned on his heel and walked back. "No, you shouldn't. It's only bad news. I meant to tell you I've received word that he let news slip—it's a game coming in two that must be played in pairs."

"A game? Chess." Something inside me warmed. He'd told me the truth.

Talen didn't appear as warmed. "Perhaps. But guess who he chose as his partner?"

"Troi?"

"No. Lord Winster."

He let the shock of that absorb before continuing. "And I can guess why. After he severed his faulty alliance with you, which were his exact words by the way, he's cozying up to your other alliance to convince him to turn away from you as well. And I don't consider you and Lord Winster to be particularly close, so he will likely succeed."

The way Talen said it sounded bad, but I didn't share the sentiment. "I don't mind losing Lord Winster's alliance. In fact, he's doing me a favor."

"He's not. After the fiasco you pulled with the stolen bracelet, it appeared as if you bested a king. But since then, Bastian has formed two new alliances, is growing close with yours, and is the sole owner of the next clue leading to a great power. It makes you look weak."

"You running off to his home to beg for the clue won't look good for you either," Odette chimed in.

"We all did that," I argued.

"We all did it *once*. Once is fine. Twice is desperate."

I tried not to let my emotions show, but a numb feeling sat heavy in my heart. Whatever Bash had once felt for me, he'd turned it all into motivation to best me. But if he could get new alliances, so could I.

"Then I will not go see Bastian. I will go see a different king."

15

RAIN FELL IN SHEETS. COLLECTING on my dress, soaking into my hair until my curls were a draggled mess by the time the chariot descended.

I looked around, unsure the chariot brought me to the right place. "Is this where Thorn lives?"

For a rakish king who radiated confidence with every step, I expected something extravagant, with spindles of towers reaching the skies and gold trimming the eaves. Instead, Thorn's castle was like a storybook image of summer, right when autumn knocks at the door. Sequestered from the realm, it was redbrick and white cobblestone framing a cottage-like manor, with four wings huddled close. It was frames of oak and hazy windowpanes. It was simplicity in the coziest way, built of childhood dreams and kisses from nature. Ivy grew near large windows, big enough that the entirety of the inside could be seen. Speckles of orange and yellow marigolds dotted the pathways, with hedges creating a maze outside, and three gardens sprawled across the grounds.

I gathered my drenched skirts in hand as rain created a soft melody, keeping time with my timid steps.

Though serene, it was anything but quiet. About twenty fae mingled through the gardens, some perched on white stone benches and reading books, while others shared tea, each unbothered by the rain. Then I realized the rain didn't touch them. Not even water from the sky could disrupt the splendor of the fae. Some tended the flowers, but they stopped to shake my hand as I stepped from the chariot.

"It's an honor to meet you, my Queen," they would say. "Thorn speaks so highly of your character."

"Thank you." I took them in breathlessly. There was not an ingenuine smile among the lot, which made the gesture easy to match. "Is King Thorn here?"

"He's in the parlor." One pointed me toward the manor. I thanked him and moved that way.

The rain left a rippling pattern on the stones, as if I moved across a lake, until I came upon glass doors. Wrought metal in an ivy pattern clung to the glass, letting me see through to a room coated in plants and orange firelight.

I knocked before letting myself in. As I entered, I spotted Thorn seated in the center of the room, facing the looming gothic windows to the north, iron detailing creating images of gargoyles and crowns in the glass. He held a slender, black paintbrush in hand.

Thorn leapt to his feet, dropping the brush. "Queen Althea! You grace me with your presence."

"There is no need to stand, Thorn. I think we are beyond formalities."

But he didn't return to his seat. Instead, he crossed to kiss both my cheeks. I wondered if the display was for my sake or a show for those behind us so they knew their king was cozy with a queen. He backed up and brushed water from his suit jacket. "You are soaked. Let's get you a cocoa."

"In a moment. First, I want to see what is happening. Are you painting?" I headed to the easel he'd set up in the center of the room. His grin turned bashful as I sat on the little wooden stool to inspect his work. Sleepy trees created a border, each one bending inward to create a cove, where a thick stump sat with its roots partially pulled from the ground. Chess pieces sat atop, their bottoms cleaved into the oak.

"It's meant to show the complexity of the realm," Thorn explained. "With each root holding us in one place, while we stretch for more. Each time we move, parts get intertwined with others, making it all connected in twisted ways."

"That's beautiful," I breathed.

"It's nothing like your artwork." Thorn pulled a sheet over it, which made me wince as it stuck to the wet paint. "I'm only dabbling. But you've convinced me to try."

Something flittered inside me. I'd convinced a fae king to paint. *Let's see if I can convince him of more than that.*

I rose. "Bastian revealed the next part of the clue."

Thorn took his time to reply as he appraised me. "Back to calling him Bastian now? Has the fire truly dwindled?"

I ignored that. "It's a game to be played in pairs."

By his expression, this was not news to him. He was already informed. He began to stroll the room. "And you wish to be my partner?"

I stood in place as he made a wide circle around me. "I wish for more than that. I wish to be your alliance."

He halted, and even the flickering fire stilled for a moment, as if the entire room hushed to listen. Slowly, Thorn faced me with a twinkle of intrigue in his eyes. "Why?"

"Because there's no reason not to." I withheld the many reasons I had to make an alliance—including healing the land by restoring the power to the queens and showing Bash that I could carry on. There was no need to make negotiations any harder than necessary. Instead, I leveled my eyes at him as if this were of little importance to me.

He did likewise. In moments like this, it was harder to forget that I was but a mortal in a fae realm, and he was a king. His stature dwarfed my own, and now that he wasn't in movement, his gaze felt like it bore into my skin. From how his lips curved upward, he was aware of my discomfort.

"An alliance with me would be very different from your connection with Bastian," he said. "I need not convince the realm that I can love, nor do I need them believing I've found my queen. Our alliance would be built on one thing alone—your promise that any information you retrieve about this Gamemaster's riddles, you will share with me."

Any information? Unease shook me, but I willed iron into my spine. If I did this, I might be handing him the seventh king's power. "And you will promise me the same."

"I'll do no such thing. You need this alliance more than I do."

He was right. But if I was to get anything from him, this would be my only chance. "Then in return, you will offer me three smaller things."

His eyes sparked, though not with anger. It appeared to be amusement. "I needn't offer you anything. You came here prepared to make an alliance, no matter the cost."

"I never do things no matter the cost," I refuted. "I have no problem walking out that door, but I hope you'll first hear my requests."

He spread his arms, and I breathed freer.

"One—you will give me three stars and not tell a soul whom they are from." His mouth opened as if to ask a question, but I stopped him. "Two—you will send Eliza flowers every other day, left at the foot of the palace with no note. Again, you will not tell anyone whom they are from."

This time he got in a word. "Why?"

There was no harm in telling him. "I want the realm to believe she has suitors galore. The Mortal Queens are short on alliances, but this will make us appear wanted."

"But I'm not to send you flowers?"

"I'll already have you," I reminded him. "Eliza is less connected. I need it to appear differently."

He crossed his arms and regarded me. "These are simple requests. What is the third?"

"A bigger one. Upon my final day in this realm, if I've yet to find a way to live, you will help me get to the mortal realm."

My first two requests were easy, but the third snapped him from his calm demeanor. "No," Thorn said, his voice ragged. "You'd die anyway."

"I know, but it gives me a chance to see my family again first."

He backed up, as if distancing himself could make me rescind the request. "It's running away."

"It's knowing when to give up. The final day, I will accept I have no future. You will spare me a death in this land."

I knew the fae loved their Mortal Queens. I knew it hurt to lose us. But I also knew it wouldn't hurt to lose me a day sooner, and it would mean everything if I could see my family once more. This wasn't a request I was willing to bend on.

It took him a while to finally nod. "As you wish, my Queen."

I swallowed the satisfaction. "We have an alliance then?"

He extended his hand, and it met mine. "We are aligned."

As soon as our hands separated, he reached up toward the hanging ivy and curled his fingers into a fist. When he opened them, three stars rested within. "The first of our agreements is fulfilled."

He waved his hand, and the stars were captured within a glass orb. He passed it to me.

"Don't forget." I put a finger to my lips. "No one can know where these came from."

"No worries about that," Thorn assured me. "When I make a promise, I never forget."

I brought the three stars back to the palace, where Odette waited in the throne room for someone's return. "Am I the first?" I asked.

She nodded. I looked over my shoulder to the realm, wondering where Eliza was and if Talen could keep her from trouble. She'd been gone for hours. I was certain queens had fallen in less time. Fear blossomed in my chest like one of the flowers in Thorn's home, but it was a wilting black flower that would bring nothing good. How long should I wait before I was allowed to panic?

"Who gave you stars?" Odette asked.

I lifted them, refocusing myself. Only kings could steal stars from the sky, and I bet she could guess which king had done this. The one who was *not* currently mad at me. "These are to be put in Eliza's throne, the same as mine were, and we will tell no one who gave them to her."

They glittered as I let them waft to her outstretched hand. Her face lit up with their glow. "Both of our queens will show that they can bend the will of a king."

"Exactly," I confirmed. "And let them wonder how she did it. The king in question is sworn to secrecy on the matter."

She took the stars across the room to Eliza's throne, where she drew them out one by one and placed them in the arched back. "And is this mystery king now in alliance with you?"

"He is." I looked at the stars with a smile. "For I am a queen who bends the will of a king."

Odette's gaze fixed on something past my shoulder, and I turned, expecting to see Talen or Eliza. Instead, a shining golden note fluttered to the ground in the courtyard. I pushed past the doors to pick it up.

A black brocade design marked the corners, stretching inward to the center, where a single pawn stood, its design stamped into the parchment. I was vaguely aware of Odette watching over my shoulder as I opened it.

The words, in elaborate calligraphy, stretched across the page.

YOU ARE INVITED TO MERLLON MANOR. THE GAME IS AFOOT.

16

PER ODETTE'S INSTRUCTION. I
changed into a slender gown of gold and brown, with skin-tight
long sleeves and layers of wavy skirts that weighed down my steps.
I wouldn't have put up with it if it didn't make me look so regal.
When showing off my new alliance, I wanted to look powerful. I'd
scored two kings so far. And tonight, I planned to talk to every
other one so the realm knew I had them all in the palm of my hand.

Before leaving the palace, I noted one thing—the darkness had
fully lifted.

I'd satisfied the realm enough that power was coming back to the
queens. It was like confidence seeping back into me, strengthening
my steps until I felt worthy of this dress.

I strode to my chariot and gave the direction. Merllon Manor. It
took off, flying me toward the unknown.

The unknown came into view a few minutes later. It was a
jungle. Any light it might have held remained captured behind an
impenetrable canopy of lush trees. The size was nothing more than
a few acres, like a dome of green plated against a sky of black. As
we neared, black spindles came into view, their tops reaching just
above the leaves.

We descended at a harrowing speed. I gripped the rails.

"Slow down," I begged the chariot. It failed to listen. I repeated the words louder, to no avail. I'd just crouched in the chariot to brace for impact when a whooshing sound surprised me. I peeked over the crossbar. The trees had separated.

The chariot let out a chipper flutter of sounds, as if laughing at me.

"You might have warned me," I muttered. It chirped back.

Darkness swarmed for mere moments before we broke through the thick branches and leaves, entering a cleanly groomed land of shortly cut grass, straight paths of stone, and rows of lanterns hanging from posts. We set down among the paths, and I lifted my eyes to the manor.

It was a thin manor, lacquered black from the first door to the highest turret, with every window propped open. A dim light seeped out.

"Wish me luck." With my invitation in hand, I stepped from the chariot.

As I made my way to the door, other chariots descended until a small crowd of us entered the manor together. Thorn was the last to arrive among them, and he walked over to join me. A golden basket greeted us, and I dropped my invitation inside.

"Welcome," the Gamemaster called. I searched to see her. The manor, as soon as we entered, had opened its jaws to deposit us directly into a large, circular room with grey pillars. I didn't care for the way in which cracks ran through them, making the entire thing appear as if it would crumble at a moment's notice.

Two oddities about the room stood out, both of which I tried to take in quickly, as if I were as familiar with the realm as the kings around me. First, the room had no back wall. Instead, it opened to the jungle, a mossy carpet below and a canopy of trees above my head.

The second was the chessboard. *Board* wasn't the right word for it. It was a chess *plaza* crafted into the ground with checkered squares, each wider than the length of my arm. It took up the entire space, making one thing very clear.

There would be no chess pieces here.

We were the players.

The Gamemaster stood in the white king's position, watching us drift in. Bastian was here, dressed in a maroon suit and white cravat. Lord Winster strode beside him with a smug grin. Talen followed soon after, splitting away to pace the room, staring at the board as if he played out the game in his mind.

Everyone filtered into the room and spread out. The Gamemaster beheld us with pride, maintaining a determined silence like the still of night. She didn't speak again until the clicking of heels came from outside. Then she smiled. "There is our second queen. All the players are now in play."

Every head turned to look as Eliza strolled into the parlor, her white skirts fluttering around her, coupled with the magnificence of her long green cloak. She kept the top of it pulled over her head, so her face remained hidden by shadows. She looked only at the Gamemaster. The gesture made her appear perfectly comfortable among the gaping stares.

Since she wouldn't look my way, I glanced to Talen. He gave me a subtle nod that told me all was well.

I grinned inside. Eliza was making her entrance to the realm exactly how she wanted it to be. Dramatic and calm. I adored that.

The others seemed to as well. Most of the lords broke into a susurrus of whispers, with many of the kings joining them. Thorn held himself back, adopting an austere look as if nothing could surprise him. Bash was studying her, as if he could discover all he needed to know from the tight draw of her shoulders.

As she held us transfixed, Eliza twirled a white letter between her fingers. "I was invited to play a game."

"And we are delighted to have you, my Queen," the Gamemaster said. She stole the attention back as she swept out her arms, letting the sleeves of her gown sprawl to the floor. "The game is one you all know well. Chess. Impress me, and you stay in the larger game."

The implication of her words struck me. "And if we don't impress you?"

She smiled with a gleam at my question. "Then, just like in

chess, some of you will be knocked off the board, and our game will continue without you."

The revelation sent a frenzy through the crowd, bigger than Eliza's appearance had. The consequences of today's match were higher than I'd guessed. It didn't matter so much that we won. It mattered if we were removed from the game and could no longer compete for the power of the seventh king.

For some, the game ended today.

"Where are the pieces?" someone inquired.

The Gamemaster tilted her head, as if disappointed it had to be asked. "You are the pieces." She stretched a long arm toward Eliza. "Our white queen—D1, please."

I wondered if she directed Eliza first to see if she knew the squares. She did. She waltzed directly to the white square and planted herself upon it. Thanks to Cal's teachings, Eliza was more prepared for this than I was. Quite likely, I would be the least skilled player on the board.

As I had that thought, the Gamemaster looked at me. "And our black queen—D8."

The marble echoed beneath my steps as I took my place, then looked up to meet Eliza's eyes. We would be opponents today, but I wished her every bit of luck. It would be tricky to impress the Gamemaster in these positions, as some of the least touched pieces in the game, especially for the first half. But we were the most powerful, so our opportunity should come.

"I will grant our queens the privilege of selecting their kings. Queen Eliza, whom do you select?"

"King Brock."

She spoke as if she'd anticipated the question, but from his curious expression, Brock hadn't anticipated her selection. Regardless, he proudly walked to Eliza's side. They exchanged a few words before something he said made her laugh.

My turn. "I choose my ally, King Thorn."

The subtle drop of news shook the crowd, and even Bash reacted, shifting to look between Thorn and me. His jaw tightened.

Thorn soaked up the shock as he took his place beside me. Once that was done, the Gamemaster examined the rest of the players.

"You all need to pick a partner. I assume by now you have chosen them?"

Shuffling took place as partners found one another, and sure enough, Bash had selected Lord Winster. From the sly way he looked at me, Winster was no longer my ally. It made me all the more confident in my choice to align with Thorn.

King Brock's partner, King Arden, entered the chessboard to stand beside Brock. Eliza remained the only one without a partner. The Gamemaster lifted a brow. "Could you not find a partner fast enough, or do you not want one?"

"I don't trust anyone enough," Eliza replied simply.

"Then you will find this much harder, but very well." The Gamemaster took turns passing between us, stopping to touch each ear and whisper as she did. When she approached Thorn and me, she placed a delicate finger to my skin. "*Eskali leon*," she whispered. Then repeated the gesture to Thorn.

I knew enough of the language of the night from my mother to translate. *Bind them.*

When the Gamemaster was finished, she faced the board. "King Arden, A1. King Bastian, A8. Though I hear we may have a new king soon."

She spoke the words so casually, yet they struck me like lightning. A new king? Was Bash losing his kingdom so easily? My eyes swung to Bash, searching for a reaction.

"I am still king," Bash declared as he stepped purposefully upon the board.

"What does she mean?" I whispered to Thorn.

"Have you not heard? Half of his lords revoked their allegiance. If more follow, he loses his status as king."

My stomach twisted. "Who gets it?"

"The one they are pledging themselves to. His father."

From the tilt of his smile, this pleased Thorn, but it gutted me. The dire situation was my fault, for revealing the bracelet Bash had stolen. He'd lose his kingdom because I hadn't trusted him. I tried to catch Bash's eye, but it remained pointed away.

The Gamemaster directed them to the two white rook positions, and placed the remaining two kings on black rooks. Then she filled the others in, the lords and two of the three House representatives, until Talen was the only one left. I examined the board. Eight pawn places remained open, three black and four white, and one black bishop.

"As for Talen, who I hear will soon be a Head of the House of Delvers, congratulations are in order. To honor you, I give you the place of the queenside bishop—C8."

Apparently, I learned all my information from the Gamemaster's offhanded comments now. For a second time, my stomach sank as the room clapped. Talen made the slow walk to my side, guilt stricken across his face despite the applause.

"You took the position," I whispered sharply.

He cleared his throat. "It comes with a great pay increase. Odette and I will need it to buy the land she wants."

"So Odette knows?"

"There wasn't time to tell her. Two months, at the longest, then I retire."

I hoped he was telling the truth.

The Gamemaster remained off the chessboard, out of play. She circled it, waving her hand, as eight pawns sprouted from the ground. "The pawns are moveable by any player of their color. As for the rest of you, you will move when you want to, attempting to play the game together. You'll notice your partner is on the same side as you. I have bound your minds for the duration of the game, allowing you to strategize. Remember, your goal is to prove yourself a worthy player if you wish to remain in our game."

She'd bound our minds? I tested it.

Can you hear me?

Thorn's voice came. *Clear as day.*

I pushed everything else away. Bash losing his throne. Talen once again choosing the lure of power. Everything had to go. All that remained were the black and white squares in front of me, and the players who stood upon them.

Good. Let's win this.

We had to.

17

ELIZA LIFTED A HAND FIRST. MOVING a pawn forward. Before I could match the gesture, one of my knights moved. I identified him as Thomas, the House of Berns Representative I chose not to align with my first day here. I steadied my hand.

He's going to be eager to prove himself, Thorn spoke in my mind.

We all are, I thought back.

Eliza moved the second pawn. It was a simple start, and I wondered if the other kings and lords let her move the first two to see what she could do. Surely they wouldn't relinquish control for long.

As soon as it was our turn, I flung up a hand to move a pawn.

Their knight moved out.

I've always wanted to win by walking the king, Thorn said.

I'm not the best piece to set you up for that.

As we spoke, the kingside bishop moved out. A ripple went through us. It was King Vern, and he exchanged a glance with his partnering player, King Leonard. They must be plotting something. We all were. The trick would be to somehow correlate those plans.

This couldn't be called chess. It was more of a blind guessing game—for both the opponent's side and ours, while simultaneously fighting for control of the three black pawns who could be moved by anyone on our own team. They'd be easily sacrificed to serve our own good.

Cal hadn't prepared me for this. Not even Troi could have prepared me for this.

After a while and a few lost pawns, the rook near Thorn tugged on his jacket. They nodded and swapped places. Castling. I was grateful for the mind bond that allowed us to still talk when he wasn't beside me.

Did you have a reason for that? I asked Thorn.

I assumed he did.

He'd better.

At my other side, Talen leaned forward to whisper to the knight. "You should advance."

The knight shook his head.

Talen leaned back with a frown. I tried instead. "We need you out there," I whispered to the knight. It was a lord I didn't recognize. Sweat lined his brow.

"I don't want to be knocked out."

Talen groaned, then moved diagonally four spaces.

Eliza moved out.

With the next step, I did as well. The queens were in play.

Eliza moved a pawn forward, placing it near one of our lords acting as a pawn. Hungrily, he moved out to claim the marble piece. As he did, it dissolved away.

But Eliza's move freed up her path, and as queen, she charged forward to claim our bishop.

The Gamemaster's eyes gleamed. "The first person has been taken."

The bishop hung his head as he took his spot to the side. He'd played too ambitiously. Or perhaps that was what the Gamemaster wanted. Who was to say if he would be removed from the larger game? Surely courage was awarded more than docile minds?

It was as if Eliza's move broke the caution across the board, and we all played more aggressively. Pieces bent to whisper together, players advanced, and Thorn and I kept our mind bridge wide open to plan a hundred ways to victory.

Their knight finally moved. *It's open*, Thorn said.

I quickly claimed the open spot before another black piece could advance. Bastian moved another of the white pawns next, placing it near our knight.

We had a plan for me here, but then our rook shifted and ruined it. I heard Thorn groan in my mind.

We can still do this, I told him.

Let's put pressure on their king. Retreat three squares.

I did and saw Brock squirm. He'd wandered out on the board more than I thought he would as a king, but he was never one to play small games.

Bastian moved next, placing him two squares from me. Our eyes met, and this time he didn't look away.

Someone on our side advanced, but I was unsure who. Thorn spoke into my mind, but Bash was mouthing something, so I focused on him instead. He'd been quiet for so long that I would take anything he offered.

I shook my head. I didn't understand. Instead of repeating, Bash studied me intently, as if seeing me for the first time, and his gaze felt like the first fall of rain after a drought. Someone moved again, but, once more, I couldn't register who.

Then Thorn shouted, "Cooper, stop! The queen is vulnerable."

That commanded my attention. I studied the board quickly. Lord Winster had played, putting him in a good position to take me. I should have moved this turn, but I had been too focused on Bash. If Thorn hadn't stopped Lord Cooper in his tracks, I would be taken next.

Heat flooded my cheeks. Bash had tricked me.

Move back left two, Thorn said. *And keep your chin high. You've nothing to be ashamed about.*

But I did. I'd let myself lose focus. Bash, to his credit, didn't bask in his small victory. His face remained as inscrutable as ever as I withdrew two spaces. I breathed deeply. *We need to get Bastian off the board.*

Happily.

Thorn moved next, and Eliza countered.

The setup came easily enough, and for the first time, several of our pieces worked together to put us in place to get Bastian out. The loss of their rook would bode well for us, and I'd focus much better without the heat of his eyes upon me. But before we could put the final piece in position, King Brock spoke.

"Queen Althea, I call upon my final favor."

It was as if all time stopped. I'd owed Brock a favor for almost a year. Now was a beastly time to call upon it.

I looked to the Gamemaster. "Can he interfere with the game like that?"

"Do you owe him a favor?"

With my teeth grated together, I nodded.

"Then it is fair."

Eliza shifted to speak to King Brock, but he paid no attention to her. "I call Althea to D3."

Right beside him.

The weight of owing someone a favor had been like a bitter taste in my mouth, constantly reminding me I wasn't free. Yet I'd rather hold that weight for eternity than be thrown from this game. But there was nothing I could do. So, with as much dignity as I could manage, I marched to D3.

With Brock's next move, he took me.

My stomach soured. I felt every eye on me as I walked from the board.

I was out. I looked to the Gamemaster to see if she was impressed with Brock, and therefore disappointed with me. I could glean nothing from her eyes.

You played well. She won't hold that against you, Thorn said.

Time will tell. You should bait the knight with a pawn to clear the path to their rook.

Through the staggered bodies, I saw Thorn grin. *Good idea. If they'll listen to me.*

Pieces were getting out more often now. People weren't moving unless they could take a piece, and it took several minutes for anyone to play at all, leaving lots of time for me to think about the moves I'd made and reflect on how easily I'd been distracted.

Once, Bastian glanced to me but then quickly looked away.

Disappointment collected inside until it was all I was made of, and I could hardly stand to be there as the game continued when I'd been so easily taken out. The only reprieve came when Thorn moved a remaining pawn, our bishop advanced, and the words finally came.

"Checkmate," Thorn said.

Eliza handled the loss with grace, bowing to the other players. She'd played well and had nothing to fear.

Though we'd won the chess match, every piece faced the Gamemaster to hear who had won *her* game. She flourished her hand, and the remaining pawns disappeared. "You all played well. But not all can advance. I have eighteen clues, and there are twenty-four of you."

I knew what would happen. I would not advance. I hadn't earned it today.

But to my surprise, she held a richly dyed blue envelope to me first. "Our two queens will advance. You both carried yourselves nobly today."

Eliza's gaze skipped to mine, and I knew we thought the same thing. Only one of us deserved this. Yet we both took the envelopes. My fingers trembled to open mine, but I composed myself.

"The kings all earned their place as well. King Brock, you impressed me the most, willing to call in your favor to advance yourself. Though you did not win, you showed me you are willing to do whatever it takes to play. King Thorn, you proved yourself a leader. And King Bastian, you put aside your cracked heart to focus on the board. All of you are worthy competitors."

Bastian didn't meet my gaze as he took his envelope.

The kings and queens would advance, but six of the lords did not, as well as the other two representatives. Talen was the only one to move forward.

The eight removed from the game carried the shame with grace, but quickly departed. As soon as they were gone, we ripped into the envelopes.

The thick parchment shone in the moonlight. Upon it, in gold ink, were three words.

WHAT'S MY NAME?

I looked up. "Your name?" I asked the Gamemaster.

But she had disappeared.

Do you know her name? I tested. Only silence remained, and Thorn didn't look my way. Our minds were our own again, then. That was a relief.

"Does anyone know her name?" I asked out loud this time.

By the shifting glances and deep silence, it seemed no one did.

I tucked the note away. This time, I determined not to make a fool of myself. I'd find her name first.

I quickly turned from the parlor to walk through the double glass doors leading to the courtyard. I passed tall hedges, searching for my chariot, until a hand grabbed my arm. My head snapped to the side to see Bash just as he pulled me into the hedge maze.

"What are you doing?" I whispered.

"I wanted to speak with you." He glanced left and right, then led me around the corner to press us into a small crevice. Branches poked my back, and the scent of pine filled my nose. I should be angry, but all I could do was feel how close he was and wonder if this was another trick.

"You don't need to apologize for earlier," I told him. "You were playing the game."

Bewilderment crossed his face.

I blinked. "You didn't intend to apologize."

"As you said, I was playing the game."

My heart fell. "Then what did you want to speak about?"

He looked over me fleetingly, while I soaked in the sight of him. His maroon suit paired well with his cream-colored shoes, and he'd exchanged his six earrings for one that ran as a continuous loop through each hole. In the dim light, his golden mask appeared almost black. Yet his eyes carried a glint that hadn't been there while we played chess. It made my heart beat faster.

Was his accelerating as well? Did being near me make him as weak as I felt?

But his tone was all business. "What information did you sell at the market?"

I gaped at him. Did he think I would give that up so easily? Being this close made it difficult to think clearly, but I wasn't daft. "I won't say."

"You can't say, can you?" Bash guessed. He exhaled. It was as if he was sorting through a problem, searching for answers. The look was so far from the cold stare I'd been getting recently that it gave me hope.

"What's wrong?" I asked.

"The information sold for a high price. Yet no one claims to have received it."

"They are biding their time, I suppose."

"That's what I'm afraid of. That they have something worth biding their time for. Have you thought through every possible way this could be used against you?"

"I'll be fine."

"Thea, something is off. I'm nervous for you."

The way his eyes searched mine was like the day he showed me the snow. Like all he wanted was to look at me forever. The tenderness touched me, giving me courage to reach for his hand.

"You don't even know what the secret is."

My heart jolted as his hand came up to brush against my cheek. "I know that secrets are only secrets because they have the power to hurt someone. I want to be certain that isn't you."

Then he stepped back, his hand sliding from mine, leaving coldness behind.

"Bash," I choked. He paused. I wished he would stay. We could figure out this next clue together, and every one after it. Instead of voicing my desire, I simply said, "I miss you."

His glance fell to my lips before turning away. "This isn't easy for me either. I loved you with everything I had."

"Then love me still." I was nearly pleading. Tears sprang to my eyes. "You must realize I never intended to hurt you."

"I do," he said. And the small way he smiled made me fall in love all over again. But he continued, "It took a while, but I realized you didn't mean to ruin me. Yet it doesn't change our situation—I am fae and you are mortal. I'm protecting us both by keeping away. Please understand. There cannot be a future for us."

Though his words were true, I wished he hadn't said them. I wished instead we could ignore such things and pretend like the rest of eternity was ours. Anything was better than nothing.

But Bash was walking away.

My heart bled after him.

I glanced to the note in my hand.

WHAT'S MY NAME?

If I solved this riddle, along with every subsequent one, and if the power of the king saved me, then hope wouldn't be obsolete. I would take hold of it and secure a future for myself.

"I will solve this for us," I promised and left the hedge maze behind.

18

ELIZA. TALEN. AND I ARRIVED IN
tandem at the Queen's Palace, where Odette waited on a balcony.
Upon spotting us, her lithe figure disappeared into the chambers.

We'd have but moments before she swept out the front doors.

I looked at my friend—my first alliance. "Lord Talen."

It wasn't a question. It was a sharp accusation.

He winced. "They don't go by lord."

I waited pointedly.

He sighed. "It happened rather quickly, and there wasn't time
to discuss with Odette."

"You and I both know what her opinion would have been, so I
rather doubt you should use that excuse on her."

Talen shifted his gaze toward the doors. "Everything I do is for
our future. She will understand."

I doubted she would, but it didn't feel polite to say so.

"What happened?" Odette asked breathlessly as she came
running up to us.

"The most difficult chess game of my life," Eliza replied. She
was prying jewels from her hair and dropping them in her pocket
before going for the pins. "I wanted to yell at everyone to follow one

plan, but they all had their own ideas for how to move. That game could have been won half an hour sooner had we worked together."

"As it was, you didn't win at all," Talen said.

To that, Eliza flashed her note. "I got this, didn't I? That means I won. Though . . ." Her attention landed on me, and I frowned.

"I was wrongly played. That shouldn't have been legal for Brock to bring in outside favors."

"I happen to agree with you," Talen said. "But you played well before that."

"Not well enough to remain in the game," Eliza said. From how Talen cast his eyes downward, he agreed with her. It was expected though. I had far less experience playing chess than all of them. Perhaps the Gamemaster took that into account as she judged us? And my team had won in the end. I might not need to be as suspicious about remaining in the game as I was, yet something still tugged at me, telling me it wasn't right.

"Some of the players were removed?" Odette guessed.

I nodded. "Eight. Two representatives and six lords. But I was not. Something kept me in the game, and I don't trust what—or who—that was."

"Whatever it was, we can be grateful for it. King Brock was impressed at how you went with grace and is interested in aligning with you," Talen said.

My first thought was no. He'd been the one to trap me in the palace for six months, barter with Talen's heart, and force me out of the chess match. He played honestly and wasn't malicious in his games, but still. "I don't trust him."

"There's much goodness in him, I can tell." Eliza surprised me by speaking. She'd gone weeks without interacting with the realm, and after one day she was chummy with a king?

"Then you align with him."

"No. But if I were to align, he'd be the one."

I sighed. I already had one alliance with a king. Two might be more trouble than they were worth. "I'll think on it," I told Talen.

"Though, Eliza, I believe you owe us a tale about your time in the realm. Illusion Point isn't for the fainthearted."

"We'll leave you two to talk," Talen said. "Odette?" He offered his arm. Odette glanced at Eliza like she wanted to hear the tale as well, but I didn't miss the urgency in Talen's eyes as he led her away.

I waited until they were out of earshot. "I hope things work out between them."

Eliza finished removing the pins and collected them in her palms, shaking her hair free. It made sense to move inside, but the night air carried a breeze that cooled my cheeks like a welcomed kiss, so I made no move to retreat. Eliza settled beside the stream to remove her shoes and dip her feet into the water, looking after Talen and Odette. "It's not often that fae marry, is it?"

"Not usually. I only know a few who are. In this realm, marriage is binding. And since they live so long, they regard the union with the highest sanctity."

She remained quiet, swirling her fingertips through the stream, leaving me to guess at her thoughts. I tried anyway. She'd returned from Illusion Point and from an elaborate chess game where we were the pieces, yet she appeared unfazed by both ordeals. If she'd made bad deals, they didn't seem to weigh on her enough to share with me.

Eliza and I had never been close. This past month, we'd spoken more than we ever had in our lives. Though we'd lived near each other, she was always focused on Cal, and I was focused on my painting. I had no right to know her inner thoughts, yet I longed for them. Perhaps because we were both trapped here and I'd just spent a year with Gaia who hadn't deemed it fit to try to escape, but I craved knowing someone else fought just as hard as I did to leave.

As time went on, I grew more convinced that this fate was not one I could escape alone.

I sat beside her, and she looked up. "Have you heard of any fae who left the realm?"

Finally. These were the questions we needed to be asking. "As far as I know, only the ambassadors hold that power, and they can only use it once a year."

"But they always come back. Do you think they have the power to leave and stay gone? Or, more importantly, to take another with them, then leave them behind?"

"I haven't heard of it happening, but we could devise a plan to force an ambassador to return us to the mortal realm and see what happens." As I said that, the memory of something Bash once told me came to mind, and I deflated. "Actually, they've tried sending mortals back."

Eliza lifted a brow, but from my frown, she guessed the ending. "She died."

"Right at the two-year mark. We could still try. I'd rather die there than here."

"I'd rather not die at all." She quieted again. I thought back to what I'd asked of Thorn, to find a way to get me to the mortal realm before I died. Perhaps I should amend the deal to include Eliza. She might prefer a year with Cal over a year here, especially if survival couldn't be obtained in either realm.

"I heard stories at Illusion Point," Eliza said. She withdrew her feet from the stream to cross them beneath her. "Ones given freely in hopes of acquiring my trust. Stories of Mortal Queens gone by. Tales of the kings."

"I'm sure they have glorious tales."

"They said a king disappeared."

"The seventh king," I reminded her. "No one knows where he went."

Eliza raked her gaze across the night sky, as if the king would appear at any moment, showing us where he'd been hiding. In all likelihood, he'd been killed for something. Kings have many things some deem worth killing over, and similar fates had befallen rulers in our land. But if he'd lived, I liked to imagine something like Odette's dreams—a small farm, a peaceful life. After escaping the chaos of the realm, he ought to have something harmonious.

But it'd been years, and no one had found him.

"A queen has never taken the power of a king before," Eliza said. "But if we held the power of a fae, we might survive the fate of a mortal."

"That's the hope. Not just for one to survive, but for all. It has to be strong enough for that."

She shook her head, not bothering to brush away the blonde strands that fell over her eyes. "We are missing something. I just can't figure out what."

"Let me know when you do." I stood. "Because I've been here for a year feeling like I'm missing a hundred things, and the answer to our survival could lie with any of them."

"We will find the key to our survival." She spoke with the certainty I'd felt when I first arrived.

Her words ignited a second memory, and I struggled to grasp it. Eliza collected her shoes and left while I remained there, staring into the sky, trying to uncover why her words had jolted me.

My mind settled on the word *key*.

The king is the key.

Had the old queen, Cottia, been here when the seventh king went missing? Was it possible he was the king she spoke of? My attention roved over the endless stars in search. If I found him, would he save me?

Additionally, how could a king hide from all the fae?

"No one from his staff left. I asked once. It was only him," I recalled, hoping if I spoke the words out loud, an answer would come. "And without help, how would a king know how to farm the land? Where to get fresh water? How to hunt?" *And how is it no one has found him yet?*

My gaze fell downward. Toward my realm.

They couldn't find him because he wasn't here.

A fae king hides in the mortal realm.

The idea ran wild, and I grasped at strings to pull it into a cohesive theory. Our vast lands provided ample sequestered places to hide. Places where no one would know to look. And we didn't know to look. It was a possibility. From what Bash had told me, kings didn't have the power to travel to the realm on their own. He'd need the power of an ambassador. If he'd succeeded, it meant an immortal dwelt in the mortal realm. That was the sort of thing that drew attention. We'd have heard about it.

That was the thread I focused on, for it was the one that could offer proof. If a king lived on the five islands, there might be a sign.

I felt as if I were Cal going over one of his puzzles. I reached for answers, exploring errant ideas before letting them go. Handsome men who didn't fit in. Ones who were stronger than others. Ones who were smarter. Military leaders. Mathematicians. Someone who didn't age at a normal rate.

"We weren't looking," I went on. "You wouldn't hide from us. You lived among our people. Where?"

Names came to mind, but there'd be no way to test my theory from here. I had no proof with me and no way to get any. How could I know if a fae had lived among the mortals when I was trapped away in the fae realm?

There must have been a sign that a fae lived among us mortals.

I had something from the fae realm. I lifted my arm.

My blood.

The breezed chilled. Air tightened in my throat. This revelation— it felt too big for me. Too much to take in. Yet I was utterly helpless, unable to prevent it from crashing into me all the same, stealing my breath and my identity in one cruel, swift move.

I couldn't look away from the blue of my veins. "It's fae blood."

There was the proof. The sign lived inside my body, guaranteeing that at one point, a fae lived among the mortals.

I'd fallen apart before. When Mother disappeared. When I was chosen as queen. When I lost my chance to escape the fae. But never had I fallen apart so quickly and put myself back together in a seamless way that felt right.

This information would sell for far more on the market.

I knew who the fae king was. And he'd handed me half the puzzle himself.

Father told me he was fae.

It had to be him. The way he carried himself around the other officers from the center island was too proud, like he'd always been above them. He'd defied the pause of time when I used my watch, when even the other fae hadn't.

Because he was no ordinary fae. He was a king, and part of this realm belonged to him.

Therefore, part of it belonged to me.

I lifted my head. Now I didn't look at the realm as something I was dragged into, but as something that was my birthright. It belonged to me just as much as the mortal realm did, and it called to me because it lived within me.

And the power of the seventh king was by rights mine. *Because I am the daughter of the fae king.*

I strapped the title on like armor, preparing myself for battle. It protected me. It strengthened my mind and spirit, knowing both realms were my home. There were questions, why he left and how he did so, yet the sweet taste of victory upon solving one riddle filled me with the promise that I'd collect the other answers over time.

Mortal Queens had not been strong enough to save themselves. But the daughter of a fae king? She was strong enough.

I'd drag my father back to this realm if I had to, and I'd make him transfer his power to me. Whatever it took.

19

I'D INTENDED TO TELL THE OTHERS, but Talen and Odette couldn't be found, and Eliza had already gone to sleep. I blew out the last, dying candle and slipped beneath the fleece blankets beside her. She had Antonio in her hand. I looked fondly at the soldier toy, wishing my brother goodnight.

My thoughts wandered. My paintings in the mortal realm depicted family more often than not, yet I'd avoided painting their images here. It spared my heart from seeing them, but perhaps Eliza would appreciate it if I drew them. She carried their ghosts anyway. I might as well give her something tangible.

Though, as I drifted to sleep, it was not Cal's or Malcom's faces that lulled me, but the image of my father in a golden crown.

I woke a little later to the click of a door shutting.

I sat as Eliza stirred. "What is it?"

"Something's there," I whispered. A frame rested in the bone-white moonlight. Rectangular, thin, and tall.

Eliza rose, her eyes on alert.

"It's a picture." I swung my feet to the floor and crossed to retrieve the wooden frame and take it to the scant moonlight by the window. Had I realized sooner, I'd have stirred gentler to keep Eliza asleep. But now she was awake as well, standing beside me and looking over the image of a queen trapped in her bedchamber and crying at her door. Tears marred her cheeks.

Eliza crossed her arms. "What a thoughtful, warm gift that is."

"It's more of a gift than you realize," I told her. "This is the only Mortal Queen to survive."

"These are your mysterious messages?" Eliza examined the painting with far more interest. "Do they show how she lived yet?"

"I hope we are about to find out." I collected her hand in mine and braced before the image. "Ready?"

Without hesitation, she nodded, and for the first time, I brought someone into the painting with me.

Our bedchamber exploded with light from the chandelier above, candles surrounding the room with the scent of lavender and smoke.

No, I realized. The smoke was from the door.

Dhalia was attempting to burn it down.

The flame licked the wood, crawling upward before dissipating. Dhalia groaned, grabbed a candle, and tried it again. Heat licked her fingers, igniting the urgency within her. Each time, the flame went out. She pounded against the lock, burning her hand.

Dhalia screamed and tried again.

What's happening? I heard Eliza's voice in my head.

We are inside her body as one. Everything she sees, touches, or feels, we feel it too.

There was a pause, then, *She's afraid.*

Dhalia was trapped inside this room by a fae king, Ulther. Or possibly by her first alliance, Morten. There is a chance she kills him.

This will be uncomfortably interesting, Eliza replied.

Then we both went silent, for someone was outside the door.

Dhalia scrambled to her feet, cradling her burned hand. "Who is it?"

"It's Morten."

"Go away," she gritted out. "You liar."

They were in love, I explained.

That's not love I feel in her. It's hatred.

Hence the possible murder. Which I greatly did not wish to witness.

"I can't get this door open," Morten called. From the way it rattled, he tried over and over again. "Did Ulther trap you?"

Dhalia didn't reply. She moved to the window and stared down, wondering how far of a drop it was. Twenty meters, she guessed. I tried to correct her. It was farther than that.

Morten pounded against the door. "Dhalia, can you hear me? I will get you out!"

She went to the door and spoke through it. "So you can give me another cursed ring?"

"Ring?" Morten tried the door again. "Ulther helped me get that ring! Dhalia, please. I would never trick you. I love you endlessly."

Her breathing evened. She stared at the door. "I don't know whom to trust."

"Trust me."

The fight within Dhalia faded.

She gave up easily, Eliza commented.

This realm has put her through a lot. She doesn't have much fight left.

Dhalia lifted her hand to the door. "Can you get me out?"

The handle jostled again. "It won't budge." Morten's frantic voice seeped through the wood.

Dhalia looked around. "Morten," she said urgently, "perhaps the window?" As her gaze swept outside, her heart sped up. She placed her palms against the grating stone windowsill and peered at the courtyard. Fae gathered there, circling the three ambassadors.

She planned to leave at Choosing Day, I told Eliza. *Morten was to go with her.*

It looks like they need to get out soon.

Yes. I pondered the situation. Ulther trapped her here for a reason. The ambassadors would wait, but not forever. Soon they'd depart for the fae realm to collect a second queen, and they'd return. Dhalia wasn't needed for that. King Ulther's only possible reason for trapping Dhalia this day must have been to keep her from escaping into the mortal realm, for he was aware of the plan.

But the fae loved the queens. If they thought the queens had a chance of living, they would sacrifice anything to give them that chance, even if it meant losing them to the mortal realm. Talen had proved that by giving up his glass heart for me. Bash had told me over and over. Try as they might, the fae could not resist the urge to love their queens. So for Ulther to deny Dhalia the chance to live . . .

It broke the rules of the realm for a king to wish a queen to die. It didn't line up. I was missing something.

A sharp snap bit the air. My thoughts halted. Dhalia spun, and I felt a gasp tear from her throat. The door she'd been trying so determinedly to burn down had suddenly come alive with flames, and the hungry tentacles of orange and yellow darted upward at an alarming speed, claiming the boards. Beneath the heat, the wood turned black. The fire would make quick work of the door. Dhalia only needed to wait, and she would be free.

Just as success seemed near, a terrified cry broke from the hall.

Dhalia's heart seized. "Morten?" She fell to her knees as close as she dared to the door. "Morten, what is it?"

"My hand is stuck," he panted. "I'm stuck to the door!"

In panic, she ignored the searing pain to grab the handle and yank it. The wood held tight, refusing to give. The metal heated quickly, soon burning her palm, but she didn't let go. Eliza and I both cried out, feeling every ounce of the agony.

Morten's screams fell silent.

The fire died.

"Morten?" She called his name, but no reply came. "Morten!"

Her desperation grew until she was throwing her weight against the door to knock it down. The planks groaned. Encouraged, she tried again. With the third attempt, the door gave, and she fell with it to the ground, patting out the remaining flames that had scorched her arm.

Outside was the same corridor I'd seen every time I opened

my own door, but it was charred black. The fire kept to the door rather than spread into her chambers, but out here, it had ravaged the corridor, burning banner and stone and tapestry until all color had faded and smoke clouded the air. Silence locked the corridor.

Too silent.

Dhalia crawled off the door and, with trembling hands, moved aside the planks. Morten lay below, but the fire had claimed him. She needn't check his pulse to know he was gone.

Dhalia looked for far longer than I had the stomach for.

Hot tears rolled down her cheeks. Loud footsteps caught her attention, and she hunched like a gargoyle, waiting, while her fingers reached for a broken shard of wood.

King Ulther appeared with three other fae following. "Dhalia," Ulther said, his eyes widening in what could only be faked terror. He scanned the scene. "We saw the flames. What have you done?"

"What have *I* done?" she choked. "You with your games and your lies and your tricks!" She hurled the piece of wood at him. The other three fae ducked.

But King Ulther drew near and looked at Morten. "Oh my, is he dead?" He gestured to his companions. "Go tell the others. I will take care of the queen." They hurried away. "Come, my dear," Ulther said loudly. "Let's get you cleaned up."

When the other fae were out of earshot, King Ulther's expression changed. "It didn't have to be this way," he said in a low voice.

She threw a second piece of the broken door at him. "You killed the only one I loved!"

He boldly approached, managing to drag her back into her room while remaining immune to her small punches against his chest. He waved his hand at the doorway until a second door appeared, perfectly in place. As if nothing had happened.

"I never wanted to hurt Morten. Listen to me, my Queen! He wasn't supposed to get hurt. But he couldn't save you, and he knew that. *I* can."

"I don't want anything from you," Dhalia hissed.

"You want to live, don't you?"

She gave a reluctant nod, but kept her lips in a firm, mean line.

"Then come to Illusion Point."

"I'm not going anywhere with you." She looked at him through eyes brimming with tears.

"You must go to Illusion Point. I told you. I'm going to save you."

The vision ended, and we were yanked back to reality.

The darkness of our room set back in, paired with a hollow silence. Eliza put a hand to her chest, steadying her breath as tears streamed down her cheeks. Meanwhile, I stared at the door. This was the one King Ulther had created. It still stood after all this time. I tried not to think of Morten, to find the clues within the vision to help me escape, but my mind kept going back to that moment. My eyes squeezed shut.

Eliza finally spoke. "I don't think I like these visions. Are they always like that?"

"That's the first time someone has died in one." The words felt strange, and my knees felt weak. It was the first time I'd ever heard someone die, and it was as if a tender piece of innocence had been ripped away. I'd never be free of that sound in my head. I swallowed. "But the complexities were all the same. As if teasing us with the answer to our survival while giving us nothing."

I rose, turning away from the wretched painting. Now that we'd watched it, the corners had turned black as if they had gone through the fire too. An odd sensation prickled me.

"It's close, though," I breathed. "I can feel it. The next painting will show us how she survived."

There was no use in going back to bed, I grabbed my cloak and sandals. No more waiting for paintings. This last one gave me a clue all on its own.

Eliza watched me, her hand on her stomach as if steadying it. "Where are you going?"

"Illusion Point. An answer lies there."

20

ELIZA ELECTED TO JOIN ME. A decision for which I was grateful. I didn't care to be alone after the experience we'd just had. As the chariot took us toward Illusion Point, I thought of Dhalia and kings and puzzles that could never be solved.

Being the late hour of night, the skies remained fairly unoccupied, with only one other chariot spotted at a distance going the other way. We descended upon Illusion Point in silence, until I instructed, "Take us directly to the big chess board. I don't care to walk through town tonight."

The chariot obeyed. We came upon the statues of kings and the stands cleaved into the ground, all overlooking the grand game of chess. The kings of the realm were all preoccupied with the Gamemaster's game and, just as before, the board sat empty.

The entire place had a deserted look to it. We touched the ground, and I stepped off.

"Did you come here when you visited Illusion Point?" I asked Eliza.

"No, but I wish I had. It's beautiful."

"Bets are made at this table." I approached to slide a finger over its smooth surface. "I won a friendship with Thorn here, and a favor from Brock. That's how Talen got his glass heart back."

"I'm not surprised he gave up his heart for you in the first place," Eliza said. "He seems like someone who'd give up everything for those he loves."

"Almost everything," I mumbled.

That wasn't fair. He would give it all up for Odette. I refocused on the task at hand—uncovering what about this place would free us.

Eliza kept close to me, picking up fallen chess pieces at random to roll in her palm. Meanwhile, I dug into every crevice, every chip in the stone thrones, and every seat in the stands. I located three separate keyholes—one in Brock's throne, one on the side of the chessboard, and one on the ground between the queens. But no keys. I prodded at the locks anyway until I had to accept they would not be opened by my poking.

"I always thought this realm would be a dream."

Eliza's sentiment was not lost upon me. "Yes, I know." I glanced at her and said gently, "I'd appreciate help if you can muster it."

She was quiet a moment. "This will not be solved by our eyes, but by our minds."

I heaved a breath and sat on one of the two thrones for the queens, where green ivy crawled up the spires to contrast the iron. "And what has your mind wrought?"

"It's discerned that it's quite late. We are both clearly emotional after watching . . ." Her voice trailed off, and she began again. "If there was something here to be seen, someone would have seen it by now."

I didn't want to admit she could be right. I was tired of searching for answers and for once I wanted one to come easily. How do the queens survive? How do we unlock the power of the seventh king? Where was my mother? All the questions wore me down until I couldn't remember the last time I hadn't been haunted by at least one of them.

"I wanted to come to the fae realm so badly," Eliza went on, her voice distant. "I had such big visions for how splendid it would be.

If it weren't for our inevitable deaths, and the blocked access from home, it would be." She let a chess piece roll from her hand. "I should have taken Cal and Malcom and run before my name could ever be read."

"We all should have run together after both our names had been called."

I glanced at the fallen chess piece, the black queen. Lifeless eyes stared back at me. She'd landed on the third keyhole, sitting directly between our seats. The way her scepter was fashioned to point, it was almost long enough to place in the keyhole.

Better than my fingers. I picked it up.

Eliza watched multiple failed attempts. "Try the king," she mocked after the seventh or eighth time.

I started as Cottia's words returned to me. *The king is the key.*

With energy I'd never possessed at this hour of the morning, I ran to the chessboard and swooped up both kings. Eliza sat up at my sudden frenzy. "It was just a jest."

"The king is the key," I muttered, then louder, "It will work."

She looked at me as if I were crazy but bent closer when I tried.

To my great delight, it worked.

I could have cried. I had solved something. What, I didn't know, but it must have been important for Cottia to write about it.

With trembling breaths and a thrumming pulse, I pulled on the lock. It lifted as a panel, the entire slab of stone rising to slide backward, revealing a dark stairwell. Dim light illuminated the bottom.

Eliza and I stood and stared.

Then we descended.

The smell hit first, like bread left unbaked. Stale and thick. Next was the texture of the air, how it clung to us with a heavy moisture. Cobwebs ran like frost up the walls, yet no creature was in sight. The way the light flickered at the other end indicated a fire, so there must be another exit for oxygen to exist down here. Or holes of sort, creating a vent.

"Hello?" Eliza called.

I froze, equally terrified and hopeful for a response. We both waited.

A slow sound came like scales on the belly of a beast dragging across the floor. I almost fled. But Eliza's steady grip gave me courage, so I continued. At the bottom of the stairs, a long hallway stretched, fitted with three oil-burning lanterns and a ground made of copper-colored cobblestones.

"It looks like the wine cellar in the governor's house," Eliza said. "The one we played hide-and-seek in when we were young."

I hadn't thought about that in a long time. We got in trouble a fair amount for sneaking in there, but we never drank anything, so we were never reprimanded badly. This felt very much the same, like we were sneaking through a place we didn't belong and would get caught any moment, dragged before the governor who would tell us we were nothing but trouble.

We turned at the end of the hallway to see what else this underground tunnel had in store, and stopped short.

Only a few paces away, the walls opened into a circular home with windows cast against a sea. Yet, there was no sea on the island. A makeshift bed had been placed on one side, with a table on the other. At least, I thought it to be a table. In truth, so many books filled the surface and floor that I couldn't be certain.

It was a room. But for whom?

Eliza silently pointed. Two feet covered in thick stockings stuck out from the other side of the books, with a chain attached to one ankle. That chain extended to the center of the room, where it had been melded to a stake with harrowing claw marks surrounding it. Not a room, then. A prison. With the prisoner still inside.

Asleep, hopefully.

We tiptoed forward, while I tried not to let hope build too quickly.

Father had suggested Mother had been captured. This would be a wonderful hiding place for her. But the realm had not been kind to me when it came to hope, so it didn't grow too large. It was more likely an enemy. We would get in trouble for this. We'd be harmed. This was a mistake.

Don't hope too much.

With our movements came the rustling of the chain, and the feet disappeared. From behind the books, a figure rose, the face half-coated in shadows from the oddly angled room. I bent, prepared to run if needed.

But the figure didn't charge. They stayed still, a slender hand lifted to their face.

"Althea," came the whisper. The familiarity of the voice couldn't be denied, and neither could the curve of her face when she stepped from the shadows and into the light.

Mother.

21

A CHASM OF SUPPRESSED EMOTIONS

flooded me, and I found myself in her bone-thin arms, sobbing.

She held me tight, her chest shaking beneath my touch. Her fingers clung to my back, and my face pressed into her clumped hair, content to stay that way forever. As if somehow my problems were solved now that I'd found my mother.

It had been five years since I'd seen her face. Five years since I'd heard her voice. Five years building up a wall around my heart, telling myself I was fine without a mother. Now the bricks all fell.

"You are doing so well," Mother whispered in my ear. I locked the sound in a box in my mind, knowing I'd repeat it many times. Mother had a huskiness to her voice that wasn't there before, paired with a feeble way of standing. I shifted back to inspect her. Haggard snags ran through her long dark hair, ones that would require hours of tending to unravel. The dim torchlight was not kind to her features, catching on the sharp cut of her cheekbones and hips, until I wondered if she had been fed more than a slice of bread a day.

"Are you well? Are they taking care of you?" So many questions, I could sit there all night and ask them.

"I am better right now than I have been in years," Mother replied.

My eyes went to the chain latched to her ankle. "Who keeps you here?"

"I don't know," she said, holding tight to my hands. Her soft brown eyes took in every inch of me, and she smiled. "So strong. My pride and joy."

My lips trembled. I could revel in the sight of her all night, but through my daze, I knew it would do me no good if Eliza and I were found here. Had we closed the door behind us coming in? I couldn't remember. My thoughts were as tangled as Mother's hair, and I had no hope of sorting them properly. "Is your captor here?"

"Whoever he is, he comes once a week with food, though he's late this week. I fear his use for me grows thin."

He. A male then. I took the first sliver of a clue and held it tight, desperate for many more. Yet Mother offered none as she kept soaking in the sight of me as if we'd reunited on a sandy shore somewhere and were in no danger, instead of in a cell with a thick chain attached to her leg. Meanwhile my chest tightened. She hadn't given useful answers, but something in her words made the dry air turn cold.

"Use?" I asked. "What does he want you for?"

Mother's lips lifted into a sad grin. "I don't know that either. Perhaps there is none. But with your time here ending . . . I suspect mine will too."

The mention of our time ending sobered me, and my questions faltered. Suddenly I had one more reason to stay alive. While my head whirled, Mother glanced over my shoulder, spotting Eliza. "I recognize you," she said.

Eliza approached. "I am Eliza Nadell. Our families used to share meals together."

"Yes, Eliza." Mother's smile grew tender. "That's right. My son was always sweet on you."

Eliza's cheeks flushed. "He still is, as I am him."

Mother's eyes brightened before shadowing. "And you are the next queen."

"Our families seem to stumble upon misfortune." Eliza's tone quickened. "Mrs. Brenheda, I must ask. How did you get into this realm? Did an ambassador help?"

Mother chuckled. "Look at the two of you. Question after question. I suppose I'd expect nothing less." She let go of one of my hands and reached for Eliza. She held the two of us with a tight grip as if we were the ones keeping her upright. When she shifted, the deep-set circles under her eyes became more visible, and my heart ached.

"There is a bridge between the realms," she said. "One that used to be open for all, its gates now open only for a few. I'm afraid they might never open again."

A bridge?

"I will try anyway." Eliza breathed fast, and I knew she was thinking of Cal. "Please, can you tell me how to open the gate?"

"It is foolhardy. The criteria is strict."

"What is it? I'll do anything it asks."

I feared more for Mother's captor coming back at any moment, especially since he was due to bring food. Yet if a blockage stood between Bash and me, and I'd heard of a gate to open it, I'd be just as desperate to get through.

Mother sighed and pulled a wobbly chair close, the spindles grating along the stone. She eased herself into it slowly, her limbs shaking ever so slightly. Once comfortable, she looked at us. "What does this realm value most of all?"

"Cleverness," I answered.

"Trickery," Eliza said.

Mother shook her head.

"Alliances?" I wasn't as certain in that, but Mother nodded.

"Specifically?"

I thought. "Smart alliances?"

But Eliza gasped as something struck her. "Marriage. Fae marriages can never be broken. It's the eternal alliance."

"Correct. The realm values marriage above all else, for it is the highest bond you can make. Once upon a time, fae could make such bonds with humans. The gate remained open for all, and marriage bonds occurred frequently."

"I hadn't realized anyone but the notorious king married a mortal," I said.

"No other kings did, and none others ended so tragically. After Queen Melody died, the gate closed, and our realms viciously tore apart. Now, it only honors those who are married."

Eliza's eyes glinted. "Any marriage? Two mortals could get into the fae realm if they are married?"

"No, they must be on opposite sides, and it will let them be reunited."

"Then how did you get in?" But I realized I knew. "Because Father is the missing fae king." Eliza's mouth fell open, and she looked at me in shock as I went on. "He belonged to this realm, so the gate made an exception to take him back." I searched Mother's eyes for proof my guess was correct.

"Did he tell you? Or is my daughter as clever as I always knew she was?"

"What?" Eliza breathed.

I covered my mouth with my hands as deep relief flooded me. I hadn't realized how much I wanted to be the daughter of a fae king until she confirmed it, but that part of my heritage filled me with pride. It connected me to this land that I loved—even when every part of it had broken me down—and gave me a sense of belonging. My hands shook. I had been right. I was the daughter of a fae king, and I belonged to the fae realm.

I turned to my stunned friend. "Father admitted he was fae. I guessed the second part."

Eliza looked between us with wide eyes. "Do you think your blood would disclose which fae your father was?"

"Perhaps," I answered, then explained to Mother. "My blood was on the market, so someone knows I'm part fae."

She pondered that, then said, "We must find a way for you both to survive quickly, before someone can entrap you here."

"Let's use the bridge," Eliza said to her, excitement rising. "You can take us there, and Thea, your father can meet us on the other side. The marriage will let us past."

"Our fate is sealed," I pointed out. "I'd die in ten months, here or there."

"It's better than staying here."

"I don't think it is," I said.

"Then stay." Eliza faced me. "Stay if you wish, but I will take a year and ten months with Cal and Malcom."

Mother's breath caught at the names. Her eyes clouded. My brothers still believed her to be dead, and she no doubt missed them as much as she missed me. "I want to see my sons very much, but let us work together so you get a life with them, not a year."

Eliza dried her cheeks, then spoke with resolve. "It is my choice to make."

I opened my mouth to argue, but the words were difficult. Mother and I couldn't promise Eliza a life with them, and there was no guarantee we would make it out of this realm alive. If Eliza wished to hold on to the small certainty she had—who was I to stop her?

As if thinking the same thing, Mother resigned. "All I can tell you is that the brightest star in the east points the way," she said.

Eliza wrapped her arms around my mother. "Thank you, Mrs. Brenheda. You have no idea what this means to me." Then, without saying goodbye to me, she turned on her heel.

"You're going now?" I asked, following a few steps in her direction. "Just like that? It won't open without Mother there."

Eliza hardly looked back. She'd reached the first torch already, then the second. "I haven't time to lose. Don't worry, Thea. I will still find a way to save us."

Then she was gone. I stared at the space she left, hoping I didn't just say goodbye to yet another queen.

"She was right. It was her choice to make."

I turned back to Mother. "But how will she open it?"

"Let her try." Chain links rattled as Mother stood. "Now, let's see about freeing you."

"And you." I crossed to the chain and knelt, following it to her ankle and pleading for my good fortune to hold fast one more time. She lifted her hem. A keyhole stared back at me, its edges sharp like the jaws of a beast.

"I don't suppose you have the key?"

I fumbled through my cloak pocket until finding the smooth surface of the king chess piece. "The king is the key," I whispered, and pulled it out. I fit it into the side of the jagged lock and turned.

It didn't budge. I tried again. And again.

"It's alright, darling." Mother rose to lift me by the hands. "I am just glad to have been found by you."

"I will free you," I promised her. "I'll find the key."

Her hands went to my cheeks to dry them, then brushed back my hair. The warmth of her touch was unlike anything I'd felt in the fae realm. It was safety. It was kindness. It was what my heart had craved. "Let us save you first, dearest. What have you uncovered?"

"Shockingly little," I admitted. A loud sound told us Eliza had reached the door, and it was difficult not to feel abandoned. "My entire time in the realm could be summarized as hardly surviving. I know our fates began with the first queen's death, and that one mortal queen has survived since then. I know I must keep my true face hidden, watch my words, and not trust the kings."

"Most of the kings," Mother clarified. "You can trust Brock."

My lips twisted in disdain. "Brock? You should hear the things he's pulled on me."

"Like locking you in your palace for six months? I heard. He told me."

That floored me. I wasn't certain which surprised me more—that Mother knew King Brock, or that he knew my mother and neglected to tell me.

"He and your father were good friends." Mother settled herself on the chair again, fixing the hem of her skirt over her thin bones. She'd lost much strength since I last saw her. Mother had grown up as I did, on the center island, where a routine part of schooling involved physical exercise. Now she appeared as frail as the flute players who visited every year, and far less cheery. I nestled at her feet like a child to hear the tale.

"Your father spoke kindly of Brock, and when I came to this realm, he was the first person I sought out. A figure ambushed me shortly after my arrival, when I'd just stepped foot in Brock's courtyard. Brock never even saw me. It wasn't until a month into your reign after all these years that he found me. Though he couldn't free me, he became a constant visitor, and when I trusted him enough, I shared that you were my daughter. He confessed the trick he'd pulled on you, and apologized, though I do believe he diminished the time to three months."

"At a price. He could have removed it entirely," I grumbled to myself. Then I sat upright. "He's known all this time where you were. Why didn't he tell me?"

"That was my doing. I know you won't understand, but I needed you focused on saving yourself, not on freeing me. If you'd known of my whereabouts, you would have been distracted from what mattered."

"I could free us both."

"I hope you do. But if you don't, I know who I want freed." Her hand cupped my cheek. "Do not worry about me, dear one. I will be fine."

I rested against her touch. "We both will," I promised her. Then I straightened. She might trust King Brock, but he'd betrayed me more than once. "What if Brock had you captured? You landed on his courtyard and were attacked. He could be behind the ordeal."

Mother chuckled, though I'd told no joke. "It is not easy to trust in this realm, but you can trust him."

"I'm not certain I can. There is a grand game taking place, promising Father's power to whoever can solve a series of riddles. Just yesterday, Brock used an owed favor to try to throw me from the game."

"That was me again. I want you out of this Gamemaster's scheme. Brock was doing me a kindness."

"Why?"

"I don't know where she came from, nor how she could promise a power that rightfully belongs to you."

"She must have Father's signet ring," I said. "If I win, I'll get his power."

"If she has the ring, why won't she keep it for herself? Think carefully, Althea. Who gives up power like that?"

I almost suggested the Gamemaster to be humble, but her theatrics didn't point to humility. There weren't many in the realm who boasted the ability to resist power, and I doubted the Gamemaster to be among them. Eliza's response came to mind. "What if she needs help unlocking his power?"

"Then I trust her even less. Games are always riveting until they take something you weren't willing to give."

"I have nothing to lose," I told her. But that was not true. I had Odette, Talen, and Bash—in a way. Now Eliza, and I supposed I wouldn't quickly trade away Thorn either. It was easy to feel alone when all I thought about were my struggles, but when I stopped to take stock, I had a band of fierce loyalty around me. Four fae in this realm whom I could not lose, plus my family back home. And now I had back my mother, and I knew if someone asked me to accept the fate of the Mortal Queens in turn for her life, I'd do it. Many things anchored me here, creating liability I wasn't willing to sacrifice in the Gamemaster's plan.

Mercifully, Mother did not call my bluff. She only sighed. "I cannot tell you what to do, for you have always been too strong-willed for that. But, please, be on guard. Can you promise me this?"

Slowly, I nodded. I would be on guard anyway. She relaxed.

I studied the room, taking time to absorb all she'd told me. I hated the thought of her in this small space alone and made note to thank Brock for visiting. Some of the kings left me alone, others sought a close friendship, but he'd done neither. Though, he always had been there like a shadow. And behind him, my mother had been there the entire time.

This realm gave me many things. Courage I didn't know I had. Strength when I wanted to give up. A sharper mind that thought before it spoke. It also gave me distrust, which I would work on. But this realm had now given me back my mother, and I'd eternally be grateful for that. If I never made it home, if I never saved the future queens, I could be grateful for coming to this realm, for it brought my mother back to my life, and somehow brought me closer to my father than I'd ever thought possible. My heart swelled.

"I didn't know you were here, yet you've had a hand over my time in this realm all along."

"More than you yet realize." She took the effort to stand again and crossed to her bed to pull out the mattress. The thin cot moved easily. Underneath, she pried up the stones of the floor to reveal a hatch. I waited as she reached in and pulled out a large canvas.

A simple golden border looked back at me, along with a half-finished black background.

At first I just blinked at her. Mother patiently waited.

The answer came slowly. The brush strokes were familiar. The dainty curves of the border. The size of the canvas. I gasped.

"The mysterious paintings?"

In a way, it wasn't surprising at all. She had taught me to paint. She had told me how illustrations convey messages that we must be clever enough to find. It made perfect sense that she had used such a form to communicate with me. Yet it still stole the breath from my throat.

"You painted them for me?"

"It was the best way I could connect with you, without you uncovering my plight."

The mystery of the paintings was one I'd accepted I'd never solve, but to know they came from my mother warmed me in a way I couldn't explain. Her words settled softly over my shoulder. "There is still much to share with you."

"Do I get the end of Dhalia's story soon?"

"I'm painting it now. But since you're here, I'll—"

Her eyes widened. A sudden chill swept up my arms.

"You must go." She knelt to stuff the canvas back under the stone and replace the bed. "He is here."

"Who?" My breathing quickened. How much room was under that cot? Perhaps I could hide there too. But Mother was already nudging me back the way I'd come.

"The one who captured me. He must not find you here. Go! Hurry."

"If he's in the tunnel, we're too late."

"He's not. I can sense when he arrives upon the island. You only have a few minutes to escape."

"I can't leave you." I clung tightly to her. "I will fight him if I must."

Mother accomplished pushing me far enough down the tunnel that she reached the end of her chain, and it held her back. She smiled sadly. "I have no doubt that you would. But you will do yourself no favors if you get trapped here with me. Go, my dear. I will be here whenever you need me."

I lingered a moment more until she begged me to leave. The desperation in her voice brought me speed, and I found the strength to run. My feet pounded as I hurled myself down the corridor and up the stairs. Cool air greeted me. Thankfully, Eliza had taken the chariot that brought us here, allowing nothing to give away my presence. The area remained empty. I wasted no time locking the door and replacing the chess piece, then I tucked myself in the shadows of the king's thrones to wait.

I needn't wait long.

Before a minute had passed, a lone figure appeared at the top of the stands, looking over the arena. His wide frame gave away his physique, and I was suddenly grateful I hadn't stayed to fight him. He took slow steps down into the heart of the chess arena, surveying all sides with eyes hidden in shadows and a face guarded by a full black mask. It was not like the masks we all wore. This one covered everything.

I pressed myself against the throne as his face turned my way. I remained there until I heard the sound of the stones grating together and his footsteps disappearing into the tunnel.

The idea of leaving him with my mother didn't sit well, but she'd been clear.

"I will return," I promised her. Then I fled.

22

I DIDN'T GO HOME. EMOTIONS clouded my mind, chipping away at every ounce of confidence I'd built up over my time in this realm and breaking it away like pieces of a clay pot, crumbling, until only chaos remained.

Who held Mother captive?

How would I free her?

How could she have been here the entire time?

Answers wouldn't come when all I stared at were questions. I tried to see past the haze. Perhaps I could convince a small band to form together and free her. We could lay in waiting and ambush the captor when he came to feed her and force him to give us the key to her chain. Or I could find a locksmith to pick it. Or someone strong enough to break it. Bash might be strong enough. He had the power of a king. Or he could join forces with Thorn and the two could work together.

I abandoned that idea. The odds of getting Bash and Thorn to work together were lower than my odds of freeing my mother.

The chariot flittered beneath my feet as if sensing my unease. Good. I wanted the whole realm to feel it. Someone had stolen my mother from me. They would answer for it. But until then, "Take me to King Brock's home."

The chariot turned sharply to the west and whisked me away.

King Brock's home sat on a small but populated island, right upon the edge of a town. It faced outward, to the skies. He possessed the smallest home of the kings that I'd seen, with no more than three levels, each one only a few rooms wide. I'd thought him humble the first time I saw the place. Now I suspected it was meant to appear unassuming so no one questioned the depth of his mind. I had underestimated him.

The early hour of dawn descended like a soft kiss, yet no lights lit the interior of his home. Even so, when the chariot landed at his doorstep, I marched off and went to pound a fist against his door. The wood rattled in response, groaning unhappily.

I pounded harder.

Brock opened the door a short while later wearing a robe tied at his waist and his forehead wrinkled with exhaustion. His gaze fell to me, and a single brow raised over the edge of his mask.

"You knew my mother was here," I accused. My throat constricted until I couldn't get a good breath. "And you didn't tell me."

He sighed and opened the door wider. "I suppose you want to come in?"

"I want to know why," I said, but I entered anyway. His home carried the scent of bread pudding, with oak details throughout the corridors and mahogany trimmings along dewy windows. A thin, creamy rug ran the length of the entryway floor, leading to a room where a dim fire burned. Brock gestured to the chairs beside it.

"Shall we sit?"

The proper way in which he spoke infuriated me. *Shall we sit?* As if he didn't cage me in my home for three months, try to pull me from the Gamemaster's game, and hide knowledge of my mother from me for a year.

I remained standing.

"I don't plan to stay long. I want to know why you decided a seventeen-year-old girl didn't need her mother."

His voice came calmly. "Because her mother insisted. And from where I stood, you didn't need anyone at all."

The frustration bubbled within. "Of course I needed my mother! I was lost! I am destined to die in a land that is not my own, where no one knows my true face, and where fae are determined to trick me at every turn. How could I not need her?"

I'd spent months tiptoeing around the fae and watching my words. It felt good to let go.

Brock matched my volume. "Who saved Talen's heart? Who convinced two kings to align with her? Who has been playing the Gamemaster's game one step ahead of everyone else this entire time? Who has won the hearts of everyone in this realm? You never needed anyone, Althea. The moment you did, I would have been there. But you were strong enough to fight for yourself, so I honored your mother's wishes."

"You never should have kept her from me."

I could never agree with that decision. Mother hadn't seen me in this realm, but Brock had. I had victories here, but I also had struggles, and he must have known that. He should have helped me. He should have helped *her*. I thought I'd had a hard time here, but my mother had been chained for five years. "If you cared at all, you would have at least fed her."

"And risked her captor taking notice? No. I fed her when I could—just enough. But who do you think brought her the canvases and paints, or delivered the messages to you? Who has been there for company for the past year? I've not abandoned her, and don't plan to. Nor did I abandon you, if you can think clearly enough to see it."

He'd been the one to deliver the paintings? Shame swarmed me. I dropped my head. "I didn't know."

"Your mother was right to keep herself from you. Since finding her, how much time have you spent thinking about how to free her versus freeing yourself?"

I could laugh. "I will save myself when she is free."

"You might not have that option. Pick one. Whom do you save?"

The way he spoke, it was as if I needed to give an answer now. But it wouldn't matter if I had all the time in the world, or only a second. I'd still land the same way. He knew my answer. Her.

His tone turned gentle. "Your mother raised you well, my Queen. But it is because of your good heart that you could not know she needed you. Because you are more important to her than freedom."

"Help me free her," I pleaded. "We will wait for the captor to visit her, then we can ambush him."

"You aren't hearing me."

"I am. I will focus on myself. But I'm allowed to think about her too. Let us at least attempt a rescue. If it doesn't work, I'll let it go."

"I doubt you will. But it's no matter. I've tried to free her more than once. The mystery captor evades me every time, and I dare not risk your life by bringing you." Authority rang in his voice, as if this were a command and not a suggestion. It made my stomach turn.

"My life is not your responsibility."

"I promised your father it was."

The words sliced through the air, stilling me. Brock sighed, running his hand over his mask before gesturing once more to the chairs beside the fire. This time, I sat.

The heat of the flame somehow cooled my anger. Brock poured two cups of lukewarm tea while I stared at the dancing embers. Intricately carved wood trimmed the hearth with black stone lining the inside, matching the shade of the curtains and the walls. Narrow paneling added dimension, while the rest of the room remained void of artwork that usually adorned mortal homes. The simplicity impressed me. No towering thrones. No majestic portraits. He was a king unlike any other.

When Brock settled beside me, I allowed him to speak.

He did so with his gaze fixed on the hearth, as if the memories lived there. "Your father and I were good friends. We grew up together, came into power together, and played the games of the realm side by side. We were unbeatable." His words faded, and it took him a while to find them again. "But he was tricked, or betrayed, or something else. He wouldn't tell me. Whatever happened, it forced him from the land, and our golden age ended."

"Who do you think tricked him?"

"I do not know. But I have been desperate to get him back to this realm ever since. It's been two hundred years since he was home."

My eyes bulged. "My father is two hundred years old?"

"He's far older than that. But a man must have some secrets."

Brock reclined in his high-backed chair with a lithe smile. I struggled to picture my father the way Brock saw him. All I remembered was a broken man, blinded by grief, who gave in to gambling to dim his pain. I'd give a lot to see him as a king.

"You may question my methods," Brock said. "But I have never done anything other than look out for you, as your father would have wanted."

"Trapping me in my home?" This time, my voice contained a hint of amusement.

He grinned. "I've never done anything *since knowing who you are.*"

I wasn't certain how to feel right then, but I could be grateful for one more person on my side. "Thank you," I said genuinely.

"Anytime. One other thing. I've removed myself from the Gamemaster's game."

I almost spilled my tea. "Why?"

"Your mother does not trust it, and neither do I. Neither does my wife, which was reason enough. I'd rather you removed yourself as well, but I am here to help if you do not."

I stared into my cup at the wilting leaves. It was hard to find my mother, then purposefully disobey the one thing she asked of me, but instinct said to stay in the game. It had something for me. "I don't think I can walk away."

"Your father wouldn't have either. This power that the Gamemaster promises, it's rightfully yours, and I will help you take it if I can." He paused, then added, "Or help your father reclaim it."

"My father wants nothing to do with the fae," I said, then

regretted it when he winced. I tried to soften my words. "He has a good life back home."

"This is his home," Brock stated. "It's always been my plan to bring him back. Regardless, if he chooses not to return, I will help you take what is yours."

I considered the possibility of him returning once again, and it thrilled me. The pieces of my family coming back together. Seeing him as a fae king and playing the games with him. Having him see me here as a queen. But whatever forced Father from this realm left a bitter taste in his mouth that soured every time he heard mention of the fae. His return was unlikely.

"Thank you," I said again. "I'll need all the help I can get to take the throne."

His eyes twinkled. "You confirm it then? You intend to remain in this realm?"

I hadn't realized what my words revealed, but his eyes lit up in a way that sent warmth into my heart. If someone had told me a month ago that Brock and I would become friends, I wouldn't have believed them. Yet there we were, with him somehow becoming someone I trusted.

"It might not be up to me if I die," I stated the obvious. "But, yes. Something about this land always felt right, even when it terrified me. I plan to stay."

He took a sip of tea. "You are your father's daughter, through and through."

Before, I would have taken that as an insult. But coming from him, I knew it was a compliment.

I rested back in the chair, balancing the teacup in my hands. The fire in my belly had waned, and exhaustion set in. I spoke through a yawn. "Tell me a story of him. One of your favorites."

His lips quirked. "Gladly. Here's the tale of how he tricked King Vern on Vern's coronation day."

So he told me. As Brock spoke, I closed my eyes, letting the warmth of the fire and the depth of his tone lull me into a quiet rhythm. And finally, after two days of exhaustion, I fell asleep.

23

WHEN I AWOKE, MY TEACUP HAD
been placed on the hearth, and the stars gleamed brightly outside,
indicating midday. I rubbed the sleep from my eyes.

"You are awake." A woman's tender voice pulled me to my
senses. I twisted to find Brock's wife sitting by the arched entrance
to the study, a red-bound book in her hands. I'd thought her
beautiful the first time I met her, dressed up in a stunning gown
with her silver hair gleaming like the moon, but in the quiet of the
day, with simple silk dressings and a kind way about her, she shone.
She closed the book. "I hope you are rested."

"I am. How long was I asleep?"

Heavy footsteps neared, and Brock appeared a moment later,
wearing a black suit with a golden cravat to match his mask and six
earrings. "A few hours. It's just past lunch."

His wife stood. "I'll go prepare food for you."

I opened my mouth to tell her that wasn't necessary, but the
pinch in my stomach stopped me. She gave a knowing smile and
hurried away before I could thank her.

I stretched my limbs, finding one sandal had fallen off in
my slumber. I bent to retie it. "Has there been any news about
Queen Eliza?"

"There has not. Should there be?"

"No, I'm sure she's fine."

But I wasn't sure. What happened if someone tried to open a gate between realms and it didn't work? If I didn't hear anything soon, I would go to the gate myself and find her. For the time being, something else interested me.

"Was it you who purchased the information I sold from the market?"

The mention of it seemed to put a sudden weight on his shoulders. "I was on my way but was too late. Someone else knows what I suspect the blood revealed—that you are part fae—and I don't trust what they will do with that knowledge."

I didn't trust it either, but before long, everyone would know who my father was when I took his throne. All I needed was the signet ring. "His ring. Do you know where it is?"

"You never take a moment to rest, do you?"

I indicated to the chair. "I rested for hours. Now it's time to move."

He sighed, but I heard a hint of a chuckle. Brock didn't have to ask which ring. "I'm afraid the location of his signet ring is a mystery he wouldn't tell me, but I know your father put it somewhere for safekeeping a long time before he left the realm. I've tried to search for it, to no avail. It would appear the Gamemaster found it."

"Do we know for certain that she did?"

"No," he admitted. "But his power rests within. No one can take it—or give it—without that."

Even so, I wasn't convinced the Gamemaster had it. I checked the pocket of my cloak to make sure the envelope was still inside, the one containing her next clue.

"Where did my father live?"

"If I could not find the ring in my two hundred years of searching, you have little hope."

"I know. Still, I wouldn't mind seeing his home. I've found my mother," I said. "Now, I think I'd like to find my father—or at least find out who he was."

Brock regarded me for a moment, then crossed the room to open the door. Cool air greeted me. "Northbound. Your father lived in the cold of the north skies in a secluded kingdom."

That sounded like him. I stepped forward as Brock held up an evelope.

"Talen asked about you. Shall I tell him you are safe, or not respond?"

I recognized the House of Delvers symbol on the parchment. "How did Talen know where I was?"

"Not much happens in the realm that your little thief doesn't know about," Brock said. I jolted at the term. It was how Talen had introduced himself to me, yet it'd been a while since someone referred to him in such a manner. "Shall I respond?"

"Yes," I said. "Tell him I am safe and will return shortly."

His wife appeared with a basket in hand. When she passed it to me, I could have melted at the savory scent coming from within. "Stuffed chicken and sugared sprouts," she said, then winked. "Plus something sweet."

"Thank you." I'd been thanking them often this morning. Was that four times already? I meant it every time. The pair had watched out for me in ways I hadn't seen, and I couldn't repay them.

She gave me a hug, and sudden embarrassment flooded me. I'd memorized the names of the kings, for they were all that mattered to me. I cleared my throat. "I don't know your name."

True to her character, she laughed in a way that told me she found no offense. "I am Illise, and I am here for whatever you need, my Queen."

"Thank you, Queen Illise." She was every bit the queen I hoped to be. Kind, graceful, and forgiving. Perhaps someday, that was who I *could* be. For now, I needed to let the cunning out a little longer.

Outside, Brock summoned a chariot, and I stepped aboard with the basket. My hand met the cusp bar. "Take me to the home of the seventh king."

At first, my father's home appeared to be a castle of ice. The palace glinted in the distance, blinding white. We neared a vast valley of snow surrounded by a cage of mountains, with my father's home in the middle of it all, standing taller than any peak.

The air turned cold enough that wrapping my cloak tighter could not save me from the chill. I'd have to explain myself to Talen when I returned with a red nose and blue fingers.

As I neared, flecks of midnight black peeked through the ice of my father's home. "It used to be stone," I realized. Perhaps his absence allowed the ice to form. Would it thaw the longer I stayed, just as the darkness had dissipated from my own palace the longer I lived there? Or would the door be frozen shut, and all I would see of my father's home were the outside walls?

The chariot descended upon a glittering bridge over a frozen stream, leading to a looming gate with spindle-like icicles opening to a sparkly path. Still clutching my basket, I stepped off.

The chariot flew away in a hurry. I blinked after it, hoping one would find me again when I needed to go home.

"It's not like chariots get cold," I whispered.

At that moment, the palace came to life. Gilded lampposts burst alive with flames licking their way through the ice. They lined the pathway to the grand stairwell pointing to the doors, where a fire formed an archway to walk beneath. Chunks of snow fell to the ground, and deep cracks indicated ice was melting. With all the light, the castle glowed even brighter.

I walked along a path of ice crystals to a circular courtyard where hedge statues were covered in ice. There were five horsemen, all facing inward to a man atop a grand steed with features much like my father's. I remained fixated on the image for some moments before moving on.

The stairs stretched high, and my feet slipped, but I made my way to the top, where two doors stood beneath the fire arch. It made the ice melt until the doors looked more like a waterfall.

I plunged my hand through the flow, ignoring the instant chill, to twist the silver knob. Ice cracked upon the hinges as they slowly creaked open, relinquishing their ancient hold. I wondered how long it had been since these doors were last opened.

With another tug, the ice relented, and the door swung open.

I was not prepared for the heat inside.

An olive-green rug coated the floor of a large hall, with pillars running parallel along both sides. Bowls of fire sat just inside, burning bright, giving the air an orange hue that reflected the stone walls. As I stepped forward, heat tinged my cheeks. Had these fires remained burning for two hundred years, or did my presence ignite them? Either way, the inside wasn't frozen at all. In fact, the room appeared as if it was still lived in, like any moment a fae would come from the corridor or walk along the hallway on the second level to greet me.

I waited, but all remained silent.

"Do you know who I am?" I wondered out loud, letting my feet sink into the rug with each step. The ceiling stretched so high, I had to tilt my head back to see it all. A mural of the night sky looked back at me. "Can you feel it?" I asked. "That the blood of your lost king has returned to you?"

I pictured him here, opening the doors for guests at a dinner party. Dancing to music while a band performed. Drinking wine and laughing with friends. But my mind refused to put a mask on him, or a crown upon his head. I could try all day, but I'd never comprehend what he was like as a fae.

I turned to the east corridor. If I couldn't picture it, perhaps the castle would show me.

The passage had high ceilings that met at a sharp point, drawing me farther inward. Each step grew warmer as if the castle were welcoming me. The walls grew less dusty. The light burned brighter. And a sweet aroma overtook the air, as if a grand feast were being prepared at this very moment. The castle might come alive for anyone, but as I ventured farther in, I pretended it was just for me—its lost heir.

The corridor turned, and I was in a square-shaped hall, with rows of armor pointing toward large, silver-plated double doors, almost begging me to open them. I couldn't resist. I pressed against the silver and pushed.

They swung open to expose the most glorious throne room I'd ever seen. Stone pillars lined the way, each set with diamonds that sparkled from the light of a chandelier. A marble floor so white, it could have been snow. A ceiling so high, none could hope to reach it. And two thrones, one larger than the other, one of silver and the other of gold. Behind them, a full-length window opened to the snowy plains outside that caught every ounce of starlight in sparkly splendor.

My feet moved as if by command, taking me to the golden throne.

I placed a hand upon it. It was far greater than my own, and I'd felt dwarfed by that one. Yet here?

Here, it was like coming home.

I could almost feel Father's presence. He'd be looking over the people with a gleam in his eyes, as if he knew something no one else did and he was waiting to see who would be smart enough to figure it out first. A sword would be at his hip, and an equally sharp smile on his lips.

How many years did he rule as king before leaving?

As long as I'd lived, Father had always held a hatred for the fae realm, which made me assume he wouldn't return if Brock asked him. But seeing this lustrous place made me question that. It was too full of beauty, of life.

If he wanted to come home, he'd need his ring.

Refocused on my mission, I left the throne room. I needed to find that signet ring.

As if rewarding me for my search, the first corridor I came to featured rows of paintings. Now, perhaps, I'd get a true vision of Father as a fae king. At first, they were all faces I didn't recognize. Places I'd never seen.

As I continued, the paintings grew harrowing.

First, a splash of black paint covered whatever once remained there.

Then a cloth concealed another.

I stopped at the third. The painting had been torn, like a jagged knife had cut through the canvas.

It showed a motherly figure, her hand on a girl's shoulder and a man beside them. But the canvas around the mother and daughter had been slashed, distorting their figures. Only the man remained unblemished.

He was who I wanted to see. He was my father.

He wore a red mask and a golden crown, his black suit tailored perfectly to show off the broad stretch of his shoulders. His smile tilted, as if he were moments away from getting in trouble. A youthful energy exuded from him, but I recognized him all the same. His pale eyes gave him away, a feature none of his children inherited. But the mother and girl had them. Family, no doubt.

My attention turned to the women. "What happened to you?"

I traced a finger along their features, wondering who they were and why they weren't here now. If there had been family to take the throne after my father left, they would have done so. Instead, it was as if the whole household had disappeared.

Around the corner, I hoped to find more paintings. Instead, I entered a corridor void of decor. From the stains on the wallpaper, paintings had once hung here, but were now torn down. All traces of his family gone.

Either things ended poorly between them, or ended poorly for them.

Whatever transpired, my father clearly wanted no reminders of his relations. And he must have done this before he left.

If the passages held no answers, I'd seek the bedchambers. The first few offered nothing but crisply made beds, mirrored vanities set with combs and brushes, as if the residents had just stepped out, and oak wardrobes bursting with outdated gowns. The silence grew unnerving as I came upon more torn paintings. These were too ripped to distinguish what they hid. I hurried on.

The next chamber—and by chamber, I meant enormous room that could house a luxurious home—lay bare, save for a massive bed placed beneath a marble arch and a grand piano, both of which were covered in white silk. The open window let a fluttering breeze through, giving the illusion of a ghost. It was proper. With or without the wind, this room was haunted.

Again, I hurried on.

I grabbed the next handle I found and turned it.

A candle burned inside, set on a brick hearth. A wolf-skin rug was spread across the floor, with a platter of grapes upon it, each one still plump. It was a stark contrast to the previous room, with every inch inviting me farther in. The fire gave a honey glaze color to the chamber, and the dark grey duvet on the bed rumpled at the edges, as if it'd been hastily made. But the painting over the bed intrigued me most. Gold edging, thin brush strokes, and my father's smiling face.

This was the kindest picture I'd seen of him yet. His light hair carried a small wave, the sides short and top longer, with a single piece carving a path to his cheek. The painter added a gentleness to his eyes that contrasted the dark palate and paired well with his crimson suit. Father stood before the throne with his hands at his sides, a nimble sword in his left hand. And then I spotted a ring. I climbed atop the bed to get a closer look.

It was nothing more than a brown band with a blue gem, but the way the light from the chandelier caught upon it to create a glow, I had no doubt it was the famous signet ring the realm searched for.

I'd never seen it in the mortal realm, so I trusted Brock when he said the ring was left behind here. Had Father given it away, or had he hidden it?

I scoured the room for more details. A goblet of wine half filled on the table. Burgundy stains on the papers surrounding it. A clutter of books beneath, some with papers sticking out. If these were once Father's chambers, the answer might be here.

"If I were a fae king, where would I hide something?" I pondered out loud.

Father would know this room far better than I could—including what stones were loose or what crevices could house a ring. I'd have to check everything.

"Why couldn't your power be from a statue?" I whispered, digging my fingers into the cracks of the hearth to see what it unveiled. Stone crumbled, giving way to nothing but empty spaces and cobwebs. "A very large statue."

I searched on. Beneath rugs, behind canvases, under the mattress as far as I could reach. I undid the bedding and checked for hallowing outside the windowsill. Finally, I turned to the books.

An Account of Chess Matches across the Ages.
Kings: When to Serve and When to Rule.
Journal of King Chasmere.

I paused. This journal was not my father's.

It wasn't long—around fifty pages in total, with ten of them tabbed. As I flipped through, I found two different forms of handwriting, one assumedly belonging to King Chasmere. From the way it was formatted with dates, it appeared to be a diary.

"You stole someone's diary?" I asked with a grin. The second set of handwriting had made a note at the beginning.

The truth, finally.

I took the journal and crossed to the hearth, where I sat with the basket of food Queen Illise had prepared for me. Once the food was spread, I opened the journal again, flipping to the first of what I guessed to be my father's tabs and notes.

The first one almost made me choke. My father had scribbled four words on the top.

Meeting the first queen.

My eyes scanned the pages to confirm, then my hands trembled. This was no mere king whose journal my father had stolen. These were the private writings of the very first king who married a mortal girl.

My fate began here.

24

Evening of the Evergreen Ball, year 312

Mortal girls came to the dance tonight, as they often do. If we don't close the bridge soon, we will have more mortals in the realm than fae. I will bring it up with my advisors later.

One of the girls was different, however. She drank no excess of wine. She refrained from that ludicrous batting of eyelashes the mortals seem so fond of. And she didn't remove her mask after ten minutes like all the others, making me wonder what lies beneath. Perhaps she hides something hideous. But I think not.

I invited her to a game of chess, and she obliged me. I proceeded to best her within minutes, but she carried the defeat well.

Perhaps the next time we meet, I may give her a lesson. Her company is quite favorable.

Before she left, she gave me her name. Melody. It even sounds like a queen's name.

The only hinderance is her friend, Briar, whose presence I can't seem to escape. If we do close the bridge, I will make certain Briar is on the other side of the gate.

Beneath the segment was my father's scratchy writing.

First mention of Melody.

While I wanted to know more about the gate, I forced myself to skip to Father's next tab. I'd read the entire journal later, but I itched to know what my father found interesting enough to note.

The second segment Father tabbed was halfway through.

Second full moon, year 314

I went back to verify that the entry was two years after the night of the Evergreen Ball.

Melody agreed to let me escort her to the Fiddler's Feast, and she stunned the realm with her grace and kindness. I do not know how long mortals take to fall in love, but for me, it took one night. My heart is hers, and it forever shall be.

For once, I thought of something other than the games of the realm and shared a pleasant evening with someone I trust to never betray me.

The only damper was Briar's presence. She kept quite close the entire evening, and nothing I did would deter her affection.

That shall be a problem for another day. Tonight will not be ruined.

The entry ended there, and the next tab skipped several entries again. Curiosity took hold, and I thumbed through the skipped pages. There was no mention of Melody in them, merely political games he'd made notes on for himself. But Father didn't find those worth noting. Only this love story.

A story that hadn't ended well. The king married the girl, but two years later, he betrayed her with another.

I flipped to the next tab.

Ninth full moon, year 314

For all my accomplishments in life, I hope to be remembered for one thing—being the first king to marry a mortal.

I had to pause. He would definitely be remembered for that.

I asked Melody to marry me last night, and she said yes. She has grand ideas for where we shall live and what our lives will be like. We already plan to trick an ambassador into giving up his power to make her fae. There is time for all that later. For now, I have a wedding to throw.

But the realm does not seem pleased. My power is weaker, my lands darker. Something has angered it.

I sought out the wisdom of the realm to uncover what I have done wrong. I sat quietly for three weeks, not moving until I could hear the whisper of the realm's voice.

The answer destroyed me. Mortals are not meant to be queens in the fae realm. This land is not theirs. It is ours.

I pled with the realm for days, begging it to allow Melody this honor. She is worthy. After three days, the realm consented—with a stipulation. It will change the fabric of our realm, creating a place meant for both. But it cannot be undone. If we do this, a mortal must always be in the land of the fae, for now it is theirs too. This shall be of no concern. The mortals are as eager as ever to visit our land, and I see no sign of that ending.

So I agreed, and the decree went out. The fae realm will always be open to mortals.

And I am getting married.

I set the book on my lap, my eyes unfocused. King Chasmere unknowingly sealed my fate with those words. *A mortal must always be in the land of the fae.* They bring us in every year because the realm depends on our existence. It wasn't quite what I'd thought—the fae feeding off us—but the concept remained. The realm demanded our presence. Due to no fault of our own, we had to come.

Father's words read:

A mortal must remain. This cannot be changed.

It wouldn't be a bad deal if the realm didn't intend our deaths. Remove that and mortals would line up across the five islands to get a taste of this world. But add in the death part . . . and it's a prison.

Even though I knew how King Chasmere and Melody's love story ended, I couldn't stop myself from reading more. Once again, it was two years before the next entry.

Fifth full moon, year 316

The past year has been blessed. The presence of a Mortal Queen causes the lands to thrive in a way they never have before. Everyone loves Melody. Not a single fae has tried to trick her yet, but rather they offer alliance after alliance, grateful for a mere moment of her time. She was made to reign.

To celebrate our anniversary, I've invited her family to join us on the cliffs for a picnic. Briar will come too. Though I've made it clear where my affections lie—with my wife—she seems to hold to me like a shadow I can't shake. Melody is gracious about it, but if it weren't for their friendship, I'd ban Briar from the land. She's too familiar for my liking.

We never closed the bridge. I suppose it is

too late now, as a mortal must forever be in our land.

The next entry wasn't more than a few lines.

Fourth full moon, year 315
With our two-year anniversary coming up, I plan to take Melody to the cliffs again. Since the fallout with her friend, it shall be only the two of us, and we will enjoy a quiet evening together. The lands continue to thrive, crops grow more plentiful than ever, and the beauty of my queen has never been more stunning.
We have much to celebrate. I am ever grateful for this life.

I paused to check the dates. This was one month before their anniversary. He didn't sound like a man who was weeks away from betraying the heart of his wife.

More invested than ever, I dug for the next tab.

Twelfth full moon, year 315

That couldn't be right. That was seven months after Melody should have died. My brows furrowed as I angled my body toward the fire for better lighting before devouring the pages.

It has taken seven months to find the strength to write down what occurred. As always, the realm went ablaze with rumors, each tale further from the truth, but my heart grew too heavy to correct any of them. I sit in my palace as ice collects outside, wondering what I could have done differently. I should have made her fae sooner. I should have closed the bridge. I never should have brought her here.

On the night of our second anniversary, I took Melody to our spot in the cliffs to celebrate our marriage. She wore a red dress with her hair down. Those are the details I don't ever want to forget. Already, I feel her slipping from my mind. She carried a basket of wildflowers, stringing one through her hair as she sang my favorite song.

Behind the steep rocks of the cliff's edge, Briar waited. She must have guessed we'd go there. I asked her to leave, but she denied me. I called for my guards, but it was too late. Briar struck out, not against me, but against Melody, taking a blade to her heart.

Her mortal body couldn't take it. I might have saved her, but Briar pushed her from the cliffs, and her body fell too fast for me to find it among the stars.

In desperation, I tried anyway. I took my chariot, scouring the skies. I searched for days. It was no use. My sweet Melody is gone.

When I returned, I found Briar had

spread vicious rumors about us. And still, she possessed the audacity to suggest marriage between us. I did what I should have done years ago—I banished her from the land. Then I retreated to my home as the realm mourned the loss of our beloved queen.

With the death of Melody, many of the remaining mortals have departed. If they all leave, we shall be breaking the rules of the realm to have a mortal here always, but I have no care. I don't know if I will ever care about anything again.

Chasmere didn't betray his queen. She died by a mortal's hand. I found myself blinking back tears.

Just like the king, my heart was heavy, mourning the loss of a queen I never knew. To lose her life over the envy of a friend was a terrible fate. Yet the loss didn't answer the remaining question. What started our fate—why do we have to die?

One tab remained. The last page.

Eve of sixth half moon, year 317

Briar has returned. She brings an army with her, all set on destroying me for killing Melody. I am not the shell of a king I was last year. Now I will fight.

Sixth waning crescent, year 317

We force the mortals from our land, every last one of them. But that was her plan. After they departed, Briar shut the gate behind her. She said now our realm will fall.

The moment the mortals are out of the realm, our lands begin to shake. Still, I will not invite them back in. The fae realm was not meant for mortals. They have no place here.

Finally, I get the approval needed. We seal the gate. It shall never open again.

Seventh full moon, year 317

The realm lashes out. It craves the presence of mortals. But we give no heed. So it steals one. As the new day begins, new land appears with a palace upon it. A courtyard sits with a black crown etched in stone. Two large thrones wait inside like angels of death, promising retribution upon us all.

And as the morning comes, a mortal girl appears in the courtyard. It is Briar. The realm informs us that we must forever have a Mortal Queen, but she will never be ours to keep.

Briar is crying, though I do not know why. She is getting everything she wanted. She is a queen in the fae land now.

I hope her reign is short. For the gates will not open, and we cannot send her back.

The entries ended, leaving me to guess what became of King

Chasmere and his broken heart. But I knew Briar's story. She ruled for two years, then she died, just as she killed Melody. For such is the fate of a Mortal Queen.

It hit me then.

The fae had it wrong. That was why father found this journal so interesting. Just as he noted, it told the true tale.

The fae did not condemn the mortals to die. The mortals did that to themselves by being jealous and wicked. They killed their own queen, then banded together to bring down the fae when they pulled their forces from the land. They brought the penalty upon themselves, provoking the anger of the realm.

This was never a punishment for the fae. It was meant for us.

And that is why it is our price to pay. Because we were the ones who committed acts of wickedness. I shut the book and held it close, going over the story again in my mind. It didn't contain the secret to our survival, but knowing the truth was a gift all its own.

And I knew then who was in charge. The realm.

If I was going to save us, I needed to prove to the realm that the mortals were worth saving. We have paid our dues a thousand times over. It was time to let us live, and we could do so in harmony again.

I took the journal to my father's bed, settling there to read it again, this time checking all the entries in between. I didn't want to miss a thing.

Soon, with King Chasmere's words in my head, I fell asleep again.

25

IT WAS ABOUT MIDNIGHT WHEN I woke, according to the clock. My sleep habits were getting dangerously off balance. I bent to retrieve King Chasmere's journal from the floor, and as I lifted it, a separate piece of parchment fell. The Gamemaster's envelope.

In the surreal aspects of the past day, I'd almost forgotten about her game. I checked the envelope.

WHAT'S MY NAME?

An idea came to mind. Perhaps my father knew this Gamemaster, and he gave her his signet ring before he left. Or perhaps it was she who tricked him, forcing him from this realm and keeping his signet ring for herself. Either way, she had something that didn't belong to her. I needed to uncover her name to get it back.

"What is your name?" I said aloud.

With a gasp, I swung my feet to the floor, resting them on the cool marble. The fire still danced as brightly as before, and I hurriedly brought the envelope closer for light. *What's my name?* The answer seemed impossible—if we thought of it as her question.

But this was not about her power.

It was about my father's.

I wouldn't know the name if I hadn't been such a nosy child, but curiosity always led me to dark crevices and into dusty journals. Once, I found a list of names stashed in a secret drawer in my father's study.

Thelonius Bren Alheda.

Theodore Bran Alheda.

Theon Bree Heda.

The list went on. Each name carried a strike through it, until the last one, where I found the name I knew him by. Theodore Brenheda. My imagination had run wild, picturing him as a spy for another country or an assassin hiding his identity time and time again. I figured if he was a spy, his true identity must be the first name listed, so I memorized it. Without that, I wouldn't know which name to guess now.

And I never would have guessed he was a fae king in hiding, moving around the five islands, taking name after name to hide the fact that he wasn't aging like we were.

"Thelonius Bren Alheda," I breathed. "That is the full name of the seventh king."

For a horrible moment, nothing happened.

Then the lettering shimmered gold and fell away like dust in my lap. Once gone, new letters appeared on the page, thinner and penned in black ink.

Tables can turn, and the king's turned sharply. Still his secrets dwell within. His harrowing tale, wrought in sorrow and pain, of death the fates did spin. Beware the maze, the tunnels, the hedge. Some things

are better lost. But a king was once wronged, and the guilty lives on. His story is now yours to uncross.

Each day seemed to bring my father back to me, piece by piece. First, the stories from King Brock. Then here, in his home. And now, a sliver more of his tale.

Harrowing. Wrought in sorrow and pain.

I'd guessed as much from the torn family paintings and rooms laid bare like empty tombs, waiting for someone who would never return. This castle wore heartbreak like an identity it couldn't shake, letting the pain seep from the walls. I wanted to solve the puzzle to uncover the next clue, but more than that, I longed to know about my father. What had caused him to despise this land so badly that he wouldn't even see the fae ambassadors when they visited?

If anyone could give me the shards of Father's tale that this riddle required, it would be Brock.

Despite the hour, I had to seek him out. The sooner I solved this, the sooner I could refocus on my mother.

As I stepped into the chilly night, a burning in my mind stilled my feet. *Any information you retrieve about this Gamemaster's riddles, you will share with me.* I bit my lip, wondering if there was any way around Thorn's binding condition. He had proved a helpful partner so far, and we'd solved the previous riddles together. But I'd discovered this all on my own and didn't need his help for the next stage either. If I hadn't made the promise to keep nothing from him, I wouldn't do so now. But promises were like iron locks here. Tight and not easily broken.

With a sigh, I threw up my hand.

Through the midnight skies, a chariot glided down to me, the same one I'd taken to get here. "You did wait," I said, patting its side. "Thank you."

The moment my feet left the ground, ice creaked behind me. I turned to see large sheets reforming over my father's home, sealing it up once more until it glittered a pale, dark blue. "Don't fasten too thick," I told it. "For I plan to return. Either with your king or as your queen."

It groaned in response. I took that as acceptance.

I spoke to the chariot. "Take me to wherever King Thorn is."

To my surprise, it took me home.

"You took me to Thorn, right?" I asked the chariot. "Because I'm not completely certain of the rules of our agreement, but I don't wish to break them." Holding up an edge of my wrinkled dress, I stepped onto the black crown embedded in the courtyard. If he was here, I might have time to change first. These clothes had seen me through a lot and were starting to smell like it.

The chariot left.

Hopefully that means yes.

The glittering double doors to the palace opened, revealing Talen in his robe with his white hair in disarray. "Our lost queen returns!"

"Why are you awake right now?"

"I can always sense when my Queen returns," he replied, as if that were the most obvious thing in the world.

"I'm sorry to have been away for so long. I have much to tell you." I took off my shoes and looked around. "First, is Thorn here?"

"He is. And you are right, you do have much to tell me." He paused, as if he expected an immediate answer for my absence.

"I would love nothing more than to get a glass of hot cider and tell you all my stories—which are unbelievable, by the way—but I'm promise-bound to speak to Thorn first. You said he's here?"

Talen sighed. "You always make poor deals when it comes to kings. Yes, he's inside."

I frowned, looking past him to the dimly lit interior of the palace, where the sweeping archways still carried hints of cobwebs and dust. "Inside my home? At night? Why?"

"He made a guest room for himself."

My stomach turned. It wasn't that I wasn't hospitable. In fact, many times I'd debated opening the palace to let more people live within it. There were numerous rooms, and I longed to see it bright and alive instead of haunted by the ghosts of queens gone by, yet taking a room in someone's home seemed like something done after being invited. Not by your own volition when the host—or hostess—was gone for a day or so. "He's bold."

"It's nothing more than a small bed and desk. I wouldn't think anything of it."

A desk? Was he planning on dealing with correspondence here? "Okay, then. The west side, I'm assuming?"

"Fifth door on the right."

Since Talen and I both had rooms in that hallway, we wandered up the stairs together. Before he could slip back into his chambers, I asked, "Is Eliza here?"

A troubled expression crossed his face. "I assumed you knew where she was."

"I . . . have a vague direction. But I'd hoped she'd returned. Can you sense if she's still in this realm?"

His brow creased further. "I'm not her ally, so I can't sense her like I can with you. But she must be in the realm. Now I'm all the more desperate to know what you've been up to."

"I'll tell you soon," I promised. Eliza should have returned. She wouldn't be able to open the gate, so there was nothing for her at the bridge. It had been a full day since we found Mother. Eliza should be back.

"Please do. Perhaps it has something to do with the mystery person who sent Eliza flowers this morning."

I hid a smile. Thorn was holding up his end of the deal. Making Eliza appear desirable would play well to the favor of the queen. Now I must hold up my end. "I'll be at your room soon."

Talen disappeared inside his chambers, while I counted five

rooms down. The fifth room had a massive oak door with a brass handle, every inch polished as if it had just been constructed. Or as if it had been waiting hundreds of years for someone to open it. I knocked as if this were his home and not mine, then waited.

Shuffling came from inside, then the door opened.

Thorn's bronze eyes found me. "My Queen. You've returned." He wore silky pants and a loosely fitted shirt, his eyelids drooping as if he were half asleep.

"I was surprised when Talen said you'd moved in," I said as I entered and took stock of what he'd done. By *a small bed and desk*, Talen literally meant a bed and a desk. Nothing else. The bed had been thrown in the corner with a simple pillow and thin blanket, the desk pushed against its end so the bed doubled as a chair. No curtains over the arched windows, no candles burning, no lush rugs underfoot. I relaxed. I'd set up tents back on the five islands more extravagant than this. The gesture no longer felt as invasive as it did considerate—he could be close to his ally.

"Say the word, and I move it all out. I only wanted to be within the premises, especially since you'd gone missing for an entire day. I feared you'd left us again." From his tone, he was asking where I'd been.

The truth rested on the tip of my tongue, but I swallowed it. The details concerning my mother were too precious to share, and while I trusted Thorn to an extent, it wasn't enough to trust the well-being of my mother with him. He needn't know any of that anyway. I only promised to share details relating to the clues.

I pulled the envelope out, now fresh with my new clue. "I was searching the seventh king's home and guessed the answer was his name instead of the Gamemaster's for the clue." I waved the riddle. "I was right."

He read quickly, then glanced up. "How did you know the king's name?"

"It was in a book," I lied.

He opened a desk drawer and rifled through papers until

procuring his envelope and whispering the name. "Thelonius Bren Alheda."

I swallowed, hoping he wouldn't notice the similarities between my name and the king's.

Just as before, the letters turned to golden dust before the new words appeared. "Good. To the best of my knowledge, no one else has this yet." Thorn read it through, his eyes moving slowly across the parchment. As he did, he absentmindedly ran his thumb along the band of his signet ring. The richness of it contrasted the simplicity of his outfit. I studied the design more closely as the chandelier light bounced off the golden flecks, bringing to life the shape of a swan twisted in a circle, its feathers forming a coven to wrap around a single midnight-blue gem. Two smaller gems made up the eyes, and those flashed, as if knowing I looked at them.

I tore my gaze back to his face just as he glanced up. "What made you think to go to the king's home?"

The lie burned inside me. "It's his power we might claim," I said. "So I wondered if I might find something there."

"Smart." But his focus lingered, as if he knew I held something back.

I cleared my voice. "You are welcome to stay here anytime. Especially if we are to solve this next clue quickly. It seems we need to find someone who wronged the king, turning his tale sad. Any guesses?" I almost slipped and said my father. I forced a smile to my face to cover it.

Thankfully, Thorn had gone back to inspecting the riddle. He shook his head. "But I know some people we can ask—ones who are far older than I." He brightened, tapping the letter against his palm. "One good thing about this, your Bastian will be at a disadvantage. He is the only remaining player in the game young enough not to have known the seventh king. Except you and Queen Eliza, of course."

"Of course." I weighed my words, running my fingers along the stone sill as if my question were simple curiosity. "You knew him, though? What was he like?"

"Not well, but I was a young prince when he reigned. I knew him enough to be afraid of him. He wasn't afraid to betray anyone to win a game." He glanced at the letter. "We have a challenge ahead whittling down his list of enemies."

The analysis didn't surprise me. Father was stone-cold in the mortal realm, and even there he was known for his desire to win. It was what helped him move up the ranks so quickly, though now I wondered if fae tricks had something to do with it. He must have had some tricks up his sleeves to avoid the mortals' notice when he'd hardly aged in two hundred years.

It was bold of him to marry at all. Mother must have known he was fae. They would have needed to tell us at some point as well, when we aged and he did not. Creating a family created a string of problems for a man hiding his identity, yet he did it anyway.

Why? Why risk it?

"Thea?"

Thorn's voice drew me from the window, and I found him with curiosity painted all over his face "What happened?"

"What do you mean?" I assessed my stance, my voice, and my mannerisms to check for what could be giving away my secrets. Things about my mother. Things about my father. Things I didn't want anyone to see. Things he seemed to see anyway.

"You just seem more thoughtful than a person usually is at"—he checked his watch—"one in the morning."

I snatched the first excuse I could think of. "I'm just tired." I resisted faking a yawn, for fear that would be too obvious. But I did slouch my shoulders and draw the length of my words longer. If I didn't leave now, he'd find a way to draw the answers from me, and I'd end up divulging everything. Even now these things pushed on the corners of my mind, begging to be communicated. Mother always told me not to keep things in, for secrets have a way of turning dark when kept from the light. But Father often said some things were best kept close, and it was his voice that won. "I should go sleep, but we will speak again in the morning."

His face fell as if I were turning him down. "As you wish."

I placed a hand on his arm before I left. "I'm grateful you're here." Questions still seemed to hang in his mind, but he drew his lips into a thin line and nodded.

"Good night, my Queen."

"Good night, my King," I replied with a joking laugh to ease the tension of the room. I didn't stay to see if it worked.

As soon as his door shut, I turned to Talen's. But a voice from inside stopped me, one that was not his. Odette had arrived.

"You should have told me right away." I didn't need to see her to know she was angry.

"Things have been hectic, but I planned to tell you when I saw you next."

Absolutely none of my business. I took two steps away.

"Becoming a Head of the House of Delvers won't save her."

I paused, quite certain *her* meant me.

"I can try!" I'd never heard Talen with such desperation in his voice. "Don't you want to do whatever we can? I've lost queens before, but this one—Odette, I can't lose this one. Not unless I try everything."

"You are losing *me*!"

Guilt made my throat swell. Talen had been with me from the first few minutes I'd arrived in this realm, and I didn't want to continue without him. I wouldn't share secrets with Thorn, but I was yearning to tell Talen everything, for he was the one I shared things with. But this wasn't his fight. And if it was causing a strain on his relationship with Odette, I didn't want him to fight it.

"She is everything to me too," Odette continued. "But I don't want to lose you both."

"I love you with all of my soul. My very heart! You have to know that. But I wouldn't be a man worthy of your love if I didn't fight for the ones around me."

"Fight for me." Odette's words were spoken in a voice much harder to hear, which was my reminder that I wasn't supposed to hear this at all. I slipped away as quietly as I could, promising myself I would find a way to set Talen free—before Odette lost him again.

26

I WASN'T TIRED. SO I PENNED A
quick note to Talen.

>   *Found my mother. She's trapped, but I'll free
> her later.*
>   *My father is the missing fae king.*
>   *Eliza went to some ancient bridge between the
> lands and hasn't returned.*
>   *Gone to find her.*

There. I wasn't keeping anything from him, but I wouldn't be
dragging him across the realm to search with me.

The more I looked at the note, the less convinced I was that it
was a good idea. I ended up tossing it in the fire. Once it burned
completely, I wrote a new one.

>   *Talen,*
>   *Could you find stories about who might have
>   wronged the missing fae king? It's important.*

A simple task that didn't take up too much time. Much better.
I set the note on the edge of my bed. The most recent painting

I'd received caught my gaze, but this time, I saw it differently. It was my mother's handiwork. If I'd known, I would have saved every painting. But I had a habit of burning things I didn't wish for others to see, which caused an unfortunate end to the other pieces she'd made. Except for the painting of Dhalia downstairs. Someday I'd free Mother, and together she and I would fill the halls with more.

First, another queen pressed on my mind. Eliza remained out there somewhere.

I changed my clothes, finding loose pants and a simple tunic, then throwing on an oversize cloak lined with ermine lining. This realm had spoiled me with fine dresses, but subtlety was my goal tonight. I put on my shoes, raked my hands through my hair, and headed for the door.

Someone knocked before I reached it.

Upon opening, I found Thorn dressed in a proper suit for the day—though it was still very much nighttime—with shoes on and a mischievous spark in his eyes. He extended an arm. I glanced at it, then at him. "How did you know I was going back out?"

"You had that look in your eye like you were craving adventure. And adventure happens to be my favorite pastime. Where to, my Queen?"

I weighed the option until deciding it could cause little damage. "Eliza went to find a rumored bridge that fae and mortals can pass through, and she hasn't returned."

He paled. "That's been closed for centuries."

"I heard that. Yet she went to look anyway, and I'm fearful about why she hasn't returned."

"We'd better hurry then." He offered his arm once more, and I took it, letting him all but pull me from my room. We descended the stairs in quick strides. "Where did she hear of this bridge?" Thorn asked as he pushed open the door.

"From Illusion Point." The man needn't know everything.

"They should have warned her." His voice held an edge.

"Warned her about what?" My heart rate sped up. "Is it dangerous?"

"That bridge only opens for those who are married and separated by realms, in order to reunite them. I do not know what the consequence would be for an unmarried soul who attempts to open it." He lifted a hand, and a chariot whisked down from the night sky to collect us. I recognized it as his—the fastest one in the realm. The first time I rode, it went so fast I felt as if my skin were being peeled away. This time, I silently begged it to go faster. "Let us hope the bridge was merciful and remained hidden from her."

I hoped that with all my heart.

The chariot took off.

We didn't know if the bridge had appeared for Eliza, but it didn't appear for us. Thorn took us through the night sky, where the air was cold enough to make me grateful for the cloak. We searched for hours, to no avail.

"If it didn't open, she would have gone home," I said.

"It couldn't open. She's unmarried."

And she wasn't home.

A horrifying third option made my stomach turn. The bridge had punished her for seeking it out.

At my concern, Thorn said, "Perhaps she went back to Illusion Point to search for another way to her realm?"

Foolish optimism flickered inside. "That sounds like something she'd do."

So we took off again.

By now, morning had fallen upon us, and the island came to life as we settled on the cobblestones. I glanced in the direction of the great chessboard, where Mother was trapped beneath, then turned my feet the other way. Knowing I was so close and wasn't going to her—it made my chest tighten.

We searched, planting innocent questions around town, asking if anyone had seen Eliza. They hadn't but were all very eager to sell us products. A vial of perfume that would never wash off? A tonic to cure lovesickness? We turned it all down.

Around midday, a sick feeling crept over me. Eliza was different from Gaia. She could handle herself. Yet I still felt an immense responsibility for her safekeeping, and I was failing.

I would have separated from Thorn to visit my mother and ask her more about the bridge, but he stayed close to my side all day.

Once, we spotted Bash. He walked through the busy streets of town, ducking beneath sparrow-tailed banners before entering a small tent, with Troi on his heels. She gave me a glance before following her brother inside, a clear warning in her expression to keep away from him.

Troi had never approved of our relationship. She saw the heartbreak it would cause him long before I cracked his heart and wanted to spare him the pain I would inevitably bring. At this point, I wondered if the pain of staying away hurt worse. It did for me.

Thorn caught me staring. "Do you want to go after him?"

I shook my head. "It wouldn't do any good. Let's refocus on something we can accomplish—the next clue. If Eliza is hiding, she will turn up when she wants to."

"Good." Thorn straightened with renewed energy and led me away from listening ears. "Who wronged the missing king? If my father were still alive, he'd know. I could ask my grandfather, but he's tight-lipped about secrets, even with me."

We paused behind an old shack to speak further. "Would he be more open with a Mortal Queen?"

"Decidedly not," Thorn grunted. "You know how pleasant I am to be around? He's the exact opposite. But I will try. It's better if I speak with him alone. Here"—he dug into his pocket—"take some coin to buy food, and I'll return shortly." He pressed three copper coins into my palm. "Are you going to galivant across the realm in search of Eliza once I leave?"

The desire to find her still echoed in my mind, but I had to accept there was nothing more I could do. "I'll be fine. I could use a warm meal and the chance to clear my head."

Looking convinced, Thorn backed away and disappeared into the crowds in the direction of his chariot.

Once more, I faced the center of the island. Everything inside me longed to return to my mother, to bring her a warm meal and make up for lost years. But her wish came to mind. I must focus on myself, not her.

As long as no one knew I'd found her, she remained safe. It was too busy now, anyway. Too many eyes to see where I would go.

It would be best not to visit again until I was certain I could free her.

Painfully, I walked the other way. Shouts rose behind me, and I whirled around. From the busy street, no one else seemed to take note. But more noise followed, a low growl followed by cheering. It traced back to the small tent Bash had entered.

I hovered as cheers came again. Now people were taking notice, and several fae filtered into the tent for whatever spectacle it held. By the sounds of it, the tent was full. Full enough that Bash wouldn't see if I entered. Or, if my luck held, Troi. As several other fae wandered inside, I joined them, ducking under a red-and-black-striped flap into the buttery glow surrounding what could only be described as a fighting ring.

True to the nature of tents on Illusion Point, the inside was much larger than the outside. The top stretched high, and the sides billowed out to allow room for stands placed at all sides, facing the ring. There, short fence posts created a barrier between the cheering crowd and two opponents.

More fae entered, bumping against me, but I stayed unmoving as I watched one of the fighters.

Bash.

He'd removed his suit jacket, leaving a thin, white shirt beneath, the corner tucked into leather pants. He kept his arms up, hands curled into fists in front of his face, looking at his opponent. With his crown gone, he looked like any other fae, and apparently his king status didn't frighten the other man—a burly fellow with quick feet, who swung hard.

Bash ducked and delivered a blow in response.

The crowd cheered.

I pressed myself closer to watch. This couldn't be Bash's first time fighting. His movements were too confident to be novice, his punch too swift. He knew just where to hit to make the other guy go down.

But his opponent gathered himself effortlessly and charged.

Breath caught in my throat and I resisted yelling out for Bash to be careful. He stepped to the side, blocking with his arms, but a second swing landed squarely in his gut. He hunched over. Sweat gathered on his brow.

Confusing emotions knotted inside—half of me appreciating the fine way Bash looked in simple attire and with that gleam in his eye, and the other half terrified he would get hurt.

"Keep your wits about you!" Troi yelled from the side. She clutched the fence posts. She had to duck as the next swing nearly clocked her. "Be quicker!"

I tugged on the sleeve of the fae nearest to me, a woman with beautiful red curls and a sharp chin. "What do they fight for?"

She took note of who I was and gave a little bow. Then she pointed to the back of the tent, where a man with jet-black hair and a long suitcoat stood, watching the fight intently. "Information." She had to shout so I could hear her. "If the winner impresses the Teller, they get to know information."

Now I was interested in the Teller. What sort of person could offer unlimited information? As the fight continued, I studied him, checking his response whenever Bash did anything particularly clever.

The next time Bash's opponent advanced, Bash met him in the middle of the arena. The man swung. Bash ducked, grabbed him by the torso, and threw him down. The man reached for Bash's feet, but he darted out of the way, then brought a knee down, pinning the man on the ground.

"Yield?"

The man struggled, eventually freeing a hand. He took a swing, but Bash clamped his own arm down, trapping the man's hand. "Yield?"

His opponent nodded.

The crowd cheered loud enough the stars must have heard.

Then all went silent as every face turned to the Teller to see if he was impressed. He stroked his chin, studying Bash. Then he nodded. More cheers.

Through the noise, the Teller spoke, his voice like wind, commanding the room. "What does the young king wish to know?"

Bash retrieved his suit coat, stringing his arms through the sleeves. I had to duck so he didn't spot me as he swiveled to face the Teller.

"I want all the information you have on deals fae made with the missing seventh king. I am searching for someone who betrayed him."

27

MY HEART SEIZED. BASH HAD understood the last riddle. Now he'd hold information I didn't have, and once more, I was falling behind.

Apparently, no one else was privy to the information he won. Which was fair. Unless I was willing to get into that arena, which I was *not*, I wouldn't get to know what the Teller said. He took Bash into a back room and shut the paneled door.

I waited outside the tent so I would know exactly how long it took the Teller to deliver the information. Bash and Troi didn't leave until thirty minutes later, walking down the street in a manner that suggested Bash had a lead. After thirty minutes, he ought to have several.

I followed as long as I could, until they mounted a chariot and took off.

There'd be little chance of following without being spotted now. I could only hope Thorn's grandfather knew something good.

Or perhaps I could convince Bash to tell me what he'd learned. I toyed with the idea of going to his home tonight, wearing a flattering dress, reminding him what he meant to me. Beg to work together. Whatever it took to win this puzzle.

Before I could run with that thought, a hand settled on my

shoulder. I twisted sharply to see a fae with the House of Delvers insignia on his palm, which he held up for me. A breeze rustled through his hair, the same white color as Talen's.

"I come from Talen," he said. His face showcased a smattering of freckles, and his tone indicated he was younger than me. With his other hand, he held up a note sealed with wax. "This is for you."

"His ability to find me is both impressive and unnerving." I took the note.

The boy grinned. "He is one of the most powerful of us."

My gaze flicked to him, but he scurried off.

I opened the note.

Eliza has returned.

Suddenly, Bash and the Teller didn't matter. I flung up my hand to summon a chariot and gave it directions to take me home as quickly as it could.

This chariot wasn't nearly as quick as Thorn's, and by the time we reached my palace, I was so jittery that my hands shook. I jumped from the chariot before it stopped moving. Several lights glowed beyond the windows. I ran through the doorway, hurtling myself up the stairs and into my bed chambers.

Talen and Odette stood inside, deep in conversation by the fire.

"Where is she?" I breathed, scanning the room. "Eliza?" The closet lay empty, and the balcony was bare.

"She will return in a moment. She's in her room."

I frowned. She hadn't stayed in that room since arriving. This was her room. "Where had she gone? Did she find the bridge?" Hearing she was safe ought to soothe me, but I needed to see her to know she was alright. When we'd searched all morning for her and found nothing, I'd feared the worst. From today onward, I would be implementing a new rule—no more running into the far corners of the sky without bringing the other along.

"We will let her explain it," Odette said.

"To all of us," Talen added. "She has been odd since returning. Very secretive."

I unclipped my cloak, catching my breath. "But she's safe?"

"She looked well," Talen confirmed.

"Good. Then she has some serious explaining to do. She's been gone for over a day. Has she eaten? Has she slept?"

"Have *you* eaten or slept?" Odette asked. "We've hardly seen you either."

I hesitated. Technically I saw—or heard—her in the early hours of this morning, but this wasn't a good time to bring that up. "I'll be better once I know if Eliza opened the bridge."

"I opened the bridge."

At Eliza's voice, we all turned. She stood in the doorway looking more radiant than I'd ever seen her, with her hair pulled up, showing off the gentle curve of her cheeks, and a joy in her eyes the realm had stripped away.

Her words shook the room. Talen reacted first. "The bridge opened? It hasn't opened in centuries."

"How did you open it?" Odette asked next.

But I asked the most obvious question. "If you opened it, why are you still here?"

Since first arriving in our realm, Eliza had made it clear she did not want to be here. Actually, she made that clear the moment the fae read her name. She would rather live out her final two years in the mortal realm than stay here and try for forever. If the bridge opened and she'd had the chance to return to the mortal realm— there was no reason she would still be here.

Eliza smiled broadly, as if she held a secret she couldn't wait to share.

"I wasn't the one who crossed the bridge," she said.

A new voice came. "I did."

Then Cal, my brother whom I thought I'd never see again, stepped from behind the doorframe to grin at me—and my two worlds collided.

28

SEEING HIM SUCKED ALL THE AIR
from my chest. I couldn't speak. All I could do was step into his
outstretched arms and hold my twin close. His chin rested against
my hair. And for that moment, I was happier than I'd ever been.

"How?" I finally asked, pulling back to look at him. My head
reached well below his shoulder now, but it was easier to wrap my
arms around him—the effects of working in academics instead of
training every day with father. The copper in his hair had darkened
until it was almost the same color as mine, but the biggest difference
was the mask he wore. Striking white, resting on the bridge of
his nose to hide the crinkles by his eyes that always showed when
he smiled.

He was smiling now.

"Look at you. Queen of the fae."

I stepped back. "Where is Malcom?"

"Home with Father," Cal replied. "He's safe." He laced his hand
through Eliza's, and she looked at him with all the happiness in the
world. This entire time, while I'd been running around trying to
solve riddles and figure out clues, she'd actually done something
of immense importance. She brought the one person here who

was practically born to play these games. How many times had I thought Cal should be here? Now he was.

Talen crossed his arms, his head cocked to the side like he was thinking. It was amusing because I'd chosen him for his similarities to my brother. Now standing near each other, they were all the more obvious. Both of them assessing the room like they could put all the pieces together without a word. Even now, Cal looked over the room as if it were a chessboard.

As if he'd solved a piece, Talen cast a knowing look at Eliza and Cal. "I hadn't realized congratulations were in order. How long?"

I frowned. "How long what?"

"Have they been married," he replied plainly.

Their eyes cut to each other with a grin.

"They're not married," I told him. "Only sweethearts."

But Talen had the same look I'd seen on Cal many times after he'd figured something out. He wouldn't be deterred from his analysis. And the truth was right there, waiting for me to take hold. The bridge only opened for those who were married and separated across realms. When Mother told us that, Eliza ran off. She knew it would work.

I gaped at Eliza. "Are you married?"

Cal spoke for her. "We've been married for a year."

My jaw dropped further. "A year!"

Odette gave a cry of delight and immediately fetched a fancy bottle of wine to celebrate the occasion. She poured a glass for each of us as Cal shared the story. "It happened shortly after you were chosen as queen. We had a spare room, so Eliza moved in to help with the house and blended into the family perfectly. We made it official right away."

"Well, halfway official," Eliza interjected. She sat on an armrest while Cal sat in the seat. They'd been comfortable together before, but the familiar way in which he stroked her skin was new. "We had a private ceremony and filled out the paperwork, but you got so busy with your apprenticeship that it never got filed. Only your father and Malcom even knew we were married."

"That's how you were still eligible to be selected," Talen said as if it was the last bit of the puzzle he hadn't figured out. "Because the governor's office had no filing."

Only unmarried women could be chosen as Mortal Queens, but now that I thought of it, Eliza had said something peculiar upon arriving. She'd said they'd made certain she couldn't get chosen. I assumed Cal had done something to rig the drawing. I wasn't entirely wrong. He had done something. He'd married her.

"I would have filed sooner, if I'd realized it would be an issue," Eliza said. "We thought I was safe from being selected, since we'd had a ceremony. Apparently, the fae don't read minds."

"Thank goodness for that." I tipped my glass.

"It's a skill I'm hoping to acquire," Talen added. Then he extended a hand. "We haven't been officially introduced. I am Talen, Thea's first alliance, Representative for the House of Delvers, and soon-to-be-appointed Head of Delvers."

"I am Cal, twin to Thea, husband to Eliza, and amateur maker of bread."

I was going to love having Cal here.

Odette offered her hand next. "I am Odette, and I will happily eat any bread you make." She sat close to Talen, suggesting they'd patched the argument from earlier. I wondered where they'd landed in regard to the part about me. But right now, with Cal here, none of that mattered. I could hand him the clue from the Gamemaster, and I bet he'd solve it in a day.

A flurry of anticipation swept over me. Cal didn't know Mother was alive or that she was here. He didn't know our father was a fae king.

Eliza's eyes danced. "If I'm a queen, and I'm your wife, does that make you a king?"

"Yes," Cal answered promptly. "I will be the first Mortal King."

Talen set down his glass like he was back to business. "Actually, I strongly suggest we keep your arrival secret. I will manipulate your ears to look fae and put the House of Delvers mark on your arm. If the realm knew a mortal boy wandered into our land, their obsession with you would steal you from us. And if they found out you were important to not just one, but both of our queens, they will seek to use you in their tricks. For your own safety, your identity should never be shared."

Talen wasn't in an alliance with Eliza, and thus far, she'd paid no mind to his advice. But she was nodding. "I've already decided that. Getting him a mask was the first thing I did. After that, we spent the day exploring the realm from a distance, and I've filled him in on everything here."

My eyes flicked to her. "Everything?"

"I left that for you," she whispered.

"What?" Cal and Talen asked at the same time.

"I'll tell you later. Both of you." And while I hadn't planned to visit Mother again until I knew it was safe, I might make an exception for Cal. The joy on Mother's face when she saw him would be well worth it.

"Do you plan to keep him hidden in the palace?" Odette asked Talen.

"No." Talen tapped his chin, then faced Eliza. "My Queen, I've offered you an alliance once before and you refused me. May I offer again? You've been hidden away for too long, but if you rise up now, you will take the realm by surprise. Continue to play the Gamemaster's game. Create more alliances. Charm the fae until we are all under your thumb, then use that power, combined with the rumored aptitude of Cal's mind, to outlast the fate of the Mortal Queens. You've already done the impossible once—bringing a mortal here. I believe you can do it again."

Cal leaned back in the chair. "What would an alliance with you do for her?"

"I vet alliance proposals. I field traps. I've disarmed four traps for Thea this week alone."

My gaze flew to him. "I didn't know that."

"You didn't need to. As your ally, I take care of things so you don't worry about them." He didn't even look my way, his attention focused on my brother like he'd found a worthy opponent. I'd pay good money to see the two of them compete in a chess match.

"What would she owe you in return?"

"Nothing. The clout of my House aligning with two Mortal Queens at the same time would be enough."

"And how do I know we can trust you?"

"I trust him," Eliza spoke, and two things happened—Cal relaxed as if that settled the matter, and Talen looked at her with surprise, then placed a hand over his chest as if trust was the highest compliment one could give. In a land such as this, it was. Trust mattered above all else.

"Is that a yes, then?" I looked between them as they nodded to each other. "What now?"

Cal's lips peeled back into a smile more genuine than any I'd seen here. He picked up his glass to take a swig, then set it down hard. "Now we play."

I've thought we could beat this realm before. But now? Now we had a chance.

29

CAL'S FIRST ORDER OF BUSINESS
was to open the palace to the realm. "I want the fae to live here,"
he said, walking into the hallway to stand at the top of the stairs
and look over the thrones below. "I want rooms with games to be
set up so I can study how they play. I want meals to be had here so
I can get to know them with their guards down. I want this palace
buzzing with so many fae that the halls never sleep."

I cast a look to Thorn's room, which was currently empty to
the best of my knowledge. "Looks like Thorn had the right idea by
moving in."

"Who's Thorn?" Cal followed my gaze.

"One of the kings," Eliza explained. "Though I didn't know he'd
moved in. When did that happen?"

"Yesterday. Uninvited," I added.

Cal lifted the corner of a brow. I'd always been jealous he could
do that. "A king? My dear sister, do you have a handsome fae king
at your beck and call?"

"She has two," Eliza said.

I shot her a look. "I have one at my beck and call, and one at
my please-don't-visit-again. But Thorn and I are not romantically

involved whatsoever. Anyway, there was talk of food. Do we even have kitchens here?"

"We do! At the back of the palace with beautiful stained glass windows," Talen said, starting down the stairs.

Cal didn't follow. "What's the story with the other king?"

How could I describe Bash? Devastatingly beautiful? Frustratingly calm in every scenario? Thoughtful and kind? Throws a wicked undercut? "King Bastian was a former alliance of mine."

"And now?" Something in his gaze softened, and it made me feel as if we were kids again, going over memories of Mother so we didn't lose her, or covering for the other as we stole vegetables from Daven's garden.

"I accidentally broke his heart, then he broke mine."

It was the only way I could describe it. Two hearts that broke, without ever wanting to hurt each other. I didn't wait for his response and went after Talen. If Cal helped us navigate this realm, I could repair both hearts by saving myself from death.

Just as my feet touched the marble floor, the double doors opened and Thorn waltzed in. He'd undone the buttons of his jacket and moved at a brisk place. He spotted me. "Thea! I've just returned from speaking with my grandfather and—" He stopped short, pointing to Cal. "You're new."

"Cristen," Cal said, extending a hand. Ahead of me, Talen twisted his hand in a small motion, and when I checked Cal's ears, they were pointed. He confidently crossed to Thorn. "It's a pleasure to meet you, Your Highness. I grew up on the outskirts of the realm, but recently joined the House of Delvers." Apparently, *Cristen* had an accent. He borrowed it from Talen, changing it slightly to be less pronounced. I had no idea if the towns on the outskirts of the realm carried any accent, but Thorn didn't bat an eye.

"He's hoping for my old job someday," Talen said. "Figured I'd show him the ropes before I leave it."

Thorn shook Cal's hand, and the tightness in my chest unraveled. "It's good to meet you. I'm going to steal Thea, if none of you mind."

"Not at all. We were just planning a party, but we can sort details with her later," *Cristen* said. I wanted to warn him against speaking with a king. Tell him to stay far away from them all. But while the twist of his smile filled with innocent excitement, his eyes were sharp as ever. He didn't even know Thorn, yet he was assessing him to find his weaknesses already.

"A party?" Interest danced in Thorn's gaze as it swung to me.

"To celebrate!" Cal swung an arm to Eliza. "The beautiful queen has just aligned with the House of Delvers, and we plan to show her off properly."

It was exactly the sort of thing Talen would say, which gave me all the more confidence that Cal could pull this off.

The group walked away, leaving me with Thorn, who watched after them. I tried to divert his focus, placing my hand on his arm. "What did your grandfather say?"

"What did Eliza say?" he countered. "I see she's back."

"She said the bridge didn't open for her, and she felt overwhelmed and needed space. It must have been good for her in some way, because she came back willing to align with Talen." I cringed inside. The lie wasn't as good as what Cal could have come up with.

But Thorn bought it. "Poor girl. I can't image the burden the queens carry. She was brave to try."

"Very true. Your grandfather?"

His focus landed on me. "Right. You'll find this interesting. It's common knowledge the king lost his sister and mother shortly before his disappearance, though no one knows how. Simply that one morning, there were two graves. Isn't that fascinating? I'm convinced that's the sad and harrowing tale we must uncover, so our question is, who killed them? For that we have three possibilities. First, King Brock. The two of them were always close, and in my experience, it's the ones closest to us who have the ability to hurt us most."

I almost refuted that idea as soon as it left his lips, but I forced myself to wait. One night of conversation and a warm meal didn't mean I could trust Brock. I tucked the name away.

"Second, rumor had it that Thelonius was involved with someone, but the relationship ended right after his family died. Coincidence?"

"Murder would be an excellent reason to break up."

"Precisely. But the third is most interesting. According to my grandfather, who knows Bastian's father well, the two of them were constant rivals."

"Thelonius and Bash's father?"

"Rivals for centuries. And when fae fight for that long . . . things get ugly."

I absorbed all three possibilities. The first was less likely, the second intriguing, and the third was far messier than I wanted to get into. Bash stole the throne from his father, which was the extent of my knowledge. I didn't even know where to find the former king. And if Bash heard that I sought out his father, what would he think?

It wasn't until Thorn spoke again that I looked up.

"It might be time to reconcile with Bash, if only to get the full story."

I couldn't sleep that night. Instead, I gathered my paints and wandered downstairs, where I lit a few torches to paint by firelight. They cast shadows as my hands moved, making it tricky to paint, but the stillness of the night soothed me.

On one side of Gaia, I sketched Eliza. The accuracy of the queens to Gaia's left would be tricky to ascertain, but at least their names would be here. For now, I finished the two I knew, and added myself to the west side.

I dipped my brushes in water to clean them, just as footsteps came down the stairs. Talen approached, holding two steaming mugs.

"Did you ever find the kitchens?" I asked him.

"We did. Odette and Eliza went to the market to stock them

while I had some time with Cal this evening. He's as delightful as you said. Quite skilled in chess too. He beat me."

"In all my life, I've yet to beat him." I dried the brushes before taking the mug of hot cocoa from Talen. "I'm sorry I wasn't around. I've been lost in my thoughts." That wasn't entirely truthful. In all honesty, I'd been reading over King Chasmere's journal again, focused on Father's notes. Which reminded me—Talen needed updating.

But first, "I heard you and Odette the other night talking about me. If you helping me is causing a problem between the two of you, then I don't want that."

Talen plopped himself down and ran a hand through his white hair, letting out a weary sigh. "It's not what you think. It's my time she's jealous for. But I'm going to do better about giving it."

"Are you certain that's all? She's not like she was before I disappeared for eight months. Ever since Gaia pressed that watch, it's as if I returned to a new realm, and she hasn't been the same around me."

Talen stared into his cup for a while before looking up.

"Remember the story I told you of one fae whose heart cracked so bad, it shattered and he died?"

I nodded. A story like that wasn't easily forgotten.

"He was in love with a Mortal Queen and couldn't save her. When she died, his heart shattered."

Now I was even more certain they should distance themselves from me. I couldn't stand the thought of even cracking hearts upon my death. But Talen continued. "Years ago, Odette was really good friends with another queen. Ruelle. As always, she died, and part of Odette's heart cracked. I was surprised she became close with you, when she'd sworn never to do that again. So if you see her become distant, it's not because she doesn't love you. But we can only become this close with the queens so often. Our glass hearts can only take so much."

This punishment for mortals would always hurt worse, but too often I discredited the pain of losing us. Over and over and over.

"But I can take it," Talen said firmly. "I can take the heartbreak, because it would hurt worse not to try to save you."

I swallowed hard. "Are you sure? The last thing I want to do is hurt you."

"I'm sure. I am your ally, and I am not giving up."

"Good, because I have news to share with you."

I told him everything. Finding my mother. Speaking with Brock. Learning who my father was. Going to his palace and finding King Chasmere's journal. I held nothing back. Talen listened to it all, his eyes growing wider by the moment.

When I finished, his cocoa was empty and mine had gone cold in my hands. He whistled. "That explains why you've done so well here. You were born to be fae."

"I'm not convinced I'd call anything I've done here 'doing well,' but thank you. It's hard keeping this a secret."

"You need to tell Cal."

"I know." I cast a look to the east side of the palace. Now that he was here, Eliza had moved to her own room, which Talen helped makeover just like he had for me. She and Cal stayed there, and my room seemed even more empty. They were only across the hall, yet she had someone at the end of the day to relax with, someone she could remove her mask for and who knew her better than anyone, while I had no one like that. I hadn't removed this mask since the fae first put it on.

As always, my thoughts wandered to Bash, and I fought them off.

"I'll tell Cal as soon as I can. How do you tell someone their mother is alive and their father is a king?"

"How do you tell someone they are going to die in two years?" Talen asked. The memory of how he told me could almost make me laugh now. He'd been so straightforward. I'd yelled at him. Then run to Gaia to form a plan.

"I told Eliza fairly soon," I said. "Though, she put most of it together on her own."

"And this news is different. You aren't telling Cal he's going to die. You are bringing his family back to him."

I drank my cocoa, thinking. Suddenly I realized that, in the joy of having Cal here with us, I hadn't thought of the ramifications. I looked at Talen, trying to keep calm. "Cal is trapped here. The gate only opened because he and Eliza were married but separated."

Talen set his cup down. "Your mother and father could still open it. But yes, your family must be careful about who goes to which side, or the bridge will stay shut. If we lose your mother, or your father meets an untimely death on his side . . . everyone will be forced to remain where they are." He eyed me. "You look overwhelmed."

I tried to find the word and landed on a hundred of them. Shocked that my father was a fae king. Blindsided that my mother was alive. Furious someone held her captive. Confused about the path forward. Bit by bit, this realm gave me pieces of its history, almost like it was promising me a future, but the pieces didn't fit together yet. I knew about the first Mortal Queen—the true story now—but it told me nothing about how I would survive. Mother gave me stories of Dhalia but hadn't yet told me how she lived. I might acquire my father's dormant power, but would that save me? As it was, I wasn't certain I could hold the power of a fae without being fae myself, and how could I know if half fae counted?

"Overwhelmed is putting it lightly. Don't get me wrong, I'm beyond grateful. I spoke to my mother for the first time in five years. I got to see the better side of my father, before the mortal realm hardened him. And now I have my brother here! But that almost made it worse. My family is whole again, so it's not just about me anymore. I have people to live for, and they are really great people. It's like"—I paused as the words got stuck in my throat. I swallowed the lump—"if I don't survive, it's like I'm letting everyone down."

"My Queen, if you die, it is *us* who let *you* down."

"You could never let me down." He truly couldn't. It was against his nature to stop searching for ways to make the Mortal Queens live.

"What do you want me to do?" he asked, his voice beleaguered.

"If there is anything I could do to save you, I'll do it in a heartbeat. Tell me how to fix it."

The words almost exactly matched what he'd said when he first told me I was fated to die in two years. *If there was anything I could do to save you, I'd do it in a heartbeat.* This time, I had a different answer. "Do whatever Cal tells you to do. He doesn't like to admit it, but he has a lot of our father in him, and we are going to need that to save us."

Talen nodded. "He's already starting. Tomorrow, I'm announcing a banquet to finally show off Eliza to the realm and declare our alliance, and we will get everyone to come. Cal will work behind the scenes to gather information about the missing seventh king—he doesn't know why," Talen added when he saw my reaction. "But it will provide an opportunity for you to speak to Bastian about his father."

I shivered at the thought of speaking to Bash again. We weren't in a position where questions about his father would naturally come up. And if I could speak with him again, his father was last on the list of things I wanted to talk about. But I shut that away to nod.

"Good. And I have a request, my Queen." Talen stood, taking both of our cups. "May I see King Chasmere's journal?"

My first instinct was to deny him, for even though the journal was not mine, it contained pieces of my father's writing, which made it dear to me. But hoarding it would do no good. "Of course. It's in my room."

Talen beamed. "Wonderful. I'm intrigued by the true story, and curious as to how it became so twisted that the entire realm believed something different to be true." He looked up the stairs longingly. "Such a priceless artifact . . ." He cleared his throat. "Plus, I could have some more insight on the text. Perhaps the answer we seek lies there after all."

30

THE PARTY THAT FOLLOWED PALED
every party I'd attended thus far in comparison. There were
fountains of liquid gold, musicians who played instruments built
of starlight, and fae swallowing fire. In the midst of it all, Eliza
accepted the tattooed crown, officially marking her reign as a
Mortal Queen, and announced her alliance with the House of
Delvers. I took it all in from my throne while hiding behind a glass
of mulled wine, so as not to steal any focus away from Eliza.

It wouldn't have mattered. I could have shown up without a
mask, and still they would all be looking at her.

Her black gown rivaled the beauty of night, with lace strung
to the neckline, sheer sleeves to cover her arms, and gilded wings
attached to each shoulder that were impossible to ignore. They
swept the floor as she made her rounds, greeting everyone by
clasping both hands over theirs, all while Cal trailed behind her.

He'd dressed similarly in the sense of no color allowed, wearing
an all-black shirt tucked into dress pants, and even exchanging his
white mask for a black one. His wild curls were the only thing not
black, and the fae focused on that to guess where he was from. *No
one in Talen's family has such coloring, yet he seems to know Talen.
Perhaps Odette's relation? But no, King Vern claims never to have*

seen him before. The outer lands then? Perhaps. But how did he rise through the ranks so fast? Do you see the familiar way the queen looks upon him as if they are acquainted with each other?

Whatever the case, was the unanimous decision, *he looks dashing—like a still night mixed with pure hope.*

I listened to it all with a straight face, but beneath the surface, I celebrated. Soon, Cal had been branded the Dashing Suitor and Eliza the Darling Queen, and together they made quite a pair. Talen, upon informing them of the whispers, instructed them to play into it. So Cal formally kissed Eliza's hand, led her in a dance, then returned to tracing her shadow as she met the realm, all while never saying a word. Eliza, meanwhile, would smile until she'd won every heart, turning often to give Cal a laugh, all while refusing to answer questions about where he was from. "I suppose he's simply a gift this realm has given to me," she answered lithely to one curious fae.

"What a gift that is," was the reply. "It seems the luck of the queens is turning." A jealous stare took Cal in, then latched on to Thorn as the king made his way to my side.

He unbuttoned his red suit to lean casually against the throne, looking bored and completely at home. His hand rested close to my shoulder. "Are you going to tell me where this secret suitor came from? Before today, she'd hardly been seen speaking to anyone else, and now she appears as familiar with him as if he were her second skin."

I didn't miss the slight disdain in his voice. Was it because of the attention Cal received, or because Thorn didn't like not knowing secrets? Likely the latter.

This was one I'd never tell. "I wish I could, but he's as much a mystery to me as anyone." I applauded with the room as the flame eater swallowed an impressive amount of fire and proceeded to blow smoke like a dragon. Cal and Eliza passed through the smoke to venture outdoors, seemingly blind to the way each head swiveled as they passed.

"I don't trust him," Thorn grumbled.

Now that Eliza had left the throne room, I stood from my seat. "You don't trust anyone."

"I trust you." Thorn offered an arm.

"You do not."

Thorn might have responded, but Bash walked in just then, and I swore that even from across the busy room, I heard the rough scrape of his boot and the fabric roll as one side of his cape fell from a shoulder. He'd dressed in the colors of his home—ore and midnight blue—and they made the warmth of his dark skin stand out. His gaze didn't hesitate. It went right to my throne. To me.

I stood like a statue until Thorn tugged my arm. "Are you coming, or shall I ask Bastian to spin so you can take in all of him?"

He hadn't the decency to say that quietly. Heat scorched my cheeks. "I'm fine."

Thorn chuckled. "I take it you will speak with him tonight?" He led me to the corner of the room to begin a slow parade about the border, filling the spaces of conversation with people as we passed. All the while, Bash remained frustratingly on the opposite side of the room, no matter how I moved.

"I'm going to try," I told Thorn. Of course, thanks to the deal I'd made with him, I'd be reporting everything back. I couldn't quite decide if I regretted that yet.

"Word of advice? Give him something. He'll be more likely to talk then."

"Give him what?"

Thorn's gaze fell suggestively to my lips and I clamped my jaw. "Oh, that. Thanks, but I think I'll do this my way."

He looked away as if bored. "Fine, do it your way. Whatever gets the king to talk." His grip on me released, sending me off, but not without a hard look. If looks could talk, this one would say, *This is your one chance. Do what needs to be done.*

I turned my back to him and sought out Bash. Talen had informed me that more of his lords were breaking away. His crown remained his, but it likely wouldn't for long. That alone would be reason to despise me, which made my steps hesitant. I had no idea what I walked into or if he would even talk to me.

Bash had paused at my painting. It was the self-portrait I'd finished recently. I approached before he could see me doing so and scanned for Troi's presence. Mercifully, I didn't spot her, although she must be nearby somewhere. His protector was never far.

My pulse raced as I neared. Out of all the kings, Bash was easily the most magnificent, and the one I could never keep away from. The very first night I saw him, he'd captured my attention the most. He asked for an alliance and I turned him down, yet he remained on my mind. Our bond formed so effortlessly, it pained me to see it now. Whatever once lay between us was now broken, and I wasn't sure I could pull the pieces together again.

"I think I did myself more justice than I should have," I remarked on the painting, making him turn.

His gaze flicked over me, almost disinterested. "It's fine."

I cringed. I could hear the old Bash in my mind. *No, you didn't give it justice enough. Your beauty could never be captured in a painting.*

"I was hoping we could speak," I said.

His focus mulled over the party, and I would have thought he hadn't heard me until he finally said, "I'm not certain that's a good idea."

"It's important, Bash. Please."

Maybe it was the use of his nickname, or the desperate way I said please, but something made him nod. He held out a reluctant arm for me. I exhaled in relief, took it, and let him lead me outside.

We stepped into the misty air. Above us came the loud pop of fireworks which had been continuous since the party began. To our left, a magician performed. To our right, acrobats. In front of us was a large ice sculpture in Eliza's perfect resemblance. Eliza herself sat at a chessboard in the middle of the courtyard, with Cal at her shoulder. A man I didn't know played against her, but as long as it wasn't one of the kings, I had faith she could beat him.

I thought to warn her not to play against a king this night, but what would coronation balls be without a mistake or two? I'd certainly made my fair share.

We were out of the courtyard and into the garden now, where shadows coated the brambles and rampant thorns grew from flowers like teeth. I glanced behind me. If anyone saw us coming here alone together, they'd assume what wasn't true. The way his hand shifted to hold mine as soon as the darkness fell around us like a curtain was not the touch of a stranger.

But as soon as we stopped walking, he dropped it, as if returning to his senses. "What is it?"

I looked around. Ivy rose high, clinging to the walls of the palace on one side. On the other, rows of white peonies hung low with the weight of their bulbs, yet reaching high enough that I suspected fae magic played a part in their growth. They provided a perfect sound barrier.

"I hear you are losing your crown."

I cringed. That wasn't how I'd wished to start this conversation. Bash backed up as if struck. "That's for me to deal with."

"If there's anything I can do to help, I would like to, Bash."

The accusation in his voice wasn't subtle. "You've done enough." I flinched. At that, his tone became less strident. "This isn't your problem to deal with. It's mine. The only way I keep my kingdom at this point is if I acquire the power of the seventh king."

My father's power.

"Speaking of that," I started. "I know you have information about the seventh king."

"Is that what this is about? You want the information I have acquired? Forget it, Thea."

He was turning, and I was losing him. Our conversation thus far had been like a stone wall. *You have to give him something.* I debated it, tilting forward on my toes. My fingers slipped around his arm to hold him back, and my mouth opened.

"My mother is here."

Once more, there I went, making poor decisions on coronation nights.

He whirled around. "What did you say?"

There was no turning back now. But I didn't want to. This was who I was with Bash, unbelievably trusting because he'd always been worth it. And even now as things remained uncertain between us, I didn't doubt he would hold this secret close. So I let it out. "My mother received word years ago that I'd be chosen, so she came to this realm to try to save me. She became trapped instead and remains chained beneath Illusion Point."

"Is she okay?"

"Yes." My throat grew tight. "Though she's not been fed well and the chains have rubbed her skin raw. I don't know what will happen to her after my two years here."

Bash drew close enough for me to see the tawny shine of his buttons and feel the warmth of his breath as he spoke. "Fae and Fates, Thea. How long have you known?"

"Only a few days, and I would have told you sooner, but . . ." He knew how things were between us.

He blew out a long breath. "How did she get here?"

I steadied myself. I had to tell him. "My father was strong enough to open the gate of the bridge from the mortal realm."

He stared at me for a moment, speechless. "How?"

Whatever strain was between us, Bash had always been my one safe place in this realm. I could trust him to bear the weight of these secrets with me. He'd been the one to find a way for me to glimpse my brothers when I needed it. He'd risked his kingdom—and now sat on the verge of losing it—for me. If we were to have any possibility of a life together, and I wanted that desperately, then I could hold no secrets from him.

I opened my mouth to tell him my father was the missing fae king, but the words wouldn't come.

Then I remembered my vow.

We'd sold the information about my father being fae. I could no longer share it freely.

"The fae king has been missing for a while," I said instead.

His brows lowered. "How's that—"

"No one seems to know where he went, but I don't think he's in this realm. Actually, I know he's not. The mortal realm seems a much more practical hiding place."

From his blank stare, I couldn't tell if he'd guessed I was setting up a puzzle for him, or if he'd decided I had lost my mind.

"My mother was always fond of the fae king. Quite, quite fond. Loved him, in fact."

I wandered close to the truth and silently begged him to see it. I spread out my hands. "Alas, I am prohibited from speaking more . . ."

Then he saw it. His forehead wrinkled in thought, and he mouthed my words again. When he got to the part about my mother loving the king, he paused. Silence stretched between us, marred only by the occasional pop of fireworks in the distance, their light flashing across the shock on Bash's face. "Are you certain?"

"Very."

"Your mother? The king?"

I nodded vigorously, nudging him on.

"And your blood being for sale on the market . . . Thea, are you related to the fae king?"

"I cannot speak on that matter," I stated, but my eyes said yes.

He backed up a pace and took me in. "You're fae?"

"Half," I corrected.

"Technicalities. That means the power of the seventh king belongs to you." He spoke faster now. "You're fae royalty." He closed the gap between us, and it was as if me telling him my secrets brought down every wall between us until we were back to what we once were. Together. Working as one. "This is incredible. Do you know what this means?"

I had a few ideas, but I shook my head.

"It means you could have held the power of the ambassador on your own. We didn't need the bracelet." He laughed. This was the very thing that drove a wedge between us and now he was *laughing*. "We made it much more complicated than it needed to be."

That plan would have turned me full fae, but there was no

guarantee it would have saved me from the fate of the Mortal Queens. It certainly wouldn't have saved a single queen who came after me.

"Then"—his eyes were alight—"you will live. I don't have to watch you die in a year."

There it was—the obstacle holding our relationship back. My death. Without it, where did that leave us? Would he welcome back the girl who hurt him, or had it just been an excuse to turn me away?

"Bash," I choked, "I know I hurt you." Although now able to speak freely, I found words even harder to say. "I know I . . . cracked your heart. But if you'd give me another chance, I really think we can have a long life together."

He had no reservations. "Let's do it, Thea. Let's save you." Bash cupped my face with his hands, standing close enough to trace his nose down the arch of mine, and desire filled me. I'd been waiting for his touch for what felt like ages. In the next moment, Bash's lips were upon mine, and I leaned into the kiss, enjoying the warmth of him once again. It was a feeling I'd never take for granted. Like magic and happy-ever-afters mixed together. He'd pulled his heart back to protect it from my death, but now determined that I wouldn't die, he'd unleashed those feelings again and his heart was mine. I swore I would protect it better this time. I'd protect it for the rest of my life.

He kissed me harder than he had before, as if making up for lost time. Too soon, he eased back. "Let's make you fae," he whispered.

"We don't know it will work," I said hesitantly.

He tensed. "Do you not want to live here?"

"Of course, I do." I latched my hands around his to keep him close. "You know how badly I want that. But I don't think turning me full fae is the answer. I'll do it, of course, to have a long life with you. But to unlock the seventh king's power will prove to the realm that queens can be clever—and that we are worth keeping alive. I think something in your father's past holds the answer. Please, will you tell me what happened between them?"

Bash exhaled, returning to his somber self. "Our fathers rose to power around the same time, making them always at odds with each other. My father took away your father's first love, and he retaliated by setting fire to half of my father's lands . . . and so on and so on. But I don't think my father was the one who hurt him most. None of the stories I know are harrowing or sad."

"Either way, we must be the ones to discover this clue."

Bash studied me. "You truly believe unlocking the missing king's power will save you?"

"More than me. It will save everyone. We won't have to protect our hearts anymore. I can stay here, forever, with you."

Bash leaned in to kiss me once more. Lighter, like soft rain and promises. "You make it very hard to stay away. I'm done trying."

Once more, I relished his touch. The way it made my heart pound, and how his arms wrapped around my back. I slid my hands to his neck to pull him closer.

When Bash leaned back, his expression turned thoughtful. "Let's focus," he said, as if he wasn't the one starting every kiss. Even though he'd stopped, his hands kept roaming over my sides, stroking my arms, keeping me near. "I might know what could be the king's greatest tragedy, yet I don't know who orchestrated it. I've heard a tale of how his mother and sister passed away one night, with their graves already dug by dawn, though the secret of their deaths remained a mystery. However, I received a clue recently. It told of a game the realm used to play, one that has long since been forbidden. It's called the War of Hearts."

The name alone sent a shiver down my spine. The fae had glass hearts. Those were not to be trifled with—especially not thrown into war.

"In this game, a maze was set up, and every player had to offer their hearts as the entry fee. They then must search the maze to find their heart again and get out before dawn. If they did, they were granted what their heart desired most. If they didn't . . ."

"The heart would be crushed," I guessed.

He nodded.

My insides twisted. "That sounds like a terrible game."

"But wouldn't you play? If you knew all you had to do was get through a maze, and you'd have the one thing your heart wanted most, wouldn't you risk it? I would." The way his gaze settled on me told me I was what his heart desired most, and heat spread to my cheeks.

He was right, though. It was an archaic, deadly game, yet I might play.

"Supposedly, a secret game took place in the basement of King Thelonius's palace the night his mother and sister died. My guess is that someone set up the game, and his family lost the War of Hearts."

31

"YOU CAN'T TELL ANYONE." BASH warned. "The fewer people who know, the better."

"Of course." But as soon as I said it, I gritted my teeth. "Actually, I have to tell one person."

Bash waited and I dreaded saying it. "Thorn."

At his name, Bash recoiled and his volume lifted. "Thorn? Why?"

"I promised him I would. It was the agreement of the alliance."

"So break the alliance."

I sighed. "How would that make me look? Right now, it's vital that I impress the realm, and aligning with and then discarding a king doesn't attribute anything good to my character."

"He's using you. You must see that."

"Everyone told me that about you," I reminded him. "And yet, I didn't listen." As soon as I made the comparison, I regretted it.

"You can't compare your relationship with me to your relationship with Thorn. I am nothing like that man."

He wasn't. Bash was calm and collected while Thorn was a wild card I could never anticipate. But he was also the one who had willingly helped me the past few weeks, and I couldn't go back on our alliance, especially when I needed the realm to believe mortals were worth saving.

"You're right. I'm sorry. Regardless, I gave him my word that I would share all details pertaining to the Gamemaster's game with him. I have no way around it."

"I cannot play this with him, Thea," Bash said flatly. "I won't."

"Who won't you play with?" At the worst possible second, Thorn stepped from behind the peonies. At that moment, I'd rather five lions had appeared than him. His lithe smile split his cheeks, and the gold buttons on his waistcoat glinted in the light of the fireworks.

Bash's eyelids narrowed in a lethal manner, and Thorn had the audacity to grin wider. "Oh. Me."

"You made Thea agree to tell you everything she found out about the game?"

"She chose to." Thorn was casual, as if it was the most natural thing in the world to wander into a conversation where he didn't belong.

I wondered how much he'd heard.

"I had to," I pointed out. "In order to gain an alliance when I had nothing. An alliance that you are overstepping, might I add. How long have you been lurking there?"

Thorn raised a brow. "I was not lurking. I've been nearby in case you needed anything. The entire realm knows you and Bash aren't exactly friendly right now." The gleam in his eye said he knew how friendly we were.

"Please go," I growled. I would have told him everything Bash told me, but right then I didn't care if I never saw Thorn again.

To my dismay, Bash was the one who began to move away. "I think I should go."

"Don't." I reached for him, but he avoided my grasp.

"I will not play this game with him," Bash said again. "I'm sorry."

Thorn put on a face of mock hurt, which made my anger grow.

"Then don't play it with him," I pled. "Play it with me."

Bash glanced between me and Thorn. "Get rid of him and I will." He pivoted and strode away.

I rounded on Thorn. "You had no right, absolutely no right, to intrude like that!"

"I heard him shout," he insisted, but I didn't buy it. I spun on my heel and marched farther into the gardens, hoping the darkness would swallow me whole until I decided what to do about Thorn. Wild thorns caught my sleeve. I yanked away, ignoring the tear.

"Thea, you must believe me. I am looking out for you."

"I didn't ask you to."

I kept walking, but he stayed with me. "Thea, would you slow down and listen! You know I don't trust him. After the nasty business with the stolen bracelet, I didn't know how he would treat you. I promise I was only on guard for your safety."

Pretty words from a pretty lying king.

"I'll admit, it was poor timing on my part." His footsteps stopped. "But you and I are united in our goal of unlocking the missing king's power, and that means you can trust me. Trust that I want this power unlocked. I would do nothing to hinder that from happening."

Was he truly so dense?

I faced him. "I'm not upset because I don't think you are as passionate as I am about solving the Gamemaster's game. I'm upset because you are tampering with my relationship with Bash, and he is not collateral I wish to wager."

"It was merely poor timing," he repeated, but I'd already turned back around. The garden transitioned into a forest, one as dark as secrets kept hidden for a lifetime, and I paused a second before plunging into it. Once inside, the noises of the night came to life—critters scurrying along the mossy floor, creatures shifting through the shadows. Every hair on my arms stood up, but I kept going. I wanted space. I wanted time to think. I wanted Bash back in my arms again. I wanted Thorn to make things right with him.

I heard no rustle of branches to indicate that Thorn followed me, and my pace slowed.

This alliance with Thorn had been necessary. He brought me this far. But if Bash was willing to risk his heart breaking again, I didn't need Thorn. Bash and I could do this alone. There'd always been something about Thorn that was too . . . perfect. His golden hair curled just right, his smile crooked in all the best ways. He was walking heartbreak and carried himself like a man who'd never been rejected. That wasn't someone I trusted.

All I had to do was figure out who orchestrated the death of my aunt and grandmother, and I would unlock the power of the seventh king. With my fae blood and Father's power, combined with the secrets of King Chasmere's journal, I had great hope for saving the queens.

Perhaps my alliance with Thorn was coming to an end.

Resolved, I turned to head back. When did it get so dark? Was the palace this way? Or would that spill me out over the edge of the island and I'd fall through the sky?

My steps slowed until I was hardly moving at all. My ears strained for familiar sounds, but all I heard was the chirping of crickets closing in.

"This is fine. I'll make it back." Even out loud, my words sounded unsure.

I attempted a confident step.

The ground gave way.

I screamed as I fell, thrashing wildly for something to grab onto, but everything passed from my fingers. Dirt sank away, along with roots and rocks. It was a cliff face, and I was sliding down.

At last, I grabbed hold of a large root and clung for dear life. My feet braced on a barely jutting, thin ledge. I shouted, then listened, then shouted more. If no one came soon, my grip would give, and I wouldn't be able to balance. I tried to see how far I'd fall, but the darkness made it difficult to tell. The above ledge was too far away to climb to. I needed help or I wouldn't make it.

I was not planning to survive a deceiving fae realm just to die by a misstep.

I shouted again.

And again, and again. Over and over until my throat was raw and my hope dwindled.

Then I heard a distant, "Thea!" It was Thorn and, in a total upending of things, right then he was my favorite person.

"Thorn! Watch out, there's a cliff!"

I heard him thundering through the forest, calling my name. I used my voice to guide him closer until his head peeked over the top of the ledge. "Hold on, Thea!" He disappeared.

"Thorn! I'm slipping!"

"I'm looking for something to pull you up with," he called. Then he swore. "There's nothing here. I'll have to go fetch a rope."

"You're a king! There must be something...magical you can do!"

"Not on the Queen's Island. It's a protection for you, but I'm limited here. Of all the cliffs for you to fall off, this was by far the worst." In any other circumstance, I'd feel protected that the kings were limited in the home of the queens, but right then, it only struck dread inside me as he said, "I'll be right back."

"I can't hold on that long! Don't leave!" Desperation clung to every tone of my voice. My hands couldn't hold the root much longer, and I was afraid it would snap soon. "Reach down your hand."

He did, but his reach was painfully short.

"What about my leg? Could you take hold of that?" Thorn shifted, this time lowering a leg as he spoke.

"No," I called back. "Still a body-length short. I can't—I can't hold on."

"You have to!" He sounded as frantic as I felt. But he wasn't the one creeping closer to their death as the air grew shallow. The scent of dirt clogged my nose until I could hardly breathe. "I can drop lower, then pull us both up. I think there's something here I can grab. Althea, don't you dare let go!"

My body trembled uncontrollably, my grip slipping.

Thorn slid down halfway and grabbed something I couldn't see. He grunted and went silent.

"Thorn?"

"I'm alright." But his tight voice said something else. Stiffly, he said, "How about now?"

I tried to reach him, but he was still too far. "I can't."

"Look, there's a rock about six inches up that appears sturdy. Reach for that. It should bring you closer."

I spotted the rock. I might be able to reach a few inches up, but not six. "It's too far."

"It's not too far. Thea, you must."

My arm cramped, and my throat closed tight. "I don't think I can." I tried and almost lost my grip.

"You have to."

I knew I had to. My mind screamed that at me. But my body was failing, and my mind wasn't persuasive enough to overcome that.

I tried again. If I were stronger, I could make it. But I'd spent a year in the fae realm and had not exercised once, so my body couldn't do what I needed it to. I gritted my teeth and tried a third time.

The root groaned and pulled farther out.

"Are you still there?"

"You'll hear my screams if I fall. Which will be soon." My voice quavered.

"There's one thing we can try." He breathed deeply. "Remove your mask."

I wasn't hearing him right. "Say that again?"

"I know it doesn't make sense, but if you remove your mask, I can order you to climb. Your body will be forced to obey. It will take very little effort on your part, and you'll scale the wall perfectly."

"No."

The answer came immediately. How could I say otherwise? This realm had warned me of many things—and I'd ignored nearly every warning. But this one I'd kept. I'd never removed my mask, even in sleep. Not even for Bash. And he'd never once asked me to. No one could have such control over me.

But was it worth dying?

"What else could you do once you know my true face?" I panted.

From the strain in Thorn's voice, he struggled as much as I did to keep a hold. "I would do nothing. I promise you. I wouldn't do a thing with the power. I promise on our alliance I won't use your true face to hurt you. I swear it. Please, my Queen, let me save you."

We were in an alliance, which forbade him from tricking me.

But he could twist things, manipulate words, or break the alliance and his words would mean nothing.

My grip slipped more, and it was all I could do to clamp my fingers tighter until my hands shook.

"I can't." The words were getting harder to speak. My vision darkened. Was it a good thing if my body went numb? I tried again to reach for the rocky ledge, but this time I hadn't the strength to let go, much less reach. Maybe if I waited long enough, someone else would come by who could help. But I wouldn't last long.

I looked down again. We were still in the middle of the forest behind my home—there had to be a ground somewhere. I could let go and take my chances with landing well.

Thorn didn't share my optimism. "Thea, it's either this or die, and I cannot lose you."

Thorn shouted, but the sound came oddly, like my ears were clouded. Like I was drifting from consciousness. Had I scraped my arms? Something sticky ran down my skin. I was going to be sick.

"My Queen!"

This was what defeat felt like. A sinking, empty feeling inside. With what strength I could muster, I pushed aside reason and used my shoulder to push off my mask.

It fell, clattering a long distance before landing somewhere below. At least now I knew the fall would have been far.

"Look at me," I croaked, and the words sounded like surrender.

I felt naked. Exposed. Weak. Wind rippled off my bare skin for the first time in over a year, and I hated every moment of it. I closed my eyes, as if that could somehow cover for the mask, as if the eyes were the only important part of my face. Thorn didn't speak, and I tried to guess what was going through his mind—all the ways he could use this against me. *I have to live. That matters most.* The thought provided little solace. What I'd just done could never be undone, and I feared the consequences almost more than I feared death.

Finally, Thorn's voice came floating to me. "You are beautiful."

I opened my eyes. He gazed down upon me, his lips parted.

I took a weary breath. "Help me."

His tone turned commanding. "Thea, you will climb up the wall and grab hold of me."

And I obeyed.

There was no possible way to explain how I did exactly what he'd ordered. I moved my arms, grabbing hold of whatever I could find, and effortlessly pulled myself higher and higher, climbing out of the dark pit. The relief was almost enough to make me forget what I'd just done.

Once high enough, I linked my arms around Thorn, and he pulled us up the rest of the way.

At the top, I rolled over, breathing heavily. The spell faded, and my limbs felt like mine again. I wrapped my arms around me, hoping that would be the last time Thorn used my true face, but I doubted it would be.

"Are you okay?" he asked in a hoarse voice.

I sat up. "My arms are a bit scraped," I answered. "But—Thorn!"

He was sprawled out on the ground, and at the top of his abdomen, a long cut cleaved his body. He waved my exclamation off as if it were nothing, but his jaw clenched hard. A wayward root or rock had sliced through his skin. I realized it must have been pressed against him the entire time he waited for me.

"Why didn't you climb back up?" I asked.

"I had to save you."

My heart went to him, and I felt less foolish for showing him my face. He propped his weight against an elbow to look at me. "I know I have made mistakes and that I'm not a perfect alliance for you. But your welfare is important to me. For you, my Queen, I would do anything."

I stood and offered him a hand. "Let's just get you back inside before you bleed anymore."

"Not like that, my Queen. You cannot." Thorn gingerly got to his feet and dug through the bushes, using the stems of leaves to fasten a makeshift mask for me. "This will fall off easily, so go directly to your room and have Talen fetch you a new mask."

"I will," I promised. "And thank you. I don't know what I would have done without you."

"I have no doubt you would have thought of something," Thorn replied, giving me his arm. But it ended up being me who supported more of his weight as we traversed through the forest with him as guide, leading us to the rear of the palace. At the door, he bid me farewell.

"I need to get this tended," he said, pulling his sticky shirt away from his skin. I winced. "And I suspect I should do so before I pass out. I trust you can make it to your room on your own?"

I hesitated. "Shouldn't you come to your room here so Talen and Odette can tend to you?"

"They are not as devoted to me as they are to you," he replied. He walked away to find the nearest clearing to throw up his hand and summon a chariot, promptly collapsing into its bed. I waited until he was gone to slip inside the door and follow the sound of music, orienting myself before slinking along the back to find my room unseen. Everything hurt. The scrapes on my arms burned. My steps were as if stones clung to my feet. All I wanted was sleep.

Talen appeared in the doorway moments after I entered my room, likely summoned by whatever strange alliance link connected us. He took one look at me and turned the lock behind him.

"What do you need?"

"A new mask," I said as exhaustion settled on my shoulders like a weight, throwing me down to the bed. "And healing ointment for my arms," I added, the words murky. I might have asked for cider as well, but I couldn't be sure if I got that out before I fell asleep.

32

THE CRACKLING OF THE FIRE WOKE

me. It burned in the hearth, keeping the room warm. By its light, I spotted two notes waiting at my bedside, one a deep black and the other sparkling opal, sealed with white wax.

Bash only sent stationary in dark colors. The other, I suspected, was from Thorn.

I opened Bash's note first.

> Thea,
>
> Allow me to apologize greatly for how I behaved tonight. It was dishonorable of me to turn away from you so quickly. If I may explain.
>
> Things between Thorn and me are complicated. Perhaps not so much complicated as simply rotten. He was the one who told King Vern to kill my sister. And he has sent and continuously sends

my father money so he may usurp my throne. Some things are written in stone, and such is the strife between us.

Still, it was poor conduct of me to allow that to hinder my relationship with you. I do not wish to advance in this game with him at my side, and seeing as how things are, he must be at yours. So, allow me to be your secret. As far as the realm will believe, we are not aligned. We are not together. But beneath the surface, I am all in. I am yours. And I will not run again. No matter how many fae kings or stolen bracelets or cracked hearts get in our way.

I am sorry I ever wavered.

Please accept my apology, and my unending support.

Yours, Bash

Him being my secret sounded nice. With everything we'd been through, I dreaded the thought of explaining our relationship to anyone else, so keeping it hidden would be less of a headache and far more fun. And, since it didn't have anything to do with the Gamemaster's game, I wasn't obligated to tell Thorn.

Speaking of Thorn. I opened his note next.

ALTHEA,

I AM SENDING OINTMENT TOMORROW TO HELP
HEAL YOUR ARMS. MY OWN WOUND IS HEALING
WELL AS I WRITE THIS.

I KNOW HOW CONCERNED YOU MUST BE THAT
I KNOW YOUR TRUE FACE. IT IS A BREATHTAKING
ONE, MIGHT I ADD. BUT I PROMISE ON OUR
ALLIANCE THAT I WILL NOT USE IT TO HARM YOU.

WHEN YOU ARE READY, WE SHALL LOOK
MORE INTO THIS WAR OF HEARTS GAME BASTIAN
SPOKE OF.

REST WELL, THORN

That confirmed that Thorn had heard some of our conversation. I could only hope his eavesdropping began there and not before.

With everything that had happened, I'd forgotten about the War of Hearts game. The final pieces of the puzzle were coming together. All we had to do was find out who had betrayed my father by setting up the game, and the answer should lead us to his signet ring. The question was there, yet how to find the answer alluded me. How do you find the one who hosted a game so few people knew existed?

My door opened and Cal stepped in, looking more like my brother from home in a simple pullover tunic than the Dashing Suitor to the Darling Queen. He put a hand to his chest when he saw me. "You're awake. Thank the fae."

"Awake, but damaged." I checked my arms, then stared. The skin tore last night, I was sure of it. Yet only scars remained, tiny white webs that ran the length of my forearms.

"King Brock healed you. Talen retrieved him as soon as you fell unconscious," Cal said. "Which was quite concerning. Especially since you weren't wearing your mask."

My hands flew to my face, but a mask rested there.

"Talen," Cal said. He sat at the foot of my bed. "Care to explain?"

"Boy problems, poor choices, and a cliff," I told him. I stretched, swinging my feet to the floor. "What time is it?"

"Late. Everyone else is asleep." For the first time, I noted the cups of cider in his hands, one of which he passed to me. The sweet apple scent hit my nose, and I relaxed.

I took the first sip, clearing my mind for what needed to come next. I'd been putting off this conversation since Cal arrived.

I could put it off a moment longer. "Tell me about last night."

Wonder filled his eyes. "It was incredible. I played chess against someone and won. It was no stakes, but still. I spoke with five of the kings and got a feel for each of them. Brock is the best of the lot, but Vern is shady. He's got a grudge against the queens that I can't figure out, so steer clear of that one. And the food! Sugar drop melts and toasted plums and glazed steaks. It puts our realm to shame."

It did. When I returned briefly to the mortal realm, everything seemed so . . . mundane. Watching Cal speak of his evening was like watching the best parts of this realm come to life. I wanted to know how he won the chess match and how he set up a stake-less match to begin with. I wanted every detail about his conversations with the five kings. But as he spoke, all I could see was the crooked crown he wore on his head, likely as a joke, but it looked just like one of the pictures of Father from his palace.

Cal should go there like I had. He should see the portraits. He should see the throne. He should read the journal.

He kept talking. "I'm eager to dive into this world more. I've got big plans for— Thea, you're shaking."

I steeled myself. "It's been a long night."

He led me to the fire where we sat down in the high-backed, tufted sofas. I took another long sip of my cider. Preparing myself. Wishing I could prepare him. Cal watched me with his brows knitted together, waiting for me to speak. I lowered the glass.

"Cal, I have two things to tell you, and both of them are . . . big."

He set down the goblet to give me his full attention. "Alright."

"There's no way to lead into this, so I'll just say it. Mother didn't die. She's alive, and she's here."

"I know." Cal didn't even blink. "Father told us shortly after Eliza was taken."

Good, then this next part wouldn't be such a surprise. "I found her."

"What?" His eyes widened, and he scooted his chair closer, as if to savor every word. "Is she okay?"

"She's alive and unharmed, generally speaking, but held captive beneath the chessboard on Illusion Point. The king piece is the key to open her door. But, Cal," I spoke quickly because the wheels in his head were visibly turning, and he'd already glanced toward the door as if ready to sprint off, "we cannot save her. She's chained to the floor, and I don't have that key. We can visit her, though." I grasped his arm. "Oh, Cal, she would love seeing you."

"Then let's go. Let's go right now, and I'll find a way to break her chain. Surely someone has welding equipment around here, or some fae power to release her."

That might work. Truly, several plans could work to free her. But what traps were laid, rigged to go off the moment her chain fell? This was the fae realm, after all. The moment she stepped from the room, would it fill with poison, killing us all? Would a sword swing from the wall and strike us down? Would it instantly alert whoever captured her, and he'd come slay us where we stood? I didn't doubt we could come up with a way to free her. It was what happened next that we didn't know, and I preferred to wait until we did. "She's not in harm where she is, and she asked that we focus on saving the Mortal Queens first."

His eyes narrowed. "Saving you and Eliza, you mean."

"That's what I said."

"It is not. Thea, tell me you aren't planning to save every queen to come after you?"

I firmed my jaw. He groaned, grabbing his cup to take an angry swig, as if that could change what I'd said. "You are impossible.

You are not responsible for everyone around you. If you find a way to free yourself, you take it."

"At what cost? Isn't it worth it to try to save everyone else?"

Cal rose. "What about the cost to you? There are people back home who are waiting for you to return. Me. Malcom. Father. You cannot abandon us."

I stood too. "The mortal realm lost me the moment I became a queen. This way, I'm assuring no other mortals are lost."

"You don't have to be the hero," he whispered as he reached out to hug me. "It's not worth it to me."

Little did he know, he'd lost me anyway. Even if I didn't die, I planned to remain here. My mind was set on that. I didn't say it, though. I simply let him hold on to me until feeling his breath slow.

"What's the other thing?"

"Hmm?" I pulled back.

"You said there were two things you needed to tell me."

"Oh, yes." I cleared my throat. Technically, I'd vowed not to share this information with any other *fae*, but Cal was no fae. The words should come easily, instead of me having to create a riddle as I'd done with Bash. I tested it.

"The second is that our father is the missing fae king who is hundreds of years old and has been hiding in the mortal realm for years."

Cal dropped his goblet and it shattered.

33

CAL AND I LEFT AT ONCE FOR
Father's palace. It was just as before, with ice formed as a shield of
armor around it, which began to melt as soon as we set foot on the
snow-ridden path, with the icicles dripping from archways to create
a toothy mouth for us to pass beneath. Cal explored the same places
I had—the corridors, the throne room, and Father's chambers. He
paused far longer in the rooms covered with sheets, then walked
slowly through it as I told him the story about the War of Hearts.

Cal grimaced. "That's a wretched way to die."

Knowing how their deaths came to be made the room even
more haunted, until I could almost feel their presence. It was regret
and broken dreams. Happy-ever-afters that never came to be. I
shivered, and it had nothing to do with the ice.

"Let's go," Cal said in a low voice. "This palace has nothing
for us now."

I didn't argue.

We arrived back home as the stars brightened, indicating the
start of a new day. I still wore my extravagant dress from the night
before, though now it hung sadly around the edges and the fabric
felt stiff against my skin. I glanced toward the gardens where Bash
had kissed me, allowing that to lift my spirits as Cal walked me to
my room. He turned to go, but Talen coughed.

We poked our heads into my chambers. Talen stood in the center with his arms crossed, wearing an expression that said we were in trouble. "Where have you been?"

I opened the door farther, finding Eliza pacing within. As soon as she spotted Cal, she exhaled.

"We went for a walk through Father's palace," I explained.

"You left without telling anyone, leaving us to find both of you gone and"—Talen swept his finger in a circle before dropping it to point accusingly at the shattered goblet on the ground—"shattered glass on the floor."

"That's my fault." Cal moved as if to clean it, but Talen put up a hand.

"I'm making a new rule. No more traipsing off through the realm without telling someone. No more late-night escapades"— he glared at me—"or running off to open dangerous bridges"—he leveled his eyes at Eliza—"without telling someone."

Eliza raised a hand. "I did tell Thea about the bridge thing."

"I approve of this new rule," I said.

Cal spoke up. "Fine. But it doesn't matter much to me, because I don't plan to be going out often. Instead, I'm going to bring some of the realm here."

"Yes, we are still preparing that."

"No, bring them today. I'm ready. They can decorate their own rooms for all I care. But starting today, the halls should be filled with so many fae that this place will never sleep again."

"I appreciate the enthusiasm, but it might take time to fill the halls."

A slow grin stretched across Cal's face. "I'll bet I get it filled by tonight."

Talen studied Cal, then grinned too. "What do you bet?"

"More glazed steak, a stable of horses, and you to teach me everything you know about this realm."

"Yes to the steak, I'll get you two horses, and I will teach you everything I can within a week. *Everything* would take a lifetime."

Cal stuck out his hand. "Done."

"And if you don't, the next time someone in your family opens that bridge between realms, you let me cross and spend two weeks in the mortal realm before bringing me back."

Their hands met. "You can spend as long as you like there."

As soon as they separated, a gleam danced in Talen's eye. "You said by tonight. The clock's ticking."

With a flourish, Cal pulled out a parchment from his back pocket. "I want this copied and delivered to every notable fae by midday."

We all gathered closer to read it.

> The king takes bishop after the bishop takes knight
> And the pawn takes a stand.
> But the queen watches all with cunning delight.
> For it was at her house that the game began,
> And it shall be at her house where I reveal the ring.
> Find the queen, win the king.

I knew Cal had brains. I didn't know he had audacity too. "You matched her handwriting. You're claiming to be the Gamemaster."

"Not claiming to be her, exactly, merely pretending that she will reveal the signet ring here. If the fae believe the game continues in your home, they will flood it—all the participants and everyone else just to watch." He flashed that smile I knew so well. "In fact, I might change the bet to say I can fill these halls before lunch."

"And when there is no clue to be found?"

"They'll look even harder. Besides, we have the next clue," Cal informed me. "I spoke to several fae last night, all eager to discuss the game with me. From what I gathered, you, Thorn, and Bash are several steps ahead of anyone else. So this isn't a complete lie."

"But we aren't willing to give up the clue."

"Naturally, but they needn't know that. I'll create a fake clue, if needed." He glanced at his wife. "Eliza, you think this is a good idea, right?"

"I love it." She'd stayed back, letting his excitement shine, but pride resided in her gaze. "It's brilliant."

That only fueled Cal. "Hear that? Brilliant."

"Don't get cocky," Talen mumbled, but his expression said he knew he'd lost. The fae would indeed flood in. I nodded my approval, deepening Cal's smile.

Talen sighed with defeat and took the note, bowing. "As you wish. Prepare yourself, for the fae are coming, and any shred of privacy we once had here shall be gone."

The fae arrived with gusto. Within the hour, every room in my hall had been claimed, and the sounds of footsteps and chatter rang from each corner of the palace.

By lunch, the kitchens were running.

By evening, there wasn't a spare room in the palace, and halls were being converted to sleeping quarters so more could stay.

I spent all day fielding questions about this new clue. Even those who weren't part of the Gamemaster's game decided they could play and were actively snooping through the palace to find a clue. Many would spot me and cheer. "There she is! We found the queen!"

"I don't have the clue," I explained. "Maybe 'queen' meant something different?"

They'd think about it, most deciding it meant Eliza, and they'd run off to find her.

I kept a slow pace as I walked the halls, seeing them come to life one after another. All I could think was how it looked when Gaia died—everything coated in darkness and cobwebs as if no one had lived here at all. That was less than a month ago. Now, it was as if this had always been a home. Talen was right—silence was a thing of the past. But despite the loss of silence, I found peace, and it spread like wings behind me. This was how things ought to have always been. Laughter in the halls. Music in the air. The queens surrounded by friends.

If queens did come after us, let them be greeted by such cheerful laughter within the walls of their home, instead of the emptiness we found. For too long this place had been a tomb. Now it was alive.

That first night was the best. We all gathered in the courtyard with blankets and cocoa, while three of the kings—Arden, Brock, and Leonard—put on a star show. We applauded as the stars danced through the sky, swaying to the music that accompanied. Bash arrived in time to see it, not to claim a room, but simply to check on me. My secret suitor. He stood across the courtyard, but every so often our eyes would meet. The first time, he smiled and gestured to everything with a nod. We'd done well.

It was possible all this would never lead to anything. Cal hoped to uncover secrets about the fae, but even if nothing came of inviting them to my home, we'd done something worthwhile. And after a year of playing games, it felt nice to do something good for a change.

After the star show, most retreated to begin a night of chess matches, Cal among them. But I took my cocoa and escaped to my room. Before I reached my door, Thorn came out of his room.

We stared at each other for a while. We hadn't spoken since last night when he saw me with my mask off, and already I feared he would use it against me. But he gave a tiny smile instead. "You look like you healed nicely."

"You too."

"I'm going to join the chess matches. Let me know if you need anything." He walked past, giving me a wide berth.

Then he was gone, and despite everything, I still couldn't figure out how far I trusted him yet.

34

THAT NIGHT. I DREAMED OF MY mother.

She was still trapped, still chained to the floor, yet dying. I somehow knew this, even as I was stuck outside, trying to claw my way through the door. I didn't get there in time. She died as soon as I pried the door open, and I never got to see her alive again.

I woke covered in sweat, my breathing rapid.

It wasn't right—me living like this while she remained a prisoner. I had to free her, and it couldn't wait.

Grabbing my cloak, I hurried into the corridor and headed for Talen's room.

"My answer is no!" Talen nearly shouted. I paused, fearing he meant me, but he spoke to someone in his room. "You cannot have my old position. You are already a House Representative."

"Of the Berns House," the person lamented. It must be Thomas, then. "I've worked hard. I deserve a better House."

"Then ask them yourself. I promise, if you ask me to put in a recommendation, it won't be a glowing one."

"For old time's sake, please."

I was making a bad habit of listening in on Talen's conversations. I turned away as I heard Talen say, "A million times, no. Now get out. I owe someone horses and don't have the faintest idea where to get them."

I didn't have time to appear as if I wasn't eavesdropping before they stepped into the corridor. Thomas scowled when he spotted me and brushed past.

Talen lifted a brow. "You ought to stop listening to my conversations."

"I was just thinking the same thing," I told him. "Consider me stopped."

Talen chuckled in a way that said he didn't believe me. "It's no matter. I don't care how many people know I don't care for Thomas. He's always been after my job, but now that I'm leaving, he thinks I'll help him get it. I won't!" He shouted the last bit down the corridor.

"I think he got the message."

"I'll believe that when he stops asking me." Talen stepped into his room, drawing me with him. A tiny bed rested in the corner with his top hat leaning on its bedrail. He had the smallest bed I'd seen for a fae, one that rivaled the size of my own in the mortal realm. But the sheer number of bookshelves made up for it. They didn't simply line the wall, they cut inward to make rows.

He had *aisles* of books in his room.

"Are any of these good?" I roved my finger over a few of the spines.

"Every single one of them is divine. Though it's my recent addition that you loaned me that is keeping me up right now. I'm fascinated by this journal."

I checked that no one lingered in the corridor and closed the door. "Did you learn anything?"

"Yes, though, is it anything useful? Time will tell. Now you tell me what you are doing in my room at the wee hours of morning."

I shared my dream with him, leaving out the details and stressing how nervous I was for Mother's safety. What if her captor wasn't feeding her? What if she was sick and needed medicine?

Talen finally put up a hand to stop me. "You are doing exactly what she asked of you. Taking care of yourself and Eliza. And we are so close, I feel it. Focus on saving the two of you, then we will go in, guns blazing, to save your mother."

"Still, I worry."

He pulled on an overcoat and set his hat upon his white hair. "Trust me, someone has gone through the effort of keeping her alive for years. They won't let her die after all that time. And we will save her soon anyway."

"You're right. She's survived for five years, and I've no real reason to believe that will change now."

"Good. Now, if you don't mind, I have a debt to your brother that needs repaying." At that moment, something loud crashed below. That would be in the main throne room. Talen sighed. "And I have another mess to clean." He wandered off while muttering about not being qualified to watch over this many fae.

The crash turned out to be the chandelier broken after someone tried to swing from it. It landed on a chessboard, shattering it in half.

Cal stood by the mess, shaking his head. "I was going to win that one."

"Have you been playing all night?"

He nodded, seeming pleased with himself. "It was worth it for the things I now know."

I brightened. "Anything about the War of Hearts?"

"No, but can I interest you in a bit of fae gossip?"

"Is it relevant to me at all?"

"No."

"Then no," I said.

He bent to retrieve the chess pieces. "Suit yourself."

Over his shoulder, I spotted Bash as he entered through the front doors, wearing a taupe suit, suede shoes, and a crimson doublet that I'd wager smelled like cinnamon. He caught my eye and gestured up the stairs. I nodded. He went first, and I remained behind to help Talen clean the broken glass, while Cal and his opponent found a different board to play on. When a few minutes passed, I disappeared after Bash.

He waited in my room, and I closed the door behind me.

"Are you alright?" he asked. I was right, he smelled of cinnamon. "I heard you got injured after I left."

"Brock healed me." I showed him my scars. "I'm fine now."

"I'm relieved. I'd hate for something to happen to my Queen." He kissed the scars, making up for the lost time between us. In his presence, the tension uncoiled inside me, letting warmth back in. Worries for my mother, thoughts of the fae crowding my home, uncertainty about Thorn—it all slipped away. Bash's grin turned boyish, like we were no longer king and queen. Like he was a boy, chasing a girl. And I was a girl, utterly smitten with him.

We made light conversation, with me asking about Troi and him asking how I felt about the entire realm moving into my home. As we spoke, he kept close, both his hands enclosing one of mine. Eventually, his smile turned downcast, until something dark brewed behind his eyes. "Thea, I need to apologize."

"But you already did. I got your note." I glanced at my bed, though he wouldn't see it from where I'd stashed it under the mattress.

"No, I need to apologize for how I acted previously. I should have trusted you when you revealed the bracelet to the ambassador. I shouldn't have pushed you away when you cracked my heart."

I winced. I knew Bash didn't keep his heart in his chest, but my hand went there all the same, as I tried not to think of the cracked glass. It pierced my own heart, what I had done to him.

"It was complicated. I lost faith in you when you didn't give me a reason to. It was fair for you to pull away." I hesitated before asking the next part. "Did it hurt?"

"My heart cracking?"

I had a flood of unspoken questions in the one I actually asked. When glass hearts broke, what did fae feel? Could they feel it through every inch of their body? Or was it nothing more than a small burn, there one moment and gone the next? Could he still feel it, the echoes of the pain? Did it haunt him while he slept? Or did he regret that, because of me, he'd never be whole again?

Once, I thought it'd be an honor to be the only one to crack the heart of the king who could not love. But now, it was my deepest regret.

"Do you remember that day in the snow?" Bash asked.

I looked up. "Of course."

"It's cold, like that. Like a sliver of ice splintering your heart, making it go numb."

At my horrified expression, he went on. "It's not terrible. And it's brief. And, Thea, you never need to feel guilty for it."

But I did. I'd taken a perfect, beautiful heart and cracked it.

"Can you forgive me?" I asked, my voice shaky.

"Already forgiven." He leaned toward me, but a knock sounded at the door. Bash put a finger to his lips and retreated to the closet, shutting the door behind him just as mine opened. Cal stuck his head in.

"Talen delivered two horses! Eliza's still asleep. Want to race?"

"Yes. Give me five minutes?"

He ducked out and I opened the closet door. Bash stood in the darkness with a mischievous smile. "I like being your secret."

"Remind me why we shouldn't tell people?" I asked as I dragged him out.

"Because knowledge comes with power, and I'd rather people not be able to use us against each other. Plus, this is entertaining." He leaned in again like he was going to kiss me, then stepped back. "Before I forget why I came, did you know your father was in a relationship with an ambassador?"

"I did, though I don't know when or with whom."

"The tall woman with silver hair."

I stepped back, startled. That one? How? She was cold and rough and unkind. Though, all those things could describe Father in the mortal realm, but I imagined him differently as a king here. I imagined warmth. I imagined kindness. And I liked to imagine him with someone who was the same way. "But she saw him in the mortal realm. Twice."

"He's a king. He can enchant his appearance."

With a start, I realized I might not know my father's true face, and that unnerved me.

"It gets interesting, though. Their relationship ended around the same time the War of Hearts took place."

I knew that too. "Do you think she had something to do with their deaths?"

"She doesn't brag about her relationship with the missing king, which would give her serious clout. Perhaps this is why. And what better reason to separate than if she killed his family?"

I shuddered. "Or what better way for her to enact revenge?"

I'd never liked that ambassador. To find she was wrapped up in all this didn't surprise me, and I could picture her hosting a deadly game to get revenge on my father for breaking her heart. Then summoning his daughter to the realm to die. She could have been behind it this entire time, playing us like puppets. She could be behind this now, hiring a Gamemaster to lure us toward my father's power. I could only fear what she had planned for the end.

"Thea," Bash interrupted my thoughts. A slow smile spread across his face. "I think we have a suspect."

35

I MET CAL IN THE COURTYARD. stepping over sleeping bodies and half-played games of dice. Morning approached, but the palace appeared to be mostly asleep for the first time since the fae had arrived. Cal took my arm and led me away from the crowd, then tossed up a hand for a chariot.

I spun, then gasped. "There are no horses here!"

Cal made no apology. "We are going to see Mother."

A chariot landed and he stepped on, but I dug in my feet. "We can't risk anyone finding out we know she is trapped. Who knows what her captor would do."

"If she dies, and I don't see her first, I won't forgive myself." Cal held out a hand for me to take, but I pushed it away.

"She won't die. Someone's kept her alive for years, so they won't let her perish now." I repeated what Talen told me.

Cal had dressed as the Dashing Suitor this morning, with his thin black mask set against copper eyes, a black suit, midnight blue cloak, and one earring glittering in his ear. It made him look stoic when coupled with his frown. "Still. I dreamed last night that she died. I need to see her. I have to."

My breath swept from my lungs. What were the odds of us having the same dream? Without saying another word, I climbed atop the chariot and grabbed hold. "To Illusion Point."

We took off.

A mist hung over the approaching island, like it knew we needed to travel in secret. Despite the early hour, we couldn't land close without someone spotting us, so we chose someplace far from the chessboard and cut a long path around the tents and hovels, sneaking like spies through the town until finding its center. I kept a wary eye, searching for anyone following, for anyone who whispered as we passed, or for anyone lurking behind corners to lock us up right alongside Mother. By the time we reached the heart of the island, I had gooseflesh over my arms and jumped with every sound.

Cal gazed in awe at the statues of the kings leading to the magnificent chessboard, where he let out a low whistle. "I'd like to play here sometime."

"Only kings and queens may play here, though matches haven't continued since the Gamemaster created the new game. Which is the one lucky thing that's happened for us." I pulled my cloak tighter around my body, keeping a careful watch.

Cal took in the thrones, looking like he wanted to inspect every inch of this place, but withheld himself. "You said the king is the key?"

"It always is," I said, finding the piece. "Let's hurry."

I wiped dead leaves from the keyhole, checking a final time that we were alone. No matter how I tried, I couldn't shake the feeling that someone watched us, and the sense made me move faster. The key twisted, the door opened, and I motioned for Cal to go down the stairs, then made sure the latch was in place behind us.

Cool, damp air swarmed us, beckoning us into darkness. My fear subsided like a retreating wave, and anticipation took its place. Last time, I hadn't known what I would find, but this time was different. I hurried down the drafty stairs, dirt swirling with each hasty step, only pausing halfway before I realized Cal had stopped.

"What's wrong?"

His chest expanded with a heavy breath. "It's been five years." His eyes glossed over.

I extended my hand. "She'll be overjoyed to see you."

"Did you know she bought me my first math book? Taught me my first equations. Showed me how to love puzzles. Everything I am, it's because of her."

"Althea?" Mother's voice wafted down the stone corridor. At the sound, Cal's head jerked up.

"Mother?"

"Who—"

We ran then, sprinting down the hallway to her. Mother stood in the center of her room, her arms already outstretched. They fell slack when she spotted Cal and her lips trembled.

He paused at the wooden architraves, resting a hand against the column, holding on as if it was the only thing keeping him upright. His height almost stretched to the ceiling, but in that moment, he looked like the thirteen-year-old boy who'd just lost his mother.

"Mother." His voice broke.

"My sweet boy." Mother's cheeks were already soaked in tears. "How is this possible?"

Cal didn't answer before stepping forward to embrace her, and they cried together. I took in the sight of them, still struggling to wrap my mind around the fact that my family was coming back together. At one time, this moment seemed impossible. Yet here we were, reunited with our mother five years after being told she was lost in a raid. Hope took root in my heart. So many other moments seemed impossible now—me living beyond this year, solving the Gamemaster's game, saving the queens. Yet, if my mother could come back from the grave, then the other tasks didn't feel as impossible anymore.

Mother brushed Cal's curls away from his face. She had to look up to see him now. "You have grown into a young man," she said, her smile wide. "A fine young man." She reached out an arm to me. "Dear Thea." The three of us nestled in a moment that held no time.

When we parted, Cal reached up to remove his mask. I chided myself for not doing that when I first found Mother and instantly followed suit.

She put a hand over her chest. "I should chastise you both for removing your masks in this realm. But I'm so grateful to really see you, both of you."

My appearance wasn't quite fair. Time in the fae realm magnified the appearance of mortals—I'd noticed that with each queen who returned the next year for the Choosing Ceremony. My skin would be clearer, my hair shinier, my lips fuller. But at the core, I remained myself. I still couldn't get that perfect arch on my smile, instead, my lips pulled back unevenly every time. My nails would always be chipped where I picked at them. And I'd always have paint stuck somewhere on my body.

Mother needed to sit down. "Tell me all about everything," she said to Cal.

"I'm married now."

Her eyes widened. "Eliza?"

He nodded, and a smile wreathed her face.

"So that's how you are here." She leaned forward eagerly. "How is Malcom?"

Cal filled her in on the details while I took in the room again, looking for any indicators of who kept her here. A platter of fruit rested on the table, half of it picked through, a basket of loaves at its side. A pitcher of water and a single glass. All basic enough to have been from anywhere. I moved on.

A canvas rested against her bed, not tucked away this time. I approached, flipping it around.

The canvas was painted.

Dhalia stood in the heart of Illusion Point, facing the thrones of the queens. King Ulther lurked behind her. Charred black singed the hem of her dress—a bitter reminder of the fire that had just claimed Morten's life—and rage still danced in her eyes.

King Ulther had told her he could save her, and it had to be on Illusion Point. That was what led me here, to Mother.

I glanced up to find her watching me. "It's the last painting," she said. "Brock was going to send it later today, but he already helped place the vision inside."

"I get to know the end of Dhalia's story?" It almost didn't feel real. I'd wanted the ending since the first painting arrived.

"In a way, you already know it," she replied. "But yes. It ends on Illusion Point."

"With a chess match?"

Her gaze darkened. "They use the island for another purpose. Marriage."

Marriage. I stared at the painting.

"Go on. We will be right here."

Cal was asking a question, but I didn't hear. I reached for Dhalia and entered her world.

The temperature change usually struck me first, but this time it was her anger. It fueled her. It seared her every thought until I struggled to keep it from mine. I felt it seep into my own emotions. Burning me.

"Dhalia."

She balled her fists at King Ulther's voice. "I will not do this."

"Morten found the only way for a Mortal Queen to live is to marry a fae king, reinstating the marriage that was broken long ago. He couldn't save you because he wasn't a king. Yet he was going to steal you away anyway."

What had he just said? I tried to process through the blinding anger coming from Dhalia.

A queen can survive by marrying a fae king.

The king is the key.

Cottia told me that. I'd used it to find the key to save Mother. But . . . Cottia came thousands of years before my mother was trapped. She couldn't have been talking about that. She had to mean something else.

The king is the key.

Mother told me what this realm valued most of all—marriage. The ultimate alliance. But mortals ruined that when they killed the first Mortal Queen out of jealousy, then evacuated the land to leave the fae to their fate.

The answer seemed too simple. There had to be a trick, or a

trap, waiting somewhere. With centuries of queens bound to this fate, this should have been easily discovered by now.

I didn't know when Dhalia's story took place, but if the answer was known, then why—

"Dhalia," King Ulther said, but his tone wasn't demanding. It was begging. "Marry me, and you will live."

"No."

"Do you want to die? My Queen, you have one year left until your death. You have the chance to live a full life." He walked around the chessboard to be near her, but she moved also, keeping the board between them.

"How could I marry you when you killed Morten? How could I live here when I hate this realm? I would rather die than stay here." From inside Dhalia's mind, I could tell she meant that.

King Ulther looked like he was steadying himself. "You will die. I guarantee that. If you don't marry me, you will die. Every other king is already married! You have no choice!"

"No!"

"When a girl says no, that means no," a smooth voice said. Dhalia glanced up, allowing me to see when my father in all his glory arrived. A surge of fear shot through Dhalia, but all I felt was wonder.

He appeared even more majestic than his portraits. Stunning white hair, pale blue eyes, and a crown of white antlers on his head. His presence made the tension in the air change, and Ulther shifted nervously. "You have returned," he said. "Where were you?"

Returned? So this wasn't my father during his glory days. He'd been missing already.

Father tapped a note in his hand. "A friend wrote me a letter, and another let me back in the realm."

King Ulther paled. "You have been in the mortal realm?"

Father paid him no mind. "Are you Dhalia?" His chariot set down and he stepped off, letting a fair distance remain between him and the Mortal Queen. She nodded, but her defenses were up. She lifted her chin.

"Who are you?"

"I am King Thelonius, but I don't fault you for not knowing that," he said with a slight smile. "I left this realm a few hundred years ago."

A few hundred years?

Interesting. That meant Dhalia was queen not too long ago. The visions were far more recent than I'd guessed.

He offered the note to her. "Morten wrote me. Is he here?"

She took the note and devoured it quickly, and I read along with her.

> *I have a request of you and shall forever be in your debt for it. I have fallen in love with a queen but cannot save her on my own. However, I've been studying the journal you left me, and I believe if you marry her, she will live. I know you care not for this world, but would you take a bride for me?*

Dhalia's stomach tightened. The hand holding the note shook. "He wanted you to marry me?"

"What?" King Ulther leapt forward to snatch the note away.

"We would not live here. I would take you back to the mortal realm, where we could live out the rest of our days."

"I could be reunited with my family?" A whisper of excitement breathed within her.

But my father winced. "It would be wiser to change your identity. I can conceal your true face from those who see it and give you a new name. We would draw too much attention as a fae king and a living Mortal Queen otherwise, and it would cause a multitude of problems."

King Ulther was protesting, urging Dhalia not to listen.

Dhalia's attention remained on my father. "But I'd live?"

"Yes. Just as Morten intends."

Dhalia's emotions weren't filled with love or excitement or

wonder, but a deep resolve settled in her heart, knowing Morten had planned this. She put her hand in my father's. "For Morten, then."

Father regarded her for a moment, and I wondered if he could see in her eyes that Morten was gone. If so, he didn't press, he simply gestured to the chariot. "Climb aboard. The path won't remain open for long."

As soon as Dhalia's foot stepped on the chariot, Ulther lunged for her. "It was meant to be me! I was meant to have the glory of saving a queen!"

Father grabbed his tunic to yank him back and received a swift punch to the face.

"You cannot swoop in and take all the credit," King Ulther growled. "Do you know how long I've been planning this?" He threw another punch, and my father ducked.

The brutish form of fistfighting had never appealed to me, but when fae kings fought, it was something else entirely. Each punch landed with the magnitude of a thunderclap, and each strike echoed through the skies. One hit would kill a mortal. The kings exchanged blows, but Father's knees began to bend with weakness, and fear crept through Dhalia.

"Did you care at all about your queen, or only your own glory?" Father challenged. He tried to end the fight by moving for the chariot, but Ulther grabbed him by the collar and hit him square in the face.

Blood seeped from Father's nose as he pushed Ulther away, swinging a leg to bring Ulther's feet out from under him, sending him to the ground. Father left him there and strode swiftly toward Dhalia and the chariot, ignorant as Ulther regained his feet.

Dhalia shouted a warning.

Father turned too late. Ulther had drawn a sword and held it at Father's chest.

"Give back the girl."

"She is not for sale."

Ulther pressed the blade forward, and Father's body hunched. It was leaving a scar. I knew because I'd seen that scar.

"Ulther, you don't want to kill me." As Father spoke, he moved his elbows inward, brushing back his cloak to reveal a dagger at his side. "Think of all we've been through."

"I'll get over it." Ulther's tone was deadly.

Father twisted, making the dagger obvious to Dhalia from where she stood behind him. She slowly stretched her hand.

"Do you even love her?" Father asked.

"This isn't about love for you, either," Ulther said. "You want the glory as much as I do. One of us will be the one to claim we wed a mortal, and it won't be you. She shall be *my* trophy—"

He staggered. Dhalia had taken the dagger and flung it with enough accuracy to strike his chest.

We were from the center island. We knew how to strike true.

The moment Ulther dropped his blade, Father stepped onto the chariot. "We need to go."

Ulther placed a hand to his heart, drawing it out. The knife protruded from within it. His head turned upward, looking at Dhalia with something inexpressible in his eyes, then the glass shattered.

As the pieces fell, so did he.

Dhalia covered her mouth with her hands and collapsed to her knees on the chariot. "What have I done?" Regret slammed into her, and I felt it as her stomach rolled.

"You did what needed to be done."

She shook her head violently. "No. He's a king. I'm . . . I'm only mortal."

"You are a Mortal Queen," Father corrected. "You rank above us all. A blow from you is lethal to anyone." The explanation provided no relief. I still felt the horror surging through her, making her vision darken. Father stepped close. "You are the only one who could have saved us both. I thank you."

Dhalia nodded, eyes blinded with tears.

"Are you ready to see your land again?" Father didn't comfort her in any physical or emotional way. Instead, he simply waited until she managed to nod. "Good. First, you'll need a new name."

She gave Ulther a lingering look, then shut her eyes tight.

"Might I suggest one?" Father asked.

"Please do." Her voice was fragile. "I can't think."

"Della."

There were times in the fae realm when I'd prided myself on being bright. But this was the daftest I'd felt since arriving, because it should not have taken me so long to realize who Dhalia was. The moment my father arrived, asking to marry her, I should have known.

Dhalia was no stranger. She was my mother.

"Della," she tried out the name. "Yes. That will work."

"And where is Morten?"

She crumpled inside. "He won't be joining us. Please, just take me home."

Father didn't ask more questions. He retrieved the note from Ulther's hand and left the dead king behind as he took my mother away. The vision left me behind as well, standing in my own skin for the first time, watching them leave. Dhalia's mask floated to the ground. She'd been freed.

They disappeared, and I was sent back to the cold cell beneath the island, where Cal and Mother watched me.

My frigid fingers released the canvas. I looked at Mother differently now. I saw the scared girl making deals with kings. I saw the love she had for Morten. I saw her pain at losing him.

"You were the queen who survived?" I breathed the words.

"I was. After this, your father and I began our life in the mortal realm."

"But how? All those stories you told us of the fae realm . . . You adored it. How could you, if you'd gone through all that?"

She drew a long breath, gazing off like my childhood rested there somewhere. "I told you those stories to rewrite my own past. By sharing the good, it helped me forget the bad. And seeing your joy, it helped the pain fade. I'm grateful for each and every story I told you."

I'd assumed she was guessing like everyone else. She truly knew. I looked again at the painting. "When was this?"

"That took place about twenty-five years ago. I am not immortal,

Thea. I will still die a mortal death, simply not as one of the Mortal Queens. The ironic part is that I ended up back in this realm anyway."

"Because of me." Then something hit me. I'd assumed someone arranged for me to become a Mortal Queen as retribution for something my father had done, but it wasn't his ties to the realm that caused this. It was my mother's. The Mortal Queen who cheated death. "I am here serving out your sentence."

Her eyes saddened. "I believe so, but I don't know who called you. King Ulther died that day, and I had no further enemies. When your father and I received the note in the mortal realm, claiming you'd one day be stolen by the fae, we worked relentlessly to figure out who wanted you. But we knew of no one. I came here right away to find out, but you know how that worked for me." She gestured to the chain.

Something else occurred to me then. It had been bothering me how Father and Mother unlocked the gate to the bridge when they stood on the same side of it—not opposite sides. Now I had a theory. The gate didn't open for their marriage. It opened because my mother belonged to the fae now, and the realm wanted her back. It was greedy with its queens, keeping us trapped here and only ever letting one escape. When she showed up to the bridge, it didn't open because of any union—it was claiming her once more.

This time, she might not escape.

"We don't know that your imprisonment is because of anything you did as a Mortal Queen." Cal was following everything with impressive speed. Or Mother had explained while I was in the vision. I still couldn't get over the fact that the girl I'd been studying for a year was my mother. She did bear some resemblance to Dhalia. Father had changed her eyes and the shape of her jaw, but the smile and nose were the same. "This could still be someone getting back at Father. I'd like to know why Eliza was dragged into it, though."

"There's a chance that was simply poor luck," I said. "I saw her name on the parchment."

"No," Cal said decisively. "We were married. Her name shouldn't have been in the bowl."

It wasn't the time to consider technicalities of paperwork that was never filed, especially when he could be right—Eliza might be another part of this puzzle, though I didn't see how. But at least now I knew how I fit. The daughter of the missing fae king and the only surviving Mortal Queen.

"So, if I marry a fae king," I ventured, "I will live?"

Mother took my hands in hers. "Yes. I had the hope that by the time you received the final message, you'd have forged enough friendships to secure a marriage to a king."

My stomach soured at the thought of a forced marriage. Mother and Father turned out happy enough, but I'd seen the way she was with Morten. She didn't have that with Father.

"From what Brock told me, this shouldn't be a problem for you," she added lightly.

I wondered if she meant Bash or Thorn.

"It won't be," Cal put in.

I shot him a look, then turned back to my mother. "But would I have to leave this realm like you did?"

Mother flinched. It took me a moment to remember her words. *I'd rather die than stay in this realm.* "You don't want to go home?"

I spoke carefully. "I've grown fond of this one."

"But she hasn't made up her mind," Cal said, sending me a look that said not to upset Mother. "Ask Bash to marry you. Or the other one. Either of them would do it."

I thought of Bash. If I married someone, it wouldn't be to save my own skin. I needed more than that. "Regardless of if I can convince a king to marry me, I have other problems. It's not so much the question of where I'll live, though I'm guessing the ambassador helped Father travel between realms, and none of the ambassadors feel such sentiment for me. But what you did, it didn't save the queens to come. I want to save all of us."

Cal groaned. "Thea has developed a hero complex since arriving here."

"Thea has developed *morals*," I corrected.

Mother examined me as if I were a puzzle she couldn't understand, while Cal was looking at me as if he understood the puzzle, he just didn't like the answer. Mother reached for my cheek. "I appreciate that you have morals. I really do. But these morals will mean nothing if you're dead."

She was wrong. *That's when they mean the most.*

"I can't walk away. Besides, Eliza can't marry a fae king, since she's already married. If I find a way to save everyone, that includes her."

That, at least, got Cal's attention.

"Those paintings I sent you were only for your salvation," Mother said. "Not the salvation of all." Then, as if her mind was made up, she stepped back, throwing a blanket over the painting to hide the image of her from a time gone by. "I'm sorry, Thea. I don't think it's possible to save everyone. Some fates cannot be undone."

She had to be wrong. There was a way—I knew it as surely as I knew my own name. But how could I explain that to her, when she had experienced the worst of this realm? Or to Cal, when he saw a realm threatening to kill his wife and his sister? They saw death. But I saw differently.

"When I look at the fae realm, I see so much possibility. I see thriving people, kind friendships, and a joy they haven't felt in centuries. I see everything it can be, including a land for both fae and mortals to live in harmony. I don't believe it's too late for that to be restored. We lived together in bliss once. We can do so again."

"Would you bet your life on it?" Mother asked.

"I already am."

36

A LETTER WAITED FOR US WHEN
Cal and I returned to the palace. It was lined with gold threads and
the unmistakable insignia of a broken heart with a serrated slash
through the center. Talen held it in the courtyard as hundreds of fae
surrounded him, whispering behind their hands. A palpable energy
thrummed through the air, centering on the letter. He extended it
to me.

I hesitated before taking hold.

"It came for everyone in the game, which now includes you,"
Talen said, giving Cal a dangerous look as he passed him a second
note. Sweat lined his brow, though it wasn't warm out. His own
opened letter sat in his pocket. Eliza stood behind his shoulder,
clutching hers.

I undid the seal.

BRING YOUR HEARTS.
LET'S GO TO WAR.

Cal and I looked at each other. I swallowed hard. The fabled
game was on again, and this time, we were the players. Bash's

words came to mind: *Wouldn't you play? If you knew all you had to do was get through a maze, and you'd have the one thing your heart wanted most, wouldn't you risk it?*

And my reply: *I would.*

Now it seemed I had no choice.

I lifted my eyes to find fear in everyone else's and uttered the words softly, as if spoken loud enough, they could bring the palace down.

"The War of Hearts."

37

THE CHARIOTS KNEW WHERE TO
go, though I debated asking mine to take me anywhere else instead.
I'd changed into a dress of red velvet and cream trim, with pointed
shoes and a confident smile that I completely faked. Cal and Eliza
took their own chariot, while Talen rode with me.

"I'm going to do it," he announced. He wore a white suit to
match his hair and a frown that said he hated every moment of this.
His gaze darted to each side, and I couldn't tell if he was trying to
figure out where we were, or if he already knew and detested the
answer. This was the first time he'd spoken in the half hour since
we'd left.

"You're going to bet your heart?" I'd been debating the same
thing, though there was one little problem—Eliza, Cal, and I couldn't
remove our hearts like everyone else. To further complicate things,
by admitting he couldn't remove his heart, Cal would be revealed
as mortal. The only solution would be for him to bow out of the
game. As for me, I didn't see a way I could be eligible. But it didn't
surprise me that Talen would play.

Would I bet my heart if I could? Likely so. Bash had said the
War of Hearts offered the heart's greatest desire, and mine was to

save all future queens. That was worth betting my heart a million times over.

"No." Talen waved a hand. "Well, probably. But I'm going to do as you suggested. I'm leaving with Odette. I've already resigned from my promotion as Head of Delvers and made plans for where we shall live. We will stay long enough for your reign to end—with you still living, of course—then we will depart for our new home."

He said it plainly, but I knew leaving everything behind wasn't easy for him. It was like asking a painter to set aside their brushes. "I'm glad for you, Talen. I know how difficult it has to be."

"I thought it'd be much harder to leave this all behind. The prestige, the titles—it was all going to my head. Now that the decision is made, I sleep better."

"You're going to have such a beautiful life," I told him. Truthfully, the image of them in a quiet town raising chickens and tending farmland didn't come naturally. But the idea of it was a tender one, filled with a life of meaningful relationships, away from trickery and manipulation. They'd grow into it, and when I needed a break from all this, I'd have a place to go. "I'll visit you."

"We'll build a room just for you, so you must come often."

Before I could promise I would, the skies changed. Stars peeled from their positions, aligning to form a path for the chariots to glide upon. High above, more stars twisted to create the words "Welcome to the War of Hearts."

My own heart faltered. Talen blanched.

"She shouldn't be able to do this," he muttered to himself.

"Only kings can move the stars," I recalled.

Talen's voice was on edge, apprehensive. "Since she appeared, I'd assumed her to be a charlatan of sorts, putting on a fun charade for entertainment. But to do this? She's far more powerful than any of us guessed, and that makes her the most dangerous person in the realm right now."

Fright wound a tight spool in my throat, making it hard to breath around. But relief also took root. The worst way for this to end would be the Gamemaster declaring it had all been a joke and she didn't have the signet ring. This display of power proved she was someone powerful enough to find a ring. Or powerful enough to take us all out as we hunted for it.

"And we are walking straight into her game."

I searched for Cal and Eliza's chariot, finding it not far ahead of us on the starry path. The chariots must have coordinated somehow, because we were all arriving at the same time, Thorn behind us, and Bash three chariots back. Troi stood at his side, his fierce protector. Good. I wanted him as safe as possible.

I faced forward as we came upon a small island, made entirely of a labyrinth. Stone walls and hedges created a maze one could get lost in for a year. I studied every detail, trying to memorize the twists and turns and dead ends and which paths led out. A futile effort. Months of study could not commit a maze of this caliber to memory.

"What happens to those who don't make it out?" I asked.

"I don't know," Talen confessed. "But I've never seen a maze of this grandeur."

"Still think you'll play?"

His voice came out sounding distant, like he was in a daze. "I think none of us will resist this."

It might be more of the Gamemaster's power at work, but something intrigued me about the layout before us, making it seem impossible to say no. I had to enter. I had to know what was inside. I had to play. I knew as soon as I stepped foot in that courtyard, I wouldn't be strong enough to not play.

With difficulty, I tore my eyes downward, focusing on the laces of my sandals. The urge subsided enough that it no longer overpowered me but remained more like a throb in my mind. Pulling me back to that labyrinth.

"If the power means nothing to you, why do you play?" I asked Talen.

"I play for you, my Queen. Because when I succeed, you succeed. Any power I gain goes to you."

The starlit path lowered to the center of the maze, finding a circular courtyard with stone of black and torches burning orange. Gargoyles sat upon pillars, each facing inward, baring sharp teeth of obsidian, and ruby red eyes flashing against the light. As we descended, it was as if we were falling into the cave of their teeth, where they would devour us all.

There wasn't enough room for the chariots to remain, so one by one they deposited us, then took off—leaving us stranded.

Everyone left a spot in the very middle, silently agreeing that would be where the Gamemaster made her appearance. We were correct. In a poof of black smoke and purple glitter, she presented herself. She wore a slender gown of deep green and gray, matching the labyrinth. Her presence always commanded the room, but today the labyrinth stole the show, with every figure swiveling to take it in, as if we could plot a way through by studying the entrances.

Five doorways stood with pillared gates of gilded architraves. Carved images jutted out from them, depictions of kings and queens. Perhaps ones who had entered here before. Perhaps some who still roamed within, looking for their lost hearts. I willed the thought away.

"Welcome, kings and queens and lords. And a new player whom I've invited to join us." She stretched an arm toward Cal. "Your name, sire?"

"I am called the Dashing Suitor."

I waited for her to press him, but she didn't. "Very well," she said and then spread her arms in that way she always did, her smile spreading as well. "Welcome to my game."

"The War of Hearts is outlawed," King Vern spoke loudly.

Her expression remained unchanged. "Then don't play."

His mouth shut. He would play. I could only fear what King Vern's greatest desire was.

What was Thorn's greatest desire? He wanted the power of the seventh king, but did he want that above all else? From what I knew of him and what he'd told me, he wanted to be a strong king who brought honor to his kingdom. He'd admitted he would cross me if it was for the good of his people. But what did that mean if someone gave him a wish? How would he use it?

My mind wandered to Bash. What did he want? Me, thankfully. But was saving me his greatest desire, or bringing his lands back to glory? His reign had been a tentative one since stealing the throne from his father, and I hadn't helped matters. If given the choice, would he choose my survival or his own glory? Was it selfish to wish he'd pick me?

Time would tell what he selected, because from the intent way in which he watched the Gamemaster, he wasn't turning down her offer.

"The rules are changed for this. I will not be offering your heart's greatest desire, because I already offer the power of the seventh king."

A murmur went through our group. The Gamemaster raised a hand to silence us. "However, you will not die if you fail. Lower reward, lower risk. I feel that is a fair trade. Your heart, though you may lose it, will remain intact."

A weight lifted from my chest. None of us would die today.

"The concept remains the same, however. Your heart is your entrance ticket. You have twenty-four hours to find it again and get out. Only the clever will continue in this game."

Twenty-four hours sounded like a fair amount of time, but in a labyrinth this size—it was like telling someone they had two seconds to ascend a triple flight of stairs. We would all try, but the odds were against us.

The fae were already reaching into their chests to hand over their hearts. I tried not to look at the cracks on Bash's when he did so. He placed himself opposite of me, keeping the appropriate distance to continue our charade. Thorn, however, kept to my side.

At last, it was just me, Cal, and Eliza who had not offered hearts.

Cal stepped forward. "I wish to remove myself from the game."

A ripple ran through the fae. "So soon?" the Gamemaster asked. "From what I hear, you love games."

"I have removed myself from the game. I will not play," Cal repeated, his voice firm and even.

Eliza spoke up. "I would like to remove myself as well."

Now I joined in the shock. But Eliza's expression didn't waver.

"Very well," the Gamemaster said. Her gaze wafted past them like they were no longer relevant. It landed on me. "And our other Mortal Queen? Do you wish to play?"

"I don't see how I could. As mortals, our hearts are pretty much stuck in our chests."

She looked pleased I'd brought that up. "Your test on cleverness begins now. Offer me something of equal value, and I will accept that instead."

"Like what?"

She tilted her head. "I can't do the work for you."

I tried to think. I could draw her a painting as I'd done for other fae, but compared to hearts, that seemed trivial. The only physical object I valued in this realm was the Antonio solder toy from Malcom. But I'd rather give up a glass heart than risk losing that.

Information, however, I had in abundance. But none of that could be reclaimed once given.

Thorn spoke up. "I will offer something for her. If I fail to find my heart, you can crush it."

I whirled around. "Thorn, no! That price is too high!"

But the Gamemaster was already nodding. "That would be acceptable."

"No." I spun back to her. "I have a soldier toy that is important to me. You can take that." But even as I said the words, I knew it wasn't enough.

"The price is already set. You are in the game. If either you or King Thorn find his heart, and you both make it back out, you both continue in the game." As she spoke, a chill ran through me that I'd just signed a contract I wasn't willing to fulfill. She went on, looking directly at me. "Besides, I very much suspect your heart is already in the game."

She cast a look toward Bash that was not subtle at all, and heat warmed my cheeks. She knew. And she was right. With Bash's heart in the game, my heart was at risk.

She lifted her hand and, all at once, the glass hearts disappeared from around her feet. "The War of Hearts has begun. Your time starts now." In another cloud of smoke, she disappeared, and the fae darted into the maze from all sides.

Bash's eyes met mine briefly before he ran into the labyrinth. Troi watched him go, then took a deep sigh. She had not bet her heart, for she was not a part of this game. Instead, she lifted an arm clad in white armor, and a chariot landed for her. I suspected she'd remain in the sky, watching us play.

Thorn tapped my arm, making me jump. "Can you whistle?"

My full attention went to him. "How could you offer to have your heart crushed?" Between me showing him my true face, and him offering to crush his heart for me, the amount of favor he was building added up. I suspected I wouldn't like the payout.

"What's done is done. Can you whistle? I say we split up and whistle if one of us finds my heart."

"What does it look like?" I asked. I'd seen Bash's heart once, but I wasn't certain I'd even know his heart if I saw it. Thorn's? I'd be guessing blindly.

"There's something about the hearts. You just know. Now, I ask again. Can you whistle?"

"Yes."

"Loudly?" Every bit of him was in motion—feet shifting, hands fidgeting, eyes darting between the labyrinth paths. Eager to begin.

"I'll keep whistling until I hear your reply, so I know you heard it," I promised.

"Perfect." He took off.

Cal and Eliza remained, their hands already in the air to summon a chariot. One appeared, gliding down to fetch them.

"You don't want to play?" I called out before they could depart. "I would have thought you'd love the Gamemaster's games."

"Oh, I want to play. But we have something else to do." Cal stepped aboard the chariot. "We are freeing Mother."

Suddenly, I couldn't see the labyrinth or feel the weight of the gargoyles' eyes upon me. My heart pounded until I couldn't think. "It's too dangerous," I managed to say.

Eliza climbed next to Cal. "Brock is going to help us, as is Odette. But think about it, whoever trapped her is likely inside that labyrinth at this moment. We can get her while they are occupied. She will have escaped before they know it."

"That's a guess. We don't know if someone in this game is her captor. The odds are—"

"Don't tell me about odds," Cal stopped me. "Odds are all I've thought of since arriving here, and this is what I know. She had a half portion of food left, meant to last two weeks, meaning her captor isn't returning today. The walls had no crevices in them for traps, and the chain could be easily broken. Our best odds at keeping Mother alive are to free her before someone finds out we know, and they kill her because of it."

"Those aren't odds! Those are guesses." I jumped aboard the chariot to force them to stay. With the small space, Cal and I stood close, and I had to tilt my neck to look up at him. "This is Mother's life we speak of. I don't think you should chance it."

"You might be queen, but I do not take orders from you." Cal's dark tone gave me pause.

He and I had always worked together to come to decisions. When to steal food for Malcom. Where to hide money so Father couldn't gamble it away. We survived, day by day, because we had each other. He'd never made a decision without me, nor I without him. Perhaps it was our year apart that stripped that away from us, or perhaps it was the different rules of the realm. Whatever it was, Cal's stance held a defiance I wasn't going to break down.

I sighed and stepped off the chariot.

"Keep him alive," I ordered Eliza. I'd told her something similar when I left for the fae realm the first time. She'd done well. I needed her to do it again. "Keep them both alive."

"I will."

"We will meet you at Brock's home when it's done," Cal said, then he threw a look toward the labyrinth. "Watch your back in there."

"Watch your back out there," I replied.

They took off, leaving me alone in the middle of the courtyard, except only then did I realize I wasn't alone. Troi had never left. She came down off her chariot.

I suspected she had a lecture for me along the lines of staying away from Bash so he didn't get hurt, like I'd heard before. Bash and I were well beyond that, but I did miss my connection with Troi. We had never been close like Odette and I were, but she was someone I trusted, for I knew exactly where her loyalties laid.

This morning, I needed her to waver from them.

"I know you are sworn to protect Bash," I started before she could get in a word. "But I promise to watch out for him in there. Meanwhile, there is someone else who needs your help, and I am shamelessly begging you to consider my request."

One brow raised. "Do you think you can protect my brother better than I can?"

"Since I can enter the labyrinth and you can't, yes."

Her voice edged. "I can protect him from the skies."

Desperation grew within me. All I could think of was Eliza and Cal's chariot gliding away, each moment building my worries.

"I haven't time to argue. Troi, my mother is in this realm, and she's not safe."

There it was. No taking it back now. With those words, I threw my trust upon her to keep the secret and bet on her kindness to go to my brother's aid. I told her the parts that were most important for now. "Someone has trapped her, and Eliza is attempting to free her tonight along with her guard." I kept my brother's identity hidden. "I fear what awaits them."

Troi studied me, then the labyrinth, leaving me to guess her thoughts. "Where is she being held?"

"Beneath the chessboard on Illusion Point. I wouldn't be asking you if I didn't fear for their lives. We have no idea who imprisoned her, nor what awaits them when they attempt to free her."

Her shoulders drew back with resolve, and her finger stretched toward the maze. "You protect the king in there," she said. "And I will protect the queen's mother."

I let out a breath. "Truly?"

She boarded her chariot. "You have a hold over Bastian's heart that I've never seen before. It's clear that to protect him, I must also protect you. You have my word."

Troi had been my saving grace many times through the months of chess and strategy training during my time of captivity last year, but this meant more to me than all of that. And her acceptance of the task felt like an acceptance of me and Bash, which I never thought I'd get from her. She didn't give me another look as she took off. I watched until she was gone and sent out a prayer of hope.

Save her. I will save him.

Then, once more, I faced the labyrinth.

A chill swept over my arms, raising the hairs. It suddenly fell too quiet. Too haunting. Like the hedges could come alive at any moment and devour us all. *Make your pick,* they seemed to say. *Or we will not let you in at all.*

The five paths stared at me. Which way had Thorn gone? Where was Bash? The gargoyles watched me, and I swore they gained wicked smiles. *Which path will you choose?* They taunted me. *The queen must choose wisely or the queen will be dead.*

Leave me alone.

I spun in a slow circle, examining each entrance, focusing on his heart, wishing it would lead me where I wanted to go. "Take me to Bash's heart," I whispered. Then I chose a path and entered the darkness. The labyrinth swallowed me whole.

38

STARS HELD NO POWER HERE. WITH
my first step, their shine disappeared, forcing me to keep my eyes
forward, where glowing marigold flowers peeked from hedges,
giving a soft yellow light to guide the path.

I wished I could have kept track of my trail in my head, but
directions had never been my forte. Instead, I made a mad dash
with my only goal being *far*. I reasoned the hearts wouldn't be
waiting close to the entrance. I kept a general sense of which route
led away and which would bring me back, and rushed onward.

Sometimes the passage was wide enough that an entire chariot
could have fit between the hedges. Other times the sides pressed in,
and I had to turn sideways and shimmy through, my back pressed
against the cool stone walls. There appeared to be no distinction
between which paths held hedges and which held stone, except the
stone ones were darker. I stuck to the glowing marigolds as often
as I could.

But the Gamemaster didn't bring us here to play safe. So the
next time the option presented itself, I chose the dark path of
stone walls.

Heavy breathing came from behind, and I pressed myself
tight against the wall to watch as King Leonard ran past, breaths

heaving, to choose the marigold path. From the desperate way he'd run, he hadn't found his heart.

We'd been given twenty-four hours. Surely no one had found theirs yet.

I wouldn't find anything by continuing to run wild. I sank to my knees and closed my eyes. *Focus*, I told myself. *Think of Bash. Find his heart.*

Everything inside me wanted to keep running. But I forced myself to stay put until I could feel the pull of his heart.

I thought of the first time I met him, how his magnificence had stunned me.

I thought of the day he showed me snow.

And the time he promised to turn me fae so I could stay with him forever.

I thought of our kiss last night.

I thought of the way my heart tumbled every time I saw him.

Then I felt it, the slight pull of a thread, tugging from my chest. It beckoned me farther into the maze, farther into the darkness. But it didn't frighten me. Instead, it felt like it called me home.

My spirits lifted. Bash's heart was calling to me.

Just as I stood, a voice spoke. "It is love that calls to you best, then."

The sound wasn't right. It was grating rocks and the rumble of a mountain.

One of the gargoyles from the entrance stood before me, licking his lips with a stone tongue, a deadly smile aimed at me. The rubies of his eyes glinted. "For other Mortal Queens, it is acceptance, or adoration. But you don't crave those things, do you? You just want him, but you want him badly enough that it blinds you to everything else."

"Who are you?" I reached down, but I hadn't carried a dagger in months. I had nothing but my fists, which would surely bleed if I punched pure rock. Worth a try, though.

The gargoyle circled me, his hunched body hopping from place to place. Fangs stuck out from his mouth, and small wings protruded from his back. His claws were gossamer gold, as shiny as they were sharp. "I am love. Or rather, that is what I can offer you. Unending love from the one you want it from most."

"He already loves me," I said, making as if to move past.

The gargoyle hissed, stilling me. "Unending love? For eternity? You are assured of that?"

No, I couldn't be assured of that. But I didn't make deals with gargoyles, and that was what came next. I tried to walk the other way before he could offer something, when he hissed again. I blinked. He'd moved directly in front of me, blocking the way.

"You have nothing to lose and everything to gain. Stay. Stay in this labyrinth for twenty-four hours, then I'll personally guide you out. When you leave, I promise the young king will love you for all eternity."

"I'm not here to play games."

"You want the blond king instead? It's no matter. I can make every single one of them love you."

"No. Let me by."

"I'm not blocking you. You can pass right through me."

Very well, then. I did. I walked right through the gargoyle, my form passing through his. Before I got two steps away, he spoke again.

"How about your father?"

I looked over my shoulder.

His eyes sparkled. "Do you wonder how he feels about you? Does he doubt if you can live up to his legacy as a fae king? If you desire it, I can make him proud."

"I don't need his approval badly enough that I'd risk another's life to get it, and that is what's at stake here." I walked away.

"Fine," the gargoyle called to me. "If I cannot tempt you, let's see what my brothers can do."

I feared what his brothers would do. But not as much as I feared what would happen if twenty-four hours ended and Bash's or Thorn's heart was still in here.

I reconnected to the thread pulling me toward Bash and I ran.

The walls grew taller the deeper I went, sometimes arching over to form a ceiling, with each new height ebbing away at my idea to scale the walls. I closed my eyes to focus on that feeling inside, telling me where to go to find the heart I desired. It might not lead me there. It could be nothing but a trick of my mind. But right now, this feeling was all I had. So I followed.

I heard nothing but the sound of my own footsteps as I walked. The labyrinth stretched for miles in each direction, so the odds now of finding someone else were low. Did the Gamemaster know where everyone was? Did she watch us as we played her twisted game? Or had she taken the hearts and run?

My mind jolted at that. No one would leave this labyrinth until they'd found their heart. And if she hadn't put their hearts in here, she'd just trapped five of the kings and several lords for twenty-four hours, leaving undisrupted access to the realm in our absence.

The ground changed beneath my feet, moss hardening into crudely cut cobblestone to create a path forward, where a glimmer of light appeared. A shining doorway of yellow and white shimmered like a deadly invitation, promising me torrid love affairs or immaculate beauty or a pool of unending wealth. The promise changed each second. But one thing remained.

The pull toward Bash's heart led me to the door.

My hand rested on the sparkly doorknob. I could stand there all day, looking for my courage, but it was my curiosity that pushed me over the threshold.

A surge of heat took hold, setting fire to my skin. Then it was gone, replaced with a chill. I stood in a small, circular courtyard with tall hedges surrounding it, only breaking for three doors—one bronze like the shine of a coin, one red like heartbreak, and one a deep purple like the malicious curl of desire. The doors all had silver knobs with gilded keyholes, and no keys in sight.

As I gaped, a creature appeared—a larger gargoyle than the first, with a slice of a smile on his lips as if he'd long waited for this day. On instinct, I stepped away. My back hit the prickly side of a hedge, but that shouldn't be right. I'd entered from that way.

I turned. The doorway behind me had transformed into a firm hedge. I was trapped, with only the three doors before me as exits.

"Let me guess, I have to choose the right one?"

The gargoyle's smile deepened, revealing sharp teeth. "They say you are the smartest queen of the century."

"Two wrong doors, one right one?"

But the gargoyle tsked his tongue. "All right doors."

"All right doors?" I asked. "What do you mean?"

"It depends on what you seek," he replied in a grating voice. "One door guarantees happiness for the rest of your life, free from heartbreak. One door promises to make your family whole. The third door is the heart you seek."

Free from heartbreak, gain my family, or find Bash's heart. I couldn't pick a bad door.

"To make it easier, I'll even tell you which is which. The king's heart is behind the red door, and I suspect he will be very grateful for you finding it." He had the audacity to wink, as if we were old friends. We might be, if he gave me Bash's heart. I liked this brother much more than the first. "Happiness is behind the purple door. The promise to piece together your entire family is behind the bronze door."

"How would you reunite us?"

He tsked again. "I don't answer specifics, but you have my word that if you walk through that door, your entire family shall live together in peace again."

I studied the doors, already knowing which I would pick. The other two were nice, but I came for the heart. The gargoyle held up a key, and I took hold, reaching for the red door. Before the lock turned, he spoke.

"One catch."

I froze.

"Whatever door you open, the other two will remain forever closed to you. By selecting one, you guarantee the other two never come to pass."

The key slid from my hand to clatter on the ground. "If I pick the king's heart, my family will never be rejoined?"

"Those are the rules."

I changed my mind. I liked this brother far less than the first. "I didn't agree to bargain those things."

"You agreed the moment you stepped foot into the labyrinth. Make your choice."

I thought hard. A life of happiness, free from heartbreak, sounded fantastic. But it would be without Bash's heart and without my family being whole. Without those things, I couldn't have true happiness, only the byproduct of the gargoyle's magic. My happiness wouldn't be genuine. On the other hand, if I didn't pick the purple door, it guaranteed heartbreak waited in my future.

For a fleeting moment, I thought it might be best to allow the gargoyle to numb my feelings and grant me eternal happiness.

I passed over the thought. The other two doors were far more important.

If I walked away from Bash's heart, he might never find it in time. And if he knew I had the chance to collect his heart and didn't take it—that might crack it further and hurt my own.

But my family.

To have my parents and my brothers with me, all in one place, that would mean everything. And Bash might find his heart on his own. Recently, it felt as if I were singlehandedly trying to bring the pieces of my family together again, and to have the certainty that it would work would be a relief. I loved Bash, but I needed my family.

"I've made my selection," I whispered, picking up the key once more. I moved it to the door I thought I wanted, but my heart twisted in my chest. This wasn't the right one.

I could live with myself if I never saw my entire family again. I couldn't live with myself if something happened to Bash's heart and he died. Before I could change my mind again, I plunged the key into the silver lock and opened the red door.

A heart sat on a pedestal inside, beneath a glass cloche. My rembling fingers reached for it. I'd found Bash's heart. He would be safe. I removed the cloche and—

"No," I uttered in disbelief. The success I'd felt ebbed away, leaving behind horror. "That's not his heart."

I snatched it, sending the cloche to the ground in shards as I clutched the glass heart close. This heart had too many cracks to be Bash's. I whirled around. "Whose heart is this?"

"King Thorn's, the one whose heart you said you would look for," the gargoyle said with a cruel grin. He had to know that wasn't the heart I searched for. He'd tricked me.

"You lied to me. You knew I wanted Bash's heart."

He tugged the key from the lock and pocketed it. "Believe me, you don't want to make an enemy of King Thorn. This is the heart you should have found."

"But it wasn't the one I wanted!" I shouted, tears in my eyes. I would have searched for Thorn's heart as soon as I'd secured Bash's. "You must show me the way to Bash's heart!"

The gargoyle snapped his stone claw and the doors disappeared. "The young king is too far away to help now." Another snap, and the walls of the hedge opened to create a pathway the direction I'd come from. "You'd better run. It is almost midday, and you need to escape the labyrinth."

I would run, but not to leave. Holding the heart near, I darted down the path, still close enough to hear the gargoyle's haunting final words.

"I hope you are happy with what you just gave up. Heartbreak waits for you, and you shall never rejoin your family again."

I was done with labyrinths and gargoyles and games that played with hearts. No matter how many times I played, I always seemed to lose.

39

I WHISTLED AS I RAN. A HIGH-
pitched noise that I hoped Thorn heard. *Leave the labyrinth, I have
your heart.* Until he whistled back, he hadn't heard me.

Then I heard it, a faint whistle. He knew I had his heart. Now
to get it out of this labyrinth. I did my best to trace a path, turning
down alleys I thought were familiar and finding others I'd never
seen before. As long as I didn't run into any more gargoyles I'd
be fine. Half an hour passed. Then an hour. I grew more frantic.
I hadn't taken this long coming in. Did I miss a turn? Was the
courtyard the other way now?

I whistled again.

I heard Thorn's echo of a reply, but he was in the opposite
direction from before. Closer, but somehow behind me.

I turned. I must have passed it.

Thorn whistled again. Then he shouted. "Thea?"

"I'm here!"

"Keep shouting! I'll find you!"

I did, and it wasn't long before Thorn swung around the corner,
his shirt unbuttoned and his hair tousled like he'd been in a fighting
ring. His gaze settled on the heart in my hands. "Thank you, my
Queen. Where was it?"

"Behind a red door," I said, carefully holding it out. He took the heart and pushed it back inside his chest.

"Much better. Now, about getting out of here . . . how wide are these walls?" Thorn stretched out his arms. Before I could reply, he said, "This will do." He flung up a hand.

"What are you doing?"

"This, my dear, is called cheating."

A few moments later, his chariot appeared, barely fitting between the walls of the labyrinth. "Clercy, my wonderful chariot. Take us to the courtyard, please," Thorn commanded. I didn't argue before stepping on. The chariot lifted us up and I tried to spot anyone else inside the labyrinth, but the paths remained too dark to see. I could see the courtyard, however, a short distance away.

The chariot, apparently named Clercy, beelined for it. We were the first to escape the maze, if this could be called escaping. As we stepped off, Thorn gave the chariot a good pat. Then he removed his heart and set it on the chariot. "Take this to its usual place, and have Saoirse make us some food, if you don't mind."

The chariot took off.

"Smart thinking," I said. "I'm starving."

"They don't call me the wise king for nothing."

I had to smile. "I've never heard anyone call you that."

He looked stricken. "Why must you do that?"

"Sorry. You are a very wise king."

"Ah, see? People saying it all the time."

I smiled again, then my expression sobered. Thorn nodded like he knew what was coming. He lifted his hand. "Go, if you must."

"I have to find him. I promise to be out before the time runs up. I'll whistle if I need to, and your sound can help guide me here."

He didn't say more, so I turned.

"Thea, wait." For a moment, I thought he was going to try to talk me out of it, or worse, use the knowledge of my true face to command me to stay, but instead he said, "Thank you for finding my heart first. I know we aren't close like you and Bastian are, but your friendship means much to me, and I appreciate the gesture more than words can say."

Guilt ate at me, but I managed to nod. "Of course. Try not to lose your heart again."

"I'll do my best."

I faced away to enter the labyrinth and chose a new direction. I started off—

And slammed into something.

I tried again and again, but something held fast like an invisible door, blocking me from entering the labyrinth. I tried another entrance. Then another. All of them remained blocked. "I don't understand," I said in frustration. "Why won't it let me through?"

"The game must be over for you," Thorn ventured. "You bargained, you played, and you got out. It won't let you play again."

"But I wasn't ready to leave yet." I banged my hand repeatedly against the wall. "You must let me through."

"Try saying please," Thorn commented.

I spun on him. "This isn't funny."

"I'm sorry, you are right. But you must trust that Bastian is clever enough to find his heart on his own."

"You needed help." I poured out my frustration on him. "What were you doing anyway? You look like you've come back from a war."

"I was fighting a gargoyle who said he could fight me or he'd go find you. As it turns out, you are my weakness. I fought him for an hour to keep you safe."

I shut my mouth.

Thorn did not. "But, by all means, risk my heart by going back in there when there is nothing you can do for Bastian, because I know he is the only king you care about. And I will stay here and let you, knowing there is nothing I could do to convince you to fight for me like you fight for him."

"Thorn—"

"I don't need an apology, Thea. I need to know you care whether my heart gets crushed, because that is what's at stake if you enter the labyrinth and don't return in time. Bastian will not die if he doesn't make it out. If you don't make it, I do."

"I do care." But I didn't care in the same way that I cared for Bash. And he was right. Bash's life wasn't at stake and his was. I moved away from the wall as if it were my choice—not because the labyrinth wouldn't allow me to return—and stood before him. He bore a cut over his left eyebrow that dripped red. A cut he got while fighting for me. "I don't want you to die, Thorn."

"Thank you." Something caught his attention and he scowled. "Looks like your king made it out anyway."

I whirled. Bash fled the labyrinth, breathing deep. I ran to him. "Are you alright? Do you have your heart?"

He tapped his chest as he nodded. "Your chariot guided me to the courtyard. Good thinking."

"Thanks," Thorn said dourly.

Bash glanced around. "Are we the first ones?"

"So it seems."

Thorn gave us our space, either prompted by his guilt over interrupting us at Eliza's coronation, or he truly was that interested in the pattern of the forsythias growing in the hedges. Either way, we had a moment of privacy, and Bash used it to step close and cup my chin in his hand. Within a heartbeat, his lips were against mine.

The kiss was short, like a stolen moment in time. Too soon he'd pulled away again, leaving behind a warmth that filled the space between us. "I'm glad you're okay," he whispered. "Now, stop looking at me like that or I won't be able to resist kissing you again, and our secret won't be secret anymore."

With difficulty, I averted my gaze. When he said things like that, I almost wanted our secret to be out. I wanted everyone to know that the king who could not love was mine.

But just then, Thorn's chariot returned. Thorn shared the food between the three of us while we exchanged tales of the labyrinth. We were finishing when King Leonard stumbled into the courtyard. King Vern followed later.

After that, no one appeared for what I guessed to be eight

hours. We dozed on the stone ground, waiting for the game to end. Thorn's chariot had fetched blankets, but it did nothing to stop the chill in my heart as I thought about Talen still being out there. Time dwindled down.

In the morning, with a few hours to go, King Arden escaped— the last king in the game.

From there, we waited on the lords. They trickled out slowly, and to my relief, Talen appeared last, without a moment to spare. As soon as he stepped into the courtyard, the Gamemaster appeared.

We'd done it. We all escaped.

She wore the same purple dress and the same cunning smile. "Good morning, kings and queen and lord. I hope you enjoyed my little game."

I was all smiles, thinking we'd won. But some of the men began shifting at her appearance. King Arden especially, wearing a grim frown.

The Gamemaster opened a little scroll and looked it over, her brilliant blue eyes growing more and more delighted. Finally, she clicked it shut. "It appears seven of you did not make it out with your hearts."

The joyous way in which she said that made my stomach drop. Seven? But we all made it out. Seven fae had left without their hearts before time was up?

"I hope whatever the tricksters offered you was worth it. As it is"—the Gamemaster snapped her fingers and the labyrinth disappeared, leaving us on flat, rocky terrain, as if nothing had ever grown there—"I now own your hearts, and I charge a high price for them."

She disappeared, leaving chaos in her wake. Without fail, everyone turned to one another in confusion, asking who didn't get their heart. Pretending to be as flabbergasted as the next person that someone might not have theirs. Seven were lying. Yet I couldn't tell who.

"As fun as this was," Thorn said, stretching his arms, "I have matters to attend to." The moment Thorn tossed up his hand for his chariot, it started a ripple of everyone else doing the same. I knew Thorn had his heart, so it wasn't nerves that led his hand.

He stepped aboard his chariot. "Thank you again, my Queen. My heart and I are indebted to you. Do you require a ride?"

"No, I'll go with Talen," I said, only half paying attention. The other half was counting kings and lords and making guesses. I didn't notice when Thorn departed.

Talen quickly occupied the space Thorn left behind and summoned a chariot.

I whispered to him so others couldn't be privy to my naivety. "I don't understand. Why would anyone leave the labyrinth if they didn't have their heart?"

"To save face," Talen replied, not looking my way. "So no one knows they lost."

I narrowed my eyes. "But you got your heart, right?"

His silence answered. He climbed aboard. "We should see how Queen Eliza fares."

He'd lost his heart? This wasn't the first time since I'd arrived in the realm that Talen had been without his heart, but this time, I feared it would take more than besting King Brock in a chess match to earn it back. What would the Gamemaster require for such an exchange?"

Silently, I stepped beside Talen and let the chariot take us away. I looked down to see Bash again, reminding myself he truly did have his heart and he was safe. He didn't show me his heart, but he left the labyrinth so early, that surely he'd gotten it.

I waited for Talen to tell his tale, but he said nothing. The silence stretched as the air turned cold, and all while Talen stood frustratingly still without a hint of nerves. Either he was unbothered, or he hid his emotions well.

It wasn't until I noted the slight purse of his lips that I took the invitation to pry.

"I can help if you need it."

"I don't think you can." His voice stretched thin.

"Were you were tricked?"

"No. Someone took my heart before I could get there." He stared forward, and I realized his stiff demeanor wasn't disinterest but deep thought. Now that the conversation had begun, he relaxed, running his hands through his hair and leaning against the rails. "I can't guess who, though. If they got my heart, they lost their own. The labyrinth only allows you to leave with one heart."

"How do you know someone took it?"

"The gargoyles appeared to offer me a deal, then abruptly changed their tune by saying I no longer had the chance at my heart. It had been taken already. They can't lie, so it must be true. I only wish I'd gotten out sooner so I could have seen who hid something in the folds of their jackets."

If the Gamemaster didn't have his heart, he couldn't collect it from her. But that meant she possessed the heart of whoever took Talen's. "We must figure out who those seven hearts belong to. One of them has yours. Maybe we can trade for it."

But Talen was already shaking his head. "You won't find a fae who would willingly admit they stole a heart or lost theirs. I suspect demands will follow."

Waiting for demands was as good as giving up. If he waited for demands, he'd prepared to give in to them. I wouldn't. Before I could say so, Talen spoke. "I don't want you involved. You have enough to face as it is. Let me deal with it alone."

"That's not how we work. We solve things together."

"Do you want to talk about your heart? I saw you slip away with Bastian the other night, and he left a note for you the next morning. Does it have something to do with why you showed up without a mask, or do we not talk about that either?"

Now I was silent. Admitting my rekindled relationship with Bash was one thing, but admitting to Talen that Thorn knew my true face felt much worse than him losing his heart. Luckily, he didn't press. "It's over, Thea. I won't get it back until they want me to."

"Can they crush it?"

"I suspect they would have done that by now. Let us hope Cal and Eliza had more favorable luck than we did."

40

ANY HOPE OF ELIZE AND CAL'S
success fled the moment we arrived back at the palace, where
Odette paced nervously beside the river and Cal and Eliza argued
nearby. Mother was nowhere to be seen.

They broke apart as we neared, Eliza wiping her red eyes and
Cal locking his jaw. At some point he'd flung his suit coat to the
ground, leaving his shirt tousled. Eliza didn't appear any more put
together. Odette wrung out her hands, but the way she looked at
Talen made me guess she was more nervous about how the War of
Hearts went than anything that happened with my mother.

She was right to be fearful.

But my focus stuck elsewhere.

"What happened?" I demanded as soon as we landed.

"It wasn't our fault," Cal started, which only fed my fears.
My mind went to all the worst possibilities and kept landing on
Mother is dead.

"She was gone when we got there," Eliza explained. "No traps
were triggered, nothing appeared out of place. But she wasn't there."

My knees buckled, and I struggled to stay upright. I'd lost her
again, and this time I didn't know where to look. I could search for
hundreds of years and still not explore every corner of this realm,

and she could very well be dead before I ever found her. Or I would be. "You never should have tried."

"It's a good thing we did! Otherwise, we wouldn't know she is missing."

"She wouldn't be missing if you hadn't gone after her," I said with certainty based on nothing. Something told me this was because we'd tried to free her. If we hadn't tried, she'd still be safe. Now she'd disappeared, and I'd never reunite my family.

"Between the two of us, we saw her twice," Eliza reminded me. Now that I was falling apart, she'd straightened and wiped her cheeks clean. "Someone probably saw us leave one of those times."

"How did it go with you?" Odette asked, her gaze on Talen.

"Later," he whispered. Odette's expression soured, but Talen schooled his expression into normalcy. "Let's think. Someone on Illusion Point might have seen something. I can ask around."

"I want to go with you," Cal interjected.

"It will make it too obvious that the information is worth something if two are asking. No, I'll go alone. In the meantime, you might receive a letter about her whereabouts, perhaps something with demands."

"You and your demand letters," I sighed.

Odette looked between us. "What does that mean?"

"Nothing." Talen sent a sharp glare my direction. "But that's the best-case scenario, because it means she's alive."

Those words silenced us all. She had to be alive. I'd like to think I'd feel different if she was dead, but all I could cling to was blind hope that my family would still be reunited someday, while ignoring the feeling that the chance for that was gone.

Hadn't I sealed the fate, though, when I chose the red door? The gargoyle said my family would never be whole again. I'd made this come to pass. If I'd chosen differently, would they have found her, alive and well, and freed her?

Movement behind Cal stilled me for a moment before I remembered we'd invited the fae to live in my home. A tall man and slender girl took a slow walk through the courtyard, their arms strung together and eyes on the slabs of cobblestone. Their gazes flicked our way more than a few times. We waited until they'd steered toward the garden to speak again.

"I'm not good at sitting around waiting," Cal said once their steps faded.

I wondered how many fae might be watching us through the windows, and how good fae hearing might be. I whispered, "Neither am I."

Yet it seemed that was all we could do. Wait, as if our mother wasn't in danger. My thoughts were on the fae now, wondering if any had overheard something they shouldn't as they dwelt in the palace. Did they linger behind my door as I told Cal of Mother? Did they know things they shouldn't simply because I forgot they lived here? Cal and Eliza wouldn't have told anyone. I could always trust Talen to hold my secrets, and I'd only told—

Sweat lined my brow.

"Did Troi show up?" I asked.

Cal frowned. "Who is Troi?"

My words came faster then, almost like a plea for them to settle my worries. She had to have been there. I saw her leave for the island. "Troi is Bash's sister. Carries five knives and has wicked aim. She was supposed to help you. Please tell me she showed up."

The alternative was something I didn't want to consider. That she'd made it there first, and she was the reason Mother was missing. That I'd told the wrong person. As confusion set in on each of their faces, my worries turned real. I'd made a mistake.

She only moved on one person's orders.

With that thought, the air turned sultry, crowding along my neck in hot swirls that moved to lodge themselves in my throat.

"Troi never came," Eliza confirmed, her eyes knowing. Knowing exactly what that meant, and exactly what I'd done.

"I understand." I grabbed hold of the chariot again and gave it orders. I'd been tricked again. I'd *trusted* again.

"Where are you going?" Cal called out.

I held the crossbar with both hands. "To fix this," I said. "I'm not waiting around for a demand letter." Tense and my mind a blurry mess, I ordered the chariot forward and it took off.

The breeze as we flew might have tempered me any other day, but now it only seemed to ice the blood in my veins until my heart had hardened by the time we reached Bash's home. Once we'd stopped moving, I was sad to see the breeze go, for the heat returned to flame my cheeks.

The picturesque palace built into stone had always comforted me with its strength, but today it resembled a dark cage rather than a haven. When I stepped into the courtyard, I hesitated.

The last time I came here was to accuse him of betraying me by giving me a bracelet that would siphon power to him. Instead, I discovered I'd cracked his heart. I could be wrong again.

But Bash was the only person I'd told about my mother, and she'd gone missing.

"Thea?"

I looked up. Bash had opened the door to this throne room and stood in the entryway dressed in a crisp taupe shirt with opal buttons.

"Tell me you didn't do it," I begged, vaguely aware that my feet were moving closer to him. If he lied, I wanted to catch it in his eyes. "Tell me you didn't take my mother."

He let the door swing shut behind him, leaving him in the open courtyard with me. Torches burned behind him, coating his expression in shadows that I needed to see through. "Take her?"

"She's gone, Bash. I told you about my mother, then the moment I informed Troi of her location, she went missing. Tell me what I'm supposed to think?"

He stiffened, his eyes growing dark. I took that as confirmation.

"Was this all because of the bracelet? Were you waiting for the moment you could get back at me?"

His silence stretched on as the muscles in his jaw feathered. It only fueled my anger.

"She is my mother, Bash. You've crossed the line. You will tell me where she is this moment."

"What does love mean in the mortal realm?"

My eyes flew wide and I drew back. "What sort of a question is that?"

"What does love mean to you?" he pressed. "Because to me, love is trust. Trust that doesn't easily surrender when doubts come and faith that isn't easily shaken. It is constant and understanding and doesn't break the moment something bad happens. Clearly, love means something different to you if you claim to love me then turn on me as soon as you think you have reason, which you've done twice now."

"You're denying it, then?"

"I shouldn't have to deny anything!" Bash snapped. He'd always been the picture of calm, even when I accused him of trying to siphon power from me. But now that restraint broke. "I would never hurt you by stealing your mother. But I can't understand how you could claim to love me, then blame me for something like that."

"You were the only one I told," I protested. "That can't be a coincidence."

He quieted, and somehow that was worse. The sight of him in the firelight was enough to make my heart jump, but I couldn't close the space between us.

I'd revealed the stolen bracelet.

I'd cracked his heart.

I'd caused him to lose his kingdom.

He had reasons galore to hate me. If I was wrong about this, I'd just delivered another blow to his heart. But he'd forgiven me for all my faults so fast. Too fast, perhaps. And I'd gone along with it because I wanted him so badly. Either he got the best of me . . .

Or he was currently getting the worst of me.

The coldness in his eyes chilled me. "Do you know how I got my heart back from the labyrinth? A gargoyle asked for a secret none of the other kings knew. Do you know what I said?"

I stood motionless, watching him.

"That I love you enough to marry you, mortal or not." He turned, walking the length of the courtyard to stare over the cliffside at the night sky. I remained planted in place, my heart beating fast. "How many times am I supposed to let you break me?" he asked in a dry voice. "How many times do I let my heart crack for you?"

I was the one who was broken. This realm had stripped away my ability to trust. "How am I supposed to know what is real and what isn't when this realm is never as it seems?"

His eyes on me were sober. "You're blaming the realm for your actions?"

Guilt buried itself in my ribs. "All I know is my mother is out there somewhere, dead or alive, and I can't think straight until I find her. I sent Troi after Eliza and she never showed up."

"Troi arrived quietly, knowing how important secrecy was to you. She overheard that Queen Eliza had discovered your mother was missing. Troi returned to inform me she was going out to search and is still out doing so."

"How do I know if that's true?"

"Because that's what love means, Thea. Trust."

My shoulders fell. "Trust doesn't come easily for me."

"Clearly," he said. "Mortal Queens weren't made to withstand our realm."

It was as if those words decided something for him, and he spoke with more determination. "I have too much at stake, Thea. No more coming to me when you are scared. No more asking for help solving puzzles. If this is love to you, then I'm done. You are nothing but a queen who will die and I will move on."

My heart sank. I had accused him of something dreadful—again. I wanted to stay and fight to make this right, but the battle already appeared lost.

Bash set his jaw and turned to the door. It opened before he could reach for it. I'd never seen anyone here other than Bash and Troi, and he claimed she was gone.

An older man with dark skin and white hair stepped out, wearing a golden crown on his head. A heavy robe rested on his shoulders, but he bore the weight as if familiar with it. The features of his face were too similar for him to be anyone other than Bash's father.

I froze.

"Bastian," his father spoke. "Do you remember where those gilded banners are that used to hang in the throne room? I'd very much like to see them hung up again."

"Not while I'm still king."

"What is he doing here?" I asked. *And wearing a crown.*

"If you'll excuse me," Bash said to me, rigidly polite. "I have work to do."

He passed inside the door, and his father gave me an unnerving smile, as if he knew all of my secrets, before following his son.

I wanted to go after Bash. He hadn't told me how brazen his father was about taking his place, and there had to still be something we could do about it. But Bash had moved out of view, leaving his father to take a preemptive seat on the throne, resting one hand over the empty cloche and watching me.

I stood there, staring at the door.

My heart felt too much to cry. Emotions had led me to act rashly, and I'd lost the one thing I wasn't willing to bargain in this realm. Yet all I could think of was the thirteen-year-old girl who woke up to find her mother missing and felt as if her world had been torn away. I was thrust back into that scared child, losing my mother all over again, and I couldn't think right until I found her.

I'd deal with the mess I made along the way later.

41

MY HOME WAS ANNOYINGLY BUSY
when I returned, a party spilling into the courtyard as fae with
goblets and laughter flittered about. I trudged through them,
entering the throne room with my head held low. A chessboard
caught my eye first, with Thorn on one side and a long line of fae
on the other, each waiting in line to play him.

Cal stood in the shadows of the arched stairwell, watching with
hungry eyes as if reading a favorite book for the first time. "It's
fascinating," he whispered to me when I approached. "The line
of fae are citizens of his lands, all asking for something. Some for
more trade ports, some for expansion of their business, others for
grains and wools, and some for things such as permission to move
or for a better home. Whatever they ask, they must play him for it.
The result of the chess match decides their fate. Can you imagine?
Your fate resting on a game of chess?"

I could. It was more than a game here.

"If they are from his lands, they should be asking in his home,
not mine," I grumbled.

At my tone, Cal turned as if pulling himself from a trance. His
face fell. "I take it whatever you set off to do didn't go well?"

"I followed a hunch," I told him miserably. "But I was wrong.

I failed." Dejection clung to the low slope of my shoulders and in the corners of my heavy frown. I tried to keep my head high so the fae didn't see their queen as defeated, but inside felt like it'd been broken too many times to hold together any longer.

"You didn't fail," Cal said, his copper eyes soft. The silver jacket he wore suited him well, making him look years older than he was, and I felt like a child beside him. "You tried. That's not failing. Failing would be if you didn't try at all." He shifted to watch the chess matches again, keeping his voice low so we were not overheard. "Father taught me that."

I didn't remember Father saying those words, but it sounded like something he would say. He'd shared snippets of wisdom often, sometimes unprompted, like the words had just come to him and he needed to share them with us. Like it was urgent that we knew.

"I never realized how much he prepared you for this realm by the way he taught us," Cal said. "But now it makes sense. He trained us hard. Not because he wanted us to fight. He knew we'd Passion elsewhere. He wanted to prepare you to be strong mentally, to know what it feels to be pushed to your limit and to continue on anyway. Did you know he bought me my chessboard with the stipulation that I teach you?"

I shook my head. I didn't know that.

"He did. And he would ask periodically how it was going. I thought he was interested in me, but now I see it was about you. Those were his only sane moments after Mother disappeared— when he would be training us or asking how teaching you went. Like he was coming out of the fog."

The hindsight this realm gave me distorted my memories of home. It changed how I saw my father, twisting it into something that could be called mercy. He was cold and distant because he needed me to learn not to rely on anyone, to trust only in myself. We went hungry so I could learn to steal and lie. I didn't get the love of a father because in this realm, I wouldn't have it. Whether or not he'd properly prepared me could be debated—I certainly hadn't felt prepared when I arrived. But one way or another, I'd survived. I guessed he could be proud of that.

Now that Cal had started on the topic, he couldn't stop. "Once you left, the fog cleared. I'd assumed it was losing you that shocked him back to us, but perhaps it was no longer having the pressure of preparing you. He'd done all he could. Whatever the reason, he was our father again, and he, Malcom, and I found a way to heal together." He glanced to me with a look of worry, as if something he'd said offended me. "We never stopped mourning you, though. We celebrated you, of course, to be chosen by the fae. But we mourned you every day."

"We are together again now," I told him, though I couldn't help but feel cheated that they got the best of Father after I was gone.

"For now," Cal said, with a tone that relayed he knew I didn't want to return to the mortal realm.

I withdrew. "It's been a long day. I'll see you tomorrow?"

He nodded, already refocused on the chess matches. From what I saw, Thorn was winning. I made my way up the stairs, past the fae who gathered there. It would take a while to get used to the palace being filled, but it added a certain amount of warmth that made me feel less alone.

I staggered into my room, exhausted, but Odette waited there with two glasses of cider and blueberry glazed crumpets, as if she knew exactly what I needed, along with two blank canvases and paints.

"I'll take a break for a short while, then I ought to search for my mother." I stripped off my shoes and ran my hands through my hair, willing myself to forget every other trouble wearing me down until Mother had been found.

"If you search, the realm will see and know there is something worth searching for," Odette reminded me, coming to take me in her arms. She always smelled of sweet wildflowers blooming after a rain. When she embraced, she held tight as if she'd hold forever if I never let go. I thought of what Talen said, how he was surprised she'd allowed herself to get close to a Mortal Queen after losing one long ago. I'd always be grateful she broke her rule for me. When she withdrew, she brushed tears from my cheeks. "The House of Delvers is vigorously—and discreetly—searching for her."

It was permission to rest, though the guilt of doing so would be difficult to dismiss. A heavy fatigue sought purchase within my bones, threatening to claim me if I didn't sleep, yet I wanted to fight it. I needed to find her.

Despite the many protests I could voice, I nodded. Then allowed her to press a glass of cider into one hand and a paintbrush in the other.

Somehow, as the next hour passed, turmoil over my worries subsided as we painted together, her drawing a glittering lake beside a sleepy forest and me painting the first family portrait I'd done in years, showing all five members of my family together. I hung it on the wall as Odette left, concentrating on it like I was making a vow.

This was more than a painting. This was a promise of a future that would come to pass—our family standing together once more. Someday.

I would not let the gargoyle's threat come true.

Talen appeared in the early hours of the next morning, shaking me awake. I sat up, heart pounding. "What is it?"

Something went wrong with Cal. Eliza is in danger. My mother's body has been found. I went through every possibility at breathtaking speed.

"Your mother," Talen said. I inhaled a terrified breath. "She's been found alive."

I flung myself from bed, grabbing my shoes. "Where?"

"Someone left her at King Brock's doorstep." I was already in my closet, reaching for the simplest dress I could find and a cloak to wear over it. Talen waited with his hat in hand, the door open. But something on his face made me pause.

"Thea"—he twisted his top hat between his fingers—"your mother . . . What you're about to find . . . It's not pleasant."

My stomach dropped to the floor. "Take me to her now."

42

THE CHARIOT RIDE TOOK MINUTES,
yet it felt like hours, and I couldn't breathe for any of it.

Cal and Eliza left at the same time, the four of us spilling into
King Brock's parlor together in the dark hours of night. Polished
stone turned to aged mahogany underfoot, and the bell of the
handcrafted clock in the foyer drowned out the sound of the
slamming door.

"King Brock?" I wandered deeper into the high corridors, the
architraves decorated with gilded beams that glittered like sharp
teeth. A pale fire burned in the hearth. My attention swung past it
all, searching for my mother. A wretched pain lodged itself in my
ribs. "Queen Illise?"

A wan light touched the chamber, originating from a hallway
to the right. Footsteps came, then the lithe form of Queen Illise,
clutching the hem of her robe. Her silky hair fell in strands over
her face, the rest of it pulled into a loose braid like a white rope,
her eyes equally drained of color. She still appeared as ethereal as
ever, but weary. Like a dying star.

Her soft voice bid us come. "Follow me, quietly."

She led us to the back of the manor, past bookshelves lining the
corridors, where wild blossoms grew from within crystal bottles.
She moved slowly. I wanted to run.

At last, Illise gestured forward. At the end of the narrow passage, a single wooden door stood open, the scent of poppies drifting out. Brock sat in a chair, keeping watch over Mother while she lay in bed, wrapped in thin linen.

"Is she awake?" I whispered. I crossed to her side.

"She's asleep."

I gently loosened the linen and folded it down. Her skin was sunken in, her body frail, but she was breathing. "Her captor simply let her go unharmed? Why?" A trick had to lay somewhere, waiting for us to find it. I reached to take her hand. At least she was here and—

My gaze flew down.

"I wouldn't say 'unharmed,'" Brock replied somberly.

Her hands were turned to stone.

"Who did this to her?"

"We do not know," Brock answered. "I tried to heal it as best I could, but her hands will never heal. I'm afraid this is permanent."

Permanent. She was alive, but she'd never paint again.

"The painting." My head swiveled to Cal. "When you went to rescue her, did you find the painting still in her room?"

"No," he replied, his skin ashen. "The paint and brushes were gone as well."

I looked to Brock next. He shook his head. He hadn't taken them. Her captor had found the painting then. That's why he did this.

"You should all get some rest," Brock said quietly. "Any of the adjacent rooms are available for your use."

As he passed, he placed a hand on my shoulder. "I'm sorry, my Queen. This realm is not usually so harsh."

It was to her.

"She is not dead," I repeated, telling myself. "We will be okay."

Once Brock had gone, Eliza went into Cal's arms. He collapsed into her as he wept. Talen silently withdrew, marching back through the corridor, ignoring the offer of a room.

I knelt beside Mother and lay my head by her side as the tears came. Once she woke, I would find a safe place for her to hide, perhaps on a farm with Odette somewhere. Someplace no one could ever hurt her again.

"You two can sleep and I'll keep watch over Mother."

Cal wiped his cheeks dry. "I'm staying."

"And I as well." Eliza pulled the armchair close, curling up in it while Cal took the other side of the bed. I hoped Mother could sense us here and know that she was safe.

We remained there through the night, one by one drifting to sleep.

I jerked awake a short while later to feel stone against my wrist. Mother's eyes were barely open, brown slits gazing at me.

Her voice rumbled like it hadn't been used in ages. "Thea."

"I'm here. You're going to be fine."

She made no indication of hearing me. "You're so grown up now. You were just a child when I saw you last."

I hesitated. Did she not recall the past few weeks? I scooted closer until my elbows were on the bed, the soft fabric of the sheets warming my skin. "Mother, do you remember who left you like this?"

Her eyes were lifted now, going to the oak beams of the ceiling. "I've been trapped for years."

Cal startled awake to rub the sleep from his eyes. When he saw Mother, he sat up. Lines marred his face from the imprint of folded linen.

"Who hurt you?" I asked again, trying to be gentle with my words so the urgency didn't frighten her. "Was it the same one who imprisoned you?"

Cal shot me a glance. "Thea, maybe now is not the—"

"He warned us there would be a price to pay, and now he is collecting," Mother continued, staring upward. "They sent us a letter in crimson ink like blood, promising to take you away. That is the price I pay. For Mortal Queens are meant to die here, but I cheated death. Now they take you, and there is nothing I can do. That is the price I pay."

Her lids fluttered shut, and the gentle stroke of Cal's thumb against her cheek wasn't enough to make her stir. He sat back and his eyes met mine.

"You will not be the price for Mother's life," he said.

But Mother was right. She had escaped death when Father took her away. Bash had said it himself—Mortal Queens were not meant to survive.

I dragged my tired body from the room and out into fresh air. *That is the price I pay.* The phrase repeated itself through my mind. Who was Mother paying the price to? There was no King Ulther in this realm anymore, yet he was the only one I knew of that she'd wronged. Who inherited his throne? Who found his body? Who could trace the death to Mother?

Those weren't the only questions I had. Time continued to tick down, leading me closer to the Mortal Queen's fate. How did I right the wrongs that occurred during the time of King Chasmere? And how could I beat the Gamemaster's riddles to reclaim my father's power? Each puzzle remained half solved, and I was stretched too thin to unravel any of them.

"Can't sleep?" A voice called to me and I looked up. Odette sat on the back patio drinking tea and watching the streets of the town outside the manor. The streets came to life with the warm hue of golden light, and for a moment, I forgot about the dark room where my mother lay, her hands never to be used again.

Just for a moment.

"I slept a little," I told her, taking an adjacent seat and accepting some tea. The flavor of black currants spread down my throat. "What are you doing here?"

"Talen told me what happened. I wanted to be here when you needed me."

"Thank you." I took my time with the second sip, trying to force my spirit to calm. The more I tried, the more my emotions rebelled, refusing to be stilled. I gave up by the fourth sip. Instead, I glanced back toward the palace, picturing it from another time, when it was strung with lights and laughter.

"Remember when I first came here? You'd dressed me in that gorgeous flowery gown and I arrived to reveal my three-month early escape from Brock's punishment. I talked with Thorn, flirted with Bash. I felt undefeatable that night. Now I feel nothing but fear."

Her hand stretched to take mine, and the feel of it grounded me. "Somehow I don't. I feel hope. Everything is going to be better than we can know."

I nodded, wishing I felt an ounce of that.

"I don't know where to begin fixing this," I confessed.

"Start with yesterday," Odette suggested. "Now that you've had the night to sleep on it, do things with Bastian still seem so dire?"

The memory of yesterday crashed into me. "Worse. I'm not certain I can repair that one."

"He would forgive you if you asked."

"He already has too many times. I don't deserve it. Last time I hurt him, it was a misunderstanding. But this time, I made an awful mistake to accuse him of such a thing, and he has every right to push me away because of it."

"If an apology won't work with words, then maybe actions. Is there something you could do to earn his forgiveness?"

I resisted telling her again how I didn't deserve his forgiveness. Bash got the worst side of me last night, the part that didn't trust and was quick to blame. Instead, I thought it over.

Was there anything I could do for him? He didn't want anything from me that I hadn't already destroyed. I couldn't ask him how to make this better. I would have to solve it on my own. He wanted the signet ring from my father. I knew that, but I wanted it too. Would I be willing to give up winning the Gamemaster's game for him, when it might be the only thing that could save me and the future queens? Meanwhile, Bash was convinced it was the only thing that could save his throne.

I paused. That might not be true.

Slowly, an idea came to mind.

"I'm going to need a lot of parchment and ink."

43

ODETTE WORKED ALONGSIDE ME. penning letters to every lord and king, telling them how stealing the bracelet from King Bastian's lords was my idea in my desperation to save myself, and he graciously helped me for my own sake, out of his love for the Mortal Queens. Then I explained how he'd valiantly saved his sister after his father had traded her away, and how he'd been there time and time again for me during my reign here. I described how thoughtful and wise of a king he was, and ended by saying he would forever be the only king I recognized for his throne, persuading others to join me in supporting his claim.

"It might not work, but it's worth a try."

"Mortal Queens have a lot of sway among the fae," Odette told me. "Knowing your allegiance lies with Bastian will convince others to follow."

We finished as Talen knocked on the door. "Is Cal here?" There was a bounce in his tone.

"He's in the next room with Mother," I said, standing to stretch. She still had yet to wake.

"Great!" Talen ran out.

Curious, I followed.

Talen was holding up two invitations, waving them in the air in the doorway. "I got them."

Cal rose from Mother's bedside where she slept. "The invitations?"

Talen tossed one his way, which Cal caught. "Two of them, for tonight. We are in."

"For what?" Eliza asked. She'd remained by Cal's side all day, only stepping out to fetch meals.

"A highly exclusive party where information will be traded," Cal read the invitation hungrily. "Specifically, information about hearts."

Each of us looked at Talen—the only one here without a heart.

He shrugged. "I'm motivated to get it back. But I have a present for you before I go." He pulled something from his pocket and passed it to me.

I unrolled the small parchment to find an oil painting, fraying at the edges but two faces still easily seen. One was my father, his sharp eyes glinting from behind his mask, brocade duvet paired with sleek gloves and a white overcoat that reminded me of the ice now enveloping his home. He stood close to a woman, his gaze fully on her, with a warmth on full display that made it impossible to deny his affection. I studied her, wondering why her pale hair and sharp chin looked so familiar.

I gasped. "That's the silver-haired ambassador!"

Talen was tenderly checking Mother. "We call her Hellen, but yes. She's an ambassador. And by the looks of it, was once favored by your father."

Cal came to my side to look over my shoulder at the painting. Hellen's figure pressed close to our father in a way that made my stomach churn, with her head tilted and a victorious smile that said she had everything she wanted in the palm of her hand.

"How close were they?" Cal asked.

"By my accounts, no one even knew they were together. Whoever they hired for this portrait must have been good at keeping secrets. But shortly after your father went missing, Hellen was publicly involved with Lord Winster, so the relationship must have ended by then."

She'd been in my house in the mortal realm with him. Hellen saw my father, yet made no note of it. Perhaps she had not recognized him with his mask off, there in the humble dwelling of the mortals, or he wore a charm of sorts. But as I continued to think, it made more and more sense why Father had always refused to attend the Queen's Day Choosing Ceremony. It wasn't just that he didn't want to see the fae. He didn't want to see *her*.

Cal peered at Talen. "Did you know our father?"

Talen stepped away from my mother's bedside. "Wish I could say I did, but not personally. I didn't become House Representative until a few hundred years after his disappearance."

I'd never get over subtle phrases like that—ones that reminded me we were not the same as the fae. We could sit with them and play their games, but they would always be something different from us. Greater, maybe. But entirely *other*.

"Where did you get this?" I asked.

"It was in the trunk Cal and I recovered," he replied.

"From Father's house. Talen and I went back there," Cal said upon my questioning look. He turned back to Talen. "I'm glad you got it open. Did you have to use fire after all?"

Talen grinned. "Only a little."

Between this and the party tonight, the two of them were becoming quite close. It was good Cal had someone to explore the realm with. He had to be careful about how much time he spent around me or Eliza before the fae grew too suspicious about his origins.

Eliza had taken the picture and was inspecting it with a furrowed brow. She held the portrait up. "If you are looking for who broke the king's heart the most, this might be the answer."

Her words took me back to the Gamemaster's game. A past flame had the ability to have cracked a heart. Yet someone had organized a War of Hearts that killed his family. Could the fae in that portrait with her hand laced through my father's be capable of such a thing?

There was only one way to find out.

Another possibility flickered in the back of my mind. If she hadn't broken his heart—if instead she had cared for it well—Father might have left his signet ring in her care. Either way, the game might end with her.

"I'll speak with her tomorrow," I said. Both Talen and Odette cringed. I took a step back. "What was that?"

Talen cleared his throat, twisting the brim of his hat between bony fingers. "Perhaps you are not the best person to do such a thing. It would require a delicate touch, that you—while filled with numerous great qualities—do not possess."

"I can be gentle," I protested.

"You can be firm," Odette corrected. "Determined. Relentless. But let me go with you and do most of the talking."

"Excellent idea," Talen said before I could comment. He placed his hat onto his head, flicking the brim down before buttoning the sides of his gold-trimmed suit. "Cal, shall we go?"

"Let me get properly dressed first." Cal gave our sleeping mother a kiss on her forehead, then kissed Eliza on his way out. She whispered for him to be careful—which he promised he would—before he slipped into the other bedroom where he kept his trunk.

Cal adapted well to this land, as I knew he would, merging seamlessly into the layers of games and manipulation that came with it. Almost as if he'd been a part of it his whole life. Eliza, in turn, thrived in him being here alongside her, in watching him take on the realm. She'd always carried a fire in her eyes, but his presence seemed to calm that and keep her grounded. She'd need that to survive two years. Sanity was easily lost in a place such as this, especially for Mortal Queens.

It was with a steady hand that she returned the picture to me, collected empty teacups, and strolled from the room while saying something about fresh air.

Odette and Talen hardly noticed her, their figures close to each other and hands intertwined.

"—and leave if there is any trouble," Odette was saying.

Talen grinned. "It wouldn't be fun if there weren't trouble."

At her stern expression, he grew serious. "I will. And when I return, I want to see sketches of those cottages you found."

I moved past them to sit at Mother's side as they continued speaking.

"Just so you know, cottage number one is my favorite."

"Cottage number one it is, then," Talen declared. "I'll return by dinner. I promise."

Then he was gone and Odette collected herself with a long sigh like she was sucking courage in from the air. It must have helped, though, for when she straightened her eyes were clearer. She looked at me. "I hope you know that when I say I can't wait to be rid of this world, I do not mean you. I mean everything else. Wars of Hearts, gambling, and trades. And the way Talen always seems to lose his heart."

"I understand," I told her truthfully. "A cottage sounds nice."

That earned a smile. "It's perfect."

I couldn't imagine the stress that came with Talen losing his heart—and to not know where it was or who held it. His heart wasn't simply his. It was Odette's as well. If it broke, I had no doubt hers would crack alongside it. But as Talen had reminded me, if someone wanted to hurt his heart, they would have done so by now. He would return safely tonight alongside Cal, I told myself.

Odette glanced out the door with a nervous tremble of her lips. "I was fine last year. But this year, it's like all I can do is worry." Her eyes clouded over. "I have too much to lose now. I don't think I can take it if I lose someone else."

I remembered that Talen told me she'd been close with a queen before and lost her. And she'd lost Talen once already—to his own thirst for power. Now she had him back, and also another Mortal Queen. But things were not always meant for keeping, no matter how hard one tried to hold on. In that moment, I could think of nothing to console her, because I could make no promise that she wouldn't lose us. But the way she looked at me was as if pleading for assurance. I tried to give it to her.

"Cal and Talen are clever. I have no doubt they will find Talen's heart, and you shall retreat to the cottage where you live a gloriously beautiful life. Meanwhile, I will be the second queen to live. And I will visit you often."

She gave a wan smile. "Thank you. I think some fresh air would do me good. Do you care for a walk through the town?"

I glanced at Mother. "I'd like to sit with her for a bit more."

Odette nodded, then paused. "You said second queen to live? I've heard stories of one who lived before, but I don't believe they are true."

"They are true. She did live." I dropped my eyes to the bed where Mother slept. "She's right here. Only you would have known her as Dhalia."

Odette gaped at me. "The murderer?"

I stiffened. "That was an accident."

Her tone softened. "I never personally met that queen. Are you're certain it's her?"

"I'm certain." My voice strengthened. "I know I'll survive because my mother did. It's in my blood."

Now Odette smiled genuinely. "Between your mother and your father, you do seem fated to live." She gave my mother a look of reverence mixed with curiosity. Her voice dipped low, like ripples meeting a shore. "I can't fathom how she did survive. It's a wonder." She cleared her throat. "However the case, I shall look forward to you living long as well, and to your very long reign."

"I'll toast to that." We smiled at each other and Odette left the room.

Alone, I brushed a hand over Mother's forehead, checking for fever. Subtle shades of pink touched her cheeks, but she wasn't waking, and I didn't know what to make of that. All I could do was hope she woke soon so we could get her home as soon as possible.

I wanted to tell Odette that Mother survived because she was wise or had tricked the kings. But in truth, she'd survived by the skin of her teeth and with a broken heart. She survived only because Father married her and took her from this realm.

If it came to it, I'd marry a king and survive the same way.

But Eliza needed another solution. One we were running out of time to find.

Mother stirred and I straightened.

Her eyelids fluttered slowly before easing open. I waited until she had noticed me. "How do you feel?"

She moaned a little, and when she spoke, it seemed painful to her. "Sore. But alive." She shifted her head on the pillow. "Where is Cal?"

I removed my mask so Mother could see my face properly. As for herself, she wore no mask, for she would not remain in this realm. As soon as she was strong enough, we planned to take her to the bridge where her presence would summon Father, who would open the gate and take her home. A day or two—that was how long I had left with her here. I would be sad to see her go, but all I could really think of was how she would be safe in two days. And nothing mattered more than that.

I yearned to ask again who had done this to her, but I feared sending her back into delirium. I squeezed her hand. "Cal is out, but he will return later tonight. He's been at your side constantly. You are at Brock's home now and you are safe."

"And you?" she asked, searching my face. "Are you safe?"

I was suddenly aware of the picture of Father with Hellen in my hand, which I surreptitiously moved to hide. "I'm safe. We're getting close to finding Father's signet ring, and then all will be well."

It was an assumption. A blind hope that becoming the seventh "king" would save me, removing me from my identity as a Mortal Queen and giving me a legitimate place in this realm. If I could convince an ambassador to give up their power for me, I'd become a fae and be fully relieved of the Mortal Queen title.

Mother had the kindness not to challenge the assumption. Her fingers pressed mine. "Thea, I'm so proud."

She wouldn't say so if she'd seen me last night, accusing Bash of horrible things with no proof.

Mother rested back into the pillow. Her words were strained

with effort to speak. "I know you want to know what happened."
Her gaze flicked to her hands before she shut her eyes tightly.

"It's alright, Mother. We can speak of it another time," I
consoled her.

It was as if she didn't hear me. "I can't seem to remember much,
but I do remember my captor going through my things with earnest
until he found the paintings. He covered his face with a full mask,
not these little things, so I saw nothing. Or perhaps I did, and he
stole the memory from me. The next thing I knew, my hands were
stone and I was in a new cage, like a birdcage in a meadow. They
gave me nothing to eat. My next memory is of being dropped at
Brock's doorstep, begging someone to help me."

"It's okay. We don't need you to remember who did this. All
will be well."

She nodded weakly, and her eyes drifted shut again. "I will
remember once I have my strength back," she whispered.

"I know you will," I whispered back. "For now, rest."

I stood, crossing the room.

"Peacocks."

I turned.

Mother peeked through half-shut lids. "I remember one thing.
While being kept in the second cage, I heard peacocks in the
distance."

44

APPARENTLY. KING BROCK HAD ALSO
attended the illusive party, so the women in the house—Queen
Illise, Eliza, Odette, and I—gathered around the large dinner table,
slowly picking at our food and glancing at the clock. Thick, blue
curtains hung open before gold-trimmed arched windows, letting
us see clearly as the stars dimmed and night fell upon us, each
minute increasing my nerves.

Queen Illise handled it better than the rest of us. She'd had
ages of practice putting on a brave face while her husband was
playing the games of the realm. She fixed herself a second bowl of
dumpling soup before lifting a brow. "Do you suppose starving will
make them return faster?"

The three of us obediently took a bite.

"That's better. My dears, they will arrive when they arrive, and
nothing we do will make that happen sooner."

My mind rested with the men, but more often than not it
wandered to Bash as I wondered if my letters had reached the lords.
Wondered if the turn of the day had softened Bash's feelings toward
me once again. The dark amber tablecloth beneath my fingertips
reminded me so much of his eyes that it became hard to look at,
and I had to lift my gaze away.

How many times do I let my heart crack for you?

"I just wish they'd hurry up," Odette fretted.

Of course, at that moment, the door swung open and the men sauntered in.

I could tell by how they walked that they'd been victorious. Cal swept in to kiss Eliza and instantly pour himself some soup, grabbing a handful of grapes as well. Talen bowed to the three queens present and tossed his hat jovially across the room. "They didn't see us coming."

Brock approached more humbly, pulling out his chair and settling upon it, but even he had a gleam in his eyes. "It was quite the night. And the two of you were most impressive. I'd expect nothing less from the son of King Thelonius."

Cal paused midbite, his grin not so victorious anymore.

Brock gave him a reassuring smile. "I guessed it when you approached your mother's bedside with as much concern as Althea. But worry not. Your family's secrets have long been mine to keep, and it is an honor to continue keeping them. And speaking of secrets . . ." He filled his goblet with a deep red liquid, then raised it in a toast. "Many secrets were traded, but ours were kept. Tonight, we have earned our drink. I was proud to play alongside you two fine men."

"What games did you play?" I asked.

"A simple game of dice," Talen put an arm around Odette as he leaned forward to speak, his eyes aglow with the thrill of the evening. From across the table, I could smell the scent of cedar and smoke coming from them. It felt a shame to have missed such a night. But my secrets were too great to risk.

Cal's were too. I sliced my gaze to him. "You left it to a game of chance?"

"It's only chance for those who don't know the game."

"You've been here for a week. You couldn't possibly know the game."

"Actually, we both do," he said between mouthfuls. "Quorilos."

Father had taught us that game a few years back. It was dice, but a handful of cards turned it into strategy as well. Just another way Father had prepared me—and unknowingly Cal—for this realm. Learning Cal hadn't blindly risked his secrets in a game of chance settled some of the unease in my stomach. "Are you going to tell us what secrets you learned?"

Talen offered the information, grinning like he'd been waiting for someone to ask. "We really shouldn't be telling anyone," he started, but his tone said *I can't wait to do so*. "We now know who five of the seven missing hearts belong to, and listen to this—there was one person who went to barter with the Gamemaster for his heart back, even though he was seen hiding one after the War of Hearts took place."

"Meaning he took someone's heart from the labyrinth, but it wasn't his own," Cal said, though it was obvious.

"And unless another chap had his heart stolen that night"—Talen paused for dramatic effect—"King Vern has mine."

I gasped, though I shouldn't have been surprised. Out of all the kings, that one was my least favorite. It was hard to like a man whose first impression included attempting to kill a prisoner and then show no remorse for it. Even at the thought, the wound in my shoulder burned from where the arrow had pierced me.

But Odette's eyes bulged. "My cousin? He wouldn't hurt me like that."

"He hasn't crushed it," Talen reminded her, taking a moment to kiss the back of her hand, as if that could whisk all her worries away. "And I don't believe him to be a vile man. Makes poor alliances sometimes, I must say, but he's not vile. My heart will be returned when he sees fit. I saw him tonight and thought to ask about it, but I'd like to see his hand revealed first."

"I'd like to see your heart safe," Odette countered.

"In good time."

Odette set her mouth in a firm line but nodded.

Brock and Illise picked at their food while we spoke, but at the first lull, Brock spoke up. "I must say, boys, I was impressed tonight. The two of you handled yourselves masterfully. Deliberate in your actions, mindful about how much you drank, and gracious to others when you won. The kind of men I'd like to surround myself with, men I'd be honored to count as a part of my lineage. To that regard—"

Brock paused to glance at his wife—unspoken words exchanged between them. She gave a small nod.

Brock stood, facing Talen. "You've proven yourself a capable master of this realm over and over. From stable boy to House Representative and now a Head of Delvers. More than that, your behavior tonight proved you are a man of character. As you know, I have no sons or daughters to inherit my kingdom, and I do not wish to pass it to someone unknown."

Odette had been holding Talen's hand, but now she dropped it and went white.

Brock inclined his head. "It would do me and my wife a great honor if you would accept the position of my heir."

Cal applauded on the table while Brock and Illise gazed upon Talen as if he were their son, waiting as anxious parents for his reply. His eyes widened as everything else about him remained frozen. The world hung in that moment, and it felt as if Talen and Odette's relationship hung with it, watching to see which way it would tilt.

I highly suspected Brock's home was not on the list of cottages Odette had picked out.

Without glancing at Odette, Talen replied graciously, "I would need to think upon it, sire. But words cannot express the honor."

Brock reseated himself with a smile, as if that was a yes. Like no one could refuse such an offer. "Very good. The paperwork will be ready for you to sign as soon as tonight."

Now Talen looked at Odette. The color had yet to return to her cheeks. Her auburn hair stood out against pale skin, while her honey eyes brimmed with tears. Talen steadied himself and faced Brock. "I will give you my answer by then."

Brock returned to his meal, unaware of Odette's discomfort.

Tension seemed to cloud the air surrounding Odette and Talen, working its way into the fibers of their courtship. The realm had a way of pulling at them, offering Talen one irresistible position after another, luring him deeper into its webs. Meanwhile, Odette tried to pull him out. There would be no compromise here. To have Odette, Talen must leave this all behind.

Perhaps some loves were simply doomed.

"Mother woke up today and spoke for a bit," I said to divert the attention. Odette shot me a look of gratitude.

Cal perked up. "What did she say?"

"Nothing of importance. The man wore a full mask, then she was in a cage. It's a lot of rambling. She still doesn't remember who is responsible. But she's getting stronger, and I think we should send her home in two days. Her marriage to Father can be used to open the bridge."

"I agree, for all sorts of reasons, but what joy it will bring her to see Malcom."

Dinner continued without event, and I tried to picture the moment when Mother and Malcom were reunited, for he had no memory of her to cling to. He would be gaining someone who, until that point, had been somewhat of an illusion. He'd finally know what it was to have a mother. But instead of being joyous, all I could think of was how the moment Mother returned to Father and Malcom was the moment I'd lose her again. In order for them to have her, I had to say goodbye. Even Cal would return home. But I never would.

I'd made my decision about where I belonged, and I wondered if Talen and I felt the same way—to have the ones we loved, we had to lose a bit of ourselves. He'd be losing the part of himself that chased power. And I'd be losing my mortal family.

Father once taught me to make a decision and not look back. He didn't realize it wasn't just advice for the fae realm—it was advice on how to say goodbye to him.

Until that moment came, I captured a mental image of this moment. A meal surrounded by those I'd miss. When Eliza and Cal had returned home, and Odette and Talen were living in their cottage, I'd still have this picture of us together to hold on to.

The image fell apart as Odette stood, sending her chair nearly toppling backward. "I need a moment," she choked. And she fled the hall.

45

DINNER ENDED QUICKLY AFTER
Odette's departure. I found Talen pacing the corridor outside
the guest chambers where Odette was staying, his black suit coat
strung over his arm, his hat on the floor. He hardly acknowledged
me as I approached.

"It's not my place to give advice," I started, but he held up a hand.

"You don't have to. I'm leaving tonight, taking Odette to marry
her, and we shall live in whatever cottage she wants. As long as I
have her."

Tension eased from my shoulders.

"I'll tell her as soon as she lets me in." Talen slumped against
the wall. "I'm afraid I've given her too many reasons to doubt me."

I braced myself next to him, looking at the shut door, grateful
I'd taken that final mental picture. It was the last dinner I'd get with
Talen and Odette for a while. With hope, we'd have many more. But
it would be different. It would no longer be with Talen as my first
alliance, nor with us trying to uncover a path to my survival. We
wouldn't be speaking of fooling kings or the latest tricks. Who were
we, with all of that stripped away?

I was eager to find out.

"She showed me her favorite cottage," I told him. "A painting of
it, at least. I think you'll like it. Wood trimming, arched doorway,

potted flowers beneath a stone awning, and vines wrapped around the eaves. A field of wildflowers grows behind it."

Talen smiled. "It sounds perfect."

A thought came to mind. "What about your heart? Will you ask for it back first?"

"I don't care about my glass heart. My real heart is in there. It's her. And I can't afford to lose her." He turned to me, and I suddenly remembered the first time I met him. It felt like forever ago. He'd been a rock for me since then, and as happy as I was for them, sadness clouded like a mist in the corners of my eyes. As if reading my thoughts, he asked, "Do you feel comfortable going on without us?"

I shrugged, trying to blink my eyes dry. "Maybe I'll see if Thomas wants to align."

"You wouldn't dare."

I shrugged again.

He pushed himself from the wall and sobered. "I better go inform King Brock that I will not be accepting. That will be a difficult conversation. Then I'll check back with Odette to see if she'll let me in. I'll make certain we say goodbye before we leave."

"Thank you," I whispered, not trusting myself to say more without my voice cracking.

He touched my arm, then strode down the corridor.

I stared after him, marveling at how simple that was. A few minutes ago, I'd been worried for them, and now they were about to begin their life together. Just like that. Talen had merely decided this was what he wanted, and he was going to chase it with his whole heart.

If their love wasn't doomed, maybe mine didn't have to be either.

I could go to Bash now, promise him of my conviction, and how I'd never hurt him again. Prove that my love wasn't going anywhere. I could do more than write letters to lords. I could grant Bash an entire kingdom on my own—mine. We could share my father's kingdom. I'd give the throne to him, if that was what it took.

It could be as simple as that. Perhaps, before the night ended, he would be mine again and I would be his.

I hurried down the corridor to fetch a cloak, dreaming of all the beautiful ways our story could end once he saw how willing I was to fight for those final chapters. I was so caught up in my fantasy I almost lost my bearings when I spotted the bright white of Talen's hair outside, not in the study with King Brock where he was supposed to be.

I shot a look behind me. Odette's door remained closed.

I approached the gilded, glass doors to peer outside. Talen stood beneath an alabaster archway, the path before him leading to a charming courtyard lined with blossoming trees that provided a small space of paradise on the side of Brock and Illise's home before the island ended and the sky began. Perfectly aligned bricks coated the ground, and Talen shifted upon them, sweat lining his brow. He'd been so confident earlier, yet now he shook.

Had he changed his mind? Perhaps Brock was saying something that changed his mind.

Yet, when I opened the door, it wasn't Brock whom Talen trembled before. It was Thomas.

Starlight gleamed against his tightly coiled red hair, illuminating the fire in his eyes. He did not appear nervous like Talen did. Rather, he stood with a wide stance and his chin tilted upward, as if he'd won some game. It wasn't until I stepped out farther, beyond the bow of branches, that I saw why.

He held Talen's heart in his hand.

The world slowed, yet there still wasn't enough time.

Thomas spotted me. "Don't come closer!" His fingers pulsed against the heart. Talen stood rigid.

Fear coursed through my veins. My own heart thundered uncontrollably.

"Thomas, what are you doing?" My voice sounded odd in my ears, as if it came from someone else. Someone terrified.

Thomas, on the other hand, sounded feral. "Taking what is mine."

"You can have it." Talen stood five paces from Thomas, eyeing his heart. "I'm leaving tonight. You can be the House Representative for Delvers. I'll give you the position myself."

"So you can return whenever you like and take it? No." His fingers tightened around the heart and Talen grimaced.

"I'll align with you!" I shouted, daring a step forward. "Eliza and I both will. No one will question your influence then."

My pleas fell on deaf ears. He looked only at Talen.

"For years, I have watched you take everything. Now, I will take what I want."

"Please." Talen's hands shook. "I have much to live for."

The darkness of the night weighed heavy. It beat down around us, anchoring me in place. I couldn't move. I couldn't breathe. I think I shouted but wasn't sure. If I dove for Thomas, he might drop the heart and break it. If I did nothing, he might break it anyway.

"There must be something I can do," Talen said. "If you let me live, I'll convince Brock to give you his kingdom. With my help, you'll be a king."

Thomas's expression soured. "With your help? Don't you see? I don't need your help anymore! I don't need anyone. I *take* now."

Talen swung his head to me. Wild fear lived in his eyes. A million memories shot between us.

Thomas placed both hands around the beating heart.

"I will take what I want," he repeated in a tone as if he were made of darkness itself.

And he crushed Talen's heart.

Death came swiftly, bringing Talen to the ground. He hit his head against the stone, but I doubted he felt it. His eyes stared blankly above.

A scream tore from my throat. I threw myself beside him to grab his hands. Shake his body. Beg him to come back.

He didn't stir. Talen was gone.

Thomas let the broken glass trickle to the ground. It was the only sound I heard aside from my screams.

"You'll be severely punished for this." White hot tears streamed down my cheeks, blurring my vision. "I'll make sure of it."

Thomas stepped closer to me. "Oh, my Queen. You will be dead within a year and cannot hurt me."

Then he swung at me, and I lost all consciousness.

46

I WOKE UNWILLINGLY. PAIN TORE
me from sleep, the kind of pain that lived in my chest and stole
all joy. There was no moment of bliss where I'd forgotten what
had happened. From the moment my body returned to its senses, I
remembered the horrible sound of Talen's pleas before his body hit
the ground. I remembered the look in his eyes. And I remembered
Odette, in her room not knowing Talen would never return.

They'd never get their cottage together. She didn't even know he
was choosing to leave for her.

Tears welled in my eyes.

"It's okay. You're going to be okay." A man's warm voice
comforted me. I focused enough to see Thorn at my side.

I blinked the tears away. "This is my room." Somehow, I'd
returned to my palace, in my chambers, with Thorn at my side.

"Yes. King Brock brought you early this morning, telling me to
watch over you. He's closed his home to guests."

I guessed Brock's true intentions. His home would be engulfed
with curious fae now that a heart had been crushed in his courtyard,
each one dying to glean fresh information about the horrible deed.
Brock had sealed his home so none could find my mother.

Thorn held my hand, tracing slow circles with his thumb,
looking at me like I might break.

I didn't want to ask out loud. "Did he tell you what happened?"

"Yes. The whole realm knows by now. Are you okay?"

No. My head throbbed, and both my mind and my body were in a daze. I'd never be okay again. Talen was gone. Talen was gone and he wasn't coming back. "I need to find Odette. She needs to know."

"She knows," Thorn said gently.

"No, she doesn't. She doesn't know how much he loved her. She needs to know." I tried to stand, but my knees gave out. "She needs to know."

I couldn't control it any longer. I hunched over, head buried in my hands, and sobbed.

Thorn sat, patiently waiting for me to calm down. He'd be waiting a long time.

When I regained control long enough to wipe my tears on my dress, a crinkle came from my pocket. With trembling fingers, I pulled out the picture of my father. I took a deep, shuddering breath. "Odette and I planned to visit the ambassador Hellen today to ask her about her relationship with . . . the missing king." I almost said my father. If I didn't get a grip soon, I'd spill my secrets. Although, right now, I didn't know if I cared.

Thorn took the small painting with great interest. "Fascinating. This painting portrays trust. She might know where the signet ring is."

I nodded, trying to collect myself. A dull throb at the back of my head reminded me I'd been struck and I rubbed the spot. "Where's Thomas?"

"Thomas?"

I chilled. "Thomas, the Representative for Berns, killed Talen. I saw him do it. Where is he?"

Thorn quickly rose to his feet. "We did not know that." He handed me back the painting. "I will organize a search for him right away. Please excuse me, my Queen. I'll return shortly so we can question Hellen together." He bowed.

The game and the signet ring were the last things on my mind. I sank back into the bed and allowed myself to grieve, wondering if the pain I felt was the same pain the fae felt when their hearts cracked, and if it would ever go away.

Thorn returned within a couple of hours with a plate of cheeses and glazed ham. "Are you feeling better?"

I'd taken a bath. I'd dressed. I'd cried. On the outside, I appeared more put together, but my insides would take much longer to heal. "Did you find Thomas?"

"Not yet, but they will. For now, we have another task. We could finish the Gamemaster's game today and earn ourselves a kingdom."

If we were right, we'd have the dilemma of who got the signet ring—him or me? But I was fresh out of emotions, so I numbly donned my shawl and followed him out the door, taking the plate of food with me.

Once more, I'd forgotten we were no longer alone in this palace. Not that anyone made a sound. All became silent as we walked past, staring at me as if they could peel the story of last night from my skin. I tried to ignore them while holding the platter of food like a shield before me, but my sigh once we stepped onto an empty courtyard gave away my thoughts.

"You get used to it after a while—always being watched. A king or queen is never alone for long, which is both a comforting and terrifying thought."

I felt alone then. Without Talen nearby, guiding me through this realm, I felt very alone.

I sat in Thorn's chariot to eat while he stood by me, recounting what had happened over the past day. "Everyone was in an uproar when King Brock discovered you and Talen in his courtyard. He commanded the whole city search for the killer right away. Luckily, the shattered heart was too far away from Talen for him to have crushed it himself, so none could doubt that it was another."

"Did anyone question if it was me?"

"Mortal skin tears easily," he said, indicating my hands. "It couldn't have been you."

Being on trial for his death would be too terrible to imagine. Did fae have trials? When they found Thomas, would my word be enough? No doubt he was in conspiracy with King Vern, who had taken the heart in the first place, so my word would be bringing down a representative and a king. Even for a queen, that asked for a lot of faith.

I shuddered to think of what the punishment would be. Banishment, perhaps, and their titles stripped. Or did the fae demand, as we did on the five islands, an eye for an eye?

A heart for a heart.

My chest tightened at the horrid thought. Even if they did such a thing, it wouldn't be even. Talen's heart was worth more than theirs combined. And what of the ricochet? Who was paying the price for Odette's cracked heart? Hers was a fate worse than his, to have to spend ages without him. A mortal life without the one you loved would be painful. The span of fae years spent missing someone would be anguish.

"What's a funeral like for a fae?" I asked Thorn in a voice hardly over a whisper. Talen deserved the best.

"Talen was—at the time of his death—a Head to the House of Delvers. That's no small feat. In a few days, the nobles of the realm will gather along with all who loved him, and we will turn him into a bright star and place him high in the skies."

"Let me be there," I begged. "So I might memorize which star he becomes and look upon it always." It would provide me solace to envision him watching over us, as if he were still here.

Thorn's hand grazed mine. "We would never deny you that." To his credit, his eyes were glazed over. He blinked them dry. "Can I ask what you were doing at Brock's home?"

"Following leads," I lied. He couldn't know about Mother. After losing Talen, I had the urge to tuck every secret I held into a box and lock it away. "He was close with the missing king, and that's how we found the picture."

Thorn watched me, and I was too exhausted to discern whether he believed me or not.

"I saw you've been sending letters pleading with lords to realign with Bastian," Thorn said casually.

He'd found the one thing that could pull me from the fog in my head. "Is it working?"

"No." His jaw ticked. "But if it makes you feel better, there was nothing you could have done anyway. His father is taking control soon."

"I should have tried harder. Should have gone to every lord in person to convince them Bash would be the better king."

Thorn didn't reply, and I recalled Bash telling me Thorn was actively trying to put Bash's father back on the throne. I clamped my mouth shut. If there was anything I could do to save Bash's throne, I must act fast. Time always moved too quickly in this realm. But any plausible ideas evaded me, like mist that couldn't form into something real, until we were nearing a rocky island only large enough for a single mansion with black stone pillars and a wrought iron gate. All time for plotting vanished.

I forced myself to focus on what we were there for. "Do we have a plan?"

"Interrogation," he said promptly. "We ask her about her relationship with the king and don't leave until we get the answer. Either she was the one who broke his heart—and therefore is the answer to the Gamemaster's puzzle—or she knows where the ring is or has possession of it herself. Either way, we will leave with something. I feel it."

I wished to feel that. But all I felt was the air turn cold as the chariot landed on the stones.

Gaps hung between each block, endless sky beneath, and we had to jump from one to the next to reach the iron gate. The message was so clear, it might as well have been painted in golden colors on the front door. *Visitors are not welcome here.*

Thorn pushed the gate open.

At least on the inside, the stones were properly sealed together, so we didn't need to fear falling to our deaths. The stubborn ground could grow nothing of beauty, leaving little to look at except the sharp spirals of the four turrets and the gargoyles that watched from the roof. Their sparkly, opal eyes gleamed as we neared, and I swore their mouths widened into those wicked smiles. I'd had quite enough of gargoyles.

"Such a homey place," I muttered.

"Hellen was never known for her warmth."

We approached a pale grey door and knocked. Then we waited.

The realm decided to show me mercy today, and when the door cracked open, Hellen stared at us from behind her silver mask, her mouth turning down. "I am not due to see you . . . ever again."

"Always a pleasure," I remarked. "Can we come in?"

Her frown said no. But the door opened to allow us through. The ambassador didn't shut the door, as if our stay would be short. Thorn noted it, and the corner of his mouth lifted.

The exterior matched the interior—colorless and cold. Dark curtains drawn over windows, hard stone floor with no rug, and a single black-framed mirror on the wall. I doubted the other rooms were warmer, but I more strongly doubted I was free to go check.

I shuffled through my mind for pleasantries we could say to lead into our questions, but Thorn whipped out the picture. He held it up between his hands, pulling back when she tried to snatch it away.

"Not many things stay secret in this realm. I must applaud the artist who drew this on his impressive silence. And you! Courting a king and not sharing the details to gain clout. Do you know what that tells me?"

"It tells you that it was none of your business," she spat. She didn't move her eyes from the picture until Thorn lowered it.

"It tells me it was real."

Hellen glared at us. "It's over now."

"Obviously." Thorn folded the painting and stuck it in his pocket.

"When did it end?" I asked tentatively.

She studied me briefly and answered sharply. "About twenty years before he went missing."

Twenty years. Unless she held some sort of grudge for that long, she wouldn't have been the one to set up the War of Hearts that killed his mother and sister. Assuming that was what broke his heart the most—she wasn't responsible.

Thorn and I exchanged glances, and I suspected we had the same thought. She hadn't hurt him.

"Did it end well?" Thorn asked.

Hellen finally closed the door, though she didn't beckon us beyond the dreary hall. "It ended . . . oddly. Toward the end, he became paranoid. He received letters from an anonymous source that he wouldn't share with me, though it was clear whatever was in them bothered him. He took late night visitors, looked over his shoulder more often, and talked about losing his throne. Which made no sense. He was obsessed with keeping it, but no one ever doubted his rule. The lords loved him. If any king was secure in his place, it was him, but whatever was in those notes frightened him enough that he feared it would all crumble. After a year of that, I couldn't take it. I ended it. Thelonius was so wrapped up in those notes that he hardly noticed when I left."

Another piece of my father to add to the puzzle, all together forming the man I never knew. This piece didn't fit with the others, but I trusted it all the same. If I ever saw him again, I'd ask about the notes.

He'd been right, though. Someone banished him, but they never got his throne. Because they never found his signet ring.

Thorn leaned forward. "Hellen, did you ever see the king again?"

"No," she said.

But I'd lied enough to hear it on someone else. Or maybe I'd made up my mind and wouldn't be deterred.

"You did. I'd wager you saw him shortly before he went missing. He was terrified of losing his throne, so he gave away the key to it—his ring. And who better to hide it with than the woman no one ever knew he courted?"

"I don't have the ring."

Thorn pressed on. "Now you've held on to it for hundreds of years. Waiting for his return. Keeping it safe until he comes to claim it."

"I have no ring. Thelonius never came to see me again."

But Thorn ran with the idea—literally. He tore through the rooms, searching her home.

"Sire, you do not have the right," Hellen said, though she didn't chase him. Something hard thudded in reply. She crossed her arms and her whisper came for me alone. "You will not find it."

"No harm in searching, I suppose," I said, unsure if I should join in the antics.

From the noise of ransacking, Thorn had moved upstairs.

"Did you ever find out who the notes were from?" I asked to break the tension that clouded the hall.

"I never did."

Her hard exterior melted with each moment Thorn searched, as if we had brought the past with us and it pained her to live through it twice. For hundreds of years, she'd kept the relationship quiet until it might have disappeared in her mind, lost among the memories. Then we arrived and forced it back into her thoughts. She appeared consumed by those thoughts—blank eyes fixed on the stone slab wall, unflinching as Thorn rummaged through her belongings upstairs.

After a moment, her lids twitched and her lips curled. She set her gaze upon me. "If you keep quiet about my former relationship with King Thelonius, I will tell you what I know about your selection."

An alliance of a sort. I wouldn't have said anything about the relationship anyway, but she needn't know that. I'd been after this information since day one, when I was informed that my selection as their new queen was anything but ordinary. I agreed without hesitation.

"Ambassadors are bound to the House in which they serve.

For me, that is Low. I lived in the House of Low for ages. I don't suppose you've ever been there, but it is not a quiet dwelling." As she told her tale, I absorbed her words. "Around five years ago, I received a letter offering me what I'd always wanted—peace. It offered this house, secluded and private, in exchange for one simple thing. Reading your name in five years."

That lined up with my father's story of how long they'd known I'd be selected. My lips parted, but she shook her head. "I don't know who sent the letter. And I didn't care. I read names every year—it didn't matter to me whose name I said. I still don't know why it was you, nor does it concern me. The past five years have been a delight and I regret nothing."

My entire life was upheaved, and she didn't care about anything other than her quiet house.

She paused, then said, "A few months ago, I received a second letter. One more task—or I'd be sent back to the House of Low."

"Read Eliza's name?" I guessed.

She confirmed it. "I got smarter this time and took a paper with her name as proof for any who questioned it."

"You didn't fight back? How do you know the same person wouldn't ask something of you next year, or the year after that?"

Her voice sharpened. "I repeat—I do not care which name I read."

My blood boiled. Nothing about being selected as Mortal Queen had turned out the way I envisioned, but at least the process was once a fair one. Now someone could make the decision themselves. Chose which girl was forced into this realm. And we were powerless to stop them, while Hellen refused to try. My future, traded for a house.

And Eliza, mercilessly dragged into this mess.

I'd been prepared to run that day at her Choosing Ceremony, but when her name rang out over the crowd, I didn't. Now there could be no doubt—she'd been chosen to keep me here. The burden of her fate was mine to bear.

Thorn's footsteps thudded down the stairs, bringing our conversation to an end.

"Are you satisfied?" Hellen asked. She stilled when she spotted the box in Thorn's hands. Silver, no larger than his palm, and trimmed in soft velvet.

"Are you stealing now?" From Hellen's sharp tone, we wouldn't be welcome in her house much longer.

The box gave a small clink as Thorn flipped it open, smiling triumphantly. I approached to see better. Inside, nestled between layers of crimson silk, lay a ring, and it stole my breath away. A brown band like the shade of a fig tree, created of three coils that spun around each other, melting in the middle to grasp a stone of ice so pure, I could see my reflection. Something irresistible tugged from within, like I was made of strings and this was the control bar, pulling me like a marionette, drawing me in. I needed it. I couldn't explain why. But my fingers itched, suddenly feeling naked without the ring.

I hadn't realized how close I was until Thorn snapped the lid shut, almost nicking my hand.

Hellen went white. "That was not there before. That box was empty."

The trance that had captured me faded away with the ring out of sight, allowing me to focus on her.

"Your lies matter not. We've found the ring." Thorn held his arm for me and made for the door, but Hellen blocked our way.

"That ring was not in my possession before, you must believe me." Wide eyes pleaded with me, her cold fingers curling around my arm. "Please, it wasn't there. I didn't take it."

I pried away from her touch. "Then you won't mind if we do."

Slowly, I registered what this meant.

It was over.

The Gamemaster's game complete.

My father's kingdom could be restored. I could reclaim what was mine.

All that was left was for Thorn and me to decide what to with the ring—would it go to him or to me?

Whoever bought the information of my bloodline from Talen

weeks ago also bought our silence on the matter, binding me from telling Thorn I was part fae, and therefore that my father was the king and the ring rightfully belonged to me. It hadn't been a problem when I was first sworn to secrecy. Now it posed an issue. And with Talen gone—a sharp pain pinched my heart at the thought—it remained unlikely I'd find who he sold the information to.

Without sharing that . . .

Thorn had technically found the ring. If he wanted to keep it for himself, I'd have a hard time stealing it.

Hellen's cries for us to believe her echoed off deaf ears as we left her home and shut the door behind us.

I wanted to ask for the ring right then but held my tongue. Thankfully, as soon as we'd bypassed the stones and stepped onto the chariot, Thorn passed it over.

"We did it," I said, opening the box once more. The invisible tug pulled at me again. "The power to his kingdom."

"Almost," Thorn said, urging his chariot onward. "It seems the king enchanted the ring. My guess? Only his bloodline can unlock the power."

For him to know that, he'd already tried on the ring. He must have done so upstairs. What would he have done if it had worked? Taken the ring and left me there?

I kept my voice even. "But he has no bloodline."

"Hence the final dilemma. Enchantments can be broken. Meanwhile, we should hide the ring."

"I'll hide it," I suggested. "People will assume I've spent the day mourning Talen, not looking for signet rings. I'll hide it while you work on breaking the enchantment."

If he suspected ulterior motives, he didn't say so. He passed the box to me, and I slid it into the folds of my cloak. "Very well. In the meantime, let's not tell the Gamemaster what we've uncovered. If she didn't possess the ring in the first place, I'm suddenly very suspicious of her antics. We keep this to ourselves, just you and me."

"Just you and me," I promised. It was a promise I fully intended to break.

When Thorn dropped me off at my home before going on to find a way to break the enchantment, I pretended to wander back inside, letting him be none the wiser when I turned around and hailed a chariot.

"Take me to King Brock's home," I commanded. "I have something very important to show him."

47

MY THOUGHTS AS I ENTERED
Brock's manor were too many to count, and each one vastly
different. I ought to find Cal and Mother, show them Father's ring.
I should go to Odette and mourn with her. I could put on Father's
ring now and take the kingdom before anyone could stop me.

I did it. I had the ring. I'd won.

Thorn would have to pry it from my hands to get it back, and
now that the Gamemaster's game was complete, our alliance could
end. I needed only to sever it and I'd owe him nothing.

Could I end the alliance on my own, or must I tell him for it to
be officially over?

My heart burned with sadness. Talen would have told me how.

"Thea?" Cal's voice found me, rooted in the foyer. It was then
that I realized I never got back the picture of Father. No matter. I
had something far better.

I drew out the box. "We should go to Mother. I have something
to show you both."

To my surprise, Mother sat up in bed when we approached, her
cheeks warm with color. Her stone hands rested in her lap. I went to
her side. "You look so much better. How do you feel?"

"Free," she said, her voice still hoarse. "Thank you for freeing me."

My gaze snapped to Cal. Freeing her? He shook his head. Her

memory was not good, then. As long as her body was healthy, I could live with her memory being weak.

"You're back." Eliza appeared in the doorway dressed in a black gown that accented the gold of her hair. From the red in her eyes, she'd been crying. "How are you?"

I knew what she meant, but I couldn't talk about Talen without crying, and right now I needed my voice. "I'm alright. Thanks to the picture Cal and Talen uncovered, I found what the realm searches for."

I opened the box so they could all see.

Cal took it first, cupping the box between his hands. "Is this what I think it is?" He twisted it to inspect from all angles, but didn't touch the ring itself. Once more, I felt the pull and wondered if Cal felt it too.

I nodded. "It's Father's signet ring."

"You did it," Eliza marveled as she took it next. "You unlocked a power greater than any Mortal Queen has known, and with it, maybe the key to our survival."

"The king is the key," I said.

Eliza passed it back and I placed it in Mother's lap.

She wouldn't have seen it before, yet she looked at it as if gazing upon an old friend. With each second, her smile grew, and I found myself staring at her. Now free and healthy, my mother had never looked so beautiful. As she stared at the ring, a tear slid down her cheek.

"The ring is Father's," I said. "If he wants it, it belongs to him."

"He'll never return to this realm. He despises it all. But he'd be honored to know his ring might save you."

"That is the hope, though we do not know if it'll do anything at all."

"I think it will," Cal said. "That phrase you said—the king is the key? I've heard it. Over and over. Like the words needed me to hear them. Somehow, a king was meant to be the key to your survival. I think this is how."

It felt too easy and somehow too complicated at the same time.

After the past year of desperately searching for the path to survival, here was the answer—to take the place of a king. Was that a simple thing at all? It felt that way, now that I had the signet ring in hand. I thought of all the queens who came before me, who didn't know what to search for. What of the queens who lived before Father went missing, who couldn't have taken a king's place without that king giving it up?

If this was the right path, I would be grateful to live. But something about the puzzle felt unsolved. Waiting for me.

I took the ring out of the box and rubbed it between my fingers, thinking over King Chasmere's story.

A king, fallen in love with a mortal girl.

The mortal girl, killed by her jealous friend.

The friend, leading every mortal out of the fae realm.

The realm that demanded there must always be a mortal within.

And finally, the Mortal Queens, doomed to forever pay the price for the first fallen queen.

The queens had come and gone, but through it all, one thing remained. The law that a mortal must always be in the fae realm. It had crumbled when Gaia and I went missing. It demanded a Mortal Queen. Yet, if the queens were so important, what value did the king hold? Why had that one phrase come to Cal and me so often?

Mother married a king and it had saved her. But it hadn't been enough to satisfy the realm.

Why?

I dropped the ring into the box, my blood turning cold. It was like a mirror shattering in my mind, the fragments piercing my skin with the sharp reality of what we'd missed. We'd been close. The answer had been right there, and it was so, so close.

The key to the Mortal Queens' survival. I'd found it.

48

MY HANDS TREMBLED AS THEY held the box, my mind aflame with the magnitude of the revelation. All these years. All the dead queens. This was what they searched for.

"A mortal must always live in the realm of the fae. That was the rule—our price for wanting to have a taste of this realm. We must always live here."

Cal looked at me strangely. "What are you getting at?"

My thoughts raced to put the pieces together. "Don't you see? The king is the key. I must marry a king and remain here, satisfying the death of the first Mortal Queen by reestablishing a happy marriage. For what does the realm value most of all?"

I looked to Mother now. She had taught me and Eliza this.

"Marriage," she replied. "The ultimate alliance."

"Exactly. The alliance broke when the first Mortal Queen died, slayed by a mortal hand. We must fix what she broke. That is why you lived even though you left the realm—because you had married a king." We'd known that part but hadn't realized how painfully close we were to the final answer. "But you left. And a mortal must forever be in the land of the fae."

Mother paled. "No. I'm not losing you."

Cal and Eliza didn't say anything. They knew I'd already been lost to the mortal realm.

If marrying a king was the price to save the queens, I'd pay it.

"Has there ever been a queen who married a king before? I want to be certain this will work before I go proposing to anyone."

"One tried," Cal said. "After I kept hearing about the king being the key, I became curious about their relation to queens, so I asked around. Kings refuse to marry Mortal Queens because marriage is eternal and Mortal Queens are not. One queen tried, though, begging all seven kings to marry her, and all refused."

"Let me guess. Cottia?"

"Sounds right. Who was she?"

"A queen from long ago whose journal I found. She knew how to free herself, but none would listen. If she had succeeded, think of the lives that would have been saved."

Mother swung her feet over the side of the bed. "There is no guarantee they will listen to you. While you are part fae, you age like a mortal. Your father and I inspected all three of you closely, and we are certain you will live a mortal lifespan. To convince a king to sacrifice an eternal bond for a mortal one would be nearly impossible."

Unless I found a way to turn myself fae.

But then I wouldn't be mortal, and when Eliza left, we'd once again be condemning the land to darkness.

"Bastian will do it for you," Eliza said.

My heart dropped. "I don't know. Things are not good between us right now, and I'm not sure he'd believe me if I explained this to him."

"Thorn then?"

Cal stepped in front of her as if doing so would block her words from reaching me. "No."

I frowned. "This isn't your choice. If Bash won't marry me, I'd take Thorn to save everyone else. I must remain and marry a king soon, before this year is out."

Cal stood firm. "Listen, Thea. Before Talen died, he and I were watching Thorn, and we don't trust him. We couldn't find anything tangible, but you can't marry him."

"This isn't about trust," I said. "It's about saving innocent mortal girls from the dangers of this realm."

"Pick any other king."

"Every other king is either married, too old, or very angry with me. If not Bash, it must be Thorn."

Mother repeated the name to herself, then suddenly stilled. "I know Thorn." Her voice was taut. "I met him when I was a young girl, though he was only a prince then." She stood on shaky legs. "Althea, he's King Ulther's son."

"The king you almost married?"

Realization slammed into me. Ulther had been adamant that Dhalia—my mother—must marry him. *To save her,* he'd said.

Had he known? And Mother discarded him because she'd been in love with another.

Mother's eyes turned fearful. "His family is not to be trusted. Thorn knows I killed his father. He appeared as your father and I rode away. He knows everything."

"But he doesn't know you're my mother. He can't."

"Who summoned you here?" Cal asked.

Blood drained from my face. "We can't know it was him."

"But he's a likely option," Cal said. "He'd have the connections to do something like that, and he's clever enough not to create suspicion."

It was like I'd been thrust into an ocean and didn't know how to swim. Ulther being Thorn's father might not change anything—or it could change everything.

If he knew who my mother was, he knew who my father was.

I looked down to where the ring glistened in Mother's hand. Thorn would have known I could unlock its power.

"This alters things," I said slowly. "But it doesn't change everything. I still must marry a king."

"We'll find another way," Mother begged.

"We already have a way." I bent to retrieve the ring, then tucked it away in the box. "But I won't go into a marriage until we have all the answers." A thought struck me. Thorn knew I'd been spending time here, and if he was the one who captured Mother, he knew where to find her. "Mother, if Thorn knows, we must get you away from here. You have to go back home." Panic made my heartbeat race. "It isn't safe for you to stay another moment."

"Things have never been safe," she said. "I can't leave my daughter behind."

"Don't think of it as leaving me," I pled with her. "Think of it as blessing me with the knowledge that you are safe. That is all I want."

"Those are just prettier words for the same thing."

"Maybe." I soaked in the sight of her, memorizing every detail. "But it doesn't make it any less true. Your place is back home with Malcom. He needs you."

Tears brimmed in her eyes. She held out her arms to me, and I sank into them, wrapped in her warm embrace. I clung to her, to the safety I felt in her presence.

"I'll stay until you are safe."

"If you do that, you risk your life, and Malcom may never get his mother back. If Thorn finds you and decides to turn more of you to stone, I'd never forgive myself."

She closed her eyes and took a long time to open them again. When she did, they were glazed. "It's a hard thing when a mother realizes her children no longer need her," she said. "I love you."

We clung to each other. "Uhnepa te," she whispered.

"Uhnepa te," I whispered back.

We pulled apart, both of our cheeks soaked with tears.

I took a few ragged breaths. Then I looked at them all. "Go to the bridge. The marriage with Father will open it, and the three of you will be home."

Cal's jaw tensed. "Now? We can't leave until we know you are safe."

"If Thorn is as dangerous as you think, you can't stay. This is the right choice. And you'll know I'm safe when Eliza doesn't die in two years as every other Mortal Queen has."

"If he's so dangerous, you shouldn't be marrying him."

That might not be up to me. I would write a letter to Bash and one to Thorn. From there, I'd let them decide my fate. If Bash wouldn't marry me, I had no choice.

Either way, this would end tonight.

To reassure Cal, I grinned. "I am more resilient than you think. Whatever happens next, I'm going to be fine."

49

I HELPED MY FAMILY PACK THEIR meager belongings into a burlap sack, then stood at the doorstep to watch them leave. Rain thundered around us. It soaked into the layers of my black tunic and dripped from the chiseled awning to create a curtain of water, glittering like diamonds. It masked the tears that claimed my cheeks.

Mother saw them anyway and held me close.

"Dearest Thea. I love you so much."

"I love you too," I barely managed to get the words out.

We separated, and losing the warmth of her touch invited the cold of the day to rush in, making purchase under my skin, nesting in my chest. I wrapped my arms around myself to summon the heat back, but only a ghost of it remained.

Eliza approached next. "I'll take care of them," she promised before I could ask.

"I know you will. You are a wonderful Mortal Queen."

Next, Cal swallowed me with his embrace, and I clung to my twin. I wished for many things in that moment—more hours with him to explore the realm, to train with him one last time. I yearned for my childhood back, to experience everything together again and savor it all the more.

But time was never on my side, and too soon it slipped away.

"I always thought you were better suited for this realm than I was," I told him when he stepped back.

His gaze roved over the streets, finding its way to the sky, where eternal stars sparkled back at us. A smile tugged on the corner of this mouth. "In many ways, it's more wonderful than the stories we heard as children." Ironically, I agreed with him, but when I first arrived, I'd thought the opposite. This hadn't been a dream. It was a nightmare dressed in silk. Cal continued, "But it's all a game to me, and now I want to return to real life."

At some point, the game had twisted into my real life, and I could no longer separate the two. They were one and the same—a game I'd willingly play forever.

But I understood his desire to leave it.

"Tell Malcom I'm sorry." My throat was swelling again. "I broke my promise to him. I can't return."

Cal wiped a tear from my cheek. "I'll explain everything to him, and he won't blame you. You are a hero, Thea, and don't you forget that."

I hoped Malcom would see it that way.

He hesitated. "Are you certain about this plan?"

I wasn't, but it was our best bet. "Yes."

"Then we'd better go." Cal squeezed me one last time, then I released him. They climbed aboard the chariot, gave me one last look, then took off. My heart bled after them.

They'd reach the gate soon and be gone.

Wearily, I dragged myself inside Brock's home. Sorrow couldn't swallow me. The day was not yet done.

I wrote letters to Thorn and Bash, which Brock sent for me. Then I spent the evening with Odette, reminiscing over memories of Talen. I told her about his final hour. She wept, holding on to me. Eventually, she managed to speak. "Thank you. Knowing he chose me in the end, it makes the pain a little easier to bear."

I suspected she'd carry the pain for a long time. I knew I would, though hers was deeper. I'd see Talen in every black top hat, in every fae with blinding white hair, in every symbol of the House of Delvers. He'd be there, just like the memories of my family, throughout all my years.

When night fell, Odette pulled herself together long enough to send a chariot to fetch one of her nicest gowns. "If you are to get married, you are going to do it while wearing this," she said, drying her eyes.

I wanted to protest until the gown arrived and the soft fabric settled in my hands. Satin sleeves split at the shoulders to drape elegantly to the waist, a bouffant, rippling skirt in creamy white, and the décolletage trimmed with sage-stained irises. It wasn't enough to make me feel like a bride—nothing could force my mind to come to terms with that—but it was enough to make me feel less hollow.

Odette nodded in satisfaction. "Are you certain you want to do this tonight? We could wait."

"For what? We've been searching for the key to my survival since I arrived. If this isn't it, then I need a new plan. If this is it, then I am freed tonight."

"This will be it," she said. "Are you sure you don't want me to come?"

"I'll find you afterward, to tell you how it went," I said. Meaning— if either Thorn or Bash showed up.

Thorn had already sent a reply, saying he'd be there. I hadn't told him why we needed to meet, but at least one person would come. Bash hadn't replied. And in his note, I'd told him everything.

Odette sniffled, wiping her face on the back of her draping sleeve. "He was so close," she choked. "So close to seeing the end to the deaths of the Mortal Queens."

Talen had missed it by one day. I reached for her hand. "I'm only here because of him. Without his guidance, I would have given up long ago."

She squeezed my hand. "I'm not sure that's true. You came into this realm defiant from day one," she said with a small smile. "But thank you for saying so." Odette retreated, opening the door. "Now go. Night is coming."

I squared my shoulders, wishing for courage to fill me. The butterflies in my stomach might be anticipation, or they might be fear.

Black is for mischief, but it is also for fear.

I'd been both.

I'd been cunning and I'd been terrified. Felt victory and defeat. This realm brought me friends, memories, heartbreak, and love. Today, it offered me another gift. Resolve. I grabbed the soldier toy off the desk to have a piece of Malcom's strength with me and shoved it in my pocket. As I marched out the door, Odette bowed to me.

"Goodbye, my Queen. Go forth, and may you finally bring salvation to the realm."

50

I COULDN'T QUITE SAY WHY I CHOSE
Father's home as the meeting place. Perhaps it was because of how
secluded it was. Or because I wanted a hint of my father's presence
at my side. Either way, I stood on the icy path beneath the frozen,
gilded gate, waiting.

And waiting.

And still waiting.

Minute by minute passed, and my heart sank with each one.
Frost prickled my fingers, clawing at my skin until my teeth
chattered like the strike of a clock and my toes grew numb. Still, I
waited. Rooted in place, trapped in a state of blind hope.

I'd told Bash to meet me two hours before I asked Thorn to meet
me, to give us time to decide together first. But as time went by and
the skies remained punctured only by stars, it became obvious he'd
made his choice.

When a chariot did show, I dared not hope. For it had been
too long. Sure enough, Thorn appeared, landing his chariot beside
mine to step onto the path. His eyes soaked in the palace.

"It's like it is sleeping," he said. "Waiting for someone to
wake it."

I swallowed my disappointment. So be it.

"I've found a way to save the Mortal Queens from dying," I said bluntly. Thorn's eyes darted to me. "I could explain it all, but the answer is this—I must marry a king and remain in this realm."

His brows set low. "And you picked me?"

No. I ended up with him. "I will not force you into this." I felt like a doll on display. Vulnerable and desperate. There'd be no way to mask the importance. No way to trick him.

Thorn approached slowly. "You would marry me, Thea?"

I willed iron into my spine. "I see no other option."

"We can go find Bastian right now, and I'm certain the young king—"

"Bash does not wish to marry me."

Surprise flashed in Thorn's eyes as heavy nausea rolled in my stomach, difficult to hold down. I must do this. There was no other way. "He had the option but chose not to marry me."

Thorn stood as still as the ice around us, watching me. He could turn me down as well, fly away and I'd be doomed. I'd be left just as Cottia was—aware of the answer and unable to achieve it. But at last, Thorn spoke.

"We are not in love. We never have been."

I shut my eyes. That was his answer, then.

"But to save you," he continued, and my lids flew open, "I will do this."

"You'll marry me?"

"I have always been a man of duty. This is no different."

Duty. That was exactly what this was. "Thank you," I replied. "We will save every other queen from dying and end the pain the fae feel upon losing them."

His gaze traveled the length of me, as if noticing my attire for the first time. He shifted. "You wish to marry *now*?"

Heat rose to my cheeks. "I saw no reason for festivities. But if this isn't to your liking . . ."

"No, this is—" He closed the space between us to take my hands, and the oddity of the touch sent unease rushing through me. He must have felt it, too, for he dropped my hands and stepped back. "Then it is my pleasure, but marriage can only take place at Illusion

Point. Regardless, there is a bonding ritual where we speak our intent, and that can take place anywhere. Then I'll send out the invitations and we will marry within the week."

"Alright," I said, my voice small. I cleared my throat. "Good." His gaze honed in on me. "Are you certain you want this?"

I couldn't afford to question my resolve. "I want to save the queens."

"That's not what I'm asking."

"Yet it is the only answer I can give."

Thorn had always been attractive, and I couldn't deny that. Yet I doubted I'd ever look upon him and not wish he were someone else. It wasn't fair to Thorn, but he knew where my affections lay. If he was to marry me, he would do so knowing the truth. I loved Bash. But I would marry Thorn because I had to.

And he would marry me out of duty to the realm.

"Then so be it," he said evenly.

But if we were to marry, I wanted the truth too. With the main problem sorted—finding a king to marry me—Cal's warning rang through my mind. I must know if Thorn had trapped my mother and summoned me here.

I would not marry a beast unknown.

If I must sacrifice my heart to save the queens to come, I needed to know where his claws were.

Thorn removed his suitcoat, twisting it into a thick chord. "The ceremony is simple. We bind our hands together and say some words." He paused. "We should dissolve our first alliance as we forge this new, eternal one."

Before I knew what was happening, he spoke. "Althea Brenheda, I end my alliance with you."

I tried not to shudder at the thought of the eternal alliance we were about to make.

I cleared my throat, withdrawing my hand when he reached for it a second time. "Before we agree to marry, we should discuss what to do with the signet ring."

His brows furrowed. "What do you mean?"

"I have my kingdom, and you have yours. But now we have a third. Who rules it?" Before he could respond, I suggested an idea. "How about this—whoever unlocks the power keeps the throne. If you find an enchantment to unlock the power before I do, you win." There. The trap had been set. If Thorn knew who my parents were, he knew I need only slip the ring on my finger and the power would enter me, held fast by my fae blood. If he didn't know, he'd find himself at an advantage when it came to enchantments.

His agreement, or otherwise, would give him away.

But Thorn merely shrugged, preoccupied again with twisting his suitcoat to bind our hands. "That sounds fair. Whoever secures the power for themselves may keep it."

I took a relieved breath. Cal had been wrong. But if Thorn hadn't summoned me to the fae realm, if he hadn't captured my mother, then who had?

I ought to be grateful I wasn't about to marry a monster, not defeated that I didn't possess all the answers yet.

Answers would come. For now, I had to do what I'd come to do. I'd been willing to do it either way. I stuck out my arm, feeling the harsh wind lash against it as I spoke. "Very well, then. I'm ready."

Thorn didn't reach for me. Instead, he let go of one side of the suit, letting it unravel. He took his time putting it back on, while my hand faltered. When he spoke, his voice sounded oily and slick. "Althea Brenheda, I command you to take out the signet ring and put it on."

A prickly sensation cascaded down my spine, urging me to obey. Forcing me. If it were anyone else, I'd be able to refuse. But he'd seen my true face. And now that we were no longer aligned, he could control me whenever he wished.

"What are you doing?" I asked between clenched teeth.

His answer was a jagged smile. "Securing the power for myself."

What had I done? My heart was in my throat, and I stood at his mercy.

"Take out the signet ring and put it on," Thorn ordered. "You will transfer the power to me."

"No."

"You can't refuse. I've seen your true face."

I hoped my smile looked fearsome. That it made him shudder. "I can't give it to you because I don't have it."

He chuckled, but the sound held no joy. "Who has it, then? Your mother? We will go to her and restore it."

"You've done quite enough to her," I said, grating my jaw. "It was you, wasn't it? The one who trapped her."

His silence offered his reply. He stormed to his chariot, the ice creaking with his steps. "I command you to remain on this island until I fetch her and bring her back."

An invisible force wrapped around my feet, rooting me there. "You won't find her," I shouted. "She's left."

He growled. "I command you to tell me where she is."

I happily answered. "She's back in the mortal realm with the ring."

Actually, I'd sent it with Cal. Either way, it wasn't in this realm. I didn't need it after all, it was too important, and it couldn't fall into Thorn's hands. I'd suspected he would try to steal it, so for the safety of the realm, I gave my father back what was his and kept it out of Thorn's grasp.

Even if it meant it was out of mine.

Thorn's cry shook the ground. "You fool! We can never get it back! With both your parents on the same side of the realm, the bridge is forever closed." For a moment, I thought he was going to slap me, but instead he paced in furious circles. "I need that power. All that work . . ."

"You had the signet ring all along, didn't you?" I asked. Hellen had been so adamant that the ring wasn't in her home. It wasn't. Thorn had planted it. "The Gamemaster—was that you too?"

"It was someone I hired," he answered dismissively. "All to get you to trust me when you unlocked the power. But now, you stupid mortal girl, it is lost."

His deception spanned deeper than I thought. Yet, if I was to live, if every future queen was to live, this man must still be my husband. Suddenly the decision wasn't so easy. The things he knew, the things he'd done . . . It frightened me. "You know who my father is, then?"

He straightened, composing himself. "No secrets between husband and wife, I suppose. Yes. I've known all along."

"Then you were the king who called me here."

"Always to serve a purpose, which is obsolete now." A calm settled over him, one that unnerved me. Then he smiled. It was a twisted, sardonic thing. "I will be the king to save the Mortal Queens from their death," he declared. "But it will not be with you. You have let me down. I shall let you die and marry the next queen."

I was out of cards, and soon out of time. "If you kill me, the realm will suffer. Eliza no longer resides in this realm. A mortal must always be here."

He waved his hand. "The realm will descend into darkness again until we can collect a new queen." From his tone, he seemed to desire it. "Then I will marry her and forever be known as the king who saved us all." He dipped his fingers into his pocket and drew out a dainty dagger, no thicker than a paintbrush. It needn't be large—it would pierce my heart all the same.

I couldn't outrun him, even if I tried. He knew my true face. He could command me to take the dagger in my own hand and carry out the act.

"And the power of the seventh king?" I grasped at straws. "Kill me, and you will never have it. Keep me alive, and I can find a way to get it for you."

Thorn stepped closer to me, dagger slowly rising. "It is already lost. And because of your recklessness, no one in this realm will ever see that signet ring again."

"I wouldn't be so sure about that."

My heart leapt. In the distance, the familiar voice sliced the air, making Thorn's skin blanch. From where I stood, it took a second to spot him. My father had returned.

He glided downward in a chariot, dressed in a striking grey

suit coat, red mask, and a wicked glare focused on Thorn. "Kill my daughter, and I promise I will make your death slow and painful."

His gaze latched on to mine briefly.

I grinned. With Father here, things didn't seem so dire.

But as Father stepped off the chariot, Thorn's dagger found its home against my neck. "Come closer, and I'll take my chances."

"I wouldn't take those chances if I were you."

This voice belonged to Cal, and I saw him coming from the west, touching down ten paces from us. Thorn's gaze snagged on something else and he grinned.

"So the signet ring found its way back to us." The ring gleamed on Father's finger. "I offer a simple trade," Thorn said. "Her life for the ring."

"I don't make deals anymore," Father responded. "Especially not with the man who kidnapped my wife."

The ice cracked around us, as if sensing its king had returned. It started to melt. As it did, a fire burned in Thorn's eyes and it fixed on me. "You still need me. You need to marry a king, and I'm the only one willing to do it. Tell your father to leave or I'll kill you."

I stood my ground, my hand slipping into my pocket as he held my gaze.

"Remove the dagger from her throat now."

This new voice jolted us both. Bash, dressed in gold, with Troi at his side.

He'd arrived.

He was *hours* late.

I sought his eyes to read his emotions, but he kept them on Thorn, boldly walking forward. Thorn retaliated by pressing the dagger firmer against my neck.

Bash paused. "Release her," he said again. "And we might spare your life."

"I make no such promises," Father interjected.

As they spoke, Cal had inched closer. Thorn spotted him, and he wrapped my hair in his hand and pulled my head back. "Not another step."

Everyone froze. Even Troi, her hands on two of the five daggers at her sides.

Thorn's chest rose and fell swiftly as he took us all in. I could hear his breath, sense the wheels churning in his mind. Feel the blade press hard against my throat. I slowly moved my hand at my side.

Thorn's oily voice washed over me, quiet and deadly. "I think it's time to cut my losses." From how he sounded, I counted among those losses. He titled his head to the side, giving me a pitied stare. He whispered in my ear, "The poor Mortal Queen, always destined to die. And no one can save her."

My hand found what it sought in my pocket, and I stole it from the darkness, bringing it to the light. "I'll save myself." I whipped the soldier figure, Antonio, up into the air, embedding his metal edges into Thorn's wrist and tearing.

He howled. The blade released, falling for me to catch.

At the same moment, everyone moved, and I ran straight to Bash. He collected me in his arms, checking the skin of my neck and wiping the hair from my face as the other three tackled Thorn.

I dared to look at him—the man I'd almost desperately married. Cal and Troi held fast to his arms, and Thorn's lips rolled up to snarl at me. The monster fully unleashed. Father put his own dagger against Thorn's back.

"It's over," Bash whispered. "You are safe."

"I should have gone straight to you in the first place," I said.

"I shouldn't have pushed you away."

My body still trembled, but his presence soothed it, until I could hardly hear my heart pounding in my ears anymore. We both shared regrets, ones that would be difficult to forgive myself for, but they stood behind us now. All I could do was promise to be better, for him and for us, and remember to hold fast to what mattered.

We'd done it. It was finished.

"The cells in my home have been empty for too long, I think," Father observed as he approached his palace. Ice continued melting, dripping water to run in streams off the island. Bit by bit, the palace was coming back to life, responding to its king.

But while Thorn's arms were held and a blade pressed against his back, I had forgotten to warn them that he could control me with his voice. His mouth was perhaps his most dangerous weapon.

And he used it while wearing a slippery grin.

"Althea, I command you to take that dagger and drive it into Bastian's chest."

"Why would she—" Bash began in confusion.

Before he could finish, I lifted my hand and drove Thorn's dagger into Bash's chest.

51

THORN HADN'T SPECIFIED HOW hard. I tried for a shallow cut, but Bash still dropped to his knees, clutching the spot where blood now dripped. The dagger lay on the ground, surrounded by red droplets that made my head swim.

"No!" I shouted, falling beside him with Troi's scream in my ears. Tears blurred my vision. "I had no choice. He's seen my true face." The tears fell. "I'm so sorry."

Shouting echoed behind me, but Thorn's voice rose above it all. "Again, Thea. Strike it deep."

I tried to stagger back before he finished, but once the order reached my ears, my muscles throbbed to obey. A metallic taste filled my mouth. I must strike again.

Bash's eyes flashed, and he grabbed the dagger before backing away. "Don't listen to him, Thea!"

"I can't help it." I sobbed the words. He moved back some more. My mind tried to throw my body to the ground, but it wouldn't listen. I couldn't stop.

Bash's eyes darted to something behind me and he shouted, "No! Stay with him. He cannot get free."

I couldn't turn to look. All I could focus on was the blade in Bash's hand and how I needed to get it so I could attack again.

It is a powerful thing to know one's true face. Guard it with your life.

Now I understood.

"Take him so he cannot command her to do worse!" Bash yelled. Father had already shoved his coat into Thorn's mouth and pressed it tight. They dragged Thorn toward the palace, casting worried glances behind them.

Bash stopped retreating.

"Please run. Get away from me," I begged Bash through my tears. Even if I couldn't get the dagger back, my hands already felt less like mine and more like weapons. "Troi, you are his protector! Save him from me!"

Ahead on the path, she stopped, looking back.

"Go," Bash ordered her.

She pressed her mouth in a firm line but obeyed.

Instead of running, Bash tucked the dagger in his belt and closed the space between us, grabbing my hands. I squirmed beneath the force of his grip.

"You have to leave me," I told him brokenly. "I can't resist the order."

"No." His voice was strained. A sickening amount of blood stained his shirt. Yet he ignored it as he reached up to the edges of my mask. "Let me give you a new order. Do you trust me?"

I nodded, making my head throb. It was like someone screamed in my mind, and all I could think of was how to rip my hands free to strike. How I could hurt him. How to obey. The terrible thoughts owned my mind, rendering me helpless against them. A prisoner in my own body.

Until Bash removed my mask, letting it fall to the ground.

Gently, he spoke. "Althea, I order you to take control of your body again and forget anything Thorn commanded—or will command—you to do."

It was like springtime rain washing away the fog. My blood stopped roaring in my head, the aches cleared from my body, and my fists uncurled. The horrid desire to harm Bash faded until only the painful memory remained, thrumming beneath the surface until that, too, was gone. Slowly, Bash released my wrists.

"Better?"

I swallowed the crisp air, letting the chill refresh me. "Thank you," I breathed.

He exhaled. "I am sorry I did that so abruptly, but—"

"You've nothing to be sorry for." I stroked his cheek. "I would have removed it willingly."

He lifted his hand to pry at his own mask.

"You don't have to."

"I want to." Without hesitation, Bash loosened his mask and let it drop next to mine.

He was stunning.

Those dark eyes regarded me, this time completed by his full cheeks and the familiar sharp cut of his jaw. The corners of his eyes crinkled with his smile, and something leapt inside me at the sight. Here he was—all of him. Perfect in every way.

Bash examined me with just as much diligence, smiling wider the longer he looked. I knew from the moment I set foot in this realm that I could never compare to its beauty, yet Bash gazed upon me as if *I* were the beauty of the realm. Like I was everything he wanted.

"Thank you," I whispered. "For this, for saving me, for"—my eyes fell to his chest—"I stabbed you! Are you okay?"

He let out a rumbling laugh. "It's already healed. Let's hope that's the only time you take a knife to me."

Behind him, the others had reached the entrance and were dragging Thorn into the palace. The doors shut with a bang, and it sounded like justice.

"I'm sorry I didn't come sooner," Bash began. "I was of two minds until Cal informed me you planned to marry Thorn if I didn't agree. That was what it took to let go of my anger, because I knew you'd be marrying the wrong man, and I couldn't let you do anything without knowing I still loved you."

Hearing the words settled any remnants of unrest within me.

"I planned to return with Cal, but the gate took longer to open than we thought, and I couldn't find a chariot to fetch me from that far away. Then your father wanted to join after hearing of your plan, and that took time. Once we arrived, Thorn was already there before you, but your father suggested we wait until he showed his hand. I'm grateful he did. Without Thorn's admittance of capturing your mother and revealing his willingness to kill you—confessed in front of four witnesses—the realm wouldn't let us hold him in the cells."

Father's palace was now as much stone as it was ice, and Thorn would be held somewhere inside. Left in the silence for whatever fate awaited him.

For the first time, when I thought of what fate had in store for me, I wasn't afraid.

I refocused on Bash. "Can you forgive me for that horrible accusation of taking my mother? I should have trusted you."

His fingers ran slowly through my hair. "It is already forgiven. Can you forgive me for rebuffing you so easily?"

Easily wasn't how I saw it. I'd practically forced him away. I placed my hand on his face. His real face. "You found your way back to me."

His mouth lowered toward mine, and it was as if we'd never kissed before. Everything else faded. There remained only him.

He parted to ask, "Do you want to marry me, my Queen?"

My heart skipped a thousand beats.

"Right now, it's the only thing I want." I lifted my chin. "But I won't force you into this just to save me. I want you to want to marry me."

"I want to marry you, Thea," he said without hesitation. "With all my heart, I want to." He kissed me again. No masks between us, no secrets, no games. Just forever.

52

PAINTING IN SOLITUDE AND PAINTING
with a crowd watching were two entirely different things. One
calmed me, the other invited a rally of questions each time I picked
up a new brush. Perhaps that was why I stole away in the middle of
the night to finish my paintings.

Bash sat at my side, a cup of steaming cocoa in his hands as
he observed. He'd snatched more stars from the sky to light the
throne room I once ruled in, though now it served as nothing but
a reminder of the fallen queens. We hid in the cover of night as I
finished painting each Mortal Queen.

It had taken ten months, but the queens deserved a place.

We'd kept the doors open to the palace, though this was no
longer my residence. Other fae lived here, bringing warmth and
cheer to what was once a place of silence and sorrow. Ushering in
a new era.

Meanwhile, Bash and I lived in his home together, starting our
own era as husband and wife.

I couldn't have stayed here anyway. It had too much of Talen
in it. Ghosts of him floated in my mind—standing at the top of
the stairs to announce our alliance for the first time, keeping me
company by my throne. He waited in every shadow and haunted
my waking moments.

Perhaps that was the real reason I came to paint at night. So I didn't see his ghost.

Shortly after bringing Father to this realm, Cal had returned to the mortal realm, this time for good. But Father remained behind and announced his presence to the fae. It came with shock, speculation, and celebration, all mixed together.

His banishment lifted, some said. *He came out of hiding from the outer stars,* others decided. But he would not say where he'd been, nor talk about his banishment. He did, however, announce me as his daughter.

It seemed Thorn had bought my blood from Talen. Father had guessed his motives. *His plot revolved around you unlocking my signet ring for him. That hinged upon your blood remaining a secret.* As more pieces came to light, I chastised myself for not seeing his deceit sooner.

Yet another reason for me to paint—to unravel the thoughts in my head, for there were many.

"It's done," I declared, leaning back. "The first Mortal Queen, all the way to the last." I gazed at them all. Most were vague, made more accurate when a fae could recall exact details, but they were all here. All together in one room. Perhaps over time I'd add to them, give each their own life instead of simple lines and colors, but such a task could take many more months. For now, at least they were here.

Bash stood to admire the portraits beside me, their expanse filling both sides of the walls. "You've honored them well. How fortunate we have been to be graced by each queen." His hand found a home in mine, despite the paint smeared across my fingertips.

"Do you miss it?" he asked suddenly. "The mortal realm?"

The first word that came to my lips was no. But it quickly shifted, molding itself into something more complicated. "I don't miss the heat," I told him. "Nor the sand. But I miss the quiet days when my family would ride camels to the depths of the island and picnic in the dunes. I miss market days. And of course, I miss my family." My voice shook a little. "I miss what I didn't have for those years. Mother with us and Father—well, his old self—together with us."

He squeezed my hand. "I guarantee you are equally missed." His eyes wandered back to the paintings. "But we are glad to have you here." He kissed my hand. "And I am elated."

We stayed for a while longer, until Bash spoke. "It's almost time."

I stole a glance outside. The stars would brighten soon as night drew its final breaths, ushering in a new year. I tried to tell myself it was a chill and not fright that made my bones shake. But if I'd been wrong, I would die as the day turned.

This was it. The final moments of my two years as a Mortal Queen.

Bash's hand found mine, and it trembled too.

"Chasmere and Melody were the first fae king and mortal to be wed," I said, reminding myself of what I'd guessed to be my salvation. "The mortals killed her and sentenced the realm to darkness by sealing themselves out."

Bash finished for me. "We undid their treachery through our marriage, and with your promise to remain here as a mortal forever."

That was the plan. Would the realm think it to be enough?

I closed my eyes, trying not to envision what death would feel like. Trying not to think of Bash's heart and how it might further crack if I died. Perhaps he shouldn't be here. He shouldn't have to watch his wife perish.

So many queens, their faces in this hall, their lives ending in tragedy. Would I follow them? Would they need to get a new queen tomorrow?

"Thea?" Bash spoke after a while. I nearly abandoned my own skin at the sudden noise. I opened my eyes to see his smile. "Morning has arrived. You did it."

I sank to my knees, pressing both hands to my chest to feel the satisfying beat of my heart. "We did it." I laughed as my vision blurred behind tears. I'd felt different once marrying Bash, as if a vulnerable part of me had strengthened, but we hadn't known for certain. Now we did. We'd done it. "We defeated the fate of the Mortal Queens."

My relief was short-lived. I might be alive, but that meant there'd be no escaping what we had planned for this morning.

I had one battle left to fight. The sentencing for Talen's death took place today.

I pushed aside my relief and promised myself I'd celebrate tonight. Sentencing those who hurt Talen felt like saying goodbye to him one final time, and for that, I needed my emotions in check.

Already, fae woke and ventured downstairs. I took another look around the room. The painted faces of all the queens stared back at me. "It is over," I whispered to them. "We are free."

I left the palace behind.

"You don't have to be there today," Bash said gently as we stepped aboard the chariot. "We can sentence the prisoners ourselves."

"I need to go." It would give me resolution. Both me and Odette.

This morning, we'd give Thorn, along with those involved in Talen's death, their punishment.

The judgment took place in the courtyard of my father's palace. The melted ice had left behind polished stone walls, marble stairs, crisp sparrow-tailed banners, and a glittering gate. We didn't open the interior for guests, and even I had only entered a few times since Father reclaimed it. He said there was remodeling to do, and that was that. The doors remained shut. Yet that didn't stop fae from collecting outside to gaze upon it, hoping for a glance of their missing king.

Fae gathered outside now, in the same place where Thorn had tried to kill me, and where Bash and I had intertwined our hands to say our intent for marriage. We were married a month later on Illusion Point, and with our vows, the first marriage between a fae king and a mortal became righted, thus ending the curse upon the queens. Finally, the realm was satisfied. So long as I remained here.

As soon as Odette and I appeared on the dais, silence locked the courtyard.

Odette swallowed hard, facing the fae. Her hand fumbled with a slip of her crimson dress.

"Will you be alright?" I whispered.

A meek nod was her only reply, but her eyes went upward, To Talen's brightly shining star.

Odette had retreated after Talen's death, living in the cottage that was meant to be theirs. I visited her several times over the past three months, always hoping she'd come back to life one of those times, but her posture was always slightly bent, and her smile couldn't reach her eyes.

My heart broke seeing her like that. If anyone needed resolution, it was her.

A trumpet sounded, sending a hush through the crowd. My father appeared in the front doors, wearing a black suit perfect for sentencing.

The crowd usually cheered at his appearance. Today, everyone was silent.

Doors to the right opened, and four guards led Thorn into the light, his wrists shackled and clothes disheveled.

Thomas came next, dressed in rags and a hard-set frown like his fight wasn't over. My stomach curdled at the sight of him.

After him, King Vern, who'd plotted with Thomas. Though a king, he'd been stripped of his crown like Thorn. Still, he kept his luxurious clothes and wore them with straightened shoulders, as if he had dignity to cling to.

His sentencing came first.

He stood before us with a scowl of a lion, listening to the charges. At the end, my father spoke. "It is clear that while he plotted to control the House of Delvers by planting Thomas in their leagues, he had no knowledge of Thomas's ploys of assassination, and therefore I cannot punish him for the murder. He will be banned from making any deals for ten years but may retain his titles."

Small claps filled the courtyard, as if there was uncertainty if this deserved applause. Odette didn't move. She watched as King Vern's hands were unbound and he made straight for the field, calling upon a chariot to take him away.

He might have justice, but his shame would be a burden upon him.

The guards grabbed Thomas next, bringing him to the front of the dais.

His list of crimes was decidedly longer.

"It is no small act to crush a heart," Father said after the list had been read. Thomas shifted his eyes, as if looking for escape. The guards at his sides offered none. "For your crimes, you are sentenced to a century in the mortal realm, where you shall learn the fragility of life, and hopefully return with more respect for it. Upon returning, you are barred from ever holding a title again."

Thomas released a puff of air, and his shoulders relaxed beneath his brocade jacket. Meanwhile, my blood ran hot. That was all? A time spent in our realm, then free to return home? I checked Odette's expression, and while a tear ran down her cheek, her face was unreadable.

I searched for Bash, standing at the front of the crowd with a worried gaze fixed on me. *This is how things are in our realm,* his expression seemed to say.

Well, I don't like it, mine said back.

I failed to come up with a suitable punishment, though. How did one compensate for a life stolen? How could such a wrong be righted? Even a century away from this realm would not be enough to soften the memory of Talen, and then Thomas would be back like a viper hiding in the bushes, reminding us of what we'd lost when we least expected it.

But judgment was not mine to pass. The kings had decided, and now my father gave their verdict. All I could do was stand like a heartbroken statue and watch as guards led Thomas back to the wooden platform, while Thorn took the stage.

I waited for what he'd do. Sneer upon the crowd. Glare at me. Fight. Instead, he stood with the calmness of a summer field while my emotions swirled like a winter storm.

Two kings on trial today. The last one received mercy, and if this one did too, I planned to rebel.

Father looked solely upon Thorn as the attendant read the list of crimes, but Bash watched me with hesitancy. Uncertainty balled into a tight fist that clenched my gut. They wouldn't pardon Thorn, right? Kidnapping Mother, threatening to kill me . . . punishment was deserved.

"You have wildly mistreated two of our Mortal Queens, who happen to be my wife and daughter," Father said. Now, Thorn stirred. "As such, Queen Althea will have a say in your punishment." My breath froze as he went on. "King Thorn will be stripped of his title and sent to the mortal realm. However, if our queen desires it, there is a transaction we can enact to grant her Thorn's fae lifespan."

His lifespan? "How?"

From near Bash, Hellen stepped forward. I hadn't noticed her before, clad in a black dress and midnight-blue cloak, but she threw back the cowl as she approached the dais.

Only an ambassador could grant a mortal the life of a fae. And to do so, they lost their status and became mortal in their place. She was willing to do this for me?

"Ambassador Hellen will be promoted to the status of king, or in this case, queen," Father announced. "She will take over Thorn's lands. Her title as ambassador will go to him, and he will give to you."

Thorn's blue eye flared. "I do not consent."

"The queens did not consent to you capturing them or using them," Father shot back without looking his way. "It is not for you to decide."

"Thorn becomes mortal," I put together. "And I become fae."

Father grinned. "You are already fae. But now you will be fully one of ours."

Though the courtyard remained still, the fae eager to hear my reply, my mind swirled with thoughts. Fae. Long life. An action that could not be undone.

One look at Bash and I had my answer. I'd take every moment I could get with him.

"You won't suffer any consequence for losing your ambassador status?" I asked Hellen.

A small twinkle appeared in her eyes at my question. "No, my Queen. I am not losing it. I am merely being promoted. It is an honor no ambassador has been given before."

Thorn protested furiously, shouting about how unfair the punishment was, how Thomas had taken a life and was getting a smaller reprimand. But he was ignored.

"Take it," Odette said beside me. "You deserve a long life."

"I want to," I told her, then lifted my voice. "But a mortal must always be present in the fae realm. That law cannot be changed. If I become fae, then the realm is without a mortal." And if I break that rule, the fate of the Mortal Queens begins again.

Father heard me. "That is why this particular day was chosen for the sentencing. For today is the Queen's Day Choosing Ceremony."

I stilled at the phrase, a shot of fear coursing through me even though the mortals no longer had anything to fear from us. We would take no more queens. We would condemn no more mortals. Before I could reply, Father gestured for Bash to join him. "My son-in-law had an idea to this regard."

Bash took a place beside me, buttoning his cream suit jacket. "I heard this plan only last night," he whispered.

"You didn't tell me?" I whispered back.

"I didn't want to sway your decision. If you choose to keep your mortal life, I won't blame you."

He faced outward. "Althea and I have spoken often about attempting to reopen the bridge between our realms, yet no answer has presented itself. Instead, I suggest we continue the tradition of Mortal Queens. We invite a mortal girl each year to live here, treat her as a queen, allow her to play the games of the realm, then take her home the next year as we select a new queen. The mortals—if willing—will get a taste of our realm but suffer no death, for our marriage has saved the queens from dying." Bash paused to smile at me. "And this way, our Queen Althea may become fae."

A murmur ran through the crowd, each fae considering it. Bash checked with me. "You know better than any of us if the mortals would like this idea. What do you think?"

I tried to process it. Mortal Queens continuing. I fought so hard to spare them from this realm, but really it was to spare them from death. I'd done that. Now they would experience what we'd always imagined—the lavish fae realm.

"We long for this land," I said. "To be invited here will allow the mortals to hold on to that dream. I don't want to take that from them."

Bash grinned. I couldn't see him with the mask on and not imagine how he looked underneath, now that I knew. "Very wise. Do you want this, then? The choice is yours."

The chance to be fae and to give the mortals a glimpse of this realm without subjecting them to death? The answer came immediately. "Yes. I accept."

Father lifted his hands. "Ambassador Hellen, I hereby promote you to the status of the seven kings, passing your title of ambassador to former King Thorn. You may take his signet ring."

The guards had to practically wrestle the ring away from Thorn. As soon as it reached Hellen's hand, she arched her back as if life entered her for the first time. Meanwhile, Thorn bellowed, wrenching against his bonds. The guards held him fast. When he stopped quivering, he stood deathly still with his head hung low.

Father continued. "Ambassador Thorn, the kings strip you of your title of ambassador and grant it to Queen Althea."

His head snapped up. "I do not willingly give up my power."

"Then you will die instead, and she will take it from your lifeless body," Father warned, a dangerous edge to his tone.

It quieted us all.

Finally, Thorn muttered, "I agree."

And with those words, power rushed into me. It came as a tingle beneath my skin, the release of breath, the strengthening of my senses. My heart stopped pounding, instead turning to glass. I could feel it as the one vulnerable part of my body, while everything else felt invincible.

Bash backed up to watch me and his smile broadened. Everyone else seemed to fade away.

"How do I look?" I asked tentatively.

"Like my forever."

53

GUARDS DRAGGED THORN AWAY

while Father retreated into his palace, leaving the door open behind him. I took it as an invitation to follow.

He gripped a satchel and stood in the center of the antechamber, waiting. I knew what the satchel meant. I wished to rewind time, turn back through those doors and pretend I didn't see him.

"No," I whispered.

His smile saddened. "It's been ten months. I need to return to the mortal realm."

"Why? Were you banished after all?"

"I was never banished," Father replied. "I merely let people believe that. But I do not belong here anymore, not when my family is in another realm."

"What of me?" The words sounded pitiful as I said them, but I didn't take them back.

"My dear Althea, you are an ambassador," he said quietly. "You can cross realms and will fetch me when your mother and Cal and Malcom are gone. Then you shall have me for ages."

The phrase almost shattered me. I'd outlive Cal and Malcom by ages. But it also gave me peace. They'd live those years with both their parents present. I'd get Father fully back someday. He'd return.

The gargoyle from the labyrinth had been right. My family would never live together in one place again. I would never rejoin them.

"I will keep your kingdom safe until then," I promised.

"Good. For it is yours now."

He stepped back, and only then did I see the remodeling he'd done. Old stones had been ripped away and replaced with new marble flooring, polished wood beams, paintings of me and Bash on the walls. Dusty curtains gone, replaced with new, warm-colored ones, windows trimmed in stained planks, and the room off to the side held an easel set in the center, facing grand windows. Everything about it welcomed me further into the home.

"You may select and furnish your room together," he said. "But the rest of the home has been made for you. Both of you. I know you have a place at his home already—"

"Thank you," I managed to say. We had a beautiful place together in Bash's home, but something about this one felt right, especially knowing Father prepared it for us. "It's perfect."

Bash entered the room. "It's time to leave," he said. "The mortals still gather, anticipating the ambassadors."

We would have to tell them the truth. All of it. Parents would learn their daughters had died, and the mortals might not wish to return to our realm. But those who wished to come would do so willingly and have my promise they'd be treated well.

"Are you ready, Ambassador?" Father asked with a wink.

I was grateful for what that meant. I'd see my family every year. My promise to Malcom to return wouldn't go unfulfilled.

We took a step, but I paused. "Wait, I still don't know one thing. Who broke your heart the most? It was a question Thorn had set up in his elaborate game. Was there an answer?"

"There was, but I doubt any other than Thorn knew it. His father."

"The War of Hearts?"

He nodded in confirmation. "Ulther had been taunting me for years with anonymous messages about stealing my throne, then he set up the game. I gave my signet ring to him during that game in an effort to keep my mother and sister safe. He killed them anyway. I lost my taste for this realm and convinced Hellen to take me away."

I gasped. "She told me she never saw you again."

Father laughed. "That doesn't surprise me. She's always been a secretive one. I doubt she'd have told you the truth, even if she knew you were my child. Do you have any other questions?"

I thought, but all my questions were answered now. "If I think of any later on, I'll ask when I see you in a year."

"I'm counting on it." Father turned to give Bash a handshake. "Take care of her," he instructed.

"I will." A look of respect passed between them. Over the past ten months, the two had grown close as my father helped drive Bash's father away from attempting to usurp the throne. Though Bash could have done it all on his own, for overnight he went from being the king with the unbreakable heart to the king who saved the Mortal Queens. Every lord wanted to pledge to him, and with our marriage, his throne became secure once more.

Father took a final look around the castle, then nodded. "Take me home."

I smiled. "As you command."

EPILOGUE

HEAT SCORCHED MY SKIN. YET I hardly felt it. I stood with the two other ambassadors, who had welcomed me with open arms, under the balcony of the governor's home. Now I understood why the fae stood in the shade. If we ventured into the sun, we might melt.

My eyes caught on the musicians from Ruen. Once, all I wanted was to be among the artists on that island. How different my life would have been, had I not been selected.

Father slipped away as soon as we arrived, but his silver hair caught my eyes, pushing a trail through the crowd.

Sure enough, the mortals had gathered, awaiting us as they did every year. I watched Father's path until it led me five rows back, to where my mother stood with Cal and Eliza on one side and Malcom on the other.

Once more, I broke protocol to press through the crowd, and soon we were entangled in one another's arms. "You did it," Cal said loudly over the roaring noise. "You survived past two years."

"I'll survive a lot longer than that," I promised.

"Yet the ambassadors still came?"

"Things have changed," I wanted to explain everything that took place, but with the excited clamor of the crowd, I wouldn't be heard. Father would need to fill them in. All they needed to know was this: "I'll be back every year. I promise."

I gave Malcom another long hug and spoke into his ear. "Thank you for little Antonio. He saved me more than you can know."

"I knew he would," Malcom said, his voice clearer than before and his head reaching higher than ever. "And I knew you'd come home to us."

"Always." This time, I didn't doubt the sincerity of my promise.

With difficulty, I tore away from my family and headed back to the stage.

Hellen had always done the speaking for the fae, and now, the other two waited for me to talk.

"How will they hear me?" I asked them.

"Just speak," the dark fae answered. "And they will hear."

I prepared to address the crowd, both terrified and excited for what I was about to do. A new time was beginning, and the veil between our worlds would grow thin. No longer would it be a secret. No longer would queens suffer. Now, our world would be shared with them.

My smile embraced them all.

"Ladies and gentlemen of the center island, I am here to find our new queen."

ACKNOWLEDGMENTS

First, I'd like to thank my previous book, *Silver Bounty*, for teaching me how difficult second books in trilogies are to write, and thus *Mortal Queens* became a duology instead of a three-book series. My sanity remained intact while writing.

Once, I believed writing to be a solitary hobby, but the years have brought countless incredible writers into my life, and you all encourage me daily. From my Omaha writing group to my social media friends, you are a constant stream of motivation for me to continue writing. I wouldn't be releasing my ninth book without you.

To all the readers—you've taken *Mortal Queens* and supported it endlessly, which I'm so grateful for. It's one thing to write a story, but it's a wholly different, beautiful thing to have readers enjoy that story. Your kind words mean more than you know.

To the team at Oasis Family Media and Enclave Publishing, thank you for all you do for my books. You help guide me through this process, and I'm grateful for your support. Huge thanks to my editors who pull my ramblings into proper sentences, and thank you to Trissina for allowing me to come to you at all hours with questions.

And lastly, to my family, who is always willing to listen to my story ideas and walk me through them, and who reads the messy first drafts I write. Thank you for believing in me.

ABOUT THE AUTHOR

Victoria McCombs is the author of The Storyteller Series, The Royal Rose Chronicles, and The Fae Dynasty duology, with hopefully many more to come. She survives on hazelnut coffee, 20-minute naps, and a healthy fear of her deadlines, all while raising four wildlings with her husband in Omaha, Nebraska.

THE QUEENS ARE MISSING.

IF SHE CAN'T TRICK THE SEVEN FAE KINGS, SHE'LL BE NEXT.

THE FAE DYNASTY

Mortal Queens

Lethal Kings

Available Now!

BEWARE THE WATERS.

THE DANGEROUS DEEP BRINGS RUIN TO ALL.

 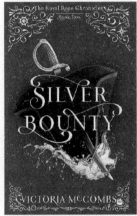 

THE ROYAL ROSE CHRONICLES

Oathbound

Silver Bounty

Savage Bred

Available Now!

www.enclavepublishing.com